EMPYREAN

Christopher Valkenburg

LIGHTHOUSE
PRESS

First edition published in 2023 by Lighthouse Press UK
www.lighthousepress.co.uk

ISBN: 978-1-7392835-0-6

Also available as an ebook.

A CIP catalogue record for the book is also available
from the British Library.

This is a work of fiction. The names, characters, businesses and
incidents herein are the products of the author's imagination or are
used in a fictitious manner. The representation of Budapest is
accurate, with embellishments. Any resemblance to actual persons,
living or dead, or to actual events is purely coincidental.

To God, my compass.
To my parents, my map.

Acknowledgements

I gratefully acknowledge the assistance of those who have, in different ways, helped me to write this book:

Rob Tomlinson, who saw the kernel and watered it.

Judit Lebrecht, for keeping me on the spiritual straight and narrow.

Dijana Dengler, for her encouragement, friendship and generosity.

Isaac Dunlap, Quan Gu, Zsuzsa Varga, Dave Pierce, Freya Nicholson, Lisa Marino and Anna Fielding, for suffering the early drafts. You made this better.

Smahajcsik-Szabó Tamás, who helped me craft a bleaker Budapest than the one we now enjoy; and Réka, for stoking the creative fire with Scoobie snacks.

Attila and Ágo Szucs; Péter and Kristina Szalai; Kafui and Mária Tse; Dan and Rose Smith; and Ferenc and Lucy Húnyar. Second family.

My mother and father, who I love more than life. Friends as well as kin.

"Redemption does not come so easily, for no one can ever pay enough to live forever and never see the grave."

—Psalm 49:8-9

Prologue

AD2132. Humanity has coalesced into six Sister Cities: Moscow, Beijing, Mumbai, Tokyo, Sydney and Budapest. These are the last bastions of civilization in a dying world. Beyond them lies the Outside: irradiated, diseased, lawless. The bomb killed most of its inhabitants. The rest succumbed to the Red Plague. The unlucky survived.

Shielded by its DOME and encircled by the Wall, Budapest remains a stronghold for 40 million Employees in the service of the Company. Here, mankind strives, neighbor against neighbor, husband against wife, for the ultimate prize—retirement to the paradise land of Empyrean and eternal life.

Budapest, October 2132

1

The Mercedes Benz Citaro O530G was an eighteen-meter, four-door city bus held together by rusted bolts and luck. It seated 50 in discomfort—58 if the babushkas kept their shopping bags on their laps—with standing room for 150. But rain had a way of fitting people into space that wasn't there.

Marci counted numbers. He knew numbers. Birth rates, death rates, SIN[1] forecasts, probability distributions. Numbers that meant life. Numbers that spelled death. It wasn't hard, but he was counting backward. Odds and evens. They changed every few sets. It was a mind game, a mental diversion designed to stave off his panic attacks. Sometimes it worked. The problem was that he was too good at it.

Two hundred. One hundred ninety-seven. One hundred ninety-four—

The bus braked hard. Marci stumbled forward, lunging for a grab rail and sullying his right hand in the process. Fighting the compulsion to fetch his sanitizing gel, he closed his eyes and willed the numbers to life.

One hundred ninety-one. One hundred eighty-eight...

At Blaha Lujza no one got off, but two dozen more passengers boarded, forcing Marci away from the exit. Dead center, he stood straddling the bendy bus's articulation plate like an overweight ballerina poised to *plié.* Was it too late to get off? Blaha had a metro stop but no SpeedWalk. An air cab was another option, but not on Monday morning at rush hour. Besides, he really needed to crack the panic attacks.

---

[1] SIN: Social Index Number.

The doors stayed open to let some rain in.

A trickle of sweat ran down his ribs.

For God's sake, get on with it!

The light above the exit flashed red. Marci sucked in a last draught of cold air from outside, bowed his head and tried a visualization.

A beach of gold. Underfoot, firm, ochre sand fringed by sea the color of tarnished bronze. He moves, dreamlike, under a sky of hammered copper like the inside of a kettledrum. This is his sanctuary, his private paradise.

The intrusion of a Tannoy: *"A következő megálló: Huszár utca."*

Huszár utca. His stop. It couldn't come soon enough.

Focus!

The sand is softer now. He feels it between his toes: a warm powder, not quite talc but comforting, the best he can imagine for a man who has never seen the ocean. Behind him, a small wooden boat nods with the ocean's heartbeat; the only sound for a thousand leagues in each direction.

The bus, shuddering over rough asphalt, broke his concentration. Marci tried to fix his bearings outside, but the windows were steamed up. Where was he? One eighty-four? No, it had to be an odd number. Or did it?

One hundred eighty-five—

A shove, the sour stench of body odor from somewhere. Marci felt his skin turn clammy. With rising panic, he pushed his way through the mass of bodies toward the exit, eliciting mumbled complaints from his fellow passengers.

"*Huszár utca,*" spoke the Tannoy.

With a groan of resentment the doors swung open, spilling out a handful of commuters. Marci Kovács found himself in the rain.

The rush hour traffic on Rákóczi út was heavy that morning, and the wet road made the noise deafening. Marci hurried to a side street, where in the portico of a closed music shop he applied antiseptic gel to hands red raw from over-washing. He lit a cigarette, but his mouth was dry and the thing tasted foul. He tossed it into the gutter and returned to the main road, holding his breath as he passed cafés and kebab shops lest the smell turned his stomach even more.

By the time he reached Keleti the rain was dancing like sparks on the sidewalk. Marci surveyed the plaza. The station had been renovated a little over a century ago in 2014 and had survived the Fuel War thanks to the DOME[2] system. But its environs had altered radically since then. Where once drab, Socialist tenement buildings—*komcsi blokkok*—blighted this part of District VIII, marvelous edifices of twisted glass, steel and concrete, the remnants of the Golden Age, now rose above the rail terminus. At their bases stood a hodgepodge of shabby, single-story shops: butchers, electronics stores, strip joints, pharmacies and fast-food outlets, each vying with one another for the attention of passers-by. Along the thoroughfare, trams, buses, taxis, private cars and air cabs thundered relentlessly through the rain.

At a Stimbooth he ordered a Kqalms shot and an antiemetic, and pressed his face against the inhalator, breathing the formula into his lungs. A vending machine dispensed his coffee, which he took to stand under the colonnade. He'd be late for work again, but Morrison could shove it.

His phone rang. A youthful, clean-shaven face appeared on the screen: his friend and fellow Adjudicant, Alex.

"Hey, Marci. You ok? Carrot-top's on the warpath."

Marci uttered an expletive. Although outranking Head of Department Fraser Morrison in both SIN and prestige, he could do without a confrontation with the irascible Scot. "I'm on my way."

"Are you at Keleti? I heard an announcement."

"Ever the detective. Have you considered a career with the Justice and Cessation Board?"

Alex laughed, giving him the appearance of a schoolboy. "With their SIN prospects? I'd never make Club 30."

Marci lit another Winterbourne. The coffee made it better this time. "You'll never make it anyway. You lack ambition."

"Nor will you if you keep turning up to work late. What happened?"

---

[2] DOME: a citywide protective shield employing Heavy Air technology.

In this case, the truth was more convenient than a lie. "Another panic attack. Fob off the little runt if he starts asking questions, will you?"

"I wouldn't worry about it. He's probably hitting the bottle and scheming his next promotion."

"In the absence of talent, people like Morrison only achieve SIN by firing everyone else."

"Make sure you're not next."

Marci hung up. A man of middle stature and regular features, he looked younger than his thirty-nine years. Slim except for a slight paunch that refused to shrink despite his efforts at temperance, he was not ill-favored. Chestnut brown hair, trim but not short, crowned a thinker's forehead. Large, soulful eyes and the mouth of a poet lent him a romantic visage, as if he had been born into the wrong age. At first glance, women would often find him attractive were it not for a demeanor of brisk aloofness and condescension which characterized his dealings with the world. Not that it mattered, he convinced himself; he was far too busy with work for any kind of dalliance.

The Kqalms was beginning to work. Turning up his collar, Marci marched across the plaza toward the main road. On second thoughts, he ducked into the underpass beneath Thököly's twelve lanes of traffic.

From a gypsy vendor he bought an umbrella drone and climbed the steps on the other side of the thoroughfare, casting it into the air. It powered up, stabilized and spread a broad plastic canopy above him, shielding him from the rain. With the machine floating overhead, Marci ducked into a side street, glad to be away from the bustle of the main road. As he did so, the blast hit.

The light came first, flashing his own shadow against the side of the building. For an instant, it seemed that through some act of Divine benevolence he had entered an alternate time frame where milliseconds were stretched to allow him to react. Instinctively he ducked, arms above his head, as he was lifted off the ground and thrown head-over-heels against the wall. He fell hard, striking his shoulder on the concrete, and rolled onto his side.

The shock wave had knocked the wind out of him. He gasped for breath, but it would not come. Sound followed light: a tremendous cracking noise, so loud it made him cry in pain, rent the air. Marci clapped his hands to his ears, to no effect; the world turned silent.

Panting, he managed to catch his breath. His lungs ached. He sat up, wincing with pain, and turned to view the devastation of Thököly út.

A hundred feet away on the far side of the street were the remnants of an articulated trolley bus, which was blown apart at its midpoint. The rear end lay in the plaza he'd just crossed, with the front section straddling a row of mangled cars, now in flames. Several had been lifted and dumped chassis up atop others, wheels turning, where they resembled dying cockroaches. Fragments of machinery, catapulted by the explosion, were strewn across the street and plaza, embedded in benches, bins and masonry. Some had struck pedestrians to gruesome effect.

His ears whining, Marci stumbled back to the boulevard on legs like gelatin. Dust hung over the street like a pall, and an awful stench reached his nostrils. Without needing an explanation, he knew it came from within the burning cars. There were other smells too: petrol and diesel from ruptured fuel tanks, and a strange odor reminiscent of fertilizer. People ran or limped, dazed and aimless, here and there. Without his sense of hearing, the scene played out like a macabre, silent parody.

Sound returned: first, a high-pitched whining, then a cacophony of car alarms, then the screaming, that awful falsetto, male and female, of those succumbing to the flames. Distant sirens joined the clangor as the emergency services scrambled from Egressy út.

In revulsion he turned away, desiring nothing more than to distance himself from the horror before him. With his umbrella drone now defunct, Marci walked through the rain, past McDonald's, and into a zigzag of silent back streets.

At Dembinsky út, Marci stopped at a convenience store, bought a coffee and a Cortiquell lozenge, and sat on a bench outside. When he went to raise the cup to his lips his hand trembled with such violence that he put the drink down without tasting it.

He returned to the shop. In a corner stood a SIN booth. It was one of the old ones, all gray and vandal-proof plastic, with a hand scanner rather than a BioField. Marci placed his palm on a pad; a bitmap display confirmed his identity by name and Employee number. The device ejected a paper ticket which read:

SIN 29, LEVEL III

Underneath was a cheery motivational message, presumably penned by some bored creative in the Company's media department. These accompanied each status index printout and were tailored to the latest hourly score. Today's was as trite and formulaic as usual:

Good morning, Márton! Level 30 is within your reach.
It's easier than you think!

Marci—only his mother had called him Márton when she was alive—crumpled the paper and threw it in a bin. It was a lie, of course. SIN 30 was always hard to get. Everybody wanted the golden ticket to The Society of Patricians, but few ever broke through. Club 30 membership numbered 118 in a population of forty million. Mythically unattainable, SIN 33 rewarded the Company's finest with the ultimate prize: eternal life and retirement in Empyrean.

The Cortiquell, reaching the synapses in his brain, kicked in with its characteristic wash of serenity. Feeling calmer, Marci resumed his journey to Hősök tere, the vast plaza presided over by the oxidized form of the Archangel Gabriel. Behind him, two semi-circular colonnades sheltered fourteen statues of note: on the left, the seven chieftains of the Magyars; to the right, an equal number of other historical luminaries.

Towering above the plaza was the Executive Team building, a pyramid of opaque, fragmented black glass three hundred feet tall, fashioned to be both imposing and inscrutable. Its nickname was the Pangolin, so dubbed because its facade resembled the animal's scaly armor.

Marci strode into the foyer past two Minotaurs[3], entered a screening chamber, then rode the elevator to the eighteenth floor. He stepped out into a large administrative office and was immediately confronted by the last person he wished to see. With a cheery salute of camaraderie, Tony Jackson swaggered over from where he had been in deep conversation with one of the new female administrators, a choice brown-eyed brunette. A waft of cheap cologne preceded him.

Tony clicked his heels together and bowed in mock reverence. "All hail the next Prefect of Budapest! To what do we owe this pleasure?"

"Morning, Tony," Marci said, trying not to break his stride, but his way was blocked by the little office manager.

"I was just telling Deborah how you'll soon be making SIN 30," Jackson continued. "There aren't too many of us high 20s around, especially here in the Exec Team. We're a rare breed."

Marci ignored the lie; Tony was SIN 20, and lucky to be that. "And I'm a little late for work, so please excuse me." He tried to move around Jackson, whose sickly-sweet perfume was already starting to cloy.

"Soon you'll not want to hobnob with us serfs," Tony said, edging closer. "Just remember to take me and Debbie to Empyrean with you when you make 33!"

Marci winced; Tony's breath was far from fresh. "I'll bear that in mind, along with your wife. Now, if you'll—"

"A little bird tells me"—here Tony turned around to ensure Deborah was following the conversation—"a little bird tells me you'll soon be up for election to The Society. Is it true?"

"Just a rumor."

"If you need any tips," Tony winked, "just let me know. I've studied the topic at length. In fact, I'm about to publish a work in the field: "Club 30: Reach for the Skies!" I'm hoping it will push me up a whole SIN point. In fact, I'm pretty sure of it."

"Tony, I—"

---

[3] Minotaur: an imposing, fourteen-feet-tall manlike appliance, armed with a mini-gun and controlled by a human operator within its exoskeleton.

"What I'm saying, my friend, is that you can't risk the election board alone. You need all the ammunition you can lay your hands on. An opportunity like this comes only once in a lifetime."

"Thanks Tony, I'll be sure to draw on your extensive experience of Level 30 when the time presents itself." Marci sidestepped him. "But now I must get to my office before I reach retirement age."

From the administrators" pool came suppressed laughter. Tony broke out into a hearty chuckle and slapped Marci on the back. "That's the spirit. Don't let the brass get you down!"

Marci, showing a thin smile, hurried across the office towards the adjacent suite.

"Always the office joker, our Marci," Tony reflected loudly. "It's good to know our top Adjudicant's a down-to-earth fellow."

A set of wide, obsidian-black steps led up between black marble walls into the heart of the Executive Team building. This was the Adjudication suite, home to MARTHA[4] and her numerous technical overseers: data analysts, systems analysts, programmers, administrative staff and, not least, Adjudicants themselves.

A short way down the hall, the marble floor had been inlaid with an annular bioreader. Marci placed himself in the center of the circle. A computer read his DNA; the red circumference turned green, and he was allowed to proceed. Eyes averted, Marci hurried past the clerical office on his left where Morrison resided.

Outside a nondescript door Marci underwent another biometric inspection and was granted access to his suite, in reality a gray-walled cubicle whose only concessions to comfort were an ergonomic office chair and a coat stand. It was a space deliberately spartan, as if the Executive Team wanted to remind its Adjudicants that despite their lofty status they were, after all, human beings like the rest of the department.

---

[4] The acronym MARTHA stands for MULTI ALGORITHM REAL TIME ASSIMILATOR. The name is taken from the Biblical account of Martha and Mary. While Mary sat at the feet of Jesus, Martha chose to busy herself in the kitchen. As the brain of the Company, MARTHA continuously monitors each Employee's life, from birth until death. Life choices and daily behavior data are sent to the supercomputer by a variety of means. MARTHA then analyses and predicts the Employee's future conduct. His SIN rating is derived from this information and is updated every few seconds.

Marci dropped off his satchel, hung up his wet jacket and, without knocking, entered the suite next door. "I should have guessed," he said. "Still wearing yesterday's shirt?"

"You can't possibly tell. The chair's in the way."

"Lei's at her mother's, which means you just picked up the same one from the floor."

Alex Pimenov swung around with a boyish grin. "It takes a bachelor to know that. Oh wait, you've got Alice."

"Hah, if only she did my laundry."

"What happened to you? You look awful."

Marci closed the door behind him. "Apart from the panic attack? I almost got blown up at Keleti."

"What?"

"A bomb on a bendy bus. If I hadn't taken the underpass I'd be dead."

Alex's mouth fell open. "Hell, Marci, that's awful. Are you ok?"

"Just a bit shaken up, that's all. Damn the Undergrounders. Someone ought to do something about the scum."

"That's Justice and Cessation's job. Are you still taking the meds?"

Marci stared at the video wall behind his friend. "For the panic attacks? Kqalms, sometimes Cortiquell. And the rest."

Alex swore. "I wish I could help."

"You can. Run some code in MARTHA that deals with Tony Jackson. He's becoming far too chummy with me."

"I could, but she'd get peeved with my stealing her glory."

Marci snorted. "Even the bloody computer wants him dead."

"Computer?" Alex looked appalled. "Only the most analytical database ever created."

"Touching. You spend more time with MARTHA than you do with your wife."

Alex grinned. "As she daily reminds me."

"Who, Lei or MARTHA?"

Alex threw a ball of paper at him. "Go and do some work before I tell Morrison you were late again."

Back in his suite, Marci logged in to MARTHA and called up the day's cases, which appeared on a bank of screens before him.

MARTHA typically worked unaided. Where liquidations were clear-cut, the computer would automatically dispatch a Justice Board cessation squad. However, where an element of ambiguity remained, an Adjudicant always rendered the final decision.

The Adjudicant was lawyer, sociologist, psychologist, data analyst, judge and jury rolled into one. His or her remit was to monitor MARTHA's decisions and, with strictest impartiality, amend them as necessary.

The premise was simple: at birth, each Employee, regardless of lineage or inherited wealth, was ascribed a Social Index Number: 10. There were no favorites; every citizen had an equal chance to further him or herself. Fare well, and he might reach the high 20s, or even the 30s. At SIN 33, he would undergo a cloning process at the city's DNA Repository before being taken far away to enjoy eternal retirement in a paradise land known as Empyrean. Just a handful of Employees had ever achieved it, and the only living SIN 33er was the incumbent Prefect of Budapest. Underperform, and the hapless citizen's SIN would eventually dwindle into single figures. At SIN 5 his life would become forfeit, and the black van of the cessation squad would be dispatched.

Marci called up the first file, that of one István Csány, 48, a Level III bank clerk. MARTHA presented his lifeline, a diagram representing the man's existence from birth. SIN changes and other notable events were highlighted on the graph.

Csány's life was not a happy one. His wife abandoned their marriage three years ago, leaving their two children with him. Spending data revealed that Csány had developed a drinking habit in the final years of his marriage, a trend which had shown no sign of abating since the departure of his spouse. Despite this, both children were doing well at school, and MARTHA predicted higher than average SIN scores for them. To liquidate Csány would jeopardize the children's academic accomplishments and their future contribution to the Company. Furthermore, both would need to be sent either to their delinquent mother or to a Company-sponsored foster home.

Marci moved between screens, reading health records, fiscal statements, employment reports and data relating to Csány's offspring. On a summary page, MARTHA proposed a course of action. Keeping Csány alive would maximize the potential of the children to become fruitful Employees, while sparing the Company welfare expenditure. She therefore suggested that Csány be placed on a rehabilitation program, undergo a workplace review, and be assigned a SIN counselor, the costs of which would be deducted from his salary. Marci approved the recommendation and requested a review of Csány's treatment and his contribution to the Company in six months" time.

The rest of the day passed without undue incident. Late in the afternoon, Marci logged out of MARTHA and knocked on Alex's door, but there was no response. Coat and satchel in hand, Marci descended to the ground floor and onto the main boulevard, where rain swept in sheets along the sidewalk.

Floating over Hősök tere, safely below the many air corridors that funneled afternoon traffic out of the city, was an airship of monstrous proportions. Its skin was formed on both sides of large video displays, visible to traffic above and below. Rotating slowly, it presented scenes of exotic charm which were quite at odds with the Monday rush hour: a river meandering through a cinnamon forest under manicured hills of tea; halls of marble, alabaster and gold, where diaphanous curtains billowed in a gentle breeze; silver platters bearing food beyond the reach of every Employee; and beautiful maidens curtsying to the camera. From loudspeakers issued gentle music and a commentary:

"A city of roses
A city of gold
A place of peace and eternal youth
Of palaces, with one your very own
The land of the Pashtuns
Flowing with milk and honey
Now the land of the chosen few
Where ancient meets modern
Where a new life begins and lasts forever
Where every need is met

And every desire fulfilled
This is your city, your destiny, your home.
This is Empyrean."

Marci, dripping wet, watched the video to its conclusion. Text appeared on the screen:

EMPYREAN
THE VERY BEST FOR THE VERY BEST *
SIN 33 REQUIRED.

* *HEALTH BUDAPEST ADVISES EMPLOYEES TO UPDATE THEIR DNA PROFILE EVERY MONTH.*

Marci stood transfixed. He'd seen the video countless times before, but still it stirred in him such a sense of longing that he never tired of watching it. Empyrean, beautiful Empyrean! The dream of every Employee! And he was just four points shy of reaching it.

Enraptured by the video, Marci failed to notice an approaching bus which, ploughing through a large puddle, sent a wash of filthy water over his legs. He stared at his wet pants, then after the bus. Cursing, he trudged to his tram stop.

From Hősök tere, the tram took him to Keleti. Despite the bombing that morning, a semblance of order had been restored: the bus, wrecked cars and mangled bodies had been removed, and Thököly út was once again alive with traffic.

Marci took a copy of the Budapest Tribune from a kiosk and caught Metro 4 to Rákóczi tér, where he disappeared into the maze of back streets known as the Palace District.

On Kőfaragó utca, a wrought iron sign depicting a cornucopia marked the presence of Objet d'Heart, an antique, bric-à-brac and curio shop, depending on one's interpretation of the stock. Marci stepped inside, his arrival heralded by the tinkling of small bells that dangled beside the door.

The musty smell of old books greeted him. Journals, novels, and literature of every ilk were stacked, piled and otherwise arranged in cases and cabinets. Others served as legs for tables bearing trinkets and knick-knacks of indeterminate age. The aisles, which were narrow at best, became impassable in places, forcing him to sidestep for fear of upsetting something delicate. Dolls' houses nestled beside muskets and elephant guns; paperweights, saucy postcards and obsolete currency filled drawers to overflowing. From somewhere unseen came the slow ticking of a clock. The shop exuded the spirit of a bygone age, and there was a tragic grandeur about the place, as if each artifact mourned its own moment of glory.

Marci moved between the rows, now and then picking up something that caught his interest. From the storage room came a short, stout man with a shock of white hair and an aquiline nose: András Horváth, the proprietor. Seeing Marci, he placed the box he was carrying on an onyx chessboard. "Marci! My favorite client!"

"You say that to all your customers."

"Only the ones who spend a lot of money in my shop. How can I help?"

"Köszönöm, csak nézelődöm."

"Just browsing, eh?" András said in disgust. "My least favorite type of customer."

Marci picked up a Matryoshka doll, which had seen better days. It rattled when he shook it. Inside, one of the set was missing. "How's trade?"

András considered the question. "Not too shabby. It seems everyone wants 19th-century English tea caddies at the moment. I don't see the appeal myself, but each to his own. Are you in the market for a tea caddy?"

"No."

"No," András repeated, as if it had been foolish to ask the question. A clatter of falling metal interrupted them, causing them both to wince.

Marci peered toward the back of the shop. "You have thieves?"

"Worse," András muttered. "I have a new employee."

"You've hired someone? I thought you were too tightfisted for staff?"

András lowered his voice. "To tell you the truth, she's a pleasure to look at, and I can always do with an extra pair of hands, so I was swayed. She's an artist or some such nonsense, which means I have to explain everything twice. Ah, speak of the devil."

Into the room came a slim woman in her late twenties carrying a box full of brass bridle medallions. Her hair, which was dark brunette, was held back by clips. Large brown eyes, a snub nose and a mouth which drooped at the corners gave her an air of pensive concentration. In a corner of the room she stopped and surveyed the merchandise already on display. She was, Marci thought, the most beautiful woman he had ever seen.

"Over there, dear," András said, pointing to the other side of the shop. To Marci he whispered, "See what I mean? I might as well be doing it myself."

Marci watched her for a moment, then picked out some Soviet-era color postcards protruding from an electric toaster. "The good old days."

András chuckled. "So they'd have you believe. I'm no Communist, but at least they didn't have SIN and the Hangman to contend with. Oh, I almost forgot. I've something special arriving soon that might be right up your street. Pedigree stuff, of course."

"A wife?"

"Even better: a Victorian bracket clock. She needs a little renovating, but nothing serious." András opened the front door. "You should head home. The curfew will start soon, and as much as I like you, I don't want you sleeping on my floor."

Marci, preoccupied with watching the shop assistant, failed to respond.

András cleared his throat. "Perhaps you'd care to stay a little longer, after all?"

Marci tucked the postcards back in the toaster. "Call me when you get the consignment."

"The machines are out," András said, looking up at the sky. "Be quick about it."

"Good night, András." He turned to the girl and managed to mumble, "Good night."

Either too busy or not interested, she failed to acknowledge him.

The rain had slackened off to a light drizzle. Under a darkening sky Marci hurried towards Gyulai Pál utca, the pedestrianized side street home to his apartment block. Overhead, low-flying sentry drones darted like steel insects between buildings, each bristling with weaponry from their undercarriage. Red and blue text bars on their bellies displayed a countdown until curfew began. Periodically, a woman's voice, crisp and officious, exhorted Employees to seek refuge. Searchlights scoured the sidewalks, but since drones could read second skin[5], the lamps served only a minacious effect.

Marci checked his watch: 18:55. He had five minutes to reach home. As he crossed Stáhly utca he was bathed in brilliant light. Fifty feet above him, buzzing like a wasp shaken in a can, a drone was reading his biodata. Marci hastened his steps. The penalties for breaching the curfew included the deduction of SIN points or imprisonment, both of which he could do without. Being shot was a more conclusive consequence. The machine trailed him for several seconds before darting away to illuminate another section of the Palace District.

From the distance came the rolling gurgle of thunder: an electrical storm[6] was nearing. Before long, AirNet—MARTHA's communication system—would be down, which meant that the Underground would soon be abroad. Marci thanked God he lived in the relative safety of District VIII.

At the end of Gyulai Pál utca stood a five story Neo-Baroque apartment building. Marci pressed his hand against a scanner panel in the wall and stepped into the lobby. Immediately, he regretted

---

[5] Second skin is the prosaic moniker for a surveillance system initiated by the Company. A faintly radioactive additive in the public water supply, when ingested, produces a mild signal which can be detected by appropriate monitoring equipment. It provides MARTHA with the precise location of all Employees.

[6] Savage and spectacular, the storms, which are the result of post-nuclear climate change, render AirNet inoperative. With both AirNet down and police drones unable to fly, a growing body of disenfranchised citizens frequently takes to the streets to loot, deface and menace Budapest. Safe from arrest, theirs is an irresistible opportunity to break free from the constraints of MARTHA and her perpetual observation. The Company's response is curfews, which only occur during such storms.

having left Objet d'Heart so soon. Attempting to drag a heavy shopping trolley up several steps to the elevator was Mária Földi, the octogenarian Housing Manager and resident Company Community officer. Widowed and childless, Mária lived in an apartment on the top floor, which afforded her both commanding views over the courtyard and limitless opportunities to report the comings and goings of her fellow residents to the Justice and Cessation Board. A doughty old bird with a will of iron, she was greatly to be feared. Fortunately, she was fond of Marci. Marci despised her.

Mária noticed him. *"Halihó, Márton! Hogy vagy?*[7] "

"Segíthetek?"[8] Marci asked, grabbing the trolley and dragging it carelessly up the steps. "Bloody hell, what have you got in here, a corpse?"

Mária grinned a toothy smile. "You are a naughty boy, Marci! I've been to the market. Cabbage rolls for dinner!"

"Nothing new there, then," Marci said under his breath.

"Tessék?"

"I said I wish we could share them."

Mária clapped her hands in joy. "I will make some extra and bring them down to you!"

"That's kind of you, but I don't want to be an inconvenience."

"It will be my pleasure, Marcim! You didn't tell me you liked them."

"My mistake."

"You hardly tell me anything," Mária said, affecting disappointment. "Sometimes I think you're a"—she lowered her voice—"a Hangman!"

Marci laughed, refusing to bite. "I'm really quite straightforward. Oh look, here's the lift."

Mária pushed her way inside, dragging the trolley after her to fully occupy the space. "I will bring you some cabbage rolls later."

"Please don't hurry," Marci replied, closing the door on her.

"Viszlát, Márton!"

---

[7] How are you?

[8] Can I help you?

"Nosy old witch," Marci said out of earshot, and headed across the courtyard.

The rain had redoubled its efforts, beating down into the courtyard and filling the drains to overflowing. Marci, whose socks and feet were already soaked, sloshed through the thin, unbroken sheet of oily water, passing a brick workshop in one corner of the quadrangle. A single window emitted wan yellow light. Inside, a loud whining noise rose and fell, as if a power tool were meeting resistance. Norbert Tóth, SIN 16 and Marci's neighbor, had finished his shift at the ammonia plant in Veszprém for the day, and was busy inside.

Marci trudged up the stairs to the third floor. A matrix of green lasers scanned him at the entrance to his apartment. Stepping inside, he removed his shoes and arranged them symmetrically beside the others in the shoe rack. In the bathroom he peeled his wet socks off, toweled his feet dry and washed his hands until they stung.

A voice came from the kitchen: "*Szia*, Marci. How was your day?"

"About the same as usual."

"I've made coffee. Would you like a cup?"

He studied his hands. They were getting worse. His doctor had prescribed some special handwash, but Marci didn't trust its sterilizing properties. He flexed his fingers; the skin broke and serous fluid appeared through the cracks. "Any messages?"

"No, but Sándor called this afternoon."

Marci entered the empty kitchen and collected his coffee from the dispenser. "Alice, make lasagna."

"As you wish."

He'd bought the apartment seven years ago when he made Adjudicant and had invested most of his salary into furnishing it. Like the other flats in the building, it was a *káder-lakás*, a former Communist Party member's residence, with large, airy rooms and high ceilings. Many owners had adapted them, knocking through walls or fitting galleries. But Marci loved the original features and had chosen to retain them.

The decor, which derived from several periods, was vintage, and despite its diversity it blended together with ease. The only concessions to convenience were Alice, his automated concierge, and a Living Wall, which presented no visible blight to the room.

Marci sat in a worn Chesterfield and lit a cigarette. "Wall on."

The lounge lights dimmed and a vast, curvilinear screen appeared in the air. "Forest."

A menu presented several options. "Summer, England." The menu faded; an evening woodland tableau encircled him. Blackbirds, unseen, sang poignant melodies; from close at hand, wood pigeons softly cooed.

"Play "The Lark Ascending"."

Marci settled back into his chair and closed his eyes. The music lulled him. Presently, he began to doze.

A noise: shouting.

He stirred. The music had finished. In the astray beside him, his cigarette had consumed itself into ashy pewter. Half asleep, he closed his eyes again.

A woman's scream, this time a louder, plaintive cry, carried from the courtyard. Marci roused himself and slouched to the front door.

The rain fell as a steady drizzle. On the fourth floor walkway a commotion was taking place. Four cessation squad officers, jackbooted and dressed in black, were trying to separate an elderly woman from her dressing gown-clad husband outside their apartment. The man, resigned to his fate, was spent and submissive. His wife, however, clung to him, and with loud wails begged the squad not to take him from her.

Marci's attention drifted to the floor above, where Mária Földi, dressed in her nightgown, peered over the balcony the better to watch the drama unfold. Below, a struggle ensued. The woman lashed out at one of the officers, who caught her by the wrist. Another pressed a medi-pen to her neck. Her grip loosened. Her legs sagged and the wailing ceased. Compliant, she was carried inside, while her spouse was led shuffling away. The remaining cessation officer emerged from the flat, closed the door and followed his colleagues out of the building.

The show was over. With an air of satisfaction, Mária Földi turned in for the night. Marci listened to the rain for a while, then retreated inside. It was never pleasant to witness liquidations, particularly when an altercation ensued.

His shoulder ached. In the bathroom cabinet he found painkillers, swallowed two with his cold coffee and settled down in front of the Living Wall, which now screened News24. The channel, run by the Company, headlined with a raid against Border defenses near Nyíregyháza. Graphic video footage showed a gang of armed Outsiders hacking two Border guards to death with machetes. The newsreel ran uncensored, but Marci, like every other Employee, had grown up seeing such reportage, and was desensitized to the horror of it.

Ticker tape text, crawling along the bottom of the screen, presented a different story:

...KELETI BLAST KILLS 68, INJURES DOZENS... UNDERGROUND CLAIMS RESPONSIBILITY...

So much for the bombing, Marci thought. All the dead got was a nine-word mention at the end of the late-night news. He'd had a lucky escape today. MARTHA would have already closed the files of the deceased. The injured would be treated and returned to work as quickly as possible. Similarly, the bereaved would be medicated and fast-tracked to normal productivity. While appalling, the bombing had some plus points: there would be sixty-eight fewer Employees wrangling for SIN 30, and a small but useful reduction in the city's overheads.

He finished a cigarette and turned in for the night. Hanging in the bedroom closet were the garments Sándor's tailor had selected for him to wear tomorrow. Marci removed the shirt and jacket and held them against himself in the mirror, inspecting his reflection with distaste. Small wonder the girl at Objet d'Heart had so conspicuously ignored him. Why wouldn't she? She was out of his league, of course. Girls like her were used to garnering the attention of finer men than him. He was just another slightly overweight punter in a bric-a-brac shop. Best to just forget her. When he reached SIN 30 he'd be someone worthy of a woman like that.

Marci lay in the darkness and stared at the ceiling. All his life he'd dreamed of crossing the river into Buda, where far away from the rank and file of Pest the SIN 30ers lived in cocooned bliss. He was close to joining them—damn close. One lousy SIN point was all he needed, and unlike the previous nineteen, this one couldn't be earned. SIN 30 was bestowed by the Prefect alone.

Everything was riding on tomorrow.

2

The air car rose over Budapest.

Marci watched the landscape below, trying his best to ignore the uncomfortable falling sensation in his stomach which had nothing to do with their flight. Next to him at the controls was Sándor Ortega, a bear of a man with a gray beard, pale-blue eyes and hair swept back in a style of timeless elegance. Ortega, 66, was a shipping magnate and President of The Society of Patricians, the elite assembly that governed Budapest.

The craft banked in a lazy arc, affording Marci a better view of the eastern shore. Pest, the ugly sister of Buda, was the workhorse of the city. Downtown, skyscrapers rose with spires like cathedrals, piercing the late September sky. Beneath them, a vast sprawl of factories, shops and tenement housing, with a spattering of greenery to break up the homogeneity. Highways, train lines, sky roads and motorways rove here and there, between, over and even through buildings, while the Danube glistened like quicksilver in the sunlight.

Sándor glanced through the starboard window. "What do you think? Quite a view, eh?"

"I never tire of seeing it," Marci said. "It's beautiful and ugly at the same time. Are the other Sister Cities like this?"

"Yes and no. Budapest has the biggest population, but Beijing outranks it for size, as does Mumbai. Personally, I prefer Tokyo. The food is less irradiated in Sydney; they fared better in the Fuel War[9] than most. Moscow has lovely women, but don't tell my wife I said so."

"It must be nice to see the world," Marci said. "I've never been anywhere."

---

[9] An overview of the Fuel War can be found in the Appendix.

"In the past, people used to travel for leisure," Sándor replied. "That was before the war, of course. Now we have SIN to focus on, and most people are afraid of venturing beyond the Border. Not that they have the opportunity, of course."

"Is it true what they say about the Outside?"

"In what respect?"

"The people. The way of life."

"It depends on who you ask. But the Company has told us what it's like, so the question is moot. In any case, why bother finding out? There are settlements in the wasteland, and I'm told some even have a semblance of order, if you can imagine barbarians capable of civility. But my business is shipping, not sightseeing." Sándor shot Marci a look. "What do you know of classic art?"

"About as much as I know of the Outside."

"Allow me to advise you. Art is much like women: some graceful, intelligent and charming to behold; many more are confusing, shallow, and brutal on the eyes. Whatever your views, remember that it's the Prefect's private collection you're viewing, and that his good opinion of you is worth far more than what he paid for the stuff, which is not inconsiderable."

"I'll try to bear in mind it probably costs more than the DOME, and nod approvingly."

"I see you already have all the makings of a Patriarch," Sándor mused. This morning he had foregone traditional Patrician attire, instead preferring a casual business look: a navy-blue jacket, pleated white shirt, tan trousers and a blue-and-brown cravat. His leather loafers exceeded most men's annual salary, and he wore the confection with the easy éclat of one for whom dressing well was an everyday occurrence.

Marci, on the other hand, felt awkwardly self-conscious in a cornflower-blue silk shirt, a Victorian-style, rust-brown jacquard vest and matching plaid cotton trousers, and high-gloss, brown lace-up boots which chafed at the heels. A mustard yellow puff tie completed the ensemble. It was an outfit which, he'd been assured, was the very height of fashion, and one that would arouse admiring envy in all he met. Marci felt like a popinjay, and was convinced he would stand out like a sore thumb.

Sándor let the car rise into the clear morning sky: two thousand feet, five thousand feet… Still the city had no end. Across the river via eight heavily guarded bridges was a different world. Buda, home to the rich, famous, and infamous, counterpointed Pest in every way. Where Pest was dirty and overcrowded, Buda was verdant, luxurious, sparse. Its denizens, the cream of society, had earned the right to dwell there, and made scant effort to conceal their wealth.

Sándor spoke into a microphone: "Budapest Air Control, private class Argo One requesting access to Buda air space, over."

A response came: "BAC to Argo One, you're cleared for Buda. Descend to three thousand and bear right on heading zero-one-zero. Have a good day, Patrician Ortega."

Sándor tapped a floating screen before him and engaged the autopilot. The vessel slowed, banked right and began its descent.

Marci drank in the landscape. From wooded hills rose fantastic buildings of every size and shape: lavish Baroque and Rococo palaces; Elizabethan priories, complete with herb gardens and hedge mazes; boxy Georgian mansions with long, sweeping drives; Art Deco condominiums in pastel shades of pink, blue and pale lemon. Among them stood the abstract and the absurd: pyramids, rhomboids, angled discs, the conical, spherical, and hexagonal. All of this lay behind a slew of roadblocks, sentry guns, surveillance and security drones, barriers, invisible sonic gates and more, provided either by The Society or the residents association. Buda the beautiful was also Buda the fortress, and sometimes it was hard to know who was protected from whom.

The craft rounded a limestone crag. Into view came a spreading Tuscan-style villa of breathtaking beauty. Tall Cyprus and parasol trees rose from a lawn of paspalum grass to pierce the sky. At the bottom of the garden, six marble landing pads awaited guests. One of them, set apart from the others, bore a crest: a gold eagle on a white background: the insignia of The Society of Patricians. With imperceptible contact the craft set down.

Sándor regarded Marci. "Well then, are you ready?"

Marci fidgeted with his neck puff. Despite the cocktail of sedatives he'd taken in lieu of breakfast, he was already feeling slightly sick with apprehension. "As ready as I'll ever be. Which is to say, not at all."

A valet appeared at the window. Sándor pressed a button and the air car's doors opened. "Come," he said, placing a giant hand on Marci's shoulder. "You'll forget your nerves soon enough."

Through fragrant gardens of jasmine, myrtle and lavender the two were escorted toward waiting buggies. Marci, who had never seen or smelled the flowers before, stopped and rubbed a lavender head between his fingers. He lifted it to his nose, sniffed it and looked at Sándor in wonder. "Are these real?"

Sándor chuckled. "Of course. They were grown from seeds taken from gene banks that survived the War."

"I can't believe all of this belongs to one man."

"Not just a man, the Prefect of Budapest! His place makes mine look like a hovel. The path we're walking on, by the way, costs over two thousand credits[10] per square foot."

Marci laughed. "That's more than I earn in a week."

Sándor raised a hand in greeting. "Here's Darius."

Another buggy halted beside them. From it stepped a spare man with a crop of light-brown hair cut short in the Greco-Roman style: Darius Rosetti, CEO of the Bank of Budapest. He wore the traditional beige robe and leather sandals of a Patrician. "I came down to find you," he said without introduction. "The Prefect hasn't appeared yet. Needless to say, we're waiting with bated breath."

Sándor embraced his friend. "Good to see you. How's business?"

"I can't complain. We have a captive market of forty-million customers, and our competition comprises Seth Anderson and Ádam Varga; both estimable Patrician, but with the combined business sense of a baboon."

"Since I trade with both of them," Sándor remarked, "I feel it prudent to withhold comment. On a different tack, allow me to introduce my protégé and friend Márton Kovács, SIN 29, one of the finest Adjudicants ever to grace the Executive Team."

---

[10] New Global Credit: an international standardized monetary unit. One credit equals one hour's manual labor, as defined in the Sister City Charter, section c5.

Darius saluted in mock reverence. "A pleasure to meet you! I hope my lifeline is secure and that MARTHA will continue to look on me with favor?"

Marci saluted in response, feeling a little foolish. "It's an honor to meet you, Patrician Darius. Unfortunately, MARTHA is completely impartial and has no favorites. But I can have a word with Data Analytics to see if they'll massage the figures for you."

Darius chuckled. "I like this fellow already, but now I fear for my SIN. Please remember that I pulled a lot of strings to get a 29er on the guest list today."

"You did no such thing," Sándor corrected. "You merely voted in favor of my proposal."

Darius showed a wintry smile. "Perish the thought that I should vote against our President."

"Well then," Sándor said, looking from Marci to Darius. "Let's not keep the Prefect waiting. Shall we?"

The shuttle car ferried them up a driveway to a broad terrace where, under an immense barber pole candy awning, waiters prepared forty tables for lunch. Steps guarded by limbless Greek statues and potted lemon trees led up to the Prefect's residence, which was even more impressive from the ground than the air. The walls, fashioned from soft rosso ammonitico limestone, stucco and exposed masonry, hid beneath hip-style roofs of terra-cotta barrel tiles. Cedars of Lebanon spread broad, horizontal branches overhead. Marci, used to breathing in Pest's polluted atmosphere, inhaled deeply. The air was rich with the scent of olive, sage, lavender, bay.

Marci, Sándor and Darius stepped through an archway into a rectangular cloistered courtyard. In the center, a series of fountains bubbled water into mosaic basins fashioned from mother-of-pearl and turquoise. Walkways to left and right provided shade. Here, heavy marble benches were arranged at regular intervals for the comfort of guests. Beside these, oversized pots confined kumquat and lemon, lavender, and verbena. Vines clung to the walls, and were cleverly irrigated by narrow channels cut into the granite floor. The passage of the water made a pleasing tinkling sound. At the far end of the courtyard, a studded oak door led further into the villa. Here, in the shadows, a minstrel played dulcet baroque melodies on a theorbo.

Sauntering here and there, talking, laughing and gossiping, were the Patricians, some in togas, others in more contemporary outfits. They varied in age, but not in gender. All were men, and all leaders in their fields: industry, commerce, the arts, sciences and politics. Each carried himself with easy confidence. Moving discreetly among them, young waitresses in kirtles served chilled white wine and hors d'oeuvres.

Marci, dazed by his surroundings, stopped short.

Sándor noted his expression and grinned. "I take it you approve?"

"It's beyond what I imagined. I didn't know such a place existed."

"Prefect Trauffaut likes to impress."

"He's certainly succeeded."

Sándor beckoned to a waitress, who brought them wine. Marci declined a canapé from another server. "The wine is a tokaji," Sándor said, "but of course not from Tokaj anymore. It's grown in the nurseries near Kőbánya. Still, I think they've done a good job. It's not far off the original."

Marci sipped the wine, which was delicate and sweet. "It seems everything is available if you have money."

"Hasn't that always been the case?"

The Patricians fell silent. Into the courtyard stepped two men. One was young, clean-shaven and elegantly dressed in an expensive navy suit. His slicked hair, parted on one side, rose in a pompadour, in keeping with the current fashion.

His companion, an elderly man, stood several inches taller, and had modestly chosen to array himself in traditional Patrician attire. The toga—white, to designate his rank—made his jaundiced pallor appear even more sickly. A gold sash hung from his shoulder, adding further distinction. Despite his enervated appearance, his bearing was distinguished, with strong, regular features, white hair swept back past his ears, a neat white beard and benign eyes. Prefect Jean-Pierre Trauffaut, leader of The Society of Patricians and premier of Budapest, extended his right hand, palm open, towards the sun. An Emperor's greeting.

As one, the Patricians bowed.

Trauffaut bade them rise, as if their deference was expected yet misplaced. "Friends, please! You are too kind. I bow to you, Patricians of Budapest. The fabric of our great city was forged by you. Together we protect the dear people of Budapest from the ravening wolves of the Outside. Yes, I bow to you, Patricians, to whom I owe so much."

The Patricians inclined their heads in appreciation.

"And I owe you an apology. For I invited you to enjoy something very dear to my heart from purely selfish motives. As someone wiser than I wrote, "pleasure has no relish unless we share it." What you are to see is the greatest private collection of classical art ever assembled. It is no exaggeration that many men gave their lives to rescue these masterpieces from the Outside, and to them I will be forever indebted. This, then, is my raison d'être: to love art and to share it with the like-minded. So then, without further ado, please follow me."

Prefect Trauffaut and his aide turned and disappeared inside. Slowly, the Patricians made their way to the door. Sándor waited for them to pass. In a tone deliberately neutral he asked, "And what do you think of our leader?"

Marci reflected on a response. The Prefect's sallow appearance was irreconcilable with the image presented by News24. "He's… taller than I imagined."

Sándor showed the faintest of smiles. "The Society has been at pains to present him in the best light possible. There are those who would monopolize any sign of weakness in the city's leadership."

Marci wondered whether an inquiry into the nature of the Prefect's ailment was appropriate. Probably not. On second thoughts, reticence might be interpreted as indifference. "I'm sorry to hear this," he said. "I hope it's nothing serious?"

Sándor acknowledged the courtesy with a nod of the head but provided no answer. "Come," he said, leading Marci to the front of the queuing Patricians, "let's see what visual feast awaits us."

The gallery, several hundred feet long, extended into pleasant duskiness under a fan-vaulted brick ceiling reminiscent of a church undercroft. The walls were fashioned from softer stuff: fawn stucco, which created a gentler ambiance in keeping with the mien of the property. From these hung priceless paintings by Michelangelo, Dürer and da Vinci. A smattering of Boticellis and Tintorettos, each arranged and illuminated for best effect, commanded equal awe.

Prefect Trauffaut wandered here and there, followed by his assistant and a flock of Patricians. He seemed in his element, taking pleasure in describing each work of art, its intent, pedigree and inspiration.

Sándor accepted another glass of wine from a waitress. He spoke to Marci: "I'll introduce you when he's less occupied. How are you feeling?"

"Nervous and excited at the same time," said Marci. "The paintings are incredible. How did he locate them?"

"With great difficulty. They were thought to be lost forever after the Fuel War, but some clever souls had stashed them away before the bombs fell. Others were in private collections, far away from cities. Once the Red Plague subsided, treasure hunters set out to recover them. Many of them died, mostly from radiation poisoning. But a handful found and returned them to the Sister Cities, making fabulous fortunes for themselves in the process."

Through the vault they strolled, passing sculptures by Donatello and Giambologna which, if viewed obliquely, might be mistaken for fellow visitors amid the toga-clad Patricians. In the center of the room, suspended beneath the ceiling by Heavy Air[11], a mural portraying the Roman god Jupiter realigning the celestial sphere, while his brothers Neptune and Pluto stood below, in attitudes less extraordinary.

Marci, his mouth sagging, stared up at it in wonder. "I don't believe it. I thought this was lost when Rome was destroyed."

"Caravaggio," Sándor said, mildly disinterested. "His only fresco, I'm told. Something about the philosopher's stone. The details escape me."

---

[11] A revolutionary advancement in physics which generates "virtual ground," against which propulsion systems create lift.

"It's not a fresco," Marci murmured. "It's oil on plaster. Frescos used pigment."

"I stand corrected."

Armand Bucco, aide to the Prefect, navigated his way toward them like mercury through a puzzle maze. Reaching Sándor he bowed a little too deeply. "How kind of you to grace us with your presence, Patrician Ortega."

The honorific, inappropriately deficient, might be forgiven in one less familiar with Society protocol. If it riled the President, he hid it well. "Palatine Bucco," Sándor greeted. "You must be in your element today."

Bucco seemed not to detect the condescension. "I confess to feeling rather spoiled. Ordinarily these works grace the main residence of the villa, where I see them every day. But I'm sure you're an authority on the Renaissance period. How do you find the collection?"

"Impressive. I was only now discussing the difficulties of gathering such an opus."

"I believe you assisted him in the case of Caravaggio's Vitruvian Man. As for the others, our Prefect's connections are equally impeccable, and he enjoys much goodwill among the Sister Cities."

"May I introduce a dear friend of mine, Márton Kovács?"

Bucco acknowledged Marci with a curt nod of his head. "You are most welcome here among the ranks of the Patricians. Any friend of President Ortega is a friend of us all."

"Marci is a SIN 29 Level 3 Adjudicant," Sándor continued. "I believe he will prove a fine addition to our fellowship."

Bucco smiled thinly. "That is a matter for The Society to decide. As you are aware, membership is exclusive, and few have joined us in recent years"—here he turned his gaze to Marci—"even if they are SIN 29 Adjudicants."

Marci flushed at the slight but held his tongue.

"And how is the running of the country going, Armand?" Sándor asked.

Bucco made a modest gesture. "I do my best. Thankfully, our Prefect and the Patricians are very supportive, and make my workload easy. Today's gathering is light relief from my normal duties, and I get to meet esteemed Patricians such as yourself."

"We are grateful for your hard work this morning," Sándor said. "But now please excuse us, as I would speak to Prefect Trauffaut."

"Very well," Bucco said. "I pray you will enjoy the rest of your visit." He bowed, then sauntered nonchalantly away.

"Obsequious little runt," Sándor muttered. "You'd think he was the Prefect himself."

Marci watched him mingle with the other guests. "He doesn't like me, for sure."

"He's not important. He's a trumped-up administrator with aspirations to become the next Prefect, which he'll never achieve since only a Patrician can be elected." Sándor surveyed the room. "Grab a drink and mingle. I'll set up an introduction with the Prefect."

Marci looked uneasily towards Trauffaut, who stood discussing an Ammanati statue. "Do I have to? Maybe we can just enjoy the exhibit?"

"I brought you here to meet the Prefect," Sándor said. "And that's exactly what you're going to do." With that, he walked off.

Marci took a glass of tokaji from a passing waiter and slunk to the side of the room. Before him hung a painting smaller than the great frescos suspended elsewhere in the gallery. The style was Renaissance but the frame was Rococo, all gold leaf and swirls. It depicted Bacchus, the Greek god of wine, leaping from his chariot to embrace Ariadne, daughter of King Minos of Crete, with whom he had fallen desperately in love. Ariadne, less than happy with Bacchus's romantic attentions, recoiled with her hand raised in deterrence. A nameplate beneath the painting dated it: 1596. Half a millennia old, give or take a few decades. Presumably this was one of the treasures Sándor had mentioned, stored away while the world tore itself apart. Who had kept it, Marci wondered? A barbarian art collector was an oxymoron; he'd just as likely use it for fuel as hang it on a wall. The painting's provenance was more interesting than the work itself.

"I find the rendition of the anatomy quite remarkable."

The voice snapped him from his reverie.

Prefect Trauffaut, attended by a flock of Patricians, offered him a long, frail hand. "Welcome, Mr. Kovács. Sándor tells me you're the finest Adjudicant in the Executive Team."

Marci stared up at him like an animal caught in headlights. He tried to speak, but his voice caught in his throat.

"From what I understand," Trauffaut continued, "the department wouldn't function without you. It seems we are in your debt." He indicated the painting. "What are your thoughts on the Titian?"

Marci's tongue felt welded to his palate. "I'm not an expert," he stammered. "I really wouldn't like to comment."

"Come now," Trauffaut coaxed, "an expert is simply one whose views concur with those of his peers. Your opinion is as valid as mine."

More Patricians had gathered around them to watch the exchange. Marci hesitated. What now? Should he follow Sándor's advice and utter a platitude, or speak his mind? His vision swam. The wine—could it be the wine? He'd only drunk half a glass.

At last he found his voice. "I'm not sure what to say. The figures are anatomically perfect, but their postures are grandiose, even for Renaissance art. Then there's the sky. I've always wondered why Titian, with so much talent for the human form, painted such a childish sky. It's as if he was having a bad day. "

Silence, save the chink of wine glasses somewhere. The Patricians, amused or uneasy, shifted their attention to the Prefect, who stooped and studied the painting anew.

Marci scanned the crowd. Where was Sándor? Couldn't he see he was drowning? If only he'd taken the President's advice and uttered some harmless pleasantry. Instead, he'd insulted the Prefect to his face in front of the entire Society.

Say something, you fool!

"It's just my opinion," he mumbled.

Trauffaut, preoccupied with the painting, spoke in a tone of quiet marvel. "Extraordinary, quite extraordinary. You're right." He turned to Marci with sudden energy. "In all these years I've never noticed such a thing!"

Bucco stepped forward and cleared his throat. "Sire," he murmured, "it is time."

Trauffaut ignored him. "Mr. Kovács, it appears your talents have been undersold. Not only are you our finest Adjudicant, but an art connoisseur. I hope when next we meet you'll share your insights into the rest of my collection." He clasped Marci's hand. "Thank you for your candor."

Before Marci could respond, the Prefect was gone, sweeping away with him his retinue.

Sándor approached. Together they peered at the painting.

"Did I say the right thing?"

"You spoke the truth, which is something few men dare to do." He broke into a grin. "We'll get you your Club 30 card yet."

Bucco tapped on a wine glass several times. "Patricians! Your attention, if you please!"

Prefect Trauffaut spoke: "My dear friends, I apologize for my fleeting presence, but I must now take my leave. Thank you once again for your company this morning. Feel to enjoy the collection further, as well as a modest repast to be served on the terrace. Until we meet again: Patricians, I salute you!"

As one, the assembly bowed low. The door to the courtyard opened; talking among themselves, the Patricians filed out.

Sándor and Marci waited for the last of them to leave before stepping out into the cloister. "While you were with the Prefect," Sándor said, "I spoke with some of the Synod. As President, I have certain privileges, one of which is to—let us say—encourage them in voting matters. Provided your acceptance speech is up to scratch, The Society has assured me it will endorse your application for membership at the next AGM."

Marci stopped short. "The AGM? That's only a month away!"

"Give or take a few days. Do you have something prepared?"

Marci shook his head. "I was hoping I wouldn't need one."

"I know you have difficulties in social settings," Sándor continued, "but all candidates are expected to give a brief talk. It's essentially a groveling thank you, but a prerequisite for approval." Taking note of Marci's dejected expression, Sándor ruffled his hair.

"It doesn't have to be a litany; in fact, quite the opposite. Most of the Patricians are only there for the food."

Marci was not encouraged. "I had no idea it would be so soon."

"*Carpe diem*," Sándor said. "Why waste time? Haven't you been working toward this all your life?"

"Yes, of course. But now it's near, I'm not sure I can do it."

Sándor led him to a bench. "Marci, how long have I known you?"

"At least since Dad died. Fourteen years ago in April."

"I remember the day well. He was a good man and a good friend. You were what, twenty-four?"

"Twenty-five," Marci corrected. "It was the year before I made Assistant Adjudicant Level I. And I'd never have done it without you."

Sándor smiled. "All I did was give you a little pep talk. And that's what I'm going to do now. Marci, you're not even forty. The world lies before you. The Society has never nominated someone at such a young age. I saw that potential in you years ago, long before your father's passing."

Marci laughed bitterly. "I wonder what he'd think of me now? I'm a nervous wreck. I can't even take the bus to work without sedatives."

"He was proud of you then, and I know he'd be just as proud now."

"Dad would have thrown a fit if he knew I was going to make Club 30. He hated the whole SIN system."

"Both he and your mother would be overjoyed," Sándor corrected, "not for your SIN, but to see you fulfill your potential. Marci, before Péter passed away I promised him I'd do everything I could to support you in life. At first it was a favor to a dying friend. Then it became a privilege. And now is your moment."

"I'm not there yet."

"You're a hair's breadth from it, and I won't see you squander the chance. This is not the time for introspection. It's time to overcome."

"That's easy for you to say," Marci grumbled. "For me it's like asking lead to float."

Have you made an appointment to see Stella Kennedy?"

Marci looked away. "Not yet."

"Then I advise you to call her," Sándor insisted. "Today, if possible. She's the best therapist in Budapest."

"Don't you think I've tried everything?" Marci cried. "Nothing works!"

"If you haven't tried her, you haven't tried everything. Another bit of Latin, the last for today, I promise: *Qui audet adipiscitur*: who dares, wins."

Marci looked across the courtyard and listened to the tinkling of water as it moved through the channels cut into the stone underfoot. The sound brought him no peace. "What happens if I can't deliver the speech?"

"It won't come to that. You're more than capable of reading half a page of text."

Marci, unconvinced, was tired of the topic. "I'll try my best."

Sándor spoke affectionately. "I expect nothing less. One little courtesy remains. I'll need to speak to the Prefect to make it official. Even though the Synod will second you, we need the Trauffaut's approval. As it happens, I'm hosting a little cocktail party at my place in a fortnight. The Prefect and István Panicucci are expected to attend. We're hoping we can solve the problem of the blasted Underground. In the meantime, start work on your speech. I'll send you some exemplars from previous nominations. Massage them a little; no one pays much attention to the content anyway." He rose. "I don't know about you, but those canapés only tease the taste buds. Shall we investigate the spread our Prefect has laid on?"

Marci followed him toward the terrace. Sándor was speaking, but Marci didn't hear the words. A month. A month to prepare the speech that would forever change his life. If he succeeded, he could leave behind Pest and his career in the Executive Team for a life of ease in idyllic Buda. If he chose to continue his career, SIN 33 and eternal life in Empyrean might one day be his.

It all depended on a few hundred words.

3

Marci strode along Gyulai Pál utca, his trench coat collars pulled up against the rain and an umbrella drone hovering overhead. Ever since his last visit to András's shop a week ago his thinking had been dominated by the girl at Objet d'Heart. Hopeless with the opposite sex, the very idea of a conversation with a pretty girl made Marci quail.

The answer lay 50% in preparation and an equal measure in self-medication. His Saturday morning had been spent agonizing in front of the bedroom mirror. A suit was too formal; tee shirt and jeans were too casual. Lacking anything arty or remotely Bohemian, Marci settled on "business casual": beige slacks, chestnut-colored shoes and a woolen long-sleeved shirt. It was an outfit that rarely saw the light of day, since at home he dressed like a slob.

Marci reached Kőfaragó utca and turned the corner. Preoccupied with his thoughts, he failed to notice a loose paving stone which, under his weight, see-sawed to hurl filthy rainwater over his shoes and pants. In disbelief he gawked at the sullied garments. Should he go home and change? He'd come this far; Objet d'Heart was close at hand. Besides, he'd steeled himself for the encounter. To the cadence of a chain of foul expletives he pressed on.

At Gutenberg Tér Marci took shelter in an archway, lit a cigarette and dabbed at his pants with a handkerchief. Across the square lay Objet d'Heart with its dimly-lit façade, which indicated neither whether the premises was open or closed; an ambiguity Marci had long-suspected was not unintentional.

He touched his neck. His pulse throbbed quick with adrenaline. Was it too late to turn back? Perhaps the place wasn't even open.

András was a law unto himself and kept hours only as the mood took him. Chances were he'd shut up shop for the weekend.

Marci smoked his cigarette, lit another and stared across the playground, where the rusting bust of József Fodor kept melancholy vigil over swings and see-saws abandoned to the rain.

Pull yourself together. She's just a shop assistant.

It was hopeless, of course. The self-talk never worked. In his pocket he found a half-used roll of Kqalms, one of which he placed under his tongue. The pills still worked, but years of overuse had dulled their effect. In response, Marci was forced to take ever-increasing doses. He was, he admitted, quite probably an addict, but had managed to stay off booze, mostly.

Get a grip, he told himself. *You're a Level 29 Adjudicant. You'll be making Club 30 soon.*

But in the end, what of it? Girls like her—he'd already formed the highest estimation of her—girls like her were above such carnal matters. No, culture and intelligence were the keys to winning the heart of such a woman. There remained, however, one obstacle that no amount of *savoir faire* could overcome. What if she found him unattractive? To that there was no answer.

He discarded his cigarette, threw a handful of peppermints into his mouth and marched towards Objet d'Heart.

The tinkling of bells heralded his arrival. Must hung in the air. The shop was silent, save the slow, steady ticking of a carriage clock. Marci closed the door behind him and hung his jacket on a coat stand. A mirror on the wall framed his face. He pushed back his hair, then ruffled it. Maybe she wasn't in today.

He moved quietly between rows of ancient desks bearing exotic wooden effigies and tatty Communist medals. An Art Deco lamp with a bottle-green shade caught his eye. Nice, but not in keeping with his apartment. A noise from the storeroom, possibly András.

It was not András. Into the room came the girl. Her hair was plaited twice at the front and wrapped around the nape of her neck; wisps fell at her ears, with another straying across her face. A white lace blouse, tawny-brown cardigan and tight wool trousers lent her an air of modest elegance. She carried a large florid vase that had seen better days. Noticing Marci she greeted him but refused to meet his gaze. *"Jó napot kívánok."*

"Jó napot," he replied, watching her try to find somewhere to put the vase.

"Segíthetek?" she asked.

"I hope so. I was wondering if the clock András mentioned has arrived?"

She tilted her head to one side to consider. "Oh yes! You're Mr. Kovács?"

"Marci. And you are?"

"I'm Erin. András popped out for a little while. I'll fetch it for you." She disappeared into the storeroom and returned with something in foam wrap. Marci made space on a chessboard and regretted his last two cigarettes. His mouth was dry and tasted foul. He tried holding his breath.

Erin removed the covering to reveal a Victorian walnut bracket clock. It was chipped in places and showed signs of woodworm, but the wood had a pleasing, flame-like swirling pattern that glowed in the dim light of the shop.

"It's beautiful," she murmured.

"May I?" Marci picked it up and examined the clock face, which was inscribed:

BIRCH AND GAYDON
153 FENCHURCH STREET, LONDON

"How old is it?" Erin asked.

"Nineteenth century. Birch and Gaydon made them between 1881 and 1933. This one's an early example. It's a bit tatty—"

"But it could be mended quite easily," said Erin.

"Yes, it could. Are you an expert on vintage clocks?"

Erin shook her head. "No. But I think it's the most fabulous thing I've ever seen. Are you really going to buy it? It's very expensive, or so I should imagine."

"That depends on how avaricious András feels today." The front door opened. "Speaking of whom…"

"Marci, dear chap," András said, shutting the door with his bottom. "I was wondering if my day could get any worse. I'm glad to see you."

Marci frowned. "I'm not sure how to take that."

András, who was carrying a tea chest, got it caught in the wind chimes. "Damn and blast it," he growled, "these bloody bells will be the end of me." He shrugged himself free. "I see you've discovered the clock a little prematurely. It's a little worse for wear, but nothing a good polish won't fix."

"'Worse for wear?' It's riddled with woodworm and it's chipped on three corners. Where did you find it? A scrapheap?"

"This is a Birch and Gaydon!" András roared. "Do you know how hard it was to come by?"

"You needn't have bothered,' Marci said. "It's not fit for anything."

András picked up the clock as he might a baby. "I knew I shouldn't have called you before I'd had it prepared; my customers only ever see blemishes. If a beautiful woman seduced you, would you refuse her attentions because of a mole on her thigh?"

"I've never been seduced by a woman, beautiful or not."

"You lack all imagination," András grumbled.

"I can imagine you're going to ask a hefty price for this."

András sighed. "Why is it that the wealthiest of customers are also the most niggardly?"

"I wouldn't know," Marci said. "Perhaps one is the result of the other?"

"Perhaps. Meanwhile, honest men work themselves to the bone to put supper on the table."

"Such is life," Marci said, glancing toward the stockroom. "Incidentally, you haven't mentioned the price."

"To put a figure on a thing of beauty such as this is vulgar."

"For the sake of avoiding vulgarity, I'm happy to take it off your hands for free."

András chuckled. "You're as ruthless a rogue as any man I've met, fine clothes and all. By the way, you have a large stain on your trousers."

"I know."

András looked about for the box. "Blast it, where's the packaging?"

"Erin has it."

"'"Erin has it"?" András looked up with an arch smile. "You work quick, my boy."

Marci felt his cheeks redden. "She was showing me the clock."

"And if she'd waited for me to return, you wouldn't have seen it in such a state and I'd have made a tidy sum. Erin! Where are you?"

Erin appeared in the doorway a little too quickly. She was already carrying the box.

"Erin," András instructed, "pack Mr. Kovács's clock and have a label made up to George Clark. Ask him to repair it as soon as possible."

"My clock?" said Marci.

"It will be yours, I assure you. Once you see it in its full glory, you won't hesitate."

"Fine. I'll reserve judgment until I've seen the lady's birthmark."

Erin turned him a quizzical look and resumed her work.

András shuffled over to his desk and handed Marci an old biscuit tin. "I know it's bric-à-brac, but I got this for free with the Birch and Gaydon. You'll probably dismiss it with equal candor, but don't say I never think of you. Help yourself while I make some tea. The girl's version is like gnat's pee."

András disappeared. Marci prized the tin lid free with his fingernails. Inside was a hodgepodge of objects wrapped in lilac tissue paper: a set of long-shanked keys, rusting; an ashtray in the style of a Kalocsa flower motif, charred in one corner; a pouch containing *pengő*, the ancient Hungarian currency; a couple of old war medals; and two contraptions of unknown purpose: a steel tube and a small black box. At the bottom of the tin was a photograph of a girl at a seaside location.

Marci picked up the black box, which looked like it might contain a wedding ring. Instead, suspended in solution, was a disc of sheer plastic, half an inch in diameter. Something resembling a pen drive served no apparent purpose.

He turned his attention to the tube. It was formed of two sections, one of which rotated, to apparently no effect. A cartoon image of a mermaid and fish among vivid corals emblazoned the exterior. Like the biscuit tin, it too had succumbed to oxidation.

Erin finished repacking the clock and disappeared into the back room. Presently, András emerged with two mugs of hot tea, which he placed on the chessboard. "It's called a kaleidoscope. Look through this end and point the other at the light."

Marci placed the device to his eye and directed the other end towards a ceiling lamp.

"Now rotate the cylinder," András instructed.

"Ha!" Marci cried. "Pretty!" He replaced it and picked up the black box.

"That," said András, "is a contact lens. Folk once stuck them in their eyes to improve their vision, can you believe? This one, however, is rather special." He removed the tray that held the lens in saline. Couched in black foam underneath was a miniature electronic device. "This is a receiver. Whatever the user sees and hears is transmitted to the receiver. Don't ask me its history because I haven't got a clue."

Erin returned with a label, which she began filling out. Marci, remembering his soiled pants, angled his leg behind the table and feigned interest in the contents of the tin. András provided commentary: "Boer war medals, circa 1899 to 1902… some old keys… an ashtray for your home, perhaps?"

Marci shot Erin a furtive glance. "I don't need an ashtray, thank you." He picked up the photo again, turning it over in the hope of an inscription that wasn't there. The word 'Polaroid' and a ten-digit code were printed on the back. "What's this?"

András leaned over and shrugged. "From the clothing and the oversaturation, I'd say it was taken in the 1980s. The background looks like Lake Balaton."

"How much do you want for it?"

"It's worthless. You can keep it, though I don't know why you would."

Marci stared at the picture. To himself he said, "I just wonder who she was… what her life was like."

Erin paused from her work and looked up.

"I've no idea," András said, sipping his tea. "Just a girl."

Marci put it back in the tin. "I'll take all of it except the ashtray."

"You're the boss. Now, about the Birch—"

"Get it fixed up, and we'll talk."

"Agreed. It'll take a couple of days. And regarding the price…"

"It's a bracket clock in poor cosmetic condition—"

"Currently in poor cosmetic condition," András corrected, "but she'll be pristine when George is finished with her. She'll fetch six hundred credits at the very least."

Marci, smiling, shook his head. "András, you live in a dream world. I'll give you three hundred since I got this can of junk for free."

András buried his face in his hands. "Why can't I find honest, decent clientele?"

"Because they'd never set foot in here."

"Very well. Since you're my best customer, I'll accept five hundred."

"Four, cash. And that's my best offer."

András's shoulders sank in defeat. "So be it. You shall have your clock for four hundred credits, and every time you wish to know the time you will see me in rags."

"An added bonus," Marci said. "But you'd never have dropped your price so quickly unless it was only worth three."

"Please don't psychoanalyze your antique dealer," András growled. "It is even more heinous a crime than your thrift. I'll take the clock to George while he's still open. May I ask for payment now? You can collect it tomorrow. Unless you'd like it delivered."

Marci and Erin's eyes met; she quickly looked away. "Delivery will be fine," he mumbled, opening his wallet. "Two hundred… four hundred."

András tucked the notes into his pocket. "Received with thanks." He looked out of the window. "It seems we must both brave the rain again. Erin, please get the door for us and say goodbye to the nice gentleman."

"Goodbye, nice Mr. Kovács," Erin said with a trace of a smile.

Marci, eyes averted, hurried out into the storm. "Goodbye, Erin."

The next day was Sunday. Marci rose early, showered and ate a light breakfast. The morning was bright and pleasant; last night's storm might as well not have happened. After collecting his medication from the local pharmacy, he strolled among the booths of the farmer's market on Gyulai Pál utca, buying such items as took his fancy and which his OCD allowed.

Laden with groceries, he climbed to the third floor of his apartment building. As he exited the stairwell, he was confronted by a small boy on a tricycle hurtling towards him: Akira Nagy, his neighbor's son. Marci leaped back, in the process dropping a loaf of wrapped bread. Akira, an expression of intense concentration on his face, sped past him without slowing.

Marci stooped and picked up the bread, cursing under his breath. Although sealed, it had made contact with the floor and would have to be consigned to the trash. Further along the walkway, Takumi Nagy squatted beside his daughter to fix her coat. As Marci approached, he raised a hand in apology. Marci waved back, underwent a bioscan and entered his flat.

The time was close to 11:00. András's message had come through early that morning: the clock would arrive sometime that afternoon. Lacking opportunity or perhaps choosing to play Cupid, the shopkeeper had entrusted its delivery to Erin, which meant the rest of Marci's day would be spent tidying the apartment.

It was foolish on several fronts. First, he kept his home clean with a fervor that would put other obsessive-compulsives to shame. Light switches, door handles and anything else prone to human contact were disinfected with missionary zeal. His kitchen and bathroom faced particular scrutiny, with Alice programmed to clean the worktops every half hour. What Marci made up for in hygiene he lacked in tidiness. There was a place for everything, even if everything was rarely in its place.

The second reason was simple: she likely wouldn't care. Aside from a single, cryptic smile as he'd left Objet D'Heart yesterday, there was nothing to suggest Erin had the slightest interest in him. But what if she did? And what if she was the type of woman who judged a man by the condition of his home? Better, he thought, to spend a few hours tidying than regret a missed opportunity. At nearly forty, he was fast running out of those.

Forty. The beginning of the end. It was a mental watershed, a box on the list of marital eligibility that would remain forever unticked. Technically, he was middle-aged. What woman of childbearing age wanted a man in his forties? Yes, time was slipping through his fingers. The more he thought about it, the more urgent the need became. He had to find a spouse, and soon.

Seeking distraction, Marci busied himself with housework, but the chores only provided a blank canvas for further introspection. Where to meet someone? Workplace romance was a breach of Executive Team protocol. He had few friends, and all were male. Bars and clubs were out, since he lacked confidence in approaching strangers.

A bigger problem remained: what would happen if a woman of interest reciprocated his attentions? The concept was foreign. He'd been single all his life and enjoyed his solitude—so he told himself. A relationship would open up a world of new and potentially difficult adjustments to his lifestyle. Better to remain single, especially now that his nomination to Club 30 was imminent—possibly at The Society's AGM next month. Preparing for it would mean long hours of concentration. This was not the time for dalliance.

Marci grew tired of dusting and had Alice brew him coffee. A large sash window with an oversized interior sill gave onto Gyulai Pál utca. He took his beverage and Winterbournes and sat watching children at play on the swings across the street. The elms that lined Gyulai Pál utca were turning color. Autumn was fast approaching, a lovely season to stroll down Andrássy út with someone special. He lit a cigarette. Fat chance of that.

His phone chimed. The screen displayed a message: "B&G ready. Delivery at 16:00 ok?"

He replied: “Is Erin bringing it?”

"Igen."

A twitch of vertigo, like a feather brushed across the cerebellum. Marci waited for it to pass. The grandfather clock in the corner chimed twice: 11:30. It wasn't too late to ask András to play postman; at least then Marci could enjoy his day free from dread.

Marci smoked his way to the bathroom, where with a cigarette hanging from his lips and one eye squinting from the sting of the smoke his reflection stared back at him. Dark, half-moon shadows hung under bloodshot eyes like the spoils of a fistfight. Below, four days of stubble sprouted from his cheeks and chin, too little to look intentional but sufficient to imply sloth. Marci disrobed, shaved and swallowed a Ketamax pill, then lay in the bathtub to staunch the blood from his razor wounds. The warmth of the water combined with the sedative began to work. At some point he sank into pleasant stupor.

He woke in tepid water to a loud, persistent chiming.

Alice, reading the shift in his brain waves, canceled the alarm. "Marci, it's 15:00. Erin will arrive in one hour."

Marci sat up. With fingers corrugated by bathwater he groped for a towel, dried himself and shambled into the bedroom, where for ten minutes he vacillated between several different outfits before settling on dark-brown slacks, a cream shirt and a beige pullover. An Nrjize tablet, washed down with the dregs of his coffee, counteracted the Ketamax.

15:30 approached. Marci paced the lounge, chain smoking. At 15:56 he lit an incense stick, gargled some mouthwash and sat in the armchair.

16:00 came and went, its passing marked by the solemn chimes of the grandfather. Where was she? Was she lost? Marci checked his phone; there were no new messages. At 16:12 he decided to send András a message, but was interrupted by the doorbell.

Marci sprang from his chair and hurried to the front door. Standing on the walkway was Erin, drenched to the skin and holding a cardboard box. Her hair was stuck to her face and water dripped from her nose and chin. She held the package out at arm's length. "Mr. Kovács, I brought you your clock."

Marci stared at her. "You're soaking."

"It's raining."

He tried to think of something to say that wouldn't sound sarcastic.

"Shall I leave it here?" Erin asked.

"Please," he said, opening the door wide, "come in. You'll catch your death of cold."

Erin peered into the hallway like a bird inspecting a baited trap.

"At least to dry yourself," he added.

Tentatively, Erin stepped inside.

Marci hurried into the lounge. "Let me get you something to dry yourself with."

Erin looked down at the pool of rainwater gathering at her feet. "I'm afraid I'm ruining your nice floor."

He returned with the towels. "Why did you go out without a coat?"

Erin set the package on the hallway table and wiped her face and hair. Her teeth chattered when she spoke: "It was only a shower when I left the shop. I thought I could make it without getting too wet."

"Alice," Marci said, "put the temperature up. And switch the Living Wall to fireplace."

"Adjusting the temperature now. Living Wall is on."

Erin peeked into the living room. "Who's Alice?"

Marci handed her another towel. "The concierge system. You're shivering."

"Oh, you have one of those?"

"You could have taken a cab."

"It's only a few blocks away. Besides, András wouldn't give me the fare." She glanced at the box. "Oh, won't you let me open it? I packed it myself, and I'd love to see it again." In anticipation of his consent, she opened the box and freed the clock along with a good few handfuls of foam beads, which fell to the floor. Marci thought she resembled a child opening a long-awaited Christmas gift.

Triumphantly she held up the Birch and Gaydon. "It looks good, doesn't it?"

Marci stepped over and took it from her. Their hands touched, and the scent of violets and jasmine filled the space between them. "It looks very good," he breathed, barely aware of the timepiece. "George has worked wonders on it."

An awkward moment, saved by the chiming of the lounge's grandfather.

"Another clock?" she said.

"Another clock."

Erin looked toward the lounge, as if considering possibilities. "May I see it?"

"Of course. Come through."

"I don't want to ruin your floor with my wet shoes."

"Take them off. The floor will survive."

Erin removed her boots and wandered down the hallway. Marci stared at them, fighting a compulsion. The urge was irresistible; he bent down and placed them symmetrical to his own.

"You really live here?" She'd stopped in the doorway, as if afraid to enter.

"Yes, I really live here," he said, walking through her intoxicating scent. In the bathroom he washed his hands, soiled from touching her shoes. He checked the mirror; his face was burning up. He ran the tap and cupped cold water to it. The man in the mirror studied him.

She's out of your league.

When he returned to the living room she was gazing at the chandeliers.

"Are these real?" she asked.

"French Regency," he said, wondering if he'd left his Winterbournes on the coffee table. "I bought them when I made SIN 25. Can I get you a hot drink? You must be freezing."

Erin made a sound of delight and hurried over to the far wall, where a large oil on canvas hung by the window. In vibrant ochre and blue it portrayed a huddle of Cornish cottages nestled among barley fields. Four-fifths of the painting were dominated by a cobalt sky; a strip of farmland occupied the bottom. She went to touch it but stopped herself. "I've only seen this in books," she said in awe. "Is this real too?"

Marci joined her. "The Piper? Yes, it's real. I'm surprised you recognize it; he was never that well-known. Do you like it?"

Erin nodded vigorously. "It's magnificent! It's almost Impressionist, and the colors are amazing. John Piper's an inspiration for my own work. You know the Museum of Fine Art would fall over itself to… But I suppose you don't want to sell it."

Marci laughed, a little uncomfortably. "Then I wouldn't be able to see it every morning."

Erin surveyed the room. "You have good taste. This place is like a palace."

"Not quite a palace, but I love old things. They make me feel at ease. What's your work?"

Erin spoke absently. "I'm an artist. It must have cost you a fortune."

Marci, despite himself, moved closer. He inhaled: again, violets and jasmine. "What do you paint?"

If she felt his proximity she didn't let it affect her. "Landscapes. And some still life. And sometimes abstracts when I'm in the mood."

Marci spoke with uncharacteristic courage. "I'd love to see your work sometime."

Erin ignored the invitation. "Oh, I forgot," she said, brushing past him into the hall and returning with an old biscuit tin. "This is for you, too."

Their hands touched again. Marci turned away. "You're freezing. Come and sit by the fire. Would you like tea or coffee?"

"Do you have hot chocolate?"

"Of course. Alice, make us two hot chocolates. Do you need a change of clothes? I don't have anything for women, but you can borrow some of mine."

Erin sat next to the fire. "I'll be fine, thanks. I'm getting warmer already."

He fetched the drinks. They sipped them in silence.

"Why do you collect all of these old things?" Erin asked. "Most people with money only like buying new stuff."

Marci considered the question. "I suppose I find them comforting. They're pieces of other people's lives. They were made by craftsmen, not machines. It's as if they have their own souls."

Erin thought about that. She said: "Why did you want that picture?"

"The Piper?"

"No, the photo in the biscuit tin. You were staring at it in the shop. You said you wondered who she was, but she's just a pretty, dead girl."

"I don't know," he replied, embarrassed by the question. "Curiosity, I suppose. What was she was like? Was she happy? Did she have a good life? Did she marry?"

Erin watched him with an inscrutable expression.

"How's your chocolate?" he asked.

"Hot. Do you live here alone?"

Marci nodded.

"It's a shame."

"Why?"

Erin cast her eyes around the room. "It's a shame to have all these lovely things and no one to share them with."

"Most people wouldn't appreciate them."

"Most people couldn't afford them."

Was she always so outspoken? he thought. "I don't go out much."

Again, an enigmatic smile. "You have high SIN, at least SIN 25. I wonder what you do?"

Marci sipped his chocolate but deigned no response.

"Hmm, a secret! How intriguing! Let me see. You live alone but in luxury. Your apartment must be over two thousand square feet here in District VIII. Pricey. And you own a concierge and a Living Wall."

Marci shifted in his chair. "I'm not quite sure—"

"So, you have money and fine furniture. You usually visit Objet d'Heart on weekday afternoons between 16:30 and 18:30—"

"How do you know that?" Marci interrupted.

"—presumably after work," Erin continued, "which means you're not self-employed. You dress well, and the fact that you're cultured probably means you work for the Company, something senior. The Executive Team, perhaps?"

Marci went to the window. "For someone who doesn't wear a jacket in a storm you're remarkably insightful." Outside, the rain fell unabated. "Looks like it's drying up."

Their eyes met.

Erin smiled faintly. "Very well, Mr. Kovács. It seems I probed a little too much. Thank you for the hot chocolate and the fire."

Instantly, Marci regretted his comment. Please don't go just yet," he said, hurrying over. "At least finish your drink."

"Thank you, but I really should get back to the shop. András will be wondering what on earth's happened to me."

In the hallway Erin and her wet shoes were reunited. Marci handed her his umbrella. "Please take this," he said. "There's no point getting soaked again."

"Thank you. Oh, I forgot something else." She handed him a Manila envelope from inside her cardigan. "I kept it there to stay dry."

"I think it would have been drier in the tin," Marci replied.

"I didn't want it to get crushed. By the ashtray."

Marci broke the seal and removed the photograph of the girl at the beach, which was unsullied by the rain. "András might be tight-fisted, but he buys premium stationary."

"I'll leave you with your eidolon," Erin said. "Goodbye, Mr. Kovács. Thanks again for the chocolate. And for showing me the Piper." With that, she hurried down the walkway.

"Please," he cried after her, "call me Marci!"

At the stairwell Erin looked back, smiled and gave him a child's wave.

Marci raised his hand in farewell, but she was gone.

For two days he floated on air, oblivious to the humdrum of everyday life and free from anxiety for the first time in years. Imperceptibly, the obsessive-compulsive disorder that made his life a living hell abated, and the intrusive thoughts that fueled his compulsions suddenly lost their power over him. Even his hands, raw from over washing, showed signs of improvement.

Other fronts were equally positive. At work, Fraser Morrison was too busy to pester him, and even Tony Jackson seemed tolerable. All because a pretty girl had shown Marci a little attention. How strange that something as simple as ten minutes with a woman could change a man's thinking! Was he really so starved of affection? Or maybe just shallow? Whatever the reason, Marci felt like a love-struck schoolboy with his first sweetheart, and hoped the feeling would last forever.

At midday on Tuesday, Alex knocked on Marci's cubicle door. "Fancy some lunch?"

Marci swung around in his chair. "Sure, I'm famished."

The two descended to the ground floor, which housed a four-hundred seat cafeteria now filled to capacity and noisy with chatter. Large windows looked out onto a landscaped quadrangle; through these, low September sunlight angled in to bathe the space with ruddy warmth.

Alex collected his meal and led them to a recently vacated table in a corner. Marci, who'd brought a packed lunch as usual, dropped into the seat opposite, sanitized his hands and made short work of his sandwiches—a feat in itself, since his OCD usually precluded him from handling food without napkins. Alex, by comparison, ate little, and remained uncharacteristically silent.

Marci waited a polite two minutes, at which point his patience expired. "You've been pushing your food around since we sat down. Usually when you invite me to lunch it's because you've something to say."

Alex stared at his lunch, which he'd arranged into its component parts on his plate. "It's no big deal. Just something data related."

"It must be important to drag me down here. What data are we talking about?"

Alex lowered his voice. "You know that model I've been working on?"

"The one that's going to get you carted off by a cessation squad?"

"It's just a model of MARTHA's architecture. Nothing sacred."

"Except that duplicating her is a capital offense. How accurate is it?"

"It's an exact replica. Subroutines, algorithms, the lot."

"Bloody hell," Marci muttered. "Go on. I know it's your golden ticket to Empyrean."

Alex pushed his tray to one side and leaned across the table. "Ok, so we know MARTHA is basically a server with a lot of automated feeds and a very clever interpretative routine."

"That's putting it mildly."

"It's all about the audience. Anyway, MARTHA takes all kinds of information about us and plots confidence intervals. The interval algorithm is relatively simple, but what she does with the data to predict our future actions is very complex[12]. If we always drink artificial coffee at lunchtime"—he indicated Marci's synthetic beverage—"and we suddenly switch to tea, we've changed our behavioral routine, and the range of expected outcomes broadens."

"Yes, yes," Marci said. "So, we've given MARTHA a surprise and the world comes to an end."

"Not quite, but that's the general idea. MARTHA's been analyzing us since birth. In fact, before our births, because she also draws on all the data she's collected about our parents, grandparents, et cetera, et cetera."

"Not forgetting second skin, biometrics and surveillance."

Alex nodded impatiently. "The point is this: our decisions as Adjudicants are based on the accuracy of MARTHA's analysis. We take lives and we spare lives based on the stats she gives us. But what if MARTHA isn't as accurate as she could be?"

Marci straightened. "That's dangerous talk."

---

[12] Conspiracy theorists speculate that MARTHA even has the ability to forecast the manner and timing of one's natural death, by means of a secret subroutine dubbed the Auspex Program. Such rumors are always denied, but form the basis for many a taboo joke. Indeed, such is MARTHA's inerrancy some suggest criminal convictions be brought on Employees whose files suggested a propensity for vice, even before the act. Liberals have so far managed to avert such a motion.

"That depends on your motives. Here's the thing: the predictive interval is key. I can improve her accuracy by at least 7%, but for that I need access to more of her files—"

"Wait a minute," Marci interrupted, "I thought you weren't using real data?"

"Ok, just a bit," Alex admitted. "I checked out all the obvious stuff—liquidation data and SIN rating correlations, predictive interval fluctuations and the like. Nothing unusual, and certainly nothing I could use to improve her accuracy. So I cast the net wider: data exceptions, flagged files—anything MARTHA can't compute."

"Go on."

Alex glanced around, then reached into his backpack and removed a paper folder, which he slid across the table.

"What am I looking at?"

"Fifteen years ago, the Justice and Cessation Board called 612 Employees to its HQ in Nyugati for questioning. None of the Employees were high-fliers; in fact, the only thing their files had in common was how unremarkable they were. Certainly not enough to justify what happened next."

"Which was?"

Alex pointed to a figure he'd highlighted at the bottom of the page. "Within a month of interviews, eighty-three of the 612 were liquidated."

"Eighty-three cessations a month is pocket change," Marci said. "The weekly average is over two thousand."

"From the same group?"

"It's about 13%," Marci said. "It doesn't mean anything."

"More than one in ten were liquidated and you say it's normal?"

"Stranger things have happened. Maybe their SIN values were low."

Alex plucked some graphs from the folder and fanned them out. "Lifeline charts of the eighty-three. The x-axis represents an Employee's lifespan, the y their SIN value from birth to death. Look at their SIN score at the point of cessation."

"This isn't possible," Marci said, leafing through them. "Cessation cut-off is SIN 5. Most of them were 15 or higher."

"Exactly. They were all liquidated within two days of each other."

"It's got to be a glitch, something wrong with your code."

"The code is good. I wrote it myself."

"Then your model is wrong. MARTHA doesn't make mistakes."

Alex took the file back. "Fine. It's all a big mistake."

The chatter in the canteen seemed suddenly louder.

"What were the interviews about?" Marci asked.

"I don't know. All I've got are numbers and a few source code annotations."

Marci spoke without interest: "Take it to carrot-top. Explain that you're trying to improve MARTHA's accuracy—"

"Which I am—"

"—and that you found the data in passing. And for God's sake don't mention your model."

"He's going to know I'm up to something. I couldn't have dug this up offline."

"Then come clean. You never know, you might make SIN 27."

Alex grinned. "I was angling more for 33. Either that or I'll be liquidated."

"Don't talk like that," Marci said. "You're the second best Adjudicant the Company has."

"I hope your shop girl appreciates your modesty."

Marci's eyes narrowed. "How did you know about her?"

Alex adopted a sinister voice. "We Adjudicants know everything! Seriously, you've told me a hundred times about some shop assistant you met."

"She's not a shop assistant," Marci corrected. "She's an artist."

"Well, well," Alex chuckled, "Chivalry's not dead. Defending her already?"

Marci gave him a withering look.

"Spill the beans then. Or do I need to pry it out of you?"

"There's not much to say. I bought a clock at Objet d'Heart and she brought it over on Saturday. It was raining, and she was soaking wet. I invited her in. She liked one of my pictures. We drank hot chocolate by the fire and talked for a while. Then she left."

Alex's face fell. "Is that it? But I guess getting a woman into your flat is something of a breakthrough."

Marci ignored the quip. "When she was leaving, she turned around and waved to me."

Alex waited. "And?"

"And what?" Marci said, rattled. "It was the look she gave me and how we spoke. It was special. Damn you, Alex! Wipe that smirk off your face."

"I'm sorry," Alex said, trying not to laugh. "I'm glad you both had a nice time. With your hot chocolate."

"Sometimes," Marci said, "I don't know why I bother telling you these things."

"Have you seen her since Saturday?"

"No. I don't have her number."

"Mistake number two."

"What was number one?"

"Not getting her to stay the night."

Marci made a dismissive sound. "Not everyone's a sexual predator like you."

Alex raised his hands in innocence. "Me? I'm married. You're the one hitting on shop assistants. Do you want to know what mistake number three is?"

"Not particularly."

Alex sighed. "You have to play her game. You're the man, for crying out loud! You chase her, she runs away and you spend all your money persuading her to nag you for the rest of your life. And you just let her go."

"What was I supposed to do?" Marci protested, "propose to her there and then?"

Alex slapped the table. "You've got to strike while the iron's hot! You can't let them slip away so easily!"

"You're sounding more like Tony Jackson every day."

"That was below the belt. I hope your shop girl appreciates your wit."

"Her name's Erin," Marci said.

"Erin. It's a pretty name. So what's your plan?"

"Plan? I don't have a—" Marci's eyes widened. "She has my umbrella."

Alex's face resembled a schoolboy who'd invented a new mischief. "Damn it, that's a genius move!"

Marci looked at him blankly. "It is?"

"Sure! You just set up your second date."

Marci began to fidget. "We haven't had a first one yet. Alex, I'm useless with women. What are we going to talk about? The Adjudicant gag order means I can't discuss work, and I don't have hobbies. Maybe I should just forget the whole thing."

Alex tucked the file in his backpack and rose to leave. "Marci, you're hopeless. Go and get your umbrella back. If you don't do something, you're going to end up a lonely old man. And don't spend the rest of the day figuring out what you're going to say to her."

"The Employee lifelines you showed me," Marci said, "how sure are you they're accurate?"

"They come straight from MARTHA's database. All I did was find and copy them."

"It's just not possible," Marci muttered. "She can't issue cessations orders above SIN 5. It goes against her core algorithms."

"I agree. But the charts speak for themselves." Alex picked up his tray. "I've got to run. My inbox is the size of the Eden project."

Marci watched his friend weave his way through the canteen. For several minutes he remained there to mull over Alex's revelation, before dismissing the whole notion as absurd.

*   *   *

"You're late."

"Fashionably."

Alex let Marci into the kitchen. "Unusual for you."

"Is Lei at home?"

"Nah, she took the kids to see their grandmother. It's just We Happy Few this evening. Say hello, boys."

Sitting at the kitchen table and engrossed in a game of poker were Csaba Mező and Akito Nakamura. Csaba, who was short, chubby and sported a crew cut, was losing his money gracelessly to the inebriated and boisterous Akito. Both greeted Marci distractedly and continued playing.

"Third game," Alex pointed out.

"But not the third beer, by the looks of it," Marci said.

"There's some left. Do you want one?"

"Coke's fine. Is Anton coming?"

"With Anton, who knows? If he is, he's going to have a fine time dodging enforcement drones, at least until the storm hits. Not to mention the Undergrounders, if they even exist."

"The mob doesn't appear until they're sure second skin is down," Akito said, inspecting his cards. "They've got some guts. I'd be worried AirNet would come back online."

Marci sipped his drink. "So long as they keep checking their phones for reception, they'll be fine. I guess when they get a signal they go home."

"They're brave," Alex said.

"Foolish," corrected Marci. "Speaking of fools, are you guys planning on hacking this evening?"

Alex grinned. "Of course! Akito's chomping at the bit. Isn't that right, Akito?"

"Huh? Yeah, all in good time. I'm about to wipe the smirk off Csaba's face."

"The poor sod's already lost forty credits," Alex observed. "Csaba, why don't you just hand over all your money now? It'll save you more pain in the long run."

Csaba, who was hunched over his cards, looked wounded. "Have you no faith in me?"

"None. Akito, when you've finished, let's go and do some hacking."

"Who's the victim?"

"Don't you remember? I thought you were going to grind the city traffic to a halt?"

"What traffic?" asked Marci. "Everyone's safe at home."

"Not everyone," said Akito. "The cops are out. News24 said MARTHA predicts riots tonight."

Alex sipped his beer. "Not in District IX."

"Better not discuss it too much with the Company man here," joked Csaba. "We'll all be sent to live in Eden."

Marci ignored that. "Is Lei coming home tonight?"

Alex shook his head. "She's staying over. Not safe to come back now."

Marci scowled. "Someone needs to tackle the Underground. They're bringing the city to its knees."

"We don't know for sure it's them," said Alex.

Akito said: "Who else can it be? It's too organized to be random. Anyway, we can always ask Anton about it. He's our cloak and dagger man."

"Speculation. On both counts." Alex finished his bottle. "Come on, Akito, time to play computer games. You've taken Csaba to the cleaners."

"Storm's not here yet. Check your signal. My phone's still got two bars, and it's Csaba to call."

"Marci, do you want to join us?" Alex asked.

"Why not?" Marci said, pulling up a chair. "If only to rid Csaba of his bus fare."

"I fold," Csaba said morosely.

The deck was cut, shuffled and dealt, and the game proceeded. Csaba, emboldened by alcohol, continued his losing streak, to the amusement of everyone but himself. In a change of tack, he began subsequent rounds by placing large blind bets, forcing his opponents to fold, and winning their blinds. On the third occasion, Csaba pushed thirty credits forward and licked his lips. "Raise."

"If you're going to bluff," Akito said lazily, "at least wait until we've put some decent money down. I fold."

"Me too," said Marci.

"I'm bored," said Alex, "and I'm out."

Triumphant, Csaba scooped up his meager winnings.

"Cut and shuffle," Alex said, grabbing another beer from the fridge. "Csaba, you're dealer."

Antes were placed and the flop cards were dealt: a jack of clubs, an eight of hearts and the two of spades.

Akito shook his head and lay his cards face down. "I'm out."

Marci inspected his hand: a jack of diamonds and a two of hearts.

The turn card was dealt: a six of spades.

"I raise five," said Alex.

Csaba met it and dealt the river card, a jack of spades. Marci, Alex and Akito placed further bets.

Csaba, his face creased in concentration, regarded his stack of coins.

Alex said, "Your money's burning a hole in your pocket, Mr. Mező."

Csaba's face was moist with sweat. "All in."

"I count that as twenty-three credits," said Akito.

Alex matched it. He glanced at Marci. "Feeling brave?"

Marci's face was inscrutable. "Quietly confident. Call."

Alex revealed his hand. "Two pairs. Twos and eights."

Marci flipped his cards over. "Full house."

"Damn!" Akito cried. "The rich get richer!"

Marci dragged his winnings toward him. "And Csaba gets sweatier."

"Csaba," said Alex, patting him on the back, "you played valiantly, but your luck ran out tonight."

Csaba was crestfallen. "I thought I'd win."

Akito spoke in mischief: "Let's see your hand."

"It's not important," Csaba replied with dignity.

Akito snatched up Csaba's cards. "Look at this joker! An ace, a three of hearts and five of diamonds."

"Csaba," Alex laughed, "you have the courage of a lion and the common sense of a drunkard."

A loud crack of thunder startled them. Akito checked his phone. "Nearly there. Signal's at one bar."

"Wait until it's dead," Alex said. "No use in taking chances."

Marci counted his winnings. "You guys are crazy. If you get traced, you're finished."

Alex held out a can of lager. "We won't."

"I've still got this."

Akito lit a cigarette. "So, Marci, what's your news? Liquidated anyone interesting this week?"

"Why bother asking?" said Csaba. "If he's an Adjudicant, he'll never admit it."

"Just think," Akito mused, "even now, Marci might be plotting our downfall. It's why I always try to lose when we play cards."

"You lose because I'm better than you," Marci said. "In any case, there are lots of jobs in the Company that are "need to know." It doesn't mean I'm an Adjudicant."

"I'd love to be a Hangman," Csaba said wistfully. "Choosing which of your poker buddies gets the chop. Alex, you work with Marci. You must know what he does."

"As Akito alluded, if he's an Adjudicant I wouldn't be able to tell you. And I think your last comment just excluded you from the role."

Akito drew on his cigarette. "Some are born to rule. I guess I'll stick to programming. My SIN micros went up a few blips this week, so I can't complain."

"We're all happy for you." Alex checked his phone. "The signal's gone."

"Mine too," said Csaba.

"Same here," said Akito.

Marci looked at his. "Like I said, you're all crazy."

"Gentlemen," Alex said, rising from the table, "I believe it's time to see what Mass Transit's server has for us. Marci, if he is indeed a Hangman as Csaba so crudely put it, will be relieved to know that we can't hack MARTHA's SIN routines. But we can have some fun with District IX's traffic management system."

"At last!" Akito cried, "some real entertainment!"

The Pimenov's lounge was a large, rectangular space made cramped by the paraphernalia of child-rearing. A wainscoting of playthings concealed the walls to waist height. Brutalist building block towers, a Georgian dollhouse occupied by astronauts, a spacecraft piloted by China dolls, sketch books and board games stacked one atop the other all competed for precious floor space. Plastic tubs filled with toys rose in columns on either side of a patio door that let out onto a narrow balcony. Alex had left the door open; a net curtain billowed in the storm wind.

The furnishings were comfortable and utilitarian. An L-shaped sofa draped with a rustic Hungarian throw filled a corner. Beside it, a glass coffee table kept tins of beer and a plate of Lei's home-baked *pogácsa* within easy reach.

At the far end of the room a computer terminal output its display to a large, wall-mounted video screen. An AirNet signal indicator, engineered by Alex and designed to measure cellular activity in much finer increments than a cell phone, rested atop the computer monitor.

Akito studied the gauge. "Dead as a dodo. Alex, log me in."

Csaba sank into an armchair opposite and availed himself of several pogácsa. "What's up, Marci? Anything of a"—his voice became silky—"romantic nature?"

"Nothing of note."

"What about that Heidi character you had the hots for?"

"She's taken."

"Ah well," Csaba said, stuffing a pastry into his mouth, "I guess it's not wise to date someone from work."

Marci moved the plate back to the middle of the table. "Not only is it unwise, it's against Company policy, especially for Adj—"

"Have a beer, Marci," Alex interrupted, thrusting a can into his hand.

"—for us Data Analysts. Besides, she's not my type."

Alex blew out his cheeks. "I'd say she was every man's type, but there's no accounting for taste."

"Honestly, I'm too busy for that sort of thing. I'll start thinking about women again when I reach SIN 30."

Csaba licked his fingers. "That's what you said four years ago when you were SIN 28. You're pushing forty."

"Forty's still young," Marci protested.

"Agreed," said Alex.

Csaba, laughing at his own joke, added: "For a sugar daddy."

Marci scowled. "I came here to relax, not to be reminded of my problems."

"You're a great guy, Marci," Alex said. "I'm sure Miss Right will come along soon enough. If not Miss Right Now."

Csaba hooted with laughter.

"That's right, Csaba,' Marci sneered, "go ahead and laugh. I hear your sister's open to all sorts of offers."

"Eh? What did you say?"

Akito turned around with a look of exultation. "I'm in!"

"Give that man a cookie!" Alex whooped. "No wait—Csaba's eaten the last one."

"Why don't you just shut up?" snapped Csaba.

Marci fingered the ring pull of his beer can with a metallic crack. "It's going to be a long night."

At a little after 23:30 Marci phoned for Executive Team transport and bade the members of We Happy Few goodnight. Akito, who had indeed managed to turn all the traffic lights in District IX green, was too drunk to reply. Csaba, satiated on pogácsa and fast asleep, snored loudly in the armchair.

At the front door Marci said, "Sorry for the slip earlier. I wasn't thinking."

"No sweat," Alex replied. "They only suspect you. Just be glad for my ninja reflexes. Is your ride picking you up downstairs?"

"With you guys hacking into government servers? Of course not. They'll meet me on Győrffy István utca."

"Be careful. A lot can happen in a block during curfew." Alex hesitated. "About what I said at lunchtime. I hope you don't think I've lost the plot."

Marci lit a cigarette. "You lost it years ago; your conspiracy theory only confirms it. Are you still planning to take your paperwork to Morrison?"

Alex didn't immediately reply.

"You're not, are you?"

"There's no harm in doing a little more delving," Alex said lightly. "You know Morrison. If it doesn't slap him in the face, he can't see the big picture."

Marci shook his head. "You're crazier than I thought. I hope for your SIN's sake your anomalies are right, but for everyone else's that you're wrong."

Alex smiled weakly. "Me too. See you Monday."

Marci descended to the street. The thunderstorm had passed; somewhere far away the skies rumbled but still spat rain here. He checked his phone, which showed four bars.

Briskly he walked briskly east toward Villám utca. As he neared the corner, a shaft of light fell upon him, so bright it transformed the raindrops around him into the likeness of silver thorns.

Dazzled, Marci stopped and looked up at the curfew drone a hundred feet above him. Its weapon bay was open and its rotary gun was already spooling. Instinctively he held up his hands.

A voice issued from the machine: "Employee 639NK381L488. Bio data confirmed. Curfew exempt."

The light cut out. A hum, the rush of wind. The drone rose and vanished into the clouds. Marci watched it disappear, then propped himself against a nearby wall until his legs felt strong enough to carry him. He set off at an ungainly run.

On Ulászló utca a black four-wheel drive waited in silence, its roof lightbar and headlamps painting the neighborhood red, blue and white. At Marci's approach, the driver stepped out, opened the passenger door and bowed. "Good evening, sir."

Marci recognized the man. "Thanks, Tomi. Miserable night."

"Ah, Mr. Kovács! That it is sir, but quiet. I guess the curfew worked."

"No riots?"

"A little trouble in District V—the usual Underground stuff. Oh, and a few snarl-ups in District IX. Something wrong with the traffic lights, apparently."

Marci flinched. "And how's your family, Tomi?"

"All tucked up in bed, sir. Looking forward to getting home myself."

"A good idea. Let's be off and you can join them."

"Best news I've had all night, sir."

4

Late on Wednesday afternoon, with rain chasing itself in sheets down Kőfaragó utca, Marci Kovács found himself sheltering under a shop porch two doors down and across the street from Objet d'Heart. Inside the breast pocket of his overcoat was the crib sheet he'd penned the night before. The document comprised a range of topics that could, upon the exhaustion of pleasantries, be employed in conversation, with contingencies for digression should circumstance dictate. The success of the crib naturally depended on Marci's remembering it; something he'd failed to do at work today due to a glut of Adjudication cases.

Spontaneity was not his forte. In lieu of this, Marci had scoured the pages of gentlemen's periodicals and compiled a list of opening gambits which would, so the articles promised, trigger in the female psyche an autonomic desire to explore more intimate prospects. A money-back guarantee provided a measure of consolation, should the method fail. Marci didn't believe it, but still scribbled two of the chat-up lines on the palm of one hand.

A more obvious and reliable source of data on Erin was MARTHA. Marci had resisted accessing her files for two reasons. First, it was unethical; he wasn't a stalker— at least not yet. Second, requesting data on personal grounds was illegal, and would breach the Adjudicant's Code of Conduct.

Alex's words from the night before hadn't helped him: "If you don't do something, you're going to end up a lonely old man." The counsel was irritatingly obvious, but had nettled Marci more than it should because he knew it better than anyone else.

He reached into his jacket and removed the crib: a single sheet of A5, folded twice. There were six in total, and underneath each were two or three bullet-pointed questions he could pose her, verbatim.

The light in the foyer was poor. Marci held the crib sheet at arm's length out of the shadow. A gust of wind, blowing through the foyer, snatched the document from his grasp and sent it fluttering down the street. In a panic he chased after it, but not quickly enough: the note rose on the air, higher and higher, then plunged into the gutter where it floated on a layer of oily water toward the drain.

Marci snatched it up. The ink had bled; his writing was illegible. He stuffed the sodden pulp into his coat pocket and wiped his hands dry with a handkerchief, which came away black. In dismay he stared at his palms. The one-liners he'd penned there were smudged beyond recognition.

Scowling in concentration, he tried to recall something—anything—from the crib. All that came to mind was a single glib cliché. Then again, they'd all been clichés. He squared his shoulders, took a long breath and strode across the street. As he reached the shop entrance his courage faltered. He stopped, wavered a moment, then marched furiously back toward Gutenberg Tér.

As before, József Fodor oxidized silently on his concrete plinth. Marci lit a cigarette and went to pace in the shelter of the cloister. Why couldn't he remember his lines? Why did he need them, anyway? He wasn't even middle-aged, for God's sake.

Damned coward. What kind of man are you?

He pressed his hands to his ears to quell the thoughts. "Shut up," he muttered, "shut up!"

It was impossible. He wasn't up to the task, and tomorrow would be no different, script or not. Filled with self-loathing, Marci swung about to head home.

"Oh, Mr. Kovács!"

Marci jerked back, ready to utter a profanity, which immediately died in his throat. Before him—inches before him—stood Erin. On the ground between them lay a hemp carrier bag whose contents had spilled onto the sidewalk.

Without thought, Marci crouched and began gathering up her groceries. "I'm sorry," he stammered. "I didn't see you."

Erin knelt beside him. "It's my lunch," she explained, holding the bag open. "Silly me, I wasn't looking where I was going."

"No, it was my fault," Marci stammered. "I was lost in thought."

"What are you doing in these parts? Do you work near here?"

Marci's heart was pounding so hard wondered if she could hear it. "Not really. I'm just…taking a stroll. And you?"

Erin, who had already deduced his reason for being here, bit her lower lip to suppress a smile. "Yes, just around the corner, at Objet d'Heart. I'm on my break, but András only gives me half an hour; in fact, I'm a little bit late. Were you going to the shop? We don't have anything new since your last visit. We usually get new things on Thursdays. That's when András goes to the flea markets or dead people's houses or the other junk shops."

Marci looked up and met her gaze, which for an ecstatic, fleeting moment she held his gaze before putting the last of her shopping in the bag.

"Well, I really must be going," she said. "It was nice bumping into you, Mr. Kovács—literally."

"It's Marci," he said, forcing a smile which might have come across as a grimace.

"Marci," she repeated. The word sounded like an apology for not using it before. For the first time in his life it sounded beautiful. "Well… goodbye then, Marci."

"I wondered if…" But his voice carried no sound, and she'd already turned away, and she moved, he thought, with that peculiar, jaunty élan common to a young woman who is supremely aware of her beauty and the preeminence it afforded her in life.

Only she'd stopped. She turned halfway and tipped her head to one side, as if considering something. "There's an exhibition this weekend at the Museum of Fine Arts," she said. "I was thinking of going."

Marci frowned. Hadn't they concluded their conversation? Why return to rub his face in her in plans for the weekend, a weekend without him? He tried to think of something caustic to say, but only managed, "The museum?"

"Yes. At Hősök tere. Shall we say noon, on the steps?" With that, she smiled, turned and hurried away down Kőfaragó utca.

Marci stared after her. What had just happened? Had she really asked him on a date? Without realizing it he'd moved across the square to stand under József Fodor's wistful metallic gaze. In his pocket Marci found his Winterbournes and the soggy crib sheet, which he tossed in a trash can. A surge of joy rose within him, a feeling so foreign that he wondered if his pills were playing tricks on him. He put the Winterbournes back without lighting up and walked home, heedless of the hastening rain.

Like a sub-SIN waiting for the Hangman's call, Marci rode out the last two days of the week in a state of crippling dread. Twice he called in sick; twice he struggled into work with the help of his sedatives. He might as well not have bothered, since he was all but useless in his duties.

On Saturday morning he rose early, dressed and made a breakfast of Cortiquells and Seromax, washed down with coffee. Hurrying out of the building, he all but bowled over Norbert Tóth, who was returning home from a night shift at the bleach factory. Marci wished him good morning and held open the door; Tóth ignored both the greeting and the gesture.

The day was pleasant. High cirrus clouds like smeared talc drifted across a powder blue sky. Marci rode the SpeedWalk to Hősök tere, around which eight lanes of traffic moved with sluggish persistence.

The time was 11:00. He was an hour early. At Városliget he bought tea from a vendor and found a bench by the lake. Already the park was busy, as Employees made the most of the late September sunshine. Joggers and cyclists competed for space on the many footpaths that dissected the grounds; children under plastic horse chestnut trees collected the first conkers of the year; by the water's edge, young parents pushed prams and strollers. Still others, in groups small and large, sat on picnic rugs taking part in SIN-enrichment classes.

Marci lit a cigarette. It would be okay. After all, hadn't she invited him here? He must have done something right. Still, there was ample scope for screwing things up. What if he froze, like last time? If Erin were forward enough to ask him on a date, perhaps she'd also carry most of the conversation.

He glanced at his watch: 11:07. Drifting over the park came a Zeppelin. Today its sides and underbelly were emblazoned in the white and turquoise color scheme of the Rapture pill. Video screens, angled down, showed an elegant couple in their sixties holding flutes of sparkling wine. Lovingly, they placed a tablet into each other's mouth. They toasted, drank.

Another scene appeared. Six teenagers stood on a low brick wall, talking and laughing together. They counted down: three, two, one, then swallowed the Rapture pill each held. In high spirits they jumped, to be frozen by the camera in mid-air.

Next, a couple lay in a hammock, seemingly asleep. Both wore expressions of bliss. The camera panned down to reveal a packet of Rapture Duo lying in verdant grass.

A logo appeared and strap line appeared:

QUICK. PEACEFUL. PAINLESS.
RAPTURE. THE GREATEST ACT OF SERVICE.

The video looped.

At a concession stand Marci bought a video tablet of the Budapest Herald. News of the Underground dominated the front page. Early that morning, a handful of members had breached the Wall near Sopron. Marci tapped on an image. Surveillance footage showed a ragtag group of Outsiders picking their way across that vast minefield known as the Field of Blood before sentry guns cut them to shreds. A gruesome centerfold featured Border guards prodding the mangled corpses with the snouts of their rifles.

Marci tossed the tablet in a trash can and strolled back to Hősök tere. The Cortiquell was now working at peak action. His mood was one of nonchalance and curious detachment from reality. At the same time, he felt rooted in the present. It was an unnatural yet pleasant experience.

After wasting the best part of half an hour in the museum gift shop, Marci took a cup of tea to the front steps and reviewed the topic prompts he'd rewritten from the other day. The approach had a fundamental flaw. Alex had once described Marci as laconic; strangers thought him aloof. In the company of attractive women he was barely articulate. If his notes were to work, Marci would have to speak, possibly at length. His hope was that Erin, like most people he knew, enjoyed talking about herself more than listening to others, and would carry the conversation for both of them.

There was a more practical concern. The cues were on his phone. Looking at it too frequently might be misconstrued as boredom.

He began to fret. What if she didn't come? He dismissed the thought. She'd invited him, after all. Which begged the question: why?

Why not? I'm a SIN 29 Adjudicant!

It was a pathetic thought. Nobody gave a damn what his slope[13] was except himself, and he had no intention of revealing either his SIN or his occupation. Respected and loathed in equal measure, Adjudicants were viewed as either idols or pariahs. Which box he ticked for Erin, time would tell.

Noon came and went. Marci toyed with the idea of another cigarette but thought better of it. He chewed some gum to mask his breath.

At 12:15 he logged into AirNet to check for messages but realized that they hadn't exchanged numbers. A search proved fruitless. Erin either lacked or had hidden her social media presence.

By the twenty-five-minute mark his mood had turned black. What choice words he'd have for her if she showed up. And if she didn't? Well then! Their next meeting would be one to remember.

---

[13] The direction of SIN, usually upward.

At half noon, convinced he'd been stood up, Marci lit a Winterbourne and began to pace. How had he been so naive? He should have seen right through her, with her saucy little walk and cryptic smile. Without even trying, she'd dealt him the cruelest blow in a woman's arsenal: raising a man's hopes only to dash them without mercy. If only he'd listened to that damnable voice in his head. The truth was that he was just another middle-aged Company man trying to make up for lost time.

Marci threw away his coffee away and took the steps two at a time. As he neared the bottom, a waft of perfume, of heady florals, enveloped him. Hurrying toward him from the main gate was Erin. If she'd moved any faster she would have tripped over herself.

A rush of excited relief mingled with his irritation. He allowed her to greet him the traditional Hungarian way—a kiss to both cheeks—with mixed enthusiasm.

"I'm so sorry for being late," she said between breaths. "Mummy's ill, and I went to visit her in Győr last night. Then the FATS[14] was late this morning. I wanted to call you, but I don't have your number."

Marci felt his rage dissipate. She looked stunning. Gone was the Bohemian look; today she wore a baby blue Kalocsa frock that perfectly complemented her light complexion. As was the custom of Hungarian women, she'd used a heavy kohl pencil to accentuate her eyes; they were large and doe-like. Her hair was loose; it tumbled thick and full of curls beyond her shoulders. Her lips were rouged a delicate red, childlike and sensual at the same time, and she looked up at him with such earnest remorse that he'd already forgiven her tardiness.

"Were you waiting long?" she asked, then laughed self-consciously. "Of course you were. I really am very sorry."

---

[14] FATS: Frictionless Transport System. A rapid underground mass transit technology in which pods travel through zero friction tubes at remarkable speeds.

"It can't be helped." Marci dropped his half-smoked cigarette behind him, hoping she hadn't noticed it. "How is your mother now?"

"She's much better, thank you. I think she just wanted some attention. I hope you haven't caught a cold waiting for me?"

"I was just getting some air. Shall we go in?"

Despite her protests, Marci bought both tickets. The two proceeded to the Marble Hall, where Coptic frescoes and mosaics, lifted from their original structures, hung above textiles, manuscripts and a multitude of other Byzantine Christian iconography.

Marci, who had no interest in the period, feigned enthusiasm for Erin's sake, and was relieved when, with a squeak of excitement, she beckoned him to the next room: the inaptly named Renaissance Hall, which contained an exhibit of French Impressionism.

The gallery was silent, save the echo of footsteps on the marble floor. A handful of other visitors drifted between works by Sisely, Degas, Monet. These, however, receded to peripheral vision, mere details overwhelmed by the minutiae of Erin's presence: the lilt of her voice, a chance brushing of hands, the trailing scent of jasmine and violets. From painting to painting they moved, ingenuous and free as children, and in Marci's mind the gallery was their universe and her his world and him her moon in orbit.

Erin took his hand and led him to the next room, where they paused inches from each other before *The Lady of Shalott.* Marci studied the painting with halfhearted attention and wondered if Erin was equally distracted.

"What are you thinking?" she asked.

Marci weighed his response in case his ecstasy was a private flight of fancy. "Interesting thoughts."

"Interesting? Tell me."

He hedged his bets and chose the painting. "Do you know the poem behind this? The lady is a maiden, imprisoned on the island of Shalott. She longs to see the court of King Arthur, but a curse prevents her from looking toward it. So she weaves a tapestry from what she sees in her magic mirror, and every night and morning she sings of her desire for Camelot."

"It seems a lonely life," Erin reflected. "What does she do for food?"

"I'm not sure; we're never told." He cleared his throat. "'And sometimes thro' the mirror blue the knights come riding two and two: she hath no loyal knight and true, the Lady of Shalott.'"

Erin frowned. "Poor Lady Shalott. You'd think someone would come and rescue her, especially when she kept the neighbors awake all night with her singing."

"Such is life."

"I'm glad I'm not a princess," Erin decided. "At least not one locked up in a tower. I'd be a bit worried in case no one came to rescue me."

Gallantly Marci said, "They'd be crazy not to."

Erin laughed off the compliment. "They might be if they knew me. I'm a total grump without my breakfast. Speaking of which, would you mind if we get some food? I'm famished."

On Állartkerti Körút they bought hot dogs and strolled into Városliget. Sunlight, mottled through dying horse chestnut leaves, played on the path before them. At the lake they found a bench and sat watching a boy of six or seven play with a toy sailing boat.

Marci eyed his hot dog with caution; as a rule, he never ate street food. "Do you feel inspired when you see the likes of Vermeer?"

"Who wouldn't be? But I can't paint landscapes, not like his. My work is Impressionist. It's hard these days because everybody wants abstract."

"You sell your work?"

"Sometimes. In fact, I've got my first exhibition soon. A friend arranged it for me. It's been a dream of mine since I was little."

"When I was a boy," Marci said, "I wanted to be a pilot, exploring the Outside. I used to imagine finding lost treasures and bringing them back to Budapest."

Erin shuddered. "That's not a dream, it's a nightmare. Aren't you scared by the stories? The cannibals and the people with smallpox?"

"I guess that was what made it appealing. I mean, the adventure."

"But we don't know if those stories are true, do we? I mean, no one's ever been there."

Marci turned her a puzzled look. “Of course we have. We’ve sent countless expeditions out over the years. Besides, the Sister City cargo barges fly over the Outside every few days.”

“But what if they aren’t? What if the people are just like us? They can't all be wild animals.”

“We know it's true because the Company says so. I have no reason to doubt it.”

“I remember singing Company songs at school assembly,” Erin recalled. “But there are other opinions. Many people are still angry that we erected the Wall. They say we’ve turned our backs on what made us great: compassion and humanity.”

“We're still compassionate,” Marci said. “We're compassionate to forty million Employees who can sleep safely tonight without worrying about being murdered in their beds by barbarians. It may not be ideal, but Budapest is one of the few places where civilization can continue like it did before the War.”

“Not quite as it did,” Erin corrected. “Now we have the SIN system.”

“Sure, and it works very well.”

They lapsed into silence. Down at the water, the boy prepared his toy boat for another voyage. The vessel, a fine square-rigged brig, was handmade. But its sails made it top-heavy, and every time he placed it in the water it rolled over to float bottom-up. The child watched in dismay as the boat began to sink out of reach.

Erin scuffed the ground in frustration. “But don't you think it's all a bit of a rat race? I mean, we spend all our lives working for SIN in order to become immortal. But hardly anyone gets to SIN 33. It just seems so meaningless.”

“We're a city state of forty million and growing,” Marci said. “The Wall is fixed; we’ve fenced ourselves in. There needs to be some kind of attrition.”

“Attrition?” Erin’s voice carried dismay. “Is that what you call it?”

“I know that the system isn’t perfect,” Marci said, “but we have limited resources. Inevitably there are winners and losers.”

“But the losers end up dead,” protested Erin. “How is that fair?”

For the first time that day, Marci felt himself becoming lightheaded. How had they got to this? Perhaps he should fall back on his crib sheet. The last thing he wanted was to shipwreck an otherwise splendid day. "All of us have an equal chance at success. It's true that some are victims, but aren't they victims of their own choices? If they fail, they have only themselves to blame." He looked across the park to where the Executive Team tower rose above the russet autumn tree line. "There may be a better way. But the fact is, the Company—the Patriarchs, at any rate—cured us of the Red Plague and gave us a safe place to rebuild our lives." He suddenly felt foolish. "I'm sorry, I must sound like a Company sales rep."

Erin laughed. "You do a bit, but you're genuine. I suppose I never thought of it that way. I'm interested in all ideas, whether or not they're popular. I don't think there's anything wrong with asking questions."

"It depends on who you ask and what you're asking."

"That sounds a little sinister."

It was his turn to laugh. "It isn't meant to. You've nothing to worry about unless you're a member of the Underground."

A breeze picked up, sending fallen leaves scrambling like surf along the footpath.

Erin rose. "I wish I could stay, but I'm teaching a self-development class this evening and I haven't done my planning." On impulse she kissed him on the cheek. "Thank you for today. It was nice, and you're sweet."

Marci reached for her, but she stepped beyond his grasp. "Did I say something wrong?" he asked. "Was it about the Company? I hope I didn't offend you."

"No, silly! I need to go anyway. It's not much, but these classes raise my SIN a little. Must avoid the Hangman for another day."

Marci watched her start off towards Hősök Tere. "Will I see you again?" he called.

She turned and smiled. "I hope so."

Marci waited until she'd gone, then lit a Winterbourne. Down at the water, the little boy had resumed his game with the sailboat. His father had rescued the sinking vessel and adjusted its sails, so that it now glided effortlessly across the surface of the lake. Marci watched for several minutes before strolling back to Heroes' Square and the SpeedWalk home.

5

Frazer Morrison, SIN 25, was a terse, acerbic little man in his early thirties with clever blue eyes and hair the color of polished copper. Despite having been born in Budapest, he had inherited a heavy Glaswegian accent and the temperament stereotypical of both redheads and Scots.

His office, a glass cubicle in the middle of the Executive Team administrative floor, was a room not befitting his authority as Head of Department, which was considerable—a fact of which he was amply aware. Dubbed by staff the "shark tank," it was obscured as far as possible with blinds, filing cabinets and other miscellanea to convey the subtle but unmistakable message that intrusions were unwelcome and likely to be met with a response dyspeptic, ungracious, or both.

The art of successful interaction with Morrison lay in timing. Mornings were bad. Lunchtime was equally ticklish. Morrison's afternoons were oft consumed by meetings which, in his eyes, served little purpose but to delay his departure from the workplace. Visitors imprudent enough to call after office hours were granted short shrift, and the insistent were rarely rewarded for their tenacity.

In light of this, Alex Pimenov timed his visit for late morning. By this point, Morrison would have cleared his most pressing business but would not yet be itching for a quiet lunch in a corner of the canteen.

Alex knocked at the door and waited an uneasy ten seconds until Morrison finally summoned him in.

"Close the door."

Alex did as he was told and waited while his boss finished something off at the computer.

"Well?"

When dealing with Morrison, candor and brevity were key. "Sir, I believe we have a problem with MARTHA."

Morrison, busy at his computer, failed to look up. "What is it, Alex?"

"I've discovered some anomalies in her database which may account for a large number of erroneous liquidations."

Morrison sat back in his chair and fixed Alex with a minatory stare. "How many?"

"Over eighty, sir."

"Sit down."

Alex looked about for a chair that wasn't there until Morrison pointed to one holding up a potted plant in the corner. Alex relieved it of the plant, sat down opposite and pulled a raft of paperwork from his folder.

"Bloody hell," Morrison muttered. "How long is this going to take?"

Alex ignored the remark. "Sir, as you know, I work with MARTHA on a daily basis. Besides my role as an Adjudicant, I also take an interest in the way she handles data. To this end, I've built a small replica of her at home in order to run some routines I've written. The purpose of the model is to improve MARTHA's predictive interval efficiency." Alex paused to read Morrison's reaction, which was inscrutable. Somewhat deterred, he continued, "The model is offline and, like MARTHA itself, provides no means to alter her data. However, she allowed me to run some homemade algorithms that seek out inconsistencies in her files—"

"Cut to the chase, Pimenov."

"I believe I've found a way to make her predictive interval computations up to 7% more accurate. But in the process, I discovered something strange. Fifteen years ago, the Executive Team questioned 612 Employees. The nature of the inquiries isn't clear. A month later, eighty-three of the respondents were liquidated. When I checked their SIN, none of them was below SIN 13, and the majority were 15 or higher." Alex licked his lips. "I have all the documents here."

Morrison lazily extended a hand, took the paperwork from him and leafed through it. "Interesting, very interesting. This model of MARTHA you've made: how accurate is she?"

"She's identical in every way."

"And you still have it?"

"It's at home, sir."

"Fine. Send across an electronic copy of the report. I'll have Data Analytics run some checks."

"Yes, sir."

Morrison placed the folder in a drawer and returned to his work. After several seconds he looked up. "Is there something else?"

Alex rose, replaced the chair in the corner and went to leave.

"One thing," Morrison said. "Have you shared this information with anyone else?"

Alex hesitated. "No, sir. No one knows except us."

"Good. Let's keep this under wraps. We don't want anyone thinking MARTHA's been sending people to early graves. Bloody hell, what a fiasco."

* * *

Budapest Jazz Club was a faux Art Deco affair of chrome, lacquer and iniquity that had outlived its neighborhood but not its sordid reputation. The venue's invitation-only membership was predicated on a minimum of SIN 27, the watershed number that separated the eminent but not-quite-there from the *haut monde*. Old money and nouveau riche alike were welcome, so long as their alibis were airtight and their dues paid.

The same was not true of guests. For the sake of commerce and expediency, these often comprised a criminal element and included traffickers, racketeers and the occasional crime lord, as well as purveyors of various discreet services. It was the haunt of the rich, the aspiring and the reprobate, and there was no shortage of applicants.

The passage of time had wrought little change to the property, and it retained much of its interwar years charm. It was a place of radiating geometric designs, of zigzags and trapezoids and triangles and rising sun motifs in colored glass; of walnut and maple veneers polished to shine like gold; and of mirrors, sconces and inlays of elongated fan design. Beneath its inverted iceberg chandeliers, which seemed to drip molten chrome and glass in suspension, the Charleston, Lindy Hop and Jive had come and gone, and those given to flights of fancy would from time to time remark that each had fused within the fabric of the club a little of their era.

Its cuisine reflected the wealth of its clientele. Herring, bream, squid and trout, farmed in the Sea of Japan and certified radiation-free, were flown over on ice and washed down with champagne from dusty bottles stored in the Club cellar. Fruit was less prohibitive. Lychees kept the Martinis flowing and pineapples the Margaritas. Both came from Mumbai. Citrus blight had killed the Beijing lemon crop that year. Peel twists were off.

Seated in a semi-circular booth of plush green velvet, Marci read the menu like a man choosing the means of his demise. Half the fare was foreign, and much of what remained his fear of food poisoning proscribed; at home, his OCD dictated his diet, which was invariably plain fare cooked by Alice.

There were bigger problems than lunch. It had been a week since his date with Erin. Rather than enjoy the afterglow of their meeting, Marci had spent the time agonizing over their conversation in the park, having convinced himself she'd never want to see him again. He had committed the ultimate faux pas of such occasions: he'd spoken the truth. Because of this, his carefully presented persona as an aesthete of liberal opinions lay in ruins. Instead, he'd revealed himself to be a dyed-in-the-wool, true blue corporate lickspittle of the worst sort, and the antithesis of everything he believed Erin to be. If he needed proof, he already had it: for the last two days he'd heard nothing from her. Their budding relationship might well have finished before it even started.

Marci put aside the menu and surveyed the room, whose curved, mirrored walls made the place seem even larger than it was. On a dais in the center of the room a pianist drifted his hands across a Steinway's keyboard to produce an inoffensive jazz piece. The melody mingled with the chinking of glasses, the gentle clatter of cutlery and the rise and fall of genteel conversation. Cigar smoke and aromatic fougère cologne filled the air: the smell of the filthy rich.

Hurrying across the room on effete steps came the maître d'hôtel, with Sándor more sedately in tow. The President was in good form, joking with the restaurant manager and patting Marci's arm as they shook hands. "I'm sorry for the wait. I had an appointment which took longer than planned."

Napkins were unfurled and placed on their laps. Sándor waved away the drinks list. "We'll have the Bollinger and a carafe of mineral water."

"Are we celebrating?" Marci asked.

"Yes, for two reasons. Firstly, my meeting was productive. I've won several major contracts with Tokyo. Secondly and more importantly, I have some good news for you." He beckoned over their table server. "Something a little more bracing on the music front, perhaps?"

"Yes, Patrician Ortega, right away."

Sándor paused. "It seems my recent visit with the Prefect was a success. We met this week for cocktails, and I raised the matter of your nomination. He speaks highly of you and has agreed to your election."

Marci clasped Sándor's hand. "Thank you, that's wonderful news. I can't thank you enough."

"That's the good part. We also discussed your speech. As I anticipated, his hands are tied by tradition. You'll need to address the Synod and the rest of The Society."

Marci's smile faded. "I thought that was coming."

"As you know," Sándor continued, "membership of The Society has two requirements: an outstanding contribution to the city of Budapest and a unanimous vote by the board. Your sterling efforts in the Executive Team have achieved the former, and thanks to a few well-placed words of mine, the latter is *fait accompli.* The ceremony will take place at the AGM in three weeks."

Three weeks, Marci thought. *It might as well be tomorrow.*

"It's good timing, for sure," Sándor continued, picking up the menu. "It will get you in before the Christmas Gala—a particularly sumptuous affair. We couldn't have orchestrated it better ourselves."

On the stage, the pianist resolved a chord and, at the whispered instructions of the waiter, broke into a new, upbeat improvisation. The champagne arrived, the bottle being presented to Sándor, who nodded in approval. "Have you decided on something? It's on me."

Marci, embarrassed by his own ignorance, said, "What do you recommend?"

"Zoli, what's the special today?"

"Patrician Ortega, today we have langoustine and grilled lobster in a garlic and peppered butter sauce, with side dishes of dill and lemon potatoes and grilled asparagus."

"Lobster used to be a luxury food," Sándor said. "Now it's both luxurious and rare." He snapped the menu shut and handed it to Zoli. "We'll both have it."

"An excellent choice, Patrician. Bon appétit."

Marci sipped his champagne—the first in his life—and savored the crisp, creamy texture. "I can't imagine some of the food you've eaten on your travels. The menu here is an enigma to me."

Sándor laughed. "There's no mystery. In the case of our lunch, the answer's simple. Since most of the world's oceans are still toxic, the Japanese created "sea ponds[15]." I don't pretend to understand the science, but they've managed to purify enough of the ocean to replenish the marine life, which they harvest offshore. Filtration units pump toxic water out of the ponds and back into the sea. They're an impressive sight."

"Tell me what it's like to travel."

"In truth, it's a little boring. As you know, we only have five trading partners, the Sister Cities. After a while you get sick of visiting the same destinations. Of course, I'm not directly involved in the shipping of goods."

---

[15] 海の池 (umi no ike): a patented Japanese farming method which utilizes small amounts of Heavy Air technology to decontaminate local seawater and provide safe breeding grounds for a range of fish and crustaceans.

"What are they like?" Marci asked. "I've always wanted to see them."

"They vary. Australia's the most civilized, after Budapest. It remained neutral in the Fuel War but the marine life's dead. They're still scraping it off their beaches a century later." Sándor sipped his champagne. "Like us, they're sealed off from the Outside and are heavily policed. Beijing sided publicly with Moscow during the War and it paid a heavy price. Unlike the Russians, the Chinese couldn't afford to buy DOME tech from us, and the capital took direct hits. When the Red Plague struck, their infrastructure couldn't cope. Things are better now, but of all the cities, Beijing is the most dismal and something of a chore to visit."

Marci, awed by Sándor's nonchalance, said, "It all sounds very intrepid."

Sándor laughed. "I certainly don't slum it, although a few more boutique hotels wouldn't go amiss; one soon tires of the Four Seasons. There's also an element of altruism at play. Without my fleet, Budapest would have a fraction of the food and luxury goods we enjoy. Speaking of which, what do you make of the Bollinger?"

"It's very nice. I suppose the Green Zone doesn't produce anything like it?"

"Nowhere in the world produces anything like it, and never will. Our Green Zone is good for staples—root vegetables, maize, wheat and the like. The hot houses produce some tropical fruit, but with so many mouths to feed they take up space that could be given over to arable farming. And we can't expand because of the Wall. We're hemmed in by our own defenses."

Zoli returned with a tray bearing two glasses of amber liquid.

"Zoli knows I'm a creature of habit," Sándor said. "Vermouth. To your health."

Marci raised his glass. "*Egészségedre.*" He lit a cigarette. "Tell me more about Club 30. You've never explained it in any depth."

"That's because much of it's secret. However, since you're soon to be elected—acceptance speech provided—perhaps I can bend the rules a little. You probably know most of it. There are 118 Patricians in a city of over forty million. So, if your math is good—which I hope as an Adjudicant it is—that means…"

Marci calculated. "Point zero, zero, zero two percent of the population."

"An infinitesimal amount. Bankers, scholars, politicians, industrialists and members of the judicial system, all elected by The Society and all recipients of a generous rewards package. You've probably heard about it through the grapevine: a liberal monthly allowance and relocation package to Buda, air corridor priority, transit visas to the Sister Cities. The list goes on."

Marci tried to hide his ebullience. "Tell me about the Club 30 card. Is it really a golden ticket like everyone says?"

"In some ways. When you join The Society, your private bank account, savings, investments and credit card balances are transferred to The Society's corporate fund management account. They remain in your name but are protected by The Society and benefit from our interest rate, currently 18% per annum. The card itself will open doors for you figuratively and literally. And it's not just the plastic, it's the Patrician's emblem. In some ways it's more powerful."

"The Aquila?"

"It carries serious gravitas." Sándor chuckled in recollection. "I was once stopped for speeding. I went to show my pilot's license but we didn't get that far. As soon as the traffic cop saw the golden eagle he bowed, apologized, and went on his way."

Zoli returned with the appropriate cutlery and laid the table.

Sándor waited for him to leave. "The Society is much more than a club. It's a brotherhood. When you're elected, you'll swear to a code of honor. The first rule is secrecy. No one outside The Society can know what we do. Given the positions and influence of our members, our discussions affect the lives of millions. The second rule is fraternity. We all help each other. All the big contracts in the city, no matter what field or industry, happen between Patricians. The same applies to the other Sister Cities."

A food trolley appeared, bearing several silver cloches. The domes were removed to reveal their lunch: lobster and langoustines flown in overnight from Hokkaido, with side dishes of fresh vegetables and warm bread rolls, with silver ramekins of butter. Basins of lemon water were also provided to cleanse their hands with. Sándor seemed ambivalent about the presentation. Marci, taken aback, stared at his plate.

"Second thoughts?" Sándor asked.

"I don't know if I should eat it or take a picture of it. It's far too beautiful to end up in my stomach."

"Enjoy it. It's a taste of things to come."

Marci picked at the vegetables. "Are these from the Green Zone?"

"Yes, they're all grown near Kőbánya. The lobster is the large, ugly creature. The langoustines are easy to deal with. Peel away the shell like so and separate the carapace."

Marci hulled the shellfish. In spite of his OCD, he placed a small amount in his mouth. "It's delicious," he said. "I've never tasted anything like it."

Sándor twisted off a lobster claw. "Now to business. I take it you've prepared your nomination speech. No? Then I suggest you begin today. It's well within your capacity and you've plenty of time. There'll be three candidates up for nomination—an exceptional number for a single meeting. The format is simple. After lunch, you'll be invited to speak. You'll tell everyone a little about your role in the Executive Team, how much you love the Company and how honored you are to be joining The Society. You'll be proposed, seconded and voted in. Afterwards, Armand Bucco will take you through the paperwork. You'll sign the vow of secrecy, provide a sample of DNA for your Club 30 card and another for The Society gene bank. The next day you'll receive your ID wallet and card."

Marci put aside his food; his appetite had left him. "You make it sound so easy."

"It couldn't be simpler. I assume you still haven't visited Stella? Go and see her. I pulled strings to get you on her books."

"I suppose it won't hurt, though I don't hold out much hope."

"We'll talk through the details of your speech over dessert. And I'll have my secretary send across those exemplars I promised."

Marci managed a smile. "Thank you, Sándor. I owe you a huge debt."

Sándor patted him on the arm. "Now let's enjoy our little repast. The somlói is out of this world." He lifted his champagne flute. "A toast: to your successful nomination to The Society of Patricians!"

Marci raised his glass. "To The Society. And to you, Sándor, my good friend!"

After a leisurely dessert, followed by cognac, cigars and a protracted discourse on the merits of contemporary jazz, Sándor dropped Marci off at Gyulai Pál before dusk. A storm was gathering; already curfew drones were circling like carrion birds under a darkling sky.

As he mounted the stairs Marci's phone chimed. Alex's image appeared.

"Marci! You'll never guess what happened today."

"Let me guess. Your SIN was slashed to 5 because of your data model?"

"Not quite. Are you sitting down?

"No, but I'll cope."

"It's all a bit of a shock. Remember Morrison called me in again? It seems the miserable git has a soft side. Half an hour ago he called me back into his office, congratulated me on my research, called me a jolly good chap and asked would I like a promotion? Needless to say, I accepted. Marci, I'm SIN 24!"

Marci frowned. "So quickly? You only presented the data this morning."

"It wasn't so quick. I've worked for months on the model."

"Of course you have. Congratulations, Alex. You've really earned it."

"There's more. The promotion's come just at the right time. Lei's pregnant."

"Alex, that's wonderful!" Marci cried. "When did you find out?"

"She took the test this morning. Isn't it great? I feel like everything's coming together."

At home, Marci arranged his shoes by the front door, washed his hands and sat in the lounge, smoking. Alex's sudden promotion troubled him. Fast tracking was rare but not unheard of. Ordinary protocol required an H.R. meeting and a consultation period lasting several weeks. A same-day SIN rise was unheard of. It was feasible that Head of Department Rieks Kruger was so impressed by Alex's initiative that he might discuss the matter with Morrison, but given the Scotsman's workload that was unlikely.

Marci turned on the Living Wall. A commercial for Seromax tablets was interrupted by News24 with an update on last night's civil unrest. Footage showed rioters looting shops in District XIII before turning on Budapest police with petrol bombs and other makeshift weapons. A police spokesman revealed that several of the agitators had confessed allegiance to the Underground, which took full responsibility for the incident. Video footage of the condemned's executions was available on demand for News24 Premium subscribers.

Marci took an instant dinner to his study and ate it in silence. He'd now have to begin the laborious process of writing his nomination speech. Perhaps he could simply tweak one of the examples Sándor's secretary had sent him? No, they would be his words, and on their merit he would gain Club 30 or fail. He stared at the blank screen of his computer. It was going to be a long night.

*   *   *

He stands in a hallway. From above the front door, late spring sunlight transfuses through a transom window of six orange segments to paint the parquet floor tangerine. To his right hang coats, children's and adult's, school satchels and umbrellas. Outdoor shoes sit in neat, ordered rows, with slippers for guests.

He moves forward, not of his own volition but as if by some slow, magnetic force. He looks down but cannot see his legs. When he passes a mirror, it reflects only the opposite wall.

From ahead comes singing: a woman's voice. She hums a melody familiar yet forgotten to him, and it mingles with washing dishes and with the soft hum of an oven.

At a sink stands a woman. She is slim but strong and bears herself with unconscious dignity. Pogácsa are baking. Their smokey, buttery aroma fills the room. A smell from childhood. Sunlight catches the woman's auburn hair. She wipes her hands on her pinafore and approaches the kitchen table, where a young girl sits drawing with crayons. The woman leans over her shoulder to inspect her work. The child looks up and speaks, but her words are silent. The woman kisses her hair and smiles. Encouraging words, also unheard.

He moves, impelled or drawn. A living room whose walls are overburdened bookcases lead to an upright piano in a corner and a gramophone, complete with flaring horn. It spins a Bakelite 78, which crackles like fire. Through the noise, a melody carries: the Adagietto from Mahler's Fifth Symphony. Outside large bay windows, lime trees unfurl tender green leaves above a side street.

On the floor sit a man and a teenage boy. The youth, sixteen, wears the navy-blue shorts and white, emblemed shirt of a school uniform. Beside him his father looks on: a man gentle in appearance, with a graying beard cut short and hair swept past his ears. He holds a pipe, which from time to time he points at something his son has written in his notepad. He asks a question. The boy throws his head back and laughs mutely.

Closer now. His father draws on the pipe, pulling the heat down again and again within the bowl. Clouds of silver-blue smoke rise toward the high ceiling, making the air heady with the scent of honey and dried fruit.

The boy's expression changes. He grabs a broad-nibbed felt pen. Clutching it like a dagger, he scratches it back and forth across the page, then rips the sheet free and hands it to his father to read.

The man, smiling, sets aside his pipe. His smile fades. The page slips from his hand. In horror he raises his eyes and looks directly at Marci.

Adrenaline like liquid voltage coursed through his veins. Marci jerked awake in bed sheets soaked with sweat, his breath coming in ragged gasps. Tears welled in his eyes, spilling into his lap when he sat up. He began to sob, huge, quaking sobs that shook his whole body. He cried without restraint, a sound of anguish: "Daddy, my Daddy!"

6

When a Mercedes Citaro failed, Transport Budapest dispatched a Volvo. When the Volvos ran out, they sent an Ikarus. On a good day, with a sprinkling of holy water and the wind behind it, an Ikarus 415T might last until noon. It was 08:36, so Marci was safe.

He counted numbers. Cumbersome, odd numbers. Sevens or nines or thirteens made the game harder, but the sequences were too familiar and he counted by rote.

Four hundred. Three hundred eighty-seven.

At Blaha Lujza, two ticket inspectors boarded and a dozen passengers immediately alighted. Marci nabbed a still-warm seat and showed his pass. A mile away, down arrow-straight Rákóczi út, lay his goal: Keleti. It would take three minutes, no more. Enough time to try his latest visualization. He closed his eyes, shutting out the world.

A beach, but different from before. It is cooler here in the shade, here where the water snakes have their holes. Nine silver birches—real trees—hide the shingle strand, their bark peeling like sunburned skin. One overhangs the river. Last year, his friends shinnied out along a bough to bomb the shallows. It was safe enough in May when the river was in flood, but not September. All summer they'd teased him for his cowardice, but they were wrong. It wasn't the fall he feared. It was the water.

The bus, crammed full, pulled out into traffic and stopped at a red on Erzsébet boulevard.

Along the shore, sunlight glitters on ripples sent by a passing ferry. The boat's wash scrubs the beach in rhythmic pulses. He feels the stones beneath his feet. They are small and warm and not sharp, but leave dimples in his skin when brushed away. Stones beneath feet, earth below blazing sun, eternity above him. He is ten.

Marci is proud. He makes fire sticks with the knife dad gave him for his birthday. He lays them at the ready beside tinder, kindling and branches. All neatly ordered, perfectly parallel—the hallmarks of prepubescent OCD. Péter lights the tinder with a pipe match. Marci adds kindling and blows on the flames. The fire sticks take; the flames rise. He claps his hands with joy. Péter smiles and ruffles the boy's hair.

Green. The trolleybus driver, riled by the delay, stamped on the accelerator, sending the standing passengers staggering back. Someone near the doors fell into the stepwell. Someone else cursed at the driver on their behalf.

Concentrate!

Now the fire is blazing. Marci places vegetables wrapped in foil into the flames. Silver nuggets in a crucible. Soon they'll be ready to eat with the *kolbász* sausage mother packed for them. A fine feast!

"A következő megálló: Huszár utca," spoke the Tannoy.

Marci felt a sickening sensation in the pit of his stomach. "One more minute," he whispered to himself. "If you can't last a minute on a bus, what hope do you have at the AGM?"

Three hundred seventy-four… Three hundred sixty-one—

The woman beside him rose to leave. As Marci rose to let her out, his vision dimmed almost to the point of blackness. His balance failed; a swirl of vertigo left him clutching for a grabrail.

He pressed the stop request button.

"Huszár utca."

The doors groaned open and Marci stumbled out. Four hundred yards east stood Keleti station and its on-demand dispensary. At an undignified, loping jog he set off, emerging five minutes later from the station concourse full of Seromax and Nauselief.

It was 09:03. Morrison would already be sniffing around the office for him. Calmer now, Marci set off on foot.

His thoughts were dark. The Society AGM was two weeks away, and his speech was nowhere near ready. To date, his best efforts had yielded half a paragraph of obsequious rhetoric which made him cringe every time he read it.

Then there was Erin. Since the time of Marci's lunch with Sándor he'd heard nothing from her. Her ambiguous silence played strongly on Marci's fears. He read and reread their texts and emails. He analyzed her old voicemail messages for tone and word choice but could find nothing to suggest antipathy on her part. Her correspondence was warm and inquiring and suggested only keen interest in pursuing the relationship. But, Marci reflected, women were women: masters of cunning and subterfuge, and predictable only in their capriciousness. It was too early to tell, but maybe Erin was different. He snorted. An unlikely prospect.

He considered a course of action. He dismissed it. It was immoral and also illegal. If caught, there would be serious repercussions. And yet, if he exercised caution, it was probably safe.

Feeling lazy, Marci hailed an air cab and minutes later was delivered to the Executive Team building. Upstairs, Morrison was busy, and Marci sneaked into his suite unnoticed.

The morning went quickly. Marci adjudicated several cases, authorizing the cessations of three Employees whose lifestyles were deemed detrimental to the Company. By 11:00 he had submitted the cases and turned his attention to routine paperwork.

At noon Marci emerged from his cubicle and descended to the quadrangle, where a small Japanese garden occupied a corner. Its centerpiece was a pond stocked with robotic koi fish, sheltered by trained acers which spread delicate russet foliage above a stone bench. Here Marci sat. From his satchel he produced a packed lunch and a paper folder. The file's cover read:

ERIN REBECCA MACSY
EMPLOYEE ID 492FR973A688
ABBREVIATED SIN PROFILE AND LIFELINE

He glanced around. He was alone. Here in the shade of the Japanese maples, the courtyard CCTV cameras could not see him.

He stared at the cover. Temptation tugged at him; equally, duty and pride pulled him in the opposite direction.

He set it aside. It was no use; he couldn't bring himself to read her lifeline. He ate his lunch and returned to the building. In the admin office he ran the documents through the shredder and headed back toward the Adjudication suite.

"All hail Patrician Kovács!"

"Oh, please no," Marci muttered, picking up speed. But Tony Jackson, hands on hips, stood between Marci and the suite, and there was no polite or impolite shortcut Marci could take.

Tony bowed low. "Greetings, exalted one!"

"Tony," Marci said without enthusiasm. Today, he noticed, the office manager was wearing a slim-fit outfit made of some stretchy stuff which showed off his muscular arms, pot belly and skinny legs to ill effect. "I see you've been working out."

Tony inspected his physique as if for the first time. "This? This is all natural. But I have had a few compliments today from the ladies," he winked. "But enough about me. A little bird told me some wonderful news." He drew near, as if to confide a great secret. "I hear your election to The Society is only weeks away. You'll be something of a prodigy, being the youngest Adjudicant to reach 30."

Marci forced a smile. The last thing he needed was for the news to go public. "Tony, if you'll—"

Tony patted him generously on the back. "We're all proud of you, old boy. In fact"—here he lowered his voice—"I'm organizing a little entertainment for this evening. Just for the boys, you know."

"I'm afraid I don't know what you're talking about."

"Girls, Márton, girls! The Honey Pot's dropped its 'no touching' rule last week. We'll have a few drinks and watch the pretty ladies dance for us."

"A strip club?" Marci said loudly. "Tonight?"

"Hush, hush, old chap!" Tony said, glancing around the room. "No need to advertise it!"

"Is it just the two of us, or is your wife coming with us?"

"Ha, ha!" Tony brayed. "No, you must have misheard me."

"Or perhaps your wife is in it?"

From the secretarial pool came stifled laughter.

Marci indicated that he wished to pass. "Excuse me, Tony. Duty calls."

Tony, now a shade of deep pink, stepped aside. "Of course, of course! Nose to the grindstone—that's how a man makes SIN!"

At 17:00 Alex rapped on Marci's door. "Fancy a beer?"

Marci turned around from his console. "Sure. Everything ok?"

Alex raised a finger to his lips. "Over a beer."

On Lendvay utca stood Duna Kocsma, a seedy little bar with booths of tatty plastic, the latest hit songs and cheap, cold beer. Marci and Alex found a corner and ordered cola and lager, respectively.

Marci lit a cigarette. "What's up? You look like you've seen a ghost."

"Maybe in the machine," Alex quipped, without humor. "What would you say if I told you the Company was covering up the liquidations I found?"

"I'd say you're still playing around with that model you made. And that you were wrong."

Alex scratched at his beer bottle label. "I had an interesting conversation with Morrison today. He told me to bring my computer into work so that I.T. can delete my MARTHA model."

"Fair enough. I've always said it was bad news."

"Think this through. Carrot-top congratulated me on discovering the anomalies, and I get a promotion out of it. Not just a micro SIN, but a whole point. That's clearly a tacit endorsement of my model. So why get I.T. to wipe it from the drive unless there's something dangerous about it?"

"That's a bit far-fetched, isn't it? Maybe they just don't like you having a private copy of the state computer on your PC."

"Okay, just hear me out. I asked Morrison if he'd learned anything about the anomalies. He said they were basically glitches, and that MARTHA's predictive interval routines sometimes play up, which we know for a fact isn't true. But that excuse, even if it's true, doesn't explain how a SIN 15 Employee became a SIN 5 reprobate in the space of two weeks without cause, and is then liquidated. And it sure doesn't explain eighty of them."

"And the cases didn't go before an Adjudicant?"

"No, but they were processed and actioned manually. Don't ask me who; no one initialed the documents."

"You mean the files were closed without being signed off by an Adjudicant?"

"Exactly. Neither were the cessation orders certified."

"That's not possible."

"There's more," Alex continued. "Morrison asked that yes-man Marcus Behrman to investigate MARTHA. Carrot-top knows that I know far more about MARTHA's architecture than anyone in Data Analytics. So why not just ask me to fix the glitches, if that's what they really are?"

"Because you're an Adjudicant, not a Data Analyst?"

Alex removed a printout from his backpack. "I ran my code again last night. The search parameters are identical to those I used before."

Marci studied the documents. "It's blank."

"Exactly. No anomalies, interviews or premature liquidations. Then I ran searches on everyone who'd been liquidated. It's the next sheet."

"There's nothing here."

"It's as if they never existed."

Marci felt the hairs on his arms rise. "Do you still have the original documents you showed me?"

"They're all at home, hidden in the bathroom."

"This doesn't make sense." Marci leafed through the papers. "Even if there was a problem with MARTHA's algorithms, she'd never just delete Employees. How many other people do they suspect are hacking MARTHA?"

"None, I assume. Marci, why the hell would they promote me to 24 and then brush off this as a computer error off unless my promotion was a payoff?"

Marci reached for another cigarette. "You're talking crazy. You found a problem. The boss, despite being a bit of a bastard, handed it over to Data and told you to stop poking around because it's illegal. You were promoted because you found the anomalies and because it was well overdue. My guess is that someone in Data was told to deal with the issue, so they just wiped the files clean. Lazy, unprofessional and criminal? Yes. A conspiracy?"

"Okay, that explains how they got rid of the problem, but it doesn't account for the cessations. Like you said, MARTHA doesn't make mistakes. If you want to kid yourself, go ahead."

Marci waved to the bartender and pointed to Alex's beer; cola suddenly wasn't going to cut it. "Then what's the alternative? That the Company's randomly killing off its own Employees and covering it up?"

"That's the point. They're not random, they're all connected to the interviews. Why are you in denial about this?"

"Questioning isn't denial."

"You've seen the paperwork. Everything's there in black and white."

"There are other explanations," Marci said, but couldn't think of one. "The Company must have its reasons."

Alex grunted. "You're turning into more of a yes-man than Behrman."

"I'm not a yes-man," Marci said mildly, "I just believe in the system. Without it, we'd be like the scum at our borders. If you work hard, you achieve SIN. It couldn't be fairer."

"So long as you're not one of the eighty-three," Alex replied. "Honestly, you sound more like News24 every day."

"And you sound like a dissenter."

The waiter arrived with Marci's beer. Marci waited for him to leave. "I was an intern in the Executive Team when Dad was taken. Three Hangmen came one evening. As far as we knew, Dad's SIN was good, but he hardly ever checked it. Besides, if you were the engineer behind the Eden Project you'd assume your SIN was safe for life. When he was liquidated, I had a choice: believe that the Company had its reasons to liquidate him, or fight the system. I chose to believe. And in all my years as an Adjudicant, I've never seen MARTHA make a bad call. Have you?"

Alex sighed. "No, which is what I've been saying all along. It's not MARTHA. It has to be someone who works for the Exec Team. Someone high up."

"Human error or bad practice," Marci said. "My explanation is plausible, at the very least."

"Plausible but unlikely." Alex drained his glass and rose. "I have to collect Lucy from her SIN enrichment program."

Marci stubbed out his cigarette. "Alex, take some advice. Go home, pack up your computer and hand it over to Morrison, then enjoy being SIN 24 with all its benefits. And please forget about this, because all it comes down to is a computer glitch and some lazy clerical work. The alternative isn't worth thinking about."

Alex tossed a credit on the table. "Enjoy your beer," he said, and walked out.

Marci waved to the server and changed his order to a whiskey.

* * *

Like pencil smudges rolled behind a diorama, the first bands of October rain crept silently across the city skyline. Marci rose early and spent all of Saturday morning confined to his study. His Society acceptance speech, while far from perfect, was beginning to take shape, and in the nick of time; the AGM was eight days away.

Events elsewhere were less productive. Since their meeting at Duna Kocsma a week ago, Alex had withdrawn, tortoise-like, from all but the most necessary communication. At first it was subtle: the odd unanswered email, or one whose brevity bordered on the terse. Their encounters became chance and infrequent, and when they occasionally found themselves in the canteen, Alex took the long route to avoid speaking to him.

Their paths finally crossed in the restroom. Alex, Marci thought, looked wan and under pressure. Feeling guilty for his heavy-handedness at the pub, Marci invited him and Lei to dinner. Alex politely declined, citing family programs. In the end, Marci realized he could only offer the olive branch so many times, and regretted even more the whole business of MARTHA's supposed anomalies.

That left the problem of Erin. Marci gave a sardonic grunt. What about her? She hadn't called him in weeks. The fact was clear: he'd blown their first and only date. What little correspondence she'd sent him was her way of letting him down gently. Erin was gone, leaving a dull pain inside him that he tried to assuage with busyness.

At midday Marci tossed a packet meal into the microwave and went to the bathroom to fetch his tablets. Gawping back at him from the mirror was a tragic figure. His sad, panda eyes, unkempt hair and three-day stubble made for a pitiful sight.

No wonder she ditched you, you ugly oaf.

From the study came a chime, which he paid no heed to. "A stupid, ugly oaf," he muttered. "She'll be sorry when I make SIN 30 and she's still sweeping trash around Objet d'Heart."

On the coffee table his phone screen displayed the last person he expected to call. He hesitated, torn between loathing and a thrill of hope. The latter won out.

"Oh, hello, Marci, it's Erin! I'm so sorry for not getting back to you sooner. I wanted to reply for ages, but I've been so busy the last few weeks. I hope you're not too annoyed with me?"

Marci was overcome by a sudden, visceral resentment at the sound of her. Without word, he marched to the kitchen and took a beer from the fridge.

"Are you there? Marci?"

"I'm busy writing my speech at the moment."

"Oh yes, of course! You have your Club 30 meeting a week tomorrow, don't you?"

Marci pulled off the ring tab with a satisfying hiss. "You remembered? How kind."

"I was just wondering if you're free tonight for dinner?" Erin continued. "I have some friends coming over, and I know they'd love to meet you." She paused. "Also, I'd like to see you."

Marci sipped his drink. "I'm not sure. I really need to finish the acceptance speech."

"Oh, I see. Marci, I know I've treated you horribly. I should have stayed in touch. I... I have issues of my own. But it was nice to meet you at the museum, and I'd like to get to know you better. Can you forgive me?"

"I'd prefer it if you didn't just disappear on me,' he said, returning to the lounge. "I know I upset you at the park, but you don't have to go silent on me."

"You didn't upset me, silly! It's my fault, but I'm going to change. Tell me how I can make it up to you!"

"I suppose I could do with a break," he mumbled. "When should I come?"

"19:00 would be perfect. My friends arrive at half past. You can help me in the kitchen."

"Send me your address and I'll be there."

Erin made a squeak of excitement. "Oh, I'm so pleased! It'll be such fun. I'll ping you my address now. *Szia*!"

Marci hung up, dropped the phone on the sofa and took another swig of beer, which had suddenly lost its appeal. How did she sway him so easily? She seemed to have it down to an art. He glanced at the Birch and Gaydon. He had two hours. He ran the bath, disrobed and resigned himself to the fact that he would never understand women.

* * *

Erin lived on Pillangó utca in Arpadvaros, a leafy district of Kecskemét favored by artists, musicians, fashionistas, and craftsmen of obscure folk art. At one time an agricultural town in the center of the Great Plain, Kecskemét had been subsumed into the capital, becoming a trendy suburb ten minutes from the city center via the FATS.

Marci took a taxi from the station to gentrified Burga utca, where a row of five-story Khrushchyovka tenement blocks built on concrete stilts provided shelter for pretentious cafés, artisanal boutiques and galleries. The once-bland, uniform structures were now renovated, each one painted with Salvador Dali designs or something arabesque.

Marci hurried through rain to the arcade, where he enjoyed a final cigarette and checked his pulse: elevated but not sinister, given the circumstances. Tonight's soiree presented him with two issues. First, he'd be expected to eat; second, he'd be doing so in the company of complete strangers. His OCD forbade the former and his social anxiety the latter. The eating aspect could be dealt with easily. He'd lie. Since he'd already had dinner he lacked appetite, but was happy to drink a glass or two of wine. This satisfied both parties. Marci would avoid food poisoning, and his host the shame of providing inadequate hospitality.

He buzzed himself into the lobby and climbed to the third floor. He was, as usual, far too early, which presented the perfect opportunity for a second cigarette. He was about to make use of it when the door beside him opened. With a yelp of delight Erin threw her arms around his neck and hugged him. "Come in—I want to show you all around!"

Marci removed his shoes, aligned them with the others in the rack and followed her into a bright, cheerful kitchen-dining room. A table was laid for four with white linen and a Kalocsa center cloth.

"It's not as grand as your place," she apologized. "My sister, Sophia, helped me to decorate it."

Marci ran the kitchen tap. "I'll just wash my hands," he muttered.

Erin waited until he was finished. "Come and see my studio."

Marci, still nonplussed by the warmth of her greeting, followed Erin to a large, cluttered room which smelled of turpentine. Paintings and sketches covered every wall; many more leaned one against the other on the floor. An easel occupied a corner; beside it stood a worktable overflowing with the appurtenances of her hobby: oils, acrylics, watercolor sets, brushes in jam jars, palette knives, and bottles of linseed oil. It was a mess, but it was an artist's mess, and thus had kudos.

True to her word, most of Erin's paintings were in the vein of French Impressionism. But rather than the joy and vibrancy typical of a Monet, hers were somber, both in theme and execution. In one, a young woman sat with her knees clutched to her chest, her head. Oppressive black clouds resembling carrion birds encircled her. In another, an outstretched hand tried to restrain a man walking unwittingly toward the black van of a cessation squad. Another portrayed a scarlet rose crushed beneath a Hangman's black jackboot.

Muted palettes conveyed a sense of hopelessness and loss; elsewhere, more buoyant color schemes evidenced swings of emotion.

One work in particular caught Marci's attention. It showed a landscape of mythic grandeur, with tall, jagged mountains and lush woodland in deep summer shadow. The focal point was a fairy-tale castle on a limestone crag, whose drawbridge spanned a river gorge. A knight on a dappled gray palfrey held aloft a lance, from which hung a heraldic pennant that rippled in the evening breeze. In the castle's highest tower, a window showed the soft glow of candlelight, but the woman for whom the knight had made his journey was gone, and his quest had been in vain.

"That's one of my attempts at fine art," Erin said. "I know it's not very good. I found the picture in a storybook at Objet d'Heart."

"You really painted this? What the hell are you doing working in Objet d'Heart?"

Erin laughed. "A girl's got to pay the bills. Oh, I forgot to tell you, my exhibition has a venue. It's at the Weber Center."

"The Weber Center?" Marci said, surprised.

"Yes. A friend of mine—Petros— helped to arrange it. Actually, you're going to meet him tonight." Erin said diffidently: "Do you like my work?"

"Very much so. It's just not what I expected."

Erin's mouth drooped. "How so?"

"It's darker than I imagined. "Bleak" might be a suitable description."

Erin laughed—a nervous sound. "Yes, it does seem that way, doesn't it? I suppose it's my hidden side coming out."

"Not so much Monet as Munch," Marci quipped. "But I'd happily have these on my walls at home."

Erin patted his arm. "Thank you, but you're only saying that to make me happy."

"No, I'm not. I mean—"

On impulse, Erin stepped close, placed her hands on his chest and kissed him: once, twice. Dazed, Marci bumped into the worktable and knocked a jar of linseed oil to the floor, where it shattered.

"I'm sorry," he stammered, looking around for something to clean up with.

Erin took a roll of paper towel from the table. Blushing, she said: "It's quite all right. Would you fetch me the dustpan and brush from under the sink?"

Marci stumbled into the kitchen, arousal stirred inside him. When he returned, Erin had mopped up most of the spillage, but the room reeked of flax. "My, my," she said, opening a window, "it's warm in here and my guests will arrive soon. I'm surprised the whole apartment doesn't smell. Whatever will they think?"

Taking the dustpan from him Erin went to pass Marci. As she did so, he slipped his arm around her waist and pulled her close. Their faces met. Desire overpowered fear. Marci kissed her, passionately. Erin let the pan slip from her hand; the glass shattered on the floor again. She placed her arms around his neck and responded to his ardor.

The doorbell rang.

"They're early," Erin breathed. "I'd better answer it."

She hurried out, Marci more slowly. From the hall came the sound of laughter and bonhomie. Into the kitchen came Erin, chattering nervously, followed by a tall, lank man with a long forehead, sharp, gray eyes and graying hair pulled back in a ponytail. A mustache, neat beard and spherical glasses lent him an air of bookish intellectualism. Pants and a shirt of jet black reinforced the cliche, while natty white loafers suggested a maverick streak. Presumably this was Petros.

Behind him, prattling furiously, was a large-boned young woman almost as tall as Petros. She had a pretty face but wore a mishmash of an ensemble clearly designed to disguise her ample figure.

Erin waited for her to fall silent but was unsuccessful.

Petros cleared his throat several times until Lydia took the hint. "Forgive me, dear Lydia," he said, "but I fear Erin's friend will think us churlish if we forego the introductions." He turned to Marci and bowed. "I am Petros Garai, at your service. The charming lady to my right is Lydia, who is something of an amateur orator, as you may already have discerned."

Lydia put her hands on her hips and gave Petros a withering look, then turned to Marci. "I'm delighted to meet you," she said, raising a hand for him to kiss, which Marci did without enthusiasm.

"And trying to get a word in edgeways," Petros continued, "is our ever-gorgeous hostess, artist and friend, Erin."

Erin lifted an imaginary skirt and curtsied.

Marci said: "I'm Kovács Márton—"

"—my boyfriend," Erin completed, slipping her arm around his waist. "Marci's quite a social phenomenon. He moves in very high circles."

Marci started to speak. "It's not really—"

"An honor," said Petros, shaking his hand. "Although I admit to confusion. I thought Lydia was the only social spectacle in our midst?"

Lydia raised her eyebrows. "Am I supposed to take that as a compliment?"

"My dear lady, could it be anything else?" To Marci he said: "Lydia is a fashion designer, as you may have gathered from her eye-catching attire. Some would call it a clash of the Titans, but I prefer to call it eclectic."

"Petros comes across as suave and educated in his funeral garb," Lydia observed. "They say that those who wear all black simply mirror their souls. In matters of fashion, he is outmoded and frightfully dull."

Petros nodded sagely. "For once, Lydia speaks the truth with brevity. I will not argue with her, mostly because I'm starving, and would prefer dinner to breakfast."

Erin said, "In which case, I'm happy to tell you that dinner is more than ready."

Petros covered his eyes. "I feel the need to apologize again for our tardy arrival."

"Please don't," said Lydia, "or we shall be waiting even longer for our food."

The meal proceeded. Erin brought them consommé with pasta shells, served with warm bread rolls. The soup only served to loosen Lydia's tongue further, and she proved even more loquacious than

Petros had implied. With exaggerated vivacity she dominated the conversation with various scandals, intrigues and tidbits of gossip.

Of particular interest to her was Marci, who unlike her proved taciturn and conducted himself with decorum. During a brief respite from her monologue, Lydia addressed him. “Marci, you are so very quiet! It's bad enough that Erin kept me in the dark about your romance. Please, don't let me hog the conversation.”

Marci, whose eyes had glazed over, bestirred himself. “What would you like to know?”

“Why, everything, of course! The more the better!”

Petros spoke: “Despite appearances, Lydia feeds not on food but on hearsay. Whatever you tell her will be recited a hundred times to her cronies, with exaggeration. In this way she enhances her social standing but not her SIN, which remains dubious.”

“Nonsense, Petros! I am a paragon of discretion! As for my SIN, I consider myself an artist, and like Erin I am above such worldly matters!”

“I'm not so elevated,” Erin admitted. “I care about my SIN very much, if only to avoid the Hangman.”

Marci spilled some soup down his shirt.

“Come, come, Erin,” Lydia chided, “such talk is in poor taste. Marci, you are still so silent! Please tell us, at least, what your occupation is.”

“Or at least where your SIN stands,” added Petros, “along with any sexual peccadilloes you're happy to share. Lydia will bleat these out with great gusto.”

“I'm afraid my life is very dull,” Marci said. “I work for the Company in administration.”

Erin touched Marci's arm. “Marci's a shooting star. In fact, he'll soon be elected to The Society.”

“The Society of Patricians?” Lydia blurted.

Marci scowled at Erin in reproof. “It's anything but certain, and something of a secret.”

“Not anymore,” Petros murmured.

Lydia regarded him with awe. “You're SIN 29? My oh my, Erin, you are a dark horse!”

Erin blushed, as much from the realization that she'd spoken too candidly as Lydia's remark.

Lydia put her cutlery down and arched her fingers. "Forgive me, Marci, but you mentioned that you work in administration. How, may I ask, does a Company administrator reach SIN 30?"

Marci felt his face burn. Why was this intolerable cow putting him in the spotlight? He'd kept his profession a secret from Erin thus far, and he certainly wasn't going to break the news to satisfy the human bovine. Sullenly he said, "I made improvements to the data models used to ensure Employee lifelines are correct."

Lydia's eyes narrowed. She was about to speak when Erin preempted her. "Marci works very hard and has been with the Company since he left university."

Lydia remained unconvinced. "I see. Well, I suppose company career men inevitably gain slope. I imagine it's a very secure line of work."

"Please forgive Lydia," Petros said. "She comes across as charming and a little dotty, but when she senses a mystery she displays the propriety of a rhino on heat."

"I'm not sure I appreciate that comparison, Petros. You can be really quite crude at times."

"Forgive me, dear lady! In a way, it was a compliment."

"I can't imagine how."

"Have we finished with the soup?" Erin asked. "In which case, Marci, please help me clear the table and we'll serve the main course."

They brought *Pörkölt* stew with tarhonya to the table, and once again the conversation found its way to the topic of Lydia, who partook liberally of the robust cabernet sauvignon Petros had brought.

Marci waited for a breach in the conversation and addressed him. "Erin told me you've organized a showing of her art at the Weber Center."

Petros nodded, dabbing his mouth with a napkin. "I have indeed. The curator, Rubin Sachs, is a close friend of mine, SIN 25, I believe. When I saw the quality of Erin's work, I felt compelled to speak with him. He was only too happy to oblige."

Erin reached across the table and touched Petros's hand. "It's so kind of you, Petros. Most artists would give their front teeth for such an opportunity."

'Nincs mit, my dear. I'm only sorry the main gallery is already taken. Rubin has promised you a side room, and I'm told agents like to step away from the hurly burly, so it might work to your advantage.'

Lydia clapped her hands in excitement. "It will be a grand affair! I will spread the news to the very finest people. Let's drink to your success, Erin! May your SIN grow ever higher!"

Erin spoke demurely: "I'm afraid my art will seem ever so frumpish compared to the other exhibits. Most of them are abstract and very eye-catching."

"The description is not necessarily complimentary," Petros said. "Although my tastes are catholic, I am old-fashioned at heart and prefer to know if I'm looking at a landscape or a bodily discharge."

Lydia tutted. "Must you be so vulgar, Petros? Such conversation does not befit the dinner table."

"My apologies. I thought we'd finished."

"Not quite," Erin said. "Lydia brought linzer biscuits. I thought we could have them with our coffee?"

Petros pushed his plate away. "An excellent idea. Let us hope she's left sufficient for the rest of us."

Lydia spoke tartly: "And let's hope the coffee invigorates in Petros a proper sense of civility."

"We can but hope," Petros said.

Marci brewed chicory and the guests retired to the living room, where they seated themselves around a coffee table. An assortment of glossy art magazines occupied the center. The cover of one depicted an Outsider family working a crude brazier.

"Good heavens," Lydia said in revolted fascination. "'Primitive art of the Outside,'" can you believe? I can't imagine who'd dare trek out there to photograph such revolting things."

"Turn to the article and you'll find the name of the author," Petros said. "Then your question will be answered."

"You know what I mean," Lydia snapped. "Look at this scene: it has a beastly charm, at the same time quaint and quite horrid."

Erin leaned over and studied the picture. A blacksmith thumped a lump of glowing orange metal on an anvil while his son worked the bellows. A woman sat nearby peeling potatoes. At her feet, two small children played naked in the dirt. "What's horrid about it?"

"Look at the state of those poor children," Lydia sniffed. "And the man—so brutal! I imagine he's creating some kind of weapon to attack us with!"

Petros gave it a cursory glance. "He's a farrier forging something, most probably agricultural equipment. I see no reason for alarm."

"How can you be so dull? They're Outsiders! Don't you watch the newsreels? The murder, the rape, the attacks on the plantations? They're not like us. They're monsters!"

Petros addressed Marci: "What is your opinion? Are they barbarians, as Lydia propounds, or just ordinary people trying to eke out a living?"

Marci, uncomfortable at being singled out, said: "I'd have to agree with Lydia. We've all seen the news footage. The Outsiders are a clear and present danger."

"Exactly!" Lydia said in triumph. "Fiends! Scavengers!"

"Then you believe News24?" asked Petros.

Marci frowned. "Of course. Why wouldn't I?"

"I consider myself a true liberal," Lydia declared, "and a lover of all humanity. But Budapest must be protected! We have enough problems with those Undergrounders rampaging throughout the city every time there's a storm. Imagine if we let the Outsiders in!"

"It's never so simple," Petros said. "Every government must have a public enemy. Without an adversary, a nation fights among itself. The Underground is a convenient contrivance."

Marci looked at Erin, who was listening intently. Catching his eye, she smiled and said, "Outsider art would certainly make for an interesting exhibition. Petros, do you think the Weber Center could be persuaded to arrange one?"

"Possibly. If people are willing to pay good money to see a dead sheep floating in formaldehyde, they'll pay to see primitive art."

Lydia, apparently bored with the topic, reclined cat-like on the sofa. The wine was having a curious effect on her. Besides becoming increasingly garrulous, she seemed to have lost her last vestige of inhibition. "A mystery remains," she said in a voice that managed to sound at once mischievous and smitten by the sound of itself, "which is that of the noticeably reticent Marci. Here he sits like an owl, refusing to enlighten us as to his profession."

"Perhaps he doesn't wish to enlighten us?" Petros suggested.

Lydia suddenly sat forward. "But I am intrigued! Dear Erin might be associating with an Undergrounder, or even worse, an Outsider!"

"I doubt it," Petros said. "He's not wearing skulls around his neck, nor carrying a bloodstained machete. Besides, he's inside, which would preclude the opposite."

"Though perhaps the skulls could be arranged?" Erin said.

Marci spoke flatly. "There's no mystery. I work in Data Analytics. I made some breakthroughs in the field which earned me my promotion."

"But you're no more than forty!" Lydia exclaimed. "Surely we all give our best to the Company, one way or another, but are we on the verge of Club 30?"

Petros said, "Lydia is about to answer her own rhetoric, it seems."

Marci's head began to swim. "There's nothing to tell. Really, nothing."

"A man in his forties, about to join The Society?" Lydia persisted. "It's astounding! Won't you at least tell us what your career path is? Or is it forbidden?"

"Calm yourself, Lydia," said Petros. "Can't you see that the gentleman is unable to answer your question?"

"But I insist! If he won't profess his employment, it must be restricted information, which in itself is a revelation!"

"Lydia," Erin said, "I think we should change the subject now."

Marci rose. "I'll see to the washing up."

"I merely ask from curiosity," Lydia complained. "What harm can come from sharing one's service to the Company among friends? Aren't we all Employees working for the greater good?"

"Lydia now enters the egalitarian phase of her soliloquy," Petros said.

"I make no apology that I am cursed with an insatiable appetite for truth!" She stretched her arm out along the back of the couch and fixed Marci with a knowing smile. "And in this case, I believe I've found it. I think you work for the Executive Team. I think you either run that department or you're an Adjudicant. No other government official could reach SIN 29 at such a young age."

Silence, at last broken by Petros. "If Marci is an Adjudicant, he would be unable to confirm your suspicion. Hence, your statement is not only redundant, but potentially embarrassing."

"Excuse me," Marci said, leaving the room.

Lydia smugly raised her wineglass to the others in a toast.

In the hallway, Erin found him locked into an OCD ritual: removing and replacing his jacket from the hook. "You're leaving?" she whispered. "Why?"

"I'm sorry, but I have to get back to my speech."

"Is it because of Lydia? She doesn't mean anything, really! She gets a bit feisty when she's drunk. Marci, why won't you tell us what you do?"

Marci opened the front door. "It was a lovely evening. I'm sorry if I spoiled it."

"Is it because of something I said?" Erin asked, bewildered. "I'm sorry for telling them about your SIN. I... I'm proud of you and wanted to show you off. Please stay! I'll call Lydia a cab and say I have a headache. Then you can tell me all about your job, and we'll never have to talk about it again."

"Why?" Marci hissed. "Why must you know my job?"

Erin shrank back—almost a cower. "Please don't shout at me."

Marci's mouth sagged. Why had she recoiled? "I didn't shout. I just don't see why it's so important to everyone. To you."

"Isn't it a normal question to ask? Like asking someone their favorite color, or what their SIN is?"

"No, it isn't," Marci said. "I don't need the world and his dog knowing what I do for a living. Why did you have to mention my nomination?"

"I said I'm sorry. But I still don't see why you're making such a big fuss about it."

Marci pressed his eyes shut; a rush of vertigo made him queasy. Telling her his profession was not only illegal, but it would also bring an end to their relationship. "It's complicated," he said. "And to be honest, I don't understand you. You ignore me for weeks, then kiss me and tell them I'm your boyfriend."

"I thought you'd like it. You did, didn't you?"

"Of course I did, but that's beside the point. I don't know if I'm coming or going with you." Marci stepped out onto the walkway. "I'm sorry, I have this damned speech to finish. Thank you for dinner."

As he strode away, he sensed Erin watching him, but did not look back.

7

The sandstorm, blown in from the Sahara the night before, had spent itself over the city and settled as thick fog, coating everything it touched. Fifteen hundred feet above it, a small, private craft was flying blind.

Marci stared out of the starboard window at where the ground should be. Every so often the city's streets, hemmed in by tower blocks and skyscrapers stained terra-cotta brown, would appear briefly through the murk, only to be swallowed up again. From this height the view resembled a scene from a trench gas attack. For Marci it was D-Day.

Sándor spoke into his headset: "Budapest Air Control, private class Argo One requesting Patrician priority access through WeatherShield[16], over."

"BAC to Argo One, you have priority. WeatherShield deactivation awaits your proximity. Re-routing other traffic now. Safe landing, President Ortega."

Sándor turned to Marci. "We'll soon be out of this filthy weather. How are you feeling?"

"Nervous," Marci admitted. "But not frantic."

Sándor smiled. "It's a walk in the park. Read your speech, then enjoy the wine and pretty waitresses."

The craft descended and crossed the Danube five hundred feet above Széchenyi Bridge. As it entered Buda airspace, the fog vanished. Above them, the sky was a dome of fiery, suffused daylight,

---

[16] WeatherShields are localized, transparent, protective particle domes that repel inclement weather. In the case of rainwater that carries sediment or fallout dirt, the DOME will not continuously clean itself. Accordingly, the transmission of sunlight through the DOME is prone to color shifts.

like the inside of an alabaster lampshade; below, the villa-studded hills of the well-heeled bathed in its orange glow.

Sándor set their destination to The Society's clubhouse on Istenhegy[17]and they descended to a pad reserved for the President. Valets hurried to help them from the vehicle.

Marci stepped out and looked across the lawn to the clubhouse, a modern building of angular design, fashioned from steel, hardwood and polyglass. The grounds were in the English style: giant, isolated oaks and cedars of Lebanon placed in a sea of electric green grass. To the side of the building, a stone path led down steps to nooks and crannies with terraces from which to view the hills of Buda and beyond.

Six shuttle vehicles waited for guests. Marci and Sándor boarded one and were conveyed under an otherworldly sky to a pavilion erected on the terrace. Three toga-clad Patricians greeted them and immediately engaged the President in conversation. Marci, feeling redundant, hung back and took stock of his surroundings.

The canopy was forty feet wide and two hundred long, striped white and gold. It sheltered a dining table equal in length, bedecked with extravagant floral arrangements of custard-yellow calla lilies, spray roses and gypsophila. A dozen waiters in starched uniforms hurried here and there, laying napkins, measuring place settings and double-checking seating arrangements. To one side of the terrace, a small chamber orchestra tuned their instruments and chatted with one another. True to Sándor's prediction, the AGM had attracted a full contingent of Society members, many of whom stood on the lawn in small groups talking loudly or welcoming old friends with exaggerated bonhomie.

Marci clutched to his chest the leather folder that contained his speech. Garbed in a suit he'd bought for the occasion, he was already sweating. He reached inside the blazer, pulled some of his dress shirt free and flapped it to air himself.

---

[17] Hill of God. The suffix *hegy* means hill in Hungarian.

From the clubhouse stepped Prefect Trauffaut. As on the occasion of his art exhibition, he wore the white robe and gold sash of a Roman emperor.

Behind him came Armand Bucco, a digital clipboard in one hand and an expression of flustered concentration on his face. Trauffaut stopped at the dining table and cupped one of the roses to his nose. He spoke instructions; Bucco hurried away.

Trauffaut's gaze fell on Marci. He replaced the flower and approached. "You'll find the toga is much more comfortable on such occasions," he said, extending his hand. "It's a pleasure to see you again, Mr. Kovács. We're very much looking forward to welcoming you to The Society."

Marci quickly stuffed his shirt back in. "It's an honor to be here, Prefect Trauffaut."

"Have you no champagne?" Trauffaut signaled to a waiter and handed Marci a flute. "It calms the nerves at such times."

"Thank you. I'm just worried my speech will disappoint you."

"Sándor showed me a copy. It's quite charming, and will go down very well." He looked past Marci and nodded an acknowledgement to someone. "You'll be fine," he added. "It's merely a formality. Excuse me: our President awaits."

Trauffaut departed. Marci, champagne in hand, slipped into the clubhouse foyer in search of the bathroom.

The concierge read his thoughts. "It's that way, sir, through the doors on the right."

Marci entered a room made of steel, frosted glass and teak. He locked the door, placed his portfolio and champagne flute on the windowsill and dug a strip of Seromax pills and another of Cortiquell from his pocket. These, his second dose that day, he washed down with the sparkling wine.

Breathe. In for four, hold for four, out for four, wait for four.

He read his watch: 13:47. Thirteen minutes until the ceremony began. As he went to leave, Marci felt his bowels loosen. Turning on his heel, he hastened for the commode. "Count the numbers," he told himself. "Two hundred… One hundred ninety-seven… One hundred ninety-four…"

Relieved, he went to the sink, inadvertently catching sight of his reflection in the mirror. He really couldn't carry off a suit. He tried picturing himself in a Patrician's robe, which was even less convincing.

Marci straightened his tie. "You can do this. Just read the script."

Someone outside tried the door handle.

Marci gripped the sink edge as a wave of vertigo threatened his balance. He looked himself in the eye.

You're a failure. You're a failure, and you're going to fail.

"Shut up," he muttered. "Shut up!"

Outside, the orchestra broke into the grandiose Anthem of Budapest. Marci hurried to the terrace, where the Patricians were making their way to the pavilion. Among them was Sándor, deep in conversation with Darius Bouwer. Marci strode halfway across the patio when, to his horror, he remembered he'd left his speech in the restroom.

The door was locked. Marci knocked and, somewhat diffidently, said: "Please, I need to get in. I've left my speech inside."

No response.

He tried again, not so gently. "Please, open the door!"

The concierge approached. "We have another restroom in the lounge, sir."

Marci swung about. "I don't need the restroom. I need my speech!"

The clerk tried the handle. "I'm afraid it's occupied."

"Of course it's bloody occupied," Marci said, heading for the lawn.

The anthem had ended. Sándor was nowhere to be seen. In the marquee, the Patricians had taken their places and were busy chatting. Marci spotted the President and a vacant chair beside him.

"I haven't got my speech," he whispered. "I left it in the bathroom, but it's locked."

Sándor spoke to a nearby waiter, who hurried away. "Sit down. He'll get it for you."

Feeling nauseous, Marci filled a tumbler with water and drank it in one go.

Sándor summoned a sommelier. "Pour him some Beaujolais." To Marci he said: 'Drink it.'

At the head of the table, Prefect Trauffaut stood and waited for silence. "Patricians, friends, and candidates, I bid you a warm welcome to our 32nd Annual General Meeting. I'm delighted to see so many familiar faces and a smattering of new ones. Today is a special occasion. Not only does The Society celebrate another year's governance of our historic city, but we are afforded the rare privilege of welcoming not one but three members into our fellowship."

There was a moment of polite applause.

"To open our meeting," Trauffaut continued, "I would like, with your kind permission, to recite a trifle from my own life; the purpose of which is not self-aggrandizement, but to share a truth which, I believe, applies to us all.

"I was born in Paris in 2063 into poverty. My father was a journalist for *Le Monde* and was commissioned as its Budapest correspondent to cover the construction of the DOME and FATS systems. When the Red Plague struck the city, my mother contracted the disease and succumbed to it some weeks later. Father coped poorly with her death. Already prone to drinking, he buried himself in his work and numbed himself with alcohol. Four months later, on a sweltering June evening, he threw himself off Széchenyi Bridge and was never seen again.

"Assuming he'd gone to a *kocsma* to drown his sorrows I stayed up all night for him to come home. The following week, one of my teachers, alarmed by my absence, called in on our apartment and found me alone. I was handed over to social services and spent the rest of my childhood in care.

"At twenty-three I graduated in Diplomatic Studies and Politics from the Weber Institute and joined the government. The Executive Team was the obvious choice; in fact, I'd chosen it as my career years before. By this stage, Grisha Ossian had outlived all the other Patriarchs and was now approaching ninety. As much as we would have loved for him to live forever, we needed to prepare for the inevitable. The city faced a population crisis, and a new approach to governance was overdue. With Grisha's kind permission, I created the Company. This was a time when modestly gifted men like me could find promotion. And I boast when I use the word 'modest.'"

Some Patricians laughed; others cried "surely not!"

Sándor turned to Marci and grimaced in disgust. Marci summoned the sommelier and asked for a refill.

"My first responsibility as Prefect," Trauffaut continued, "was to forge stronger ties with our Sister Cities. Because of that work, we now have long-established trade deals that furnish us with what we cannot produce and enable us to sell abroad what we can. My penchant for diplomacy had found an outlet. I traveled widely and lived a life that would be the envy of most. The downside was the functions I was forced to endure. To be frank, I found most of them unutterably tedious, an experience I'm sure you can relate to today. But on one occasion something happened that would change my life forever.

"I'd been invited to a particularly tiresome reception by a foreign Ambassador whose name I won't mention. Toward the end of the evening I slipped away to explore the venue: a rambling Gothic pile which had survived all three world wars. I remember it was snowing. After wandering here and there I found myself in the mansion's orangery. In the distance, music played. Oh, the inadequacy of the word! It was a sound from another world, at once majestic and exquisitely tragic.

"At the end of the conservatory stood a great hall. As if drawn by some invisible power, I approached the doorway to listen, daring not to move lest the spell be broken. The music, I later learned, was the Prelude to Wagner's "Tristan and Isolde," and if heaven is real, then this is its motif."

Sándor leaned over to Marci and whispered, "Personally, I prefer jazz."

Trauffaut, momentarily overcome, paused to check his emotions. "As I listened, I remembered my parents. They were kind, simple people who had squandered their years and had nothing to show for it. That night, I vowed that the course of my life would not follow theirs. This was my epiphany: I would dedicate my life to the preservation of culture. In so doing, I would be my parents' surrogate, bringing them the honor and meaning their lives had lacked. And what an achievement it would be! To protect man's most noble achievement. For only in art does life have beauty and meaning.

"Walking out onto the moonlit terrace, I reflected that human history is a catalog of misery and loss, most of it penned by man's own hand. But in art, humanity finds vindication and atonement for its sins. It discovers and expresses its most virtuous qualities."

There were nods of approval and several cries of "hear! hear!" among the crowd. Marci, who'd finished his second glass of Beaujolais, had heard little, and was engrossed in a distraction technique.

Trauffaut studied the Patricians ranged along the table. "How does this apply to us? Budapest is not merely a bastion of civilization, but the hope of the rest of the world. We sit in a wilderness of depravity and ignorance, surrounded by those who would destroy us and the legacy we've created. Within the walls of our great city, forty million souls look to us as children look to her mother. Let us not disappoint them. May we nurture them, may we protect them, and may we steadfastly defend their right to fulfill their potential.

"We have suffered much, yet we remain. Let us vow to rise above the errors of our past, and let us, The Society of Patricians, steadfastly protect that which circumstance has bestowed on us. For the Company is Budapest, and Budapest is the Company!"

As one, the Patricians stood and applauded. Sándor leaned over and addressed Marci. "An interesting speech, but a little too self-indulgent for my liking. By the way, there are two other nominees. You'll go last."

Marci rose, pausing to steady himself. "I think I'll try to find my speech," he slurred.

Sándor motioned for him to sit. "The waiter's already looking for it. Stay and talk to me or your neighbor. It will distract you from your nerves."

Marci, however, returned to the foyer, where he found the restroom still in use. As he raised his hand to knock, the door opened and the occupant emerged. Marci hurried inside. There on the windowsill was his leather portfolio, and inside his speech.

From the pavilion came the sound of clapping: the first nominee had concluded his address. Marci stumbled outside and crouched behind a rhododendron bush obscured from proceedings but still within earshot. Prefect Trauffaut proposed the applicant, who was seconded and duly voted into The Society.

Armand Bucco introduced the next candidate, who delivered his address. Like the first, he was proposed, seconded, and the motion carried with equal approbation: Marci's cue to return.

Marci shambled back to the pavilion and slumped into his seat as Sándor rose addressed the Patricians. "I'll keep this brief. I'm delighted to nominate Adjudicant Márton Kovács to The Society. Marci is a man of intelligence and good character, and is the finest Adjudicant to grace the Executive Team. His dedication has safeguarded the integrity and reliability of both MARTHA and the SIN system for many years. I count him as my friend. Please support him with your good wishes and your vote."

The Patricians began to clap. Marci felt his skin turn clammy and reached for more water.

"What are you waiting for?" Sándor whispered. "Go to the microphone. Thank Trauffaut and make your speech."

Marci rose slowly, feeling the weight of the room's eyes on him. Impelled by the dying applause, he staggered toward the head of the table, which now seemed further away than he remembered.

At the microphone he greeted the Prefect with a weak handshake and regarded the two hundred faces that stared back with stoic impassivity. Trauffaut had seated himself; apart from the waiting staff, Marci was the only one standing. With difficulty he removed a single sheet of A4 paper from his folder, gripping it with both hands as a choirboy might a hymn sheet. His hands were trembling. He frowned, bringing it close, then holding it at arm's length. The words, no matter how near or far he viewed them, swam in and out of vision as if alive. He blinked, wiped both eyes and tried again. Still the text glared back in defiance, a hodgepodge of meaningless black on white.

The room fell away, then righted itself. Marci grabbed the edge of the table. The vertigo, passing, left in its wake a sudden intense nausea. Discarding his speech, he grabbed Trauffaut's glass of water, drank it and leaned close to the microphone. When he spoke, no sound came forth.

Say something, you idiot. Say something. Anything!

"Two hundred...one hundred and ninety-three, one hundred and eighty-six..."

His eyes snapped open. Two hundred faces regarded him in bemused fascination. Sándor sat slumped looking away.

In a voice tremulous and barely audible, Marci addressed the gathering. "Gentlemen, Patricians and Prefect Trauffaut, I thank you for your hospitality and the opportunity to be here."

Another wash of dizziness. He reeled again, and this time Prefect Trauffaut was forced to reach up and steady him. Marci turned, swaying, and whispered, "I'm so sorry. I can't do this."

Abandoning his speech, he broke out into an undignified, loping run across the lawn. Behind him lay awful silence: the sound of humiliation.

A stone staircase led down to a secluded balcony overlooking Buda. Beneath a bougainvillea tree he found a bench where he sat panting and fought the urge to vomit.

Minutes passed; the nausea receded. Marci went to the balustrade. Beyond the WeatherShield, enveloped in orange smog, lay Pest, where tens of millions strove for SIN and a chance at the opportunity he'd just squandered.

The clouds parted. The Danube, that great dividing line between the haves and the have-nots, glinted in sunlight like a strand of copper thread. Falling away below him were Buda's verdant hills, each dotted with villas, mansions and palaces resembling precious stones couched in green velvet. Any one of them could have been his if his courage hadn't failed him. Marci leaned on the railing, his heart too full of sorrow even to cry.

Yet there was still hope. He could return to the pavilion and make his apologies, blame it on the wine or maybe even tell the truth. Would they understand? At least he'd salvage some reputation, if not his then Sándor's. Marci tried to picture the President, who with his typical suave levity was probably making light of the situation. There'd be laughter, a pleasant luncheon and something to talk about in the months and years to come, until Márton Kovács was forgotten about. For Sándor it was different. His personal nominee had walked out on him in front of the entire assembly. In a single act of cowardice, Marci had shamed himself, his friend, the Prefect and the Society.

He leaned over the railing. Eighty feet below lay a neighbor's ornamental garden. The fall would take little more than two seconds.

From the staircase came the sound of footsteps: Sándor. He approached and placed his arm around Marci's shoulders. "I spoke with Trauffaut and explained you're not feeling well. We've moved your slot to the end of the meal. Take your time, compose yourself and rejoin us."

Marci turned away in shame. "I can't do it, Sándor. I really tried. It's the anxiety. It's just impossible."

"Catch your breath. The Society will vote you in, I've made sure of it. You only have to give your speech."

"Sándor, I took more medication than I've ever done in my life. I still can't give my speech." His voice broke. "Please, I'd like to go home."

Sándor regarded him for long seconds. "You realize what this means? I can't guarantee The Society will ever grant you another audience."

"Can't they accept a written speech? Just this once?"

"You know the answer. It must be done in person."

Marci walked to the end of the terrace. Beneath a livid sky Budapest glowed like superheated metal. He'd been so close. SIN 30 was gone, along with his dream of eternity in glorious Empyrean.

8

Little Tokyo was sixty-eight blocks of structured chaos strung together with washing lines and power cables. Its core was Nyugati, a solar plexus of elevated railways, subterranean mass transit routes and converging boulevards dominated by the Justice Board's much-feared cube-shaped HQ. The district was dirty beyond description, noisy beyond tolerance and home to some ten thousand sub-SINners—unregistered citizens who lived their lives below the Company's radar—alongside three million ordinary Employees. Tonight, it seemed all of them were abroad.

A figure cut through the crowd. His face was lost inside a monastic cowl, and a wide-brimmed bush hat, pulled low, dripped rain onto his shin-length leather trench coat. Stubble flecked his chin and jawline and a cigarette hung from his lips. He moved through the heaving throng without haste, deviating from his course for no one. If his pace seemed easy, his visage was anything but. Seeing him approach, pimps corralled their call girls into the shadows. Hawkers hung back. Dressed from head to toe in black, he strode down streets of wet neon like Death among the living.

At a crosswalk, eight lanes of traffic barred his way. A whale-size Zeppelin emblazoned with the rising sun drifted overhead and bleached the city block with searchlight brighter than the noonday sun. Smaller craft moved like cleaner fish around it, firing animated adverts against the clouds: an energy drink, a sushi restaurant, a Geisha massage parlor.

A rivulet of rain ran off the airship's skin and fell to spatter against his upturned face. He didn't care. He didn't care about anything.

The lights changed. On Váci út, the scent of humanity, pleasing and foul, issued from every quarter. Heady Nag champa resins, burning in censers, flowed from spice souks; tagines of apricot, cinnamon and tamarind issued their fragrance from Moroccan bistros. Curry kiosks added cumin, coriander and onions frying in ghee to the medley. Perfume, some agreeable, some repugnant, carried on the air with diesel fumes. Amid the odor, peddlers, pushers and more reputable merchants worked their trades with brazen aplomb, selling whatever the human heart could conceive beside much that shouldn't. In Little Tokyo, everything was available for a price. The only thing free was olfactory overload.

At a tobacconist's he bought a miniature of pálinka which he finished before reaching the shelter of a strip club awning half a block away. The bouncers brushed rain from their polyester suits and sized him up. Still he didn't care. Tonight, the world could go to hell.

It had happened that afternoon, his epiphany. Resigned to either a slow, alcoholic demise or an act of absolute finality, he'd covered both bases: a Rapture pill from the pharmacy and a bottle of single malt Yamazaki from his favorite liquor store. Which he'd use first didn't matter, although it would be a crime to waste the whiskey by being dead.

He was on his way home at the time. Norbert Tóth, reeking of ammonia, had stepped off bus 8E directly in front of him. Overtaking the old bugger would be rude, if not perfectly reasonable. Dawdling behind him was equally without merit. It was then, as the two men reached their building, that enlightenment came, with the crystalline clarity of a Living Wall image. He was free.

Free! Free from the interminable pursuit of SIN, free from overtime and working weekends and tiptoeing around Frazer Morrison. He'd made Adjudicant. It was a fine achievement, but he might as well not have bothered. The Society had closed its doors on him. Never would he taste eternal life. He would die, like other men, a natural death, or strapped to a gurney in the sterile confines of Nyugati's liquidation center. Since he could be promoted no further, his SIN rating was worthless, like points accrued on a reward card whose issuer had gone broke. The only way was down, its conclusion an inevitable meeting with the Hangman. He was, arguably, already dead.

The effect was immediate. Like a heavy yoke lifted from his shoulders, his anxiety was gone. At the same moment, he was overcome by a surge of such absolute indifference toward life that he wanted to both punch Tóth for letting the front door swing back in his face and hug him from sheer joy. His miserable existence was finite. Who wanted eternal life, anyway? This one was more than enough.

A voice, ugly and low in register, broke his reverie. "Are you coming in, or are you just gonna take up space?"

Marci turned slowly and looked the bouncer up and down. "Go drink another protein shake, you moron."

The doorman, vulva-pink in the neon oozing from the club entrance, drew himself up. "What did you say?"

Marci lit a cigarette and looked out across the boulevard. Whatever had happened to him that afternoon was having a curious corollary: he felt no fear.

The bouncer swaggered over. "I asked you a question, jackass. Who are you calling a moron?"

"If you can recite the answer, you heard the question." Marci blew smoke in the man's face and brushed past him onto Teréz Körút.

Marci reached another intersection as the light turned in his favor. As he stepped into the road, a black van, breaking hard, squealed to a stop in front of him.

The side door slid open. Three men dressed in the black garb of Hangmen emerged. Before Marci could react, two of them grabbed him by the arms, while the third pulled a hood over his head. He felt his legs lift from beneath him as he was bundled inside the van, which sagged with the weight of his accosters when they climbed inside.

The door slid shut. Marci's arms were wrenched behind him; plastic cuffs cut into his wrists. A heavy weight—the weight of a man—pressed down on him, squeezing the air from his lungs. Something sharp punctured his skin. Cold discharge followed.

Rapture.

His scream woke him. Alice had already switched on the mood lights by the time he knew where he was. He sat up, groggy and disorientated and soaked in sweat and swung his legs over the bed. His knuckles were sore, grazed but not broken. The headboard was the victim.

In the living room the Birch and Gaydon pealed the dead of night. Marci slumped into the Chesterfield and stared across the room, nowhere.

He was alive—this was the unpleasant reality. His AGM debacle was also real, and so were his prospects. It had been fine yesterday. Yesterday he couldn't have cared less. Temporary insanity, perhaps. It hadn't lasted. By evening he felt numb, then desperate, then drunk. Sándor had been kind about the whole thing but could promise nothing. Society statutes made no allowance for a second stab at nomination. As things stood, the game really was over.

On the table was a bottle of Yamazaki, still three-quarters full. The glass contained mostly thawed ice, but enough booze to make him feel sick. What he needed was someone to talk to. Who? Hardly Sándor. After yesterday's ignominy, the President wasn't exactly top of the shoulder-to-cry-on league. Who else, then? Alex had taken Lei and the kids to Balaton for the weekend. Besides, they'd barely spoken since their meeting at Duna Kocsma.

Marci stared at his phone's blank display. He hesitated, then dialed a number. After six rings it went to voicemail. Feeling guilty, he hung up.

A half-minute later his phone rang.

"Marci?" The voice of an angel. "Did you call me?"

"I'm sorry. I know it's late. Can we speak?"

A pause. Perhaps the flick of a switch. "Is everything ok?"

"Not really. I—I screwed the nomination. It's all over."

"Oh, Marci… Do you want to come over?"

"Would you mind?"

Erin made a sleepy sound. "I'll put the kettle on. Don't expect me to look great."

"I'll be there soon."

Marci dressed, descended to Rákóczi út and hailed an air cab. When he reached Kecskemét the clock towers were chiming 04:00. The morning sky was still black; rain fell silent on the town.

Erin was waiting at the door. Wordlessly, she tiptoed and kissed him. "Come in," she whispered. "I've made hot milk."

He followed her into the kitchen, washed his hands and began to pace: a step forward, another back, then forward again, all the while mumbling to himself.

"Marci, what are you doing?" Erin asked.

Locked in his miserable ritual, Marci said nothing.

Erin stepped in front of him and took his hands. "Let's sit down with a nice hot drink, yes?"

A plastic, flame-effect electric fire discolored the lounge an infernal shade of orange. Marci sat hunched in the armchair and stared at the heating elements like a man hypnotized. His lips moved, but the only sound he made was a repetitive sibilant mumble.

Erin waited, perhaps unsure of what to say.

Marci completed his compulsion and lit a cigarette. "It's all over," he said at last. "I went to the AGM. I tried to speak, but the words wouldn't come out and I ran. Sándor found me in the garden. He tried talking me into going back. He said the Patricians were waiting, that they'd give me a second chance, but I couldn't." He met her eyes. "It's finished. I won't make 30."

Erin came over to sit on the armrest. "You'll make 30," she said, stroking his hair. "If you can get this far, you can reach 30."

"Sándor said there might be another chance, but he was just being kind. Now I'm stuck. I've reached the top of the tree and run out of branches. Basically, I've worked my way out of the SIN system." His voice cracked. "One minute, one lousy, bloody minute! That's all it would have taken. Now they'll all remember me as the idiot who couldn't even read his speech."

"You tried your best," Erin said. "No one can blame you for that."

Marci took her hand. "I'm sorry for walking out of your dinner party."

"It wasn't your fault. It was that dreadful woman Lydia. I wanted to punch her for being so rude."

"It wasn't just Lydia. To be honest, you're a total mystery to me. One minute you won't speak to me, the next we're an item. Why didn't you return my calls?"

Erin made an airy gesture. "Can't a girl have any secrets?"

He pulled away. "Is there someone else?"

She hesitated. "It's complicated. Sometimes I'm not sure I know myself."

Marci released her hand. "I see."

"There's no one else," she said quickly. "The problem is me."

Marci felt his stomach knot. Here was a 'Dear John' letter about to be delivered in person. "Do you care to explain?"

"I'll try, although I'm not sure it will make any sense. It happened long ago. There was a man I loved very much. I thought we'd get married and have a life together with babies and a nice house. One day I found out he was having an affair. It had been going on for months behind my back. There was a confrontation. He told me he was going to leave. I begged him to stay but he wouldn't. I waited for him, hoping he'd come back to me. but he didn't. Years later, I heard he'd got married. I guess I should have given up on him when he told me he was walking out."

"I'm sorry."

"After that, there were many men who were happy to console me. I made lots of mistakes, but there was one I promised myself I'd never make again: to get close to someone. At the same time, I still want to love someone and be loved back. So you see, there's a war inside me. Can you understand?"

Marci frowned. "Not really. Do you think I'd hurt you?"

"It's not as simple as that," Erin explained. "If I thought you were going to hurt me, we wouldn't be here now. But a lot of the time I want to be sure about things that I can't be sure about. And so the other part of me, the scared part, tells me to run away." She gave a nervous laugh. "I'm a little bit like a hedgehog when I get hurt; I want to curl up and protect myself."

Marci, always quick to assume the worst, said: "Where does that leave us?"

"I think my kissing you is the answer, silly. So that's my little secret, but I'm not the only mysterious one. Tell me the truth: why did you run away from my dinner party?"

Marci groaned. "Not this again."

"I know the obvious answer. Lydia is a nuisance, but you could have answered her question. And mine, for that matter."

Marci began playing with his lighter. "What if I couldn't tell her? What if I can't tell you?"

"That would be strange, and it would make me a bit worried."

"I promise I'll tell you when the time is right."

"Then I'll wait," Erin said. "But please tell me something now. What were you doing in the kitchen?"

Marci looked away in shame. "Do we have to talk about it?"

"No, but it scares me. You were doing it just before you left last week."

"It's called obsessive-compulsive disorder—OCD. I've had it since my mother died. Well, before then. Not that I'm counting. It doesn't mean I'm crazy."

"I'm sorry. And I never thought you were crazy."

"I'm sorry too, for waking you. I didn't know who else to call."

She kissed him. "I'm glad you did, even though it's four in the morning and I have to get up in three hours."

"You're already up."

"So I am."

They kissed again.

"It's not over," Erin said. "Sándor said there's another chance, and he's the President. If he's the President, he can call for another meeting."

Marci lay his head back and looked at the ceiling. Artex. Who had Artex ceilings anymore? In happier moments he would have laughed at the randomness of the thought. "The Society has rules. Without a speech, there's no vote."

"Then we'll just have to ask Sándor to arrange another vote. And I'll help you with the speech."

Thunder grumbled outside, somewhere far away.

Erin spoke hopefully. "Maybe there'll be a curfew."

"András won't be happy if you don't turn up."

"András is a creep. Would you like to sleep or talk?"

"Are there any other options?"

"Not at four am."

She brought blankets and pillows from her room and made a bed on the sofa. They kissed passionately, then gently.

Erin slept. Marci listened to the rain beat against the window and also hoped for a curfew. He dreamed he walked through a forest the shade of sepia with his father and the rabbit they'd caught.

When he got up, Erin was gone but had left a note on the kitchen table. The paper was coarse, handmade and brilliant white. An eagle drawn in gold ink occupied the center: the Aquila of The Society. Below it, in childish handwriting:

The real one is coming soon!

Marci returned to the lounge, propped the card on the armrest and drifted back to sleep.

* * *

Marci's failure to secure SIN 30 had a more immediate consequence than he could have expected. Somehow, the Executive Team rumor mill had gained wind of events on Istenhegy, and his presence at work the next morning confirmed the tidbit to be true: Márton Kovács had flunked his nomination, along with all hope of making Club 30.

Marci, who knew office politics all too well, arrived early by air cab and rode the lift to the eighteenth floor, hoping to cross through the secretarial pool before it became busy. He had, however, misjudged his departure time from Kecskemét. As he stepped from the elevator, he was confronted by a full complement of clerical staff, brisk with the day's freshest prattle. Registering his presence, they fell silent. A single, unanswered telephone added pathos.

Marci felt the collective gaze of the room fall on him: the sympathetic, the unsympathetic, the ambivalent. He hesitated. To retreat to the lift would compound his humiliation. Besides, he'd have to run the gauntlet at some point. Steeling himself, he marched pink-faced toward the far exit, thankful that Tony Jackson hadn't yet turned up for work.

Marci hid himself in his cubicle for an hour and failed to do anything of value. At last he logged out, informed Morrison's beleaguered secretary Moira that he felt unwell, and left for the day.

At home the lift was out of order. As he crossed the courtyard to the other stairwell, Marci's ears were assaulted by a high-pitched metallic chattering noise. The clamor came from the work shed in the corner of the quadrangle, where Norbert Tóth, heedless of his neighbors, worked a rotary saw with the door wedged open for ventilation. Spotting Marci, Tóth kicked the chock free and pulled the door closed, before resuming his handiwork.

With his teeth and nerves set on edge, Marci climbed the three flights to his apartment. Here he showered, changed clothes and set off for the Central Market.

The morning was fine. Warm October sunlight painted the spires and facades of Budapest a pleasant macaroon yellow. Marci ambled against the flow of clerical workers ascending sleepy and late for work from Astoria's subway. A tram conveyed him to Fővám Tér, where he entered Nagy Vásárcsarnok, the cavernous nineteenth century marketplace beside the Danube.

The air was rich with the scent of spices, frangipane pastries and smoke from wood ovens. The bustle of the day was yet to be; pleasant torpor hung over the place.

Marci wandered between the stalls, reflecting on recent events. Erin had been right. Surely Sándor could wrangle him another shot at nomination. Yesterday had been no more than a setback. Even if he had to wait for next year's AGM, what of it? He was still young enough to notch up his last four SIN points at his leisure. How foolish of him to succumb to despair. He would try again, and this time he'd succeed. He was Marci Kovács, SIN 29, the finest Adjudicant Budapest had ever known!

As he strolled, he felt almost woozy with inexplicable happiness. Prefect Trauffaut had described the city well. It was a bastion of enlightenment, a safe haven where every man and woman could reach their fullest potential. Trauffaut had unknowingly described Marci's life. The Company had schooled him, provided him a career and rewarded him richly for his labor. Like a loving father, it had given him everything he needed to prosper. And now he was on the cusp of attaining the ultimate prize. What privilege to serve in the congress of men like Prefect Trauffaut and President Ortega. How he loved the Company!

Sunlight, alive with dust motes, slanted from high windows to pool in the aisle before him. Marci stopped and let it warm his skin. Today the sun shone for him alone. The niggling irritations of life had fled; even the merchants whose shops he patronized seemed happier, as if they, too, were sharing in his joy. And Erin, wonderful little Erin, who had thrown him a lifebuoy in his darkest hour. How he loved her, too! He loved her, and perhaps she loved him. And if not? In time she would, of this he was sure.

Loaded with groceries, Marci proceeded to Vámház Körút and bought a bottle of Australian shiraz costing a week's salary. He took the back streets home and spent the afternoon under the tutelage of Alice, learning how to prepare dinner.

At 18:15 Marci opened his front door to Erin.

She kissed him, then held him at arm's length. "You look different. What's happened to you?"

"I'm not sure. How do I look?"

"Brighter. And at least ten years younger."

"I called in sick today," Marci explained. "I haven't had Morrison breathing down my neck."

"Hmm, I'd hope it had something to do with me coming over."

"That as well, of course. And I realized you were right: it's not the end of the world."

"That's a good attitude to have. And it suits you, this happy look." She lifted her nose and sniffed the air as a mouse might a rind of cheese. "Something smells delicious, and it isn't you. What are we having?"

"That would be "dinner," which will be ready in twenty minutes."

"Then let me help you set the table."

Despite his culinary incompetence—Marci usually lived off microwave meals—the afternoon's effort surpassed even his own modest expectations. After a starter of goulash, the two dined on poached freshwater trout in a parsley, garlic and butter sauce. The shiraz complimented the dish perfectly.

Over dessert, Erin showed Marci a flier she'd brought with her. "It's for the exhibition I told you about," she explained. "Petros gave me some to hand out."

Marci studied the pamphlet, whose graffiti font and random splotches of fluorescent ink projected a subversive message inconsistent with the venue's lofty reputation. The cover featured one of Erin's projects. "I'm impressed," he said. "Isn't this one of yours?"

"Yes, can you believe it? I was so happy when Petros showed me the proof version. Isn't it exciting?"

"Exciting, but not surprising. Your work is simply getting the recognition it deserves."

Erin brushed aside the compliment. "I think it's got more to do with Petros and his connections."

"How did you meet him?"

"At a political club last year. He works for DeLane Westland, the architectural firm. He's a bit of a dilettante, but he has a good heart and he's very keen on helping me with my art projects."

"A political club?"

"It's all very innocent. We meet on Thursday evenings near Fővám Tér. In fact," Erin added, "I was going to ask if you'd like to come to the next one?"

Marci poured them more wine. As tempted as he was to accept any invitation of hers, an evening playing canasta with Mária Földi held more appeal. "I'd like to go," he said, toying with his food, "but I have a lot of casework coming up. I think Thursday's going to be busy."

Erin laughed. "You're an awful liar. Why not just say no?"

Marci deflected the question. "How many artists will be exhibiting there?"

"I'm not quite sure. I can't imagine less than fifty. Oh, do tell me you'll come! I want to show you off to my friends. And I need you to hold my hand; there'll be lots of influential people, including agents."

"I wouldn't miss it for the world," he said, handing back the flier. "Just so long as nobody asks me about my work."

"Oh yes," Erin said flatly. "That."

"Anyway," Marci said, then put on a menacing voice, "we Hangmen aren't allowed to reveal our identities to any pretty girl who asks!"

"I hope you're joking," Erin shuddered. "I'd run a mile if I found out you had anything to do with cessations."

"Alice," Marci said, "play some jazz."

The next morning, Erin called in sick, hoping András would cope without her at Objet d'Heart. He did not take the news philosophically. "What will I do without you? The shop will go to rack and ruin!"

Erin reminded him he'd coped well enough without her in the past. "Besides," she added, "I'll have the place shipshape again in no time." András conceded her point with poor grace, and there was no more to be said.

For two days, Marci and Erin lived in a bubble, aware of the world around them but set apart from it. They did little of consequence and neither cared; for love, Marci reflected, had a strange way of transforming the everyday into the exquisite. The question of his occupation was either forgotten or left unspoken, to his relief.

In Erin's presence his anxiety symptoms went into remission to such an extent that it was Wednesday before Marci realized he'd forgotten to take his pills or visit a medibooth. Erin, too, was different. Gone was her capricious, halfhearted attitude. She now expressed a warmth and intimacy that matched Marci's.

On Thursday afternoon, Marci returned home and rode the elevator to his floor. Waiting outside his apartment was a girl of nine: Satomi Nagy. Tall for her age, she wore a white-and-green school uniform and green stockings and stood pressing the doorbell with extreme focus. Seeing Marci, she broke into a shy smile, bowed and presented him with a plastic tub. "Pogácsa," she said softly, "from mother."

Marci took the box and bowed in return. "Thank you, Satomi. Please thank your mother very much."

Satomi raised her hand to her mouth, giggled, and ran back home. Marci watched her with amusement and let himself inside.

"Welcome home, Marci. Can I fix you a drink?"

Marci kicked off his shoes and washed his hands at the kitchen sink. "Just some Assam, Alice."

"You have three new voice messages."

"Play them."

"Message received on Wednesday at 10:12: 'Kovács? Rieks Kruger. Fraser tells me you're off sick. Let me know when you'll be back in the office. MARTHA's dealing with cessations on her own. Not ideal.'"

"Thanks for inquiring after my health," Marci muttered. "Next."

"Message received Wednesday at 14:31: 'Hello Marci, I have some news regarding your Society application I think will interest you. I'll be in Moscow until Friday, so call me then, if you will.'"

Marci strode into the lounge and picked up his cell phone, but the battery was dead. "Sod it," Marci growled. "Next."

"Message received on Wednesday at 20:18: 'Marci, it's Alex. We… I need to talk to you. Something's come up. Call me.'"

Marci collected his tea and sat down with a plateful of pogácsa. Sándor had alluded to hopeful developments with The Society. Could this mean a second chance at nomination? Rieks's message, by contrast, could not have provided a starker juxtaposition to the President's, and had been left only an hour into Marci's absence from the office.

The office! The thought of it made Marci cringe. Kruger wouldn't care less about his failed nomination, but Morrison, who resented Marci's stellar career, was a different matter. No doubt he was rubbing his hands in glee. Tony Jackson presented a different problem but was of less import. More than ever, Marci thought, he needed to relinquish his life in Pest.

That left Alex's ambiguous missive. Hopefully it had nothing to do with computer anomalies.

To his great relief, Marci arrived at work the next day to find that Tony Jackson was off sick. The office manager had been on medical leave all week with an undisclosed ailment of an intimate nature. Even better, Moira reported that Fraser Morrison was working offsite, and had expressed no interest in Marci's recent absence. The good news ended at his inbox, where a four-day backlog of casework no one had bothered to reallocate had accumulated. Marci's day was mapped out.

A midmorning visit to Alex's suite proved futile. Marci tried again at noon, then sought out Alex's secretary, Emese, who could shed no light on his friend's whereabouts.

Marci took himself and his packed lunch to the quadrangle and ate without appetite, all the while watching his phone beside him. Sándor should now be back from Moscow with news that might forever change his life. At last he could wait no longer. With butterflies in his stomach he dialed Sándor's number. A flat tone designated the handset as out of range.

At 17:00 Marci logged out of MARTHA and made his way home. At Oktagon he stopped at the DNA Repository and provided a monthly blood and tissue sample. The procedure, mandated by the Company, ensured that each Employee's gene bank record was up to date, in the event he or she attained SIN 33. It was a painless, routine procedure that took less than a minute and which unfailingly stirred in Marci a sense of pride in both his own importance and the magnanimity of the Company.

He arrived home to the murmur of distant thunder and rode the lift to floor three. As he neared his apartment, a cheery voice assaulted him above. “Márton!”

Mária Földi was leaning over her railing, pointing to the fourth floor: a rendezvous instruction. Feigning ignorance, Marci peered down at the courtyard.

Mária shook her head in dismay and jabbed a bony finger at the floor below. Marci, simpering, waved off his own foolishness. It was always a pleasure to wind up the old witch.

When he got there she was waiting with a large, flat parcel wrapped in brown paper and tied with string. “It came at lunchtime.

You were at work, so I kept it safe. There's a card, too," she added, placing it on top of the package. "It was already open."

Marci stared at her for two seconds, knowing full well she'd steamed the envelope. The bitch.

Mária adopted a saucy pose. "A nice young lady delivered it. Fancy not telling me you have a secret admirer!"

Marci looked at the envelope. The handwriting was Erin's. Földi would already have added her name to the file she kept on him, just like she kept on all the residents.

"A pretty little thing," Maria added, coiling a strand of hair with her finger. "Perhaps a little young for you?"

Marci checked his anger; there was no point getting on the wrong side of an Informant. Although no one from the Justice Board would dare dabble in an Adjudicant's private life, a lie uttered in avarice could, conceivably, affect his SIN. Evenly he replied: "Excuse me, Mária. I need to make dinner."

Maria's grin faded into petulance. "Won't you open it?"

Marci turned away; he had no intention of adding his love life to the crone's repertoire of gossip. He took the steps two at a time to his floor and placed the envelope on the landing's windowsill.

Unlike the card, the package showed no signs of tampering. With fingers trembling with rage, he used his Zippo to burn through the string, then pulled away the paper to reveal a framed painting: the Arthurian landscape he'd admired in Erin's studio. It was as before, but for a significant detail: the empty chamber, high in the castle's tower, was no longer vacant. Erin had painted in a princess in regal attire who stood waiting for her deliverer. The story had been rewritten. The knight's quest was no longer in vain.

Marci opened the envelope. A card of stiff white paper showed two interlocking hearts on the front. Inside it read:

To my knight,

I hope this won't look out of place in your apartment. Thank you for rescuing me.

Szeretlek, Erin x

From the courtyard came the hideous, modulating buzz of an angle grinder. It was the final straw. Infuriated both by Mária's prying and weeks of Tóth's noise, he descended to the courtyard and marched to the workshop. Emboldened by vexation, Marci rapped loudly on the door.

The metalwork paused briefly, then continued. Marci knocked again, louder. From inside came an ugly epithet; something was replaced on a worktable with unnecessary emphasis.

The door opened three inches. Norbert Tóth scowled through the gap. "What do you want?"

Marci drew himself up. "I'd like to know what the hell you're doing in there."

Tóth looked him up and down. "Are you working for that Civic Taskforce whore? Always poking her nose into other people's business. It's like the Communist days all over again."

"I wouldn't know. It was before my time."

"Mine too," Tóth replied, "but it might as well be, what with you Company types and your snitches."

"She's not my snitch," Marci replied, wishing his legs wouldn't go weak at the first sign of conflict, "and what makes you think I'm with the Company?"

"It's written all over you," Tóth growled. "Don't worry, I'm not a spy like that *kutya* upstairs. They took poor János last month. I saw Mária standing on her balcony, pleased as punch. I bet she got a nice reward from those bastards at the Justice Board."

"No doubt," said Marci, "but you haven't answered my question. What are you doing in here day and night? You're driving half the building mad with your noise."

"It's none of your business, that's what it is. Can't a man have a little privacy? It's the only place in this damned city where I don't have a camera in my face."

Marci stared at Tóth, trying to think of something to say but failing. He turned away, uttering a curse beneath his breath.

"Be careful what you say to Mária," Tóth called after him. "She's taken a shine to you, but she's nobody's friend. And don't bother me again."

Tóth shut and bolted the door with finality. The angle grinding resumed. Fuming, Marci climbed upstairs, retrieved Erin's painting and marched towards his apartment. On the walkway, Satomi and Noémi Nagy were drawing a hopscotch grid. Seeing him, the girls stood up, bowed in unison, then giggled behind their hands.

Réka noticed Marci through the kitchen window and stepped out to greet him. "*Szia*, Marci! How were the pogácsa?"

"*Szia*, Réka! They were fantastic, as always. Thank you."

"I made a big batch of them, but the rest didn't last the hour. How are you?"

"Surviving. And you?"

Réka wiped her hands on her pinafore and glanced down at the courtyard. "Fine, but I swear Norbert's going to drive me crazy one of these days. I'm surprised Mária hasn't reported him to the Justice Board for being a public nuisance."

"Something's keeping him alive, and it's not his people skills. How's your slope?"

"Bearing up. My SIN development course is popular. In fact, I'm going to need more teachers soon. Takumi's doing well at the agency, so I hardly see him these days. He's been on some new soft drink project and hopes to make SIN 21."

"If anyone deserves it, it's you two. You're a credit to the Company."

"We try our best. Oh, Noémi, I told you not to draw on the walkway! Where did you get that chalk?"

Noémi looked up innocently. "It's not chalk. It's a marker pen. Akira gave it to me."

Réka beckoned her over and took it from her. "He's a little rascal," she told Marci, only half cross. "Kids—who'd have them?"

Marci laughed. "Not me. At least not yet."

"Your time will come. Let us know when you have an evening free. I'll make lasagna."

"Sounds terrific. Send my best to Takumi."

Marci let himself into his apartment, kicked off his shoes and carried the painting into the lounge. Standing in the middle of the room was Alex. In his day four stubble and crumpled trench coat he resembled a depressive or an alcoholic—Marci couldn't decide which. On reflection, perhaps both.

"Sorry to invade your house," Alex said sheepishly. "Seems your bioscanner still remembers me."

Marci rested the picture against a wall. "You look bloody awful, but I'm glad to see you. Fancy a drink?"

"I thought you'd never ask."

"Alice, two whiskeys, one on the rocks." He indicated to Alex to sit. "You're a hard man to track down."

"Sorry about that. I'm trying to keep a low profile, which is why I wanted to speak to you in person."

"Sounds serious."

"Can I cadge a smoke from you?"

"I thought you quit?"

"I did."

Marci tossed him his packet and lighter. "Should I feel guilty?"

"Yes," Alex said, lighting up. "But it's my choice." He coughed hard. "Damn, this tastes vile. I must have recovered better than I thought."

"They're Winterbournes."

Alex took another drag. "Vile and expensive."

"You're welcome."

"I didn't feel welcome in Duna Kocsma."

Marci fetched the whiskeys. "My turn to apologize."

"Don't. I should have stayed in touch."

"Deuce. Who's going to score the winning volley?"

"Me, probably. I've got bad news."

Marci lit a cigarette. "Game, set and match."

"Something like that." He took a folder from his backpack and spread six sheets of paper on the coffee table facing Marci.

Marci sensed *déjà vu* but held his tongue.

Alex said: "Remember you told me the anomalies I found were computer glitches, and that I should just move on with life?"

"Distinctly."

"Well, I took your advice and surrendered my PC to Data Analytics."

"A wise decision, at long last."

"Thanks, but you're jumping the gun. The night before I took it into work, I hacked Exec's mainframe one last time. What you're looking at is email correspondence between Morrison and Kruger. It began the day I told carrot-top about my research and ends ten days later. I'm guessing there were also phone calls and face-to-face meetings, but of course they don't show up here."

Marci reluctantly took up the first page, written by Morrison.

Rieks, we have an issue. One of our Adjudicants has been digging around in MARTHA and found compromising data. See attached. Can we set up a meeting?

"He got a reply within twenty minutes," Alex said. "They must have met. The next one's a follow-up."

Fraser, do some digging of your own. I want to know how this happened. Needless to say, whoever found this has to be blocked, and the data removed. And see how many other people know about it, including D.A. staff. I'll contact Taggart. Get back to me ASAP.

Morrison responded:

Rieks, can confirm that no one except Pimenov knows about this. Suggestions?

"The next one's a real gem," Alex said. "Let me read it to you. 'Call him in. I've had words with the relevant people. They'll award him a SIN point. Tell him he's a good boy and pat him on the back. Hopefully that'll shut him up. Secure his computer and block him and everyone else from these files. And watch him. He's dangerous.'" Alex raised his whiskey in salute. "So much for earning my promotion."

Marci read the next, which was dated the following evening and had been written by Fraser Morrison.

Looks like he bought it. I told him to keep the whole thing under wraps and explained away the data as glitches. He'll bring his machine in and we'll wipe it. It should be the end of the matter.

Marci looked up. "I don't believe I'm reading this."

"I couldn't find the next one," Alex said. "Maybe Kruger didn't reply. This one's from Morrison again. I quote: 'All done. Pimenov's happy as Larry. I.T. will wipe the drive. They've already blocked him from everything related to Data Analytics except where it affects his duties.'"

Marci, his voice now a monotone, read the last communication aloud. "'Good work, Fraser. Hell, I didn't sleep for days. Put checks and balances on this Pimenov character. I pulled up his record. He's a strong Adjudicant, but too clever for his own good. Dinner invitation still stands for Saturday, by the way. Annelies is making Stroopwafel for dessert.'"

He let the sheet slip from his hands. One of the lounge's window shutters swung open and closed. A storm was nearing.

Alex drained his glass. "I need a favor, a big one. I know my SIN—I checked it this morning. But SIN's meaningless if my predictive interval's broadened."

"I'm not sure how I can help," Marci said. "No one has access to their own lifeline. Imagine if Employees found out when they were going to die?"

"Point taken. But my concern is only my current interval, not when I'll cash my chips in. Unless one equates with the other."

"Don't be daft. You've just been promoted. If anything, it should have narrowed."

"That was before I accessed all of this. What if MARTHA's traced me?"

"She wasn't tracing you when you were digging for anomalies. Why would she start now?"

"Check the date on Rieks's last email, the one about keeping an eye on me. He sent it after I'd reported the anomalies but a week before I handed in my computer—exactly when I was hacking the email server. Taggart could have set up a traceroute and I'd never know." Alex sat back and crowned his head with his hands. "I should've just taken your advice and let it lie."

"Yes," Marci said, "you should have. But I still don't see what this has to do with—" His eyes narrowed. "Bloody hell, Alex, no!"

"I'm sorry, Marci. I swear I wouldn't ask unless I was desperate."

"Absolutely not. You know the rules. Adjudicants can't access their own profiles or those of friends and family. It's a capital offense."

"That's not quite true," Alex corrected. "Adjudicant protocol states: 'Adjudicants may, in exceptional circumstances, request the lifeline and profile data of any Employee, including co-workers, family members and friends, provided the petition contains sufficient burden of proof that said Employee's behavior or attitudes pose a substantive threat to the well-being of the Company, and or the city of Budapest.'"

Marci stared at him, then strode to the window to close the shutter, furious his friend should quote him regulations. This was no spur of the moment citation. The edict was an obscure by-law, the gist of which every Adjudicant knew but which was hidden away in canon. Alex would have looked it up and learned it as part of his pitch.

"I was going to ask why me," Marci said, "but I already know. You want me to run a sham investigation with you as a subject. Maybe spice it up with some known troublemakers so you don't stand out. Get your profile, then close the case, no issues found. Am I right?"

"Pretty much."

"Pretty desperate. Have you tried hacking for it? I hear it can work wonders on a man's career."

"You're funny. And of course I have. I couldn't breach the firewall. Please, Marci. Help me out."

"No. It's against Adjudicant Code of Conduct. If I'm caught, I'll lose my job. Or worse."

"Code of Conduct?" Alex laughed bitterly. "You read the emails. Conduct left the building long ago. It's a whitewash."

"Yes, I read the emails. Kruger and Morrison are covering something up, something you—we—shouldn't know about. Call it conspiracy, but we don't have all the facts. Maybe there's a good reason they're lying."

"Such as?"

"I don't know."

"Finally, we agree on something."

"Look, you got promoted. As far as Rieks and Morrison are concerned, you took the bait and left happy. In their eyes it's the end of the matter."

"So that's it, then? We just pretend nothing's happened?"

Marci went to the kitchen, removed the whiskey bottle from the dispenser and poured them refills.

"Read them again," Alex said.

"I don't need to. The first time was bad enough."

"Then help me," Alex urged. "If they know I have these, my P.I. could have ballooned by now."

Marci stared into the fire and let out a sigh. "What will you do with it?"

"The lifeline? Check to see where I stand with MARTHA."

"I meant the data. The emails."

Alex tapped another cigarette from the pack. "That depends on my predictive interval. Probably nothing much."

Marci noted the equivocation and spoke with deliberation. "I'm glad you're dropping the whole anomaly issue. You need to think of your SIN, not to mention Lei and the kids. Right?"

"Marci, something sinister's going on. A lot of people—innocent people—died for no good reason. Don't you want to know why?"

Marci regarded him with incredulity. "You're going to continue your investigation?"

"If they can do it to them, everyone's expendable, including us."

"All the more reason to quit now."

"I will. Soon, I promise."

"How? Morrison's got your computer and all your data."

Alex broke into his boyish smile. "One of them. I made a backup on my other PC. You didn't think I'd just hand it all over, did you?"

"'As a dog returns to his vomit, so a fool repeats his folly.'"

"Plato?"

"The Bible."

A peal of thunder, heavy with import, sounded loud and close.

The two men looked at each other.

Alex laughed, nervously. "Maybe it's a sign."

"Yes," Marci replied, "but of what?"

"Does that thing still work?"

"The gramophone? Sure."

Alex went over to the phonograph, picked out a record from the shelf and set the turntable to play. The 78's leader crackle morphed into the first bars of the Adagietto from Mahler's Fifth. Marci jumped up and lifted the tonearm.

"Not a fan?" Alex said.

"It was my father's favorite," Marci said. "I can't listen to it anymore."

"No sweat. In which case, a toast. To high SIN and a quiet life."

"To both."

"And a successful investigation," Alex added.

"You're a bloody fool," Marci said, raising his glass, "but you've got some guts."

9

October rains, dark with contamination from the Outside, trailed across the city skyline in gray Bezier curves.

Marci sat by the bay windows of his apartment drinking tea and watching rivulets run their course like tears down the glass. His mood was somber. The disappearance of the eighty-three Employee records might, with a generous measure of grace, be extenuated as clerical error—so he told himself. But the emails Alex had shown him were irrefutable proof. His Head of Department and the Executive Team Director had colluded to cover up what boiled down to murder.

He could almost forgive the human element, abhorrent as it was. People were people, and prone to turpitude. But MARTHA's systems were designed to protect her from manipulation. The thought that someone had exploited her was unthinkable. For Marci, it was akin to being told his non-existent wife was cheating on him.

Alex's request for his predictive interval posed a different problem. The penalty for Marci, if caught, would be harsh. At the very least, he'd be expelled from the Executive Team and stripped of his SIN; thereafter, he could count himself lucky to find work flipping burgers at a kiosk in Little Tokyo. The worst case involved a trip to Nyugati in a black van.

There was also the matter of his conscience. To infringe the Adjudicant Code of Conduct was tantamount to apostasy and was almost as repugnant as his bosses' correspondence. So the battle raged within him. The favor Alex had asked of him harmed no one, but it vied with one of Marci's few virtues: honor.

At work, Marci tried to hide his loathing for Morrison and made even more effort to avoid him. Tony Jackson returned from sick leave wan, subdued and smelling of ointment. The matter of Marci's failed nomination was never mentioned. Perhaps even he realized there was nothing to gain by riding the tailcoats of a man who'd failed to make Club 30.

Marci's casework now took on an additional aspect: the construction of a fictional investigation that would allow him to view Alex's predictive interval. A cohort of sixteen other Employees whose records showed questionable allegiance to the Company would pad things out.

Rather than access Alex's profile himself, Marci placed a formal request to submit it to Data Analytics in the hope that his transparency would lend the inquiry a measure of legitimacy it didn't deserve. He would frame the request as an investigation into 'alleged breaches of high-level security systems for unknown purposes'; a petition sufficiently truthful that it would cover his own back, if challenged. Given the risk involved, the case would have to be watertight. For this reason, to Alex's frustration, Marci worked on it with slow, careful exactitude.

Events on other fronts were just as sluggish. Sándor proved elusive, even though calls to his mobile suggested he was back within the city's cellular range. After more than a dozen attempts, Marci gave up. He would wait for the President to answer in his own good time.

Sándor's response came quite literally out of the blue. As Marci was leaving work that Wednesday afternoon, an air car sporting The Society's eagle insignia descended to a landing space in front of the Executive Team building. Marci, whose thoughts were elsewhere, failed to notice the vehicle. Only when his name was called did he notice Sándor leaning across the passenger seat, addressing him: "Are you free for an hour or two?"

Marci approached without haste. Despite whatever news the President might have, he felt a surge of unexpected resentment toward his friend; not so much for neglecting to return his calls, but in the cavalier way Sándor expected him to dance to his tune at will.

If Sándor discerned the cause of Marci's delay, his countenance provided no clue. "Climb in," he said. "I've somewhere special to take you."

Impeller motors whined into life. The craft rose with sickening speed, circled over Hősök tere, then sped west. At two thousand feet it punched through clouds like dirty rags to emerge in unbroken sunshine. Ahead lay Budaörs, where a needle-like structure pierced the sky: the Josef Jung tower.

The car docked; valets ushered Sándor and Marci to an elevator that carried them up to a vast, revolving lounge. A circular bar occupied the center of the room, with the rest of the area allocated to dining.

The style was Avante-Garde industrial. Bold primaries of lime green and white offset a bare concrete ceiling from which depended a variety of cogs, belts and pulleys. The centerpiece of the restaurant was a tarnished, semi-circular iron cog 25 feet in diameter, which rose through the floor as if it had chewed its way from below.

The Maitre d' approached. "Patrician Sándor Ortega, how wonderful to see you again. Would you care for your usual table?"

"Thank you, Charles. That would be perfect."

They were seated at a window table and brought cognac and menus. A white-gloved cigar waiter presented a humidor, from which Sándor selected a Montecristo for himself and a Cohiba for Marci, which were clipped and lit.

Sándor let the smoke drift from his mouth. "One of my rare indulgences," he said. "Even I struggle to justify the expense, but these vintage Habanos are worth every credit. Now!" he said, slapping the table, "down to brass tacks. I had words with Trauffaut last week. I explained that you were taken ill at the AGM and that you send your sincere apologies for leaving—an excuse he accepted with good grace. He wishes you a speedy recovery, which of course you don't need because you're fine. In short, The Society is happy to reconsider your application at the Christmas Gala."

Marci stared at him in stupefaction. "Oh Sándor," he cried, "I don't know what to say. Thank you!"

"Don't thank me, thank the Prefect. After I conveyed your message, it was he who suggested we offer you a second chance."

Marci clasped Sándor's hand. "I knew you'd be able to help."

Sándor smiled. "While I'm still President, the Prefect listens to me. You've got a couple of months to prepare. I suggest you memorize your speech this time."

"The speech," Marci said, suddenly crestfallen. "I'd hoped we might bypass that."

Sándor signaled to the waiter. "Charles, some champagne? The usual stuff." To Marci: "Now we have to address your problem, and there can be no circumventing it. The Gala draws Patricians like gannets to a pilchard factory. You'll deliver your address to a full house, just like last time."

Marci nodded slowly, trying to phrase something diplomatic. "Sándor, I can't thank you enough. You've gone beyond the call of duty for me. But I can't deliver the speech. I tried my best the last time and look where it got me."

A flicker of irritation crossed the President's face. "Come now! It's a second chance, and certainly the last you'll have. I've pulled strings for you, and I'm depending on you to deal with this issue." He removed a business card from his wallet. "Call her," he said, gently. "She's the best therapist in Budapest."

Marci read it. "Stella Kennedy, Psychocerebral Therapist."

"At worst, you waste an hour and thirty credits. At best, you find a cure for your mental health issue. Worth a try?"

Marci nodded in obedient resignation. "Worth a try."

Charles returned with their champagne and two coupes.

"Don Perignon, the 2002 vintage," Sándor told Marci. "I prefer the '82 but needs must." He waited for the head waiter to leave. "Forgive me my manner, Marci. You're like a son to me. I want you to make Club 30 as much as you do. Trim down the speech. It doesn't have to be a saga."

Marci acquiesced. "I'll work on it. And I'll contact Stella." He smiled. "I won't let you down again."

"You didn't let me down. We simply delayed your election." Sándor raised his glass. "A toast! To your successful therapy, your good health, and to your election to The Society of Patricians!"

"And to you, Sándor, my faithful friend!"

* * *

The Weber Center was a Brutalist block of concrete and iridescent glass that had survived the fall of Communism, the Great War and the redevelopment of Budapest. It had endured several makeovers, including a ruthless emasculation of soft curves and pastel shades wrought on it by liberal architects. The last overhaul was restorative: it once again resembled chiseled coal.

Marci signed in at the lobby, passed a pair of Minotaur units and through a security chamber, and descended a flight of steps to the Grand Hall. Two hours into proceedings, it was filled to capacity. Erin's work, she'd told him, would be displayed in a smaller gallery, but the exhibition catalog provided only room names, not artists. Ambitiously, he searched the faces in the crowd, but could not find hers.

A waiter served him chardonnay, which he took to a corner of the room, the better to appraise his fellow guests. These, in Marci's estimation, fell into two camps. The first appeared an insipid lot, all black turtlenecks and cravat-sporting tweed blazer types. Critics, perhaps? The others were of a different ilk: loud, flamboyant and dressed in garments that would give macaws migraines. Erin's friend Lydia came to mind. Was she was coming tonight? At 6"1 she'd stand out like a totem pole wrapped in tie-dye. Hopefully a bus had hit her. It would take a big bus.

Marci edged around the side of the hall, wondering if, in his navy suit, he might be mistaken for a gallery attendant. By chance he noticed Erin a short distance away, trapped in conversation with a tall Somali man in a silk kaftan.

Catching sight of him, she excused herself and apologized her way across the room toward Marci. "I'm so glad you're here," she said, throwing her arms around his neck. "Mummy and Daddy and Sophia can't make it. I was beginning to think you wouldn't, either."

"I wouldn't miss it for the world," Marci said, without conviction.

She adjusted his tie. "Don't you look handsome in your suit?"

"I feel like a penguin at a Mardi Gras parade."

"Well, you made an effort. That's what counts."

The comment, Marci thought, inspired no confidence. "Is Petros coming?"

"He's already here."

"Alone?"

"Yes. Why?"

"He's far too chummy with you," Marci said. "Is he single?"

Erin laughed. "He has a wife. At least, I assume he has. Are you jealous?"

"Not at all."

She kissed him. "You fibber. Let me show you some important people."

Hand in hand they navigated the hall, Marci's anxiety alleviated by her presence. Tonight she wore a knee-length black dress, black stockings and tiny patent black shoes. Some of her hair, heaped up in curls, had been allowed to fall to the nape of her neck. Her skin was pale and luminous, and she exuded youthful vitality. If her art didn't garner attention, still no one would forget her tonight.

In a salon to one side of the hall hung a dozen canvases. Marci recognized half of them from Erin's studio, although the other six suggested identical provenance.

Milling about in the center of the room was an equal number of visitors, among them a tall fellow dressed in a black turtleneck and a tweed blazer: Petros Garai.

"My dear fellow," he said, grasping Marci's hand, "how very nice to see you. You'll be relieved to hear that Lydia can't make it tonight."

Marci smiled. "What a disappointment. I hope no one else will ask me about my line of work."

"No one here is remotely interested in you, me or even the Prefect himself. Despite appearances, this is not a social gathering; rather, a therapeutic outlet for the uncomfortably rich. Earlier, I watched some misguided fool surrender six hundred credits for a canvas, blank but for a blob of gangrenous yellow-green paint in one corner."

"Some would call it art," Marci said.

"Some would. I call it vapid and self-absorbed, which describes most of this evening's attendees."

"I hope you don't include me in that category," Erin said.

"Nor me, for that matter." The remark came from an elegant woman of middle years.

Erin made introductions. "Marci, Petros, this is Juliana De Vries, a very influential agent."

"And only slightly vapid," Juliana added, glancing at Petros. "In my line of work I must be impartial at all times. Perhaps this is what the gentleman means."

Petros bowed. "Naturally, my comment was not directed at you, madam. I see I have committed a social gaffe. Excuse me while I admire Erin's work."

"Please forgive my friend," Erin said. "He has a wicked sense of humor but a heart of gold. It's because of Petros that my work's on show. Marci, do you think I'm vapid?"

"Dressed as you are, no one could call you dull."

She kissed his cheek. "You always say the right thing."

Juliana and Erin fell into conversation. Marci, feeling surplus to requirements, moved away to study Erin's paintings, all of which conveyed a subtle sense of sadness or loss, although these qualities were hard to define.

One particularly abstruse piece caught his eye, as much for its impalpable meaning as its texture. The oils, which were laid on thickly, had been applied by hand or other body part in a frenzied release of energy. Bright vermilion clashed with pumpkin orange and olive green, blending to create, to Marci's tastes, new and unpleasant hues. A plaque below the work read 'Project 62.'

Marci stepped back and cocked his head.

"It won't help," Petros said, appearing at his side. "It's the right side up; you can tell from the autograph. And don't ask me what it means. Only the artist understands such work, and even then, not always."

"I recall you mentioned something similar about a landscape or a bodily—"

"I remember it well," interrupted Petros. "In this case, I shall refrain from making the comparison, although its appearance suggests an unorthodox approach."

Marci's phone chimed: a message from Alex. He'd read it later.

"You must be very proud of Erin," Petros said. "Her work has an honesty that sets it apart from the rest of the exhibition."

"I am proud of her. But when it comes to art, I'm a complete heathen."

"My dear fellow! Erin tells me your home is an epitome of good taste."

Marci said sharply, "What did she say, exactly?"

Petros raised his hands in surrender. "Nothing scandalous! Only that you surround yourself with the finer things of life. I am, by the way, an architect. I suspect we have more in common than you might imagine."

"So she told me." Marci looked around the gallery for an excuse to escape but could find nothing that didn't seem contrived. He turned his attention to Project 62. "It's kind of you to include her in the exhibition. She'd very much like to find an agent."

"In the sphere of culture, there are no guarantees. Van Gogh produced over nine hundred paintings but sold only one before committing suicide. Such is the travesty of art."

"That's not very encouraging. Did he sell any more after he was dead?"

"Considerably. And perhaps therein lies a valuable lesson."

"I hope it won't apply to Erin."

"You hope what won't apply to me?" Erin said, joining them. "I hope it's not something unpleasant."

"I'm lost with double negatives," Marci confessed.

Petros said: "The gist of it is that we wish you every success in your career."

Erin lowered her voice. "Your wish may already be coming true. Juliana has just agreed to represent me."

Marci scooped her off her feet. "Erin, that's wonderful news!"

"My heartfelt congratulations," Petros said, embracing her when she was free. "I should speak to Rubin. Perhaps he can move your work into the main hall."

"Thank you Petros, but I don't want anyone else to know just yet, in case I get a better offer."

"Who said artists were vapid?" Marci muttered.

"I can't imagine," Petros chuckled. "Erin, you have the cunning of a fox."

"Thank you, Petros! At least, I think I do."

"On a different tack," Petros said, "I was hoping to catch you both together. As Erin may have mentioned, I run a little social club on Thursday evenings. It's no great affair. We discuss current events of a political nature. Erin tells me you might be interested in joining us?"

Marci fixed Erin with a gelid stare. "She did?"

Erin slipped her arm through his. "Marci is ever so clever," she said brightly. "I think he'd enjoy our meetings."

"As a man of influence," Petros said, "you're just the sort of fellow we're looking for. You'd be our only SIN 30 member."

"SIN 29. And I'm not one for socializing. I doubt I'd add anything to your meetings."

"That's because you spend too much time at home," Erin chided. "Oh, do say you'll come! Even just for one meeting. For me, Marci. Please?"

"Fine," Marci said, sullenly. "Just this once. But don't expect me to say anything."

"Oh, I knew you'd say yes!" Tiptoeing, she kissed him, then hugged Petros. "Thank you for all your help, Petros. I wouldn't be here without you."

Petros blushed. "When faced with such charm, what man could refuse?"

Erin looked past them both. "There are two more agents I need to throw myself at. Would you excuse me? And please wish me luck."

Petros spoke gallantly: "You won't need it, my dear." To Marci he said: "I, too, must take my leave. I promised Rubin we'd discuss yet another overhaul of the building's exterior. See you on Thursday at seven."

"It will make for an interesting evening," Marci replied.

10

The Eden complex, located in south-central Budapest, was a series of twelve parallelograms tilted at 28 degrees, reaching 1300 feet tall at their highest peaks and resembling a dozen shards of differing-sized glass dropped upright into the ground. Hailed as an engineering marvel, it was a dizzying spectacle of sublime walkways, sky-high shopping malls and gravity-defying architecture.

Access to Eden was provided by a fleet of buses, three trams, a SpeedWalk, and a subway which stopped directly underneath the city. From here it continued to its terminus at Békéscsaba, where agricultural workers transferred to a dedicated shuttle service which would convey them to the nurseries and plantations of the Green Zone.

Alex Pimenov stepped from the carriage and rode the escalator to Plaza One, a concourse of colossal proportions at the base of Eden's tallest tower: Eden One. The time was a little after 17:30, and the place hummed with rush hour activity. Office workers hurried home, or on to the next meeting; others lounged with colleagues in restaurants and wine bars to tattle or forget the day. Farm laborers, in smocks clean or dirty depending on their shifts, grouped outside *pékárusok*[18] to do likewise.

Alex, who had never set foot in Eden, walked to the center of the atrium and looked up in wonder. A quarter of a mile above, Eden

[18] bakery kiosk

Ones quadrilateral form converged steeple-like at a glass sky deck. Not a religious man, Alex nevertheless wondered whether he was experiencing the same sense of awe that, half a millennium ago, pilgrims must have felt on first entering a far-flung cathedral.

At a news kiosk he bought an Adaptive Text pamphlet and a pair of disposable HUD glasses, which were synced to map data sent to his phone. In the center of the plaza stood a café. Alex ordered coffee and opened the guide, which was made of disposable electronic paper which altered its content based on the reader's location. He read:

To the first-time visitor: welcome to Eden, the city within a city and one of the wonders of the engineering world! As you sit here in Plaza One no doubt marveling at its scale and grandeur, rest assured you're in good company. Nearly a quarter of a million residents feel the same. Built in 2083, it once housed the 20,000-strong construction team employed in building Budapest's FATS and DOME. These days it accommodates the city's agricultural workforce, which labors tirelessly to provide us our food. Fifty years on, and Eden is still the linchpin that holds our great city-state together!

He turned the page, where the text took on a less triumphant tone.

Newcomers may reasonably assume that the usual norms of society apply here. Not so! Due to chronic underinvestment by the Company, Eden has learned to rely on its own resources to survive, and is proud to boast of its semi-autonomous status. By all means enjoy the comfort and relative safety of Eden One, but do not be warned: the rest of the enclave does not live up to its name! Official law enforcement is minimal and is confined to a single office three hundred yards north of where you sit. It is understaffed and overworked. Do not rely on it for anything other than life-or-death predicaments, which may be both frequent and many. Eden is not known as 'The Lair,' 'The Slum,' and 'New Babylon' for nothing.

Alex grunted; the book was unusually candid.

Navigating Eden can be a daunting prospect at the best of times. Do not be alarmed! Even Edenites lose their way! Remember, though, that not all is as it first seems, and care must be taken when exploring this cultural gem. Here, then, are three tips for a safe visit:

1. Never attempt to travel Eden unaided. You will quickly become lost in a rabbit warren of corridors, passageways, SpeedWalks and alleys, staircases, escalators and elevators—not all of them interconnecting—which link floors that are confusingly similar, if not identical, to one another. In short, the map and HUD you bought, Alex, are invaluable to your safe passage.
2. To reiterate, do not rely on the local constabulary. Law enforcement operates a token presence. Eden is, to all intents and purposes, controlled by serious organized crime. To avoid abduction, police officers conduct their beats in groups of three or more. If you find yourself in trouble, resort to the time-tested means of problem-solving: pay. In Eden, as elsewhere, money eases a multitude of trials.
3. Take advantage of freedom from MARTHA but live wisely! Eden's crime syndicates long ago discovered ways to hinder second skin technology. This means Edenites enjoy liberties denied Employees in the rest of Budapest. Although this has attracted many reprobates, remember that most Edenites are loyal and hard-working citizens. Do not judge them by their habitat. Remember, too, that the Company has spies everywhere. MARTHA always gets her man!

Alex tossed the pamphlet on the table. A waitress served him coffee lukewarm and weak. He smoked a cigarette, left a tip and departed. Near the metro escalators he paused. It wasn't too late to go home. Lucinda and Huang had pre-SIN development class, which meant Alex and Lei could enjoy a couple of hours together with that nice bottle of Merlot she'd won at the work party raffle.

He looked up at the atrium again. He'd come this far; he might as well see his mission through. He donned his navigation glasses and followed the arrow that appeared in his field of vision to an elevator full of rowdy farm workers, which rushed them up sixty-five floors to a landing. A SpeedWalk conveyed him to Eden Four, where another SpeedWalk carried him over dizzying heights to Eden Nine.

After several minutes and a confusing labyrinth of alleyways, Alex found himself in a run-down tenement block. Gray concrete walls mitigated by fluorescent graffiti led in all directions. A staircase ran up a floor to a row of nondescript flats that clung like barnacles over a precipitous drop. Halfway along the passage was Apartment 9-43. A sign on the door read 'Viktor Romanov.'

Alex removed his glasses and ran his fingers through his hair. Today he wore a tie—a pet hate of his—which now felt constrictive. His hands, he noticed, were damp with sweat. Nerves, of course, and with good reason: although Romanov's profile made no mention of him being an Informant, the same might not be true of his neighbors. Eden's mafia would surely love an Adjudicant for a trophy.

Alex corrected his slouch, took a deep breath and pressed the doorbell.

Nothing. After a respectful thirty seconds he tried again.

There was no response. He turned away, happening to look over the walkway railing. Astroturf the size of a postage stamp provided scale. The park was so far below him he couldn't even make out the trees. Alex wrenched himself away from the guardrail. Some people had a problem with confined spaces; for him it was heights.

He stared at Romanov's door. MARTHA's file listed him as a subway foreman. If he was working days, he should be home by now. Alex was about to try the bell a final time when he heard a key turn in the lock. Bolts slid back: one, two. The door opened six inches: the length of a chain lock.

A face appeared. *"Tessék?"*

"Jó napot kívánok. You are Viktor Romanov?"

The man spoke with caution. "I am."

"My name is Alex Pimenov. I'm investigating an inquiry carried out fifteen years ago by the Justice and Cessation Board. I understand they questioned you at Nyugati."

Romanov regarded him as if roused from slumber. "And you are?"

Alex shot a nervous glance along the walkway and showed his ID.

"An Adjudicant?" Romanov's eyes widened. "Is this about Kristoph?"

"It's about your interview. I realize it was a long time ago." Alex again looked toward the stairwell. Had he heard something? The whole damn place, labyrinth that it was, seemed to echo.

Romanov appeared trapped by indecision.

"Please, Mr. Romanov. It will only take a few minutes."

The door closed on him. The chain rattled and the hallway appeared. Romanov looked out: left, right.

"I'm alone," Alex said, hurrying inside.

Romanov bolted the door and led Alex into the most dismal kitchen he'd ever seen. A narrow table and two plastic chairs occupied a space beside a barred window, which was too opaque to see through. Alex wasn't sure if it was cloudy by design or from want of cleaning, but the rest of the room testified to the latter. A Formica work surface, its veneer peeling away at the lip, supported predictable clutter: a mug tree of chipped cups which dangled like old fruit; an electric kettle glazed at the spout by a limescale patina; half a jar of instant coffee, budget brand; and a two-ring electric travel hob. A decrepit fridge provided rattling background ambiance. The room's extractor fan, equal in volume, fought bravely to keep the funk of stale cigarettes at bay.

Romanov sat down and motioned Alex to the chair opposite. He was lean and taut, like a manual worker who labored hard but ate little. His age? Indeterminate. Fifties or sixties, probably. His head was shaved—recently, or so it seemed—and sloped to a narrow brow as lined and furrowed as the metro tracks he worked on. Listless eyes, set deep in shadows, registered pain, or resignation, or both. They were eyes that had seen too much and had forgotten nothing. He was, Alex thought, the most broken-looking human he'd ever met.

From skin gray as mortar sprouted three-day stubble. Romanov lit a cigarette and scratched at it. "You'll have to excuse me. I was sleeping when you called, and I'm only half awake."

"I'm sorry to disturb you," Alex said. "Are you unwell?"

"I'm an engineer. I work nights on the metro." His eyes flicked at a wall clock. "I should get ready to leave soon."

"Then I'll keep this brief." Alex removed a file from an attaché case he hadn't used in years because he despised it only slightly less than wearing a tie. "According to our records, you, along with a large number of other Employees, were interrogated in 2117 by the Justice Board. I'm trying to establish the purpose of the interviews."

"I was hoping you could tell me. No one ever said why." Romanov frowned. "If you're an Adjudicant, why are you asking me this? Isn't the information in MARTHA?"

Alex smiled awkwardly, hoping the engineer would interpret it as professional embarrassment for the clerical error, rather than shame for the lie he was about to tell. "We've had some technical issues with MARTHA that have only just come to light. Mine's really a fact-finding role."

Romanov was coming to his senses. "Is this an official inquiry? It seems strange the Justice Board would send an Adjudicant to visit me at home. Especially in Eden."

Alex skirted the question. "I work for the Executive Team, not the Justice Board. Please tell me what you can remember."

"It was fifteen years ago. I don't recall the details. They asked a lot of questions about my son."

"Your son?"

"Yes. I was there for ten hours and we discussed nothing else." Romanov tapped his fingers on the table in a quiet drumroll. "Mr. Pimenov, I'm sure it's very important, and I don't want to get into any kind of trouble with the law, but I already went through all of this a very long time ago."

Alex spoke with sympathy. "I understand. And you're right—the information should have been documented. But it wasn't, which is why I'm here." He waited ten seconds while Romanov said nothing and stared at the table. In a strained voice, Alex added: "I should mention that failure to cooperate in an Executive Team investigation will negatively affect your SIN."

"My SIN?" Romanov chuckled himself into a hacking cough. "Forgive me. I stopped caring about SIN long ago." He went to the fridge and took out two cans of Borsodi. "Do you want one?"

"Not on duty, thanks."

Romanov cracked open the other. "I'll tell you what I told them. My wife and I had a son: Kristoph. We'd tried for years to have kids until he came along. He was our world, an only child. Kris loved music. It took me and Natalyia six months to save up enough to buy him a violin. He played it all the time; wanted to become a concert virtuoso or some such. We worried about his SIN, but he was fourteen and had his whole life ahead of him. Soon after that Natalyia died."

"I'm sorry. What happened?"

"She was liquidated. She went into Pest one morning to the DNA Repository and never came home. I got the letter the next day. I suppose we should have seen it coming; she was a housewife, not a career woman." Romanov took another swig. "There wasn't a bad bone in her body. Begging your pardon, but it shouldn't have happened, not to her."

Alex lowered his eyes. He understood now why Romanov didn't want to speak to him. "How did your son take it?"

"It hit him hard. He stopped playing, even stopped eating. Stayed in his room and wouldn't speak to me for days. One evening I got back from work and found him in the hallway in the dark, speaking to someone. I don't know if he was praying or talking to his mother. I felt awkward, like I was interrupting something. I tried speaking to him, but he just carried on like I wasn't even there."

"It can't have been easy, seeing him like that."

"I never saw him cry," Romanov reflected. "Guess he got that from me. Not very good with emotions, myself. Boys don't cry, and all that. I thought he'd get over it, eventually."

"Did he?"

"Up to a point. He started hanging out with friends again, even started talking. Not much, mind, and only when I asked him something. One day he comes home full of questions about the Outside, and what was it like? Of course, I don't know, only what's on TV. Some of the farm workers tell stories, but nobody gets past the Wall, so who can say?"

"It's not unusual for children to ask such questions," Alex pointed out. "Why do you mention it?"

"Because he hardly spoke about anything else. When your son's been mute for six months, you notice."

"Point taken. Please continue."

Romanov returned to his seat, extinguished his cigarette and lit another. "Anyway, after a while Kris went back to school. His sleeping got better. He started eating again. I thought we was back to normal. Then one afternoon he didn't come home. I called the school. They said he hadn't showed up. At first I thought he was just bunking off with his mates. Then it gets late. I was on duty that night. There's no phone signal in the tunnels when the power's down, so I couldn't check on him. When I got back in the morning, he wasn't here."

"Did you contact the police?"

"Of course, but they're useless. They told me to come back in a week and they'd file a missing person report. I went to the school. They did some phoning round, called the parents. His friends hadn't got home either. So I spoke to this guy, he's local mafia, a nasty piece of work, but he's got connections, better than the cops. He said he'd get to the bottom of things for me. He wanted money, of course, a lot of it. I gave him all my savings. Two weeks later I see him coming out of some swanky clothes shop in Eden Four, dressed up like a peacock. I asked him if he'd found Kris. He said, 'who the hell are you?' and if I ever approach him again it'd be me who goes missing. He was my last hope."

"Did you hear back from the Justice Board?"

Romanov shook his head. "I went to Nyugati two weeks after Kris disappeared to see if he'd been liquidated. He hadn't. I asked if they could find him using second skin? They said because it doesn't work here in Eden, they couldn't tell if he died here."

"And there was no record of second skin transmissions outside Eden?"

Romanov shook his head again.

"And you haven't heard anything more in fifteen years?"

"Fifteen years..." Romanov spoke the words as if he'd only just realized how long it had been. "They say it gets better with time, but it doesn't. I think about him every day. Where is he now? Is he alive? Sometimes I think he's dead. He probably is." Romanov stared into space. "Do you know what it's like not to know? To wake up every morning hoping yesterday was just a bad dream? Sometimes I'd beg God to tell me Kris was dead, that the Justice Board was wrong and that I'd find a letter waiting for me in the hall. That's when the guilt hits. On good days it's worse. How can I say I love Kris if I'm enjoying a few drinks with the lads? How can I say I miss him if I forget him for an hour or two?" He finished his beer and glanced at Alex. "You think I'm an alcoholic?"

"I don't think anything."

"It used to help me sleep, the booze, but not anymore. To be honest, the insomnia's a blessing in disguise; when I sleep, I dream about him. In my dreams he's still young, somewhere far off, somewhere happy. Sometimes Nataliya's with him, but it's a place I can't reach. When I call to them they don't hear me. Every night I go to work in the tunnels and wonder if I walk far enough into the darkness I'll see Kris there. If we'd had power that night and my phone had worked... When you showed me your Adjudicant badge I thought you might know something. But you don't, do you?"

"No. Did the Company offer you any therapy?"

"Yes, for a price, of course. They said my productivity was down and docked my wages for a two-week bereavement course. Told me to throw all Kris's stuff out and focus on building my SIN back up. I told them they could go to hell and quit the program. I've kept his room the same as the day he left. Haven't even washed the sheets so I can remember how he used to smell. Sometimes I go in there to remember. Not that I ever forget." He half rose. "Do you want to see it? I was thinking it might help you find him, but after this long I suppose there's no point."

Alex pointed to a photograph taped to the window. "Is that him?" Poorly composed and overbright, it showed a teenage boy and a woman, presumably Natalia, sitting under a café awning somewhere.

"That's Kris on his birthday, the year he went missing. We went out for ice cream. Kris loved ice cream."

Alex stared at the image. How could he tell the man there was no hope? "Is this the original? I don't want to deprive you of it."

"Take it. I've got five albums full of them." Romanov put his cigarette out. "I hope this answers all your questions. There's nothing more I can tell you. I have lung cancer. Soon I'll die. Then I'll be with them."

Alex removed the photo, slipped it into Romanov's file and rose numbly to his feet. "Mr. Romanov, thank you for your time. Unless I hear news of your son, I will never disturb you again."

Outside, darkness had settled over Eden. Alex let himself out, closing the front door gently on Romanov's wretched world. In the bleakest of moods he donned his navigation glasses and strode to the stairwell.

An elderly woman, shopping caddy in tow, huffed her way past him to the landing. As he passed her, she paused to watch him disappear, as Kristoph once had many years prior, into the labyrinth of Eden.

* * *

Marci and Erin ran the short distance from the Fővám Tér tram stop to Csarnok Tér, their umbrella drone too small to shelter both of them from the hail that pelted District IX. Erin, excited by the prospect of attending Club Bohém, chattered without pause. By contrast, Marci was tense and tight-lipped, and for good reason: Adjudicants, like other senior civil servants, were expected to be above politics, and articulating their opinions in public was strictly prohibited. With just two months until Society's Christmas gala, he could ill afford a scandal. Once again, Erin had bent him to her will.

There was another reason for his taciturnity. Come what may, tonight he would reveal his occupation to her—with potentially irreversible consequences.

Café Primo was the venue for their meeting. It occupied a courtyard address separated from Csarnok Tér by a high archway, and here they stopped for Erin to brush hail from Marci's jacket and provide ancillary improvements to his appearance.

"Not bad," she said, pleased with her work. "You're quite a catch. A little grumpy, but still a nice prize for me to show off."

"I hope I stack up well against tonight's political heavyweights," Marci grumbled.

"You'll do. I know you don't want to be here but thank you for coming."

"Don't expect me to say anything. And whatever you do, don't tell anyone else I'm SIN 29."

"I promise." She kissed him. "Are you ready?"

"Let's get this over and done with."

Inside, they ordered coffees and proceeded to a back room, where chairs for thirty had been arranged in two concentric semicircles. At the front stood Petros, in conversation with three middle-aged women.

Erin led them to their seats, greeting acquaintances on the way. Marci, anxious and lightheaded, ignored them and ensured he sat at the far end of the row, convenient to an exit.

Petros called the meeting to order. "Good evening, everyone, and thank you for braving the dreadful weather. I'd like to begin proceedings by extending a special welcome to my friend, Márton Kovács, here with the ever-delightful Erin Macsy, whom you already know."

Marci glowered at Petros. So much for a low profile.

"By way of opening," Petros continued, "perhaps we could introduce ourselves? Name and occupation? I'll begin: Petros Garai, architect and art lover."

"Zoli," a tall, ascetic-looking youth in the front row said. "I'm a student at ELTE."

Beside him sat a girl whose dyed green was shaved just short of the scalp. "Zsuzsi, also at ELTE. Political Sciences major."

Next, a timid-looking woman half-raised her hand for permission to speak. "I'm Marysia, a human resources coordinator. Should we mention our SIN?"

"That won't be necessary," said Petros.

Others made themselves known until only Marci and Erin remained.

"I'm Erin, an artist and shop assistant."

"Kovács Márton." Marci hesitated. "Clerical worker," he added, feeling Erin's eyes bore into the side of his head.

Petros, who was aware of Marci's high SIN, evinced no reaction. "Welcome to Club Bohém, one and all. For the sake of our newcomers, allow me to explain what we are not. We are not a political movement. We are not dissidents. We advocate no action and receive no remuneration from the Company, the Underground, the Guild of Abattoir Workers or anyone else. We exist to facilitate open and honest dialogue on the political status quo and whatever else takes our fancy. To those who are politically thin-skinned, I ask for your tolerance. There is nothing treasonous about well-meaning discourse, even if some ideas run at a tangent to our own. Such differences of opinion are part and parcel of healthy debate, and can only help but enrich our understanding of the world we live in.

"One rule governs our proceedings. Whatever is said between these walls remains here. To this end, and for our mutual protection, please be aware that recording devices are not permitted and that you were screened for such when you entered this room."

Marci spoke in a hushed voice: "I thought you said these meetings are all a bit of harmless fun?"

"Petros can be a little bit overcareful at times," Erin whispered.

"Last week," Petros continued, "we enjoyed a spirited discussion on the now weekly riots that plague the city and the Undergrounders who are alleged to instigate them. Zoli, you made an interesting comment, which we lacked time to cover."

Zoli sat bolt upright and darted a nervous glance left and right before answering. "I believe it was a question, rather than a statement. I asked if the riots and bombings are genuinely organized by the Undergrounders, or whether this is a ruse by the Company?"

"And why would the Company do such a thing? Anyone?"

"*Casus belli?*" Zsuzsi suggested. "Every society needs an enemy. For us it's the Undergrounders and the Outsiders. No one gets killed, and we only have News24 to feed us what it wants us to believe. In short, how do we know it's true?"

"Zsuzsi has made an interesting point," Petros said, "one which perhaps many of us have thought but never dared to say out loud. I open the floor for comments."

Marci studied the faces of those present: ordinary folk of various ages and diverse backgrounds. A little naive, perhaps, as in Zsuzsi's case, but otherwise harmless.

No one spoke. Marci, feeling awkward for Petros, reminded himself that he was here to please Erin, not to contribute to the conversation.

Petros surveyed the group. "No one? I—"

"What I don't understand is why the Underground is bombing people in the first place," Zsuzsi said. "I mean, if they want to win people to their cause, then starting riots and blowing up buses doesn't seem like the best way of going about it."

Marysia spoke in hushed speculation. "I heard the Undergrounders are in collusion with the Outsiders. They want to let the barbarians in to kill us and to destroy the city!"

"You said something, Marci?" Petros inquired.

"I was clearing my throat."

"Marysia's been reading the gossip columns again." So spoke Attila, a mountain of a man with a face of granite, who wore his office shirtsleeves like shrink wrap. "All this talk of revolution's nonsense. Everyone knows what the alternative is: anarchy."

"It would be interesting to know what Outsiders are really like," Erin mused. "I mean, what if they're ordinary people, just like us?"

"Why wouldn't they be?" asked Zsuzsi. "Fifty years ago, our grandparents were living there. Were they also barbarians and cannibals? The only difference now is that we live on this side of the Wall."

"Fifty years ago we had the Fuel War," Marci heard himself saying. "It was a completely different situation."

"Really? I don't see how. They're human beings like us."

"They've been living without law and order for half a century," Marci said. "If their food's run out, why wouldn't they practice cannibalism?"

"Bloody savages, that's what they are," Attila muttered. "We're cooped up here like chickens in an abattoir while they roam free. I say we take the fight to them, reclaim a few more thousand miles of land and stop relying on the Hangman to keep our population in check."

Zsuzsi regarded the two of them with disgust. "You sound like the Budapest Tribune! Have you no compassion? We should be embracing our brothers and sisters on the Outside, not slaughtering them at the drop of a hat."

"Drivel," Marci replied. "Compassion is protecting our communities from roaming gangs of murderers and rapists. While you and your friends debate the merits of utopian socialism over a bottle of rosé, our Border guards are sacrificing their lives for your liberal nonsense."

"Nonsense? Loving my fellow human beings isn't nonsense! It's common human decency. How can you justify gunning down women and children as keeping us safe?"

"Maybe Zsuzsi has a point," Erin said softly. "Our city, our way of life—they've been bought at the expense of the Outsiders. We used to be a place that people flocked to. Now we've become a fortress, killing those who want to share in what we have."

Marci looked at her askance. "You believe this too? That we should open our doors and let them in?"

"I'm saying that perhaps they're not the enemy that we're led to believe."

Marci spoke crisply: "Let me tell you what would happen if we adopted Zsuzsi's approach. Within two days of deactivating our defense systems we'd have thirty thousand Outsiders in the city. They have no food, no education, no money and no ethics. Our welfare system doesn't support the unemployed because doing so would foster a culture of dependency, nor is it geared up to provide humanitarian aid. They'd be children in a candy shop. They would loot, steal and kill to get what they need. Within a month, half a million more would have shown up, all doing the same. Reactivating the Wall is now too late. For every eighty Employees there's one Outsider, whose sole purpose is to take as much as he can—food, medicine, human life—from the city that's shunned him and his family for two generations. The police won't be able to stop him, and if you think the Undergrounders are bad, try someone motivated by five decades of deprivation. It would be utter chaos."

"Hear, hear!" declared Attila. "Maybe we can arrange some kind of scrap between the two of them? It would kill two birds with one stone."

"I find your comments flippant and offensive," Zsuzsi sniffed, "and not in the spirit of Club Bohém."

Petros arched his fingers and spoke reflectively. "An interesting assessment of yours, Marci, and one which I suspect might prove true. Marysia, in response to your comment let me allay your fears. No such cabal exists between the Underground and the Outsiders. The Wall, for all its divisiveness, prevents such an alliance.

"So the Underground is real then?" asked Zoli.

Petros blinked; evidently, he'd spoken rashly. He pursed his lips and seemed to consider whether or not to answer the question. "I can tell you two facts. The Underground is real, and they play no part in the bombings."

"That's a bold statement," Marci said. "How do you know this?"

"And who's responsible?" asked Zoli.

Petros spread out his hands. "Now we enter the realm of speculation."

"It's all speculation," grunted Attila.

Erin said, "But you think it's the Company?"

Petros's smile was strained. "My function here is to facilitate intelligent discussion, not to provide absolute truths."

"So far we've had neither," Marci muttered.

Zsuzsi spoke tartly: "I'm surprised you'd recognize either. Whether it's a government ruse or not, the fact remains that there are many decent, hardworking Employees who feel disenfranchised by our political system and have no legitimate means to vent their frustration."

"Is that what they teach you at ELTE," Marci asked, "or is it something you thought up all by yourself?"

Petros intervened: "To answer Erin's earlier question: the media's portrayal of the Outside as a lawless wasteland is far from accurate. In fact, I have it on good authority that structured, civilized society much like our own exists in many places beyond our Wall."

"Who is this 'good authority,' Petros?" Marci asked. "The Company has almost no data on the Outside. We stopped flying patrols over thirty years ago, and our access to satellite imagery is extremely limited. Any remarks about "civilized societies" are complete conjecture."

Petros smiled. "There is information, if you know where to find it."

Marci spoke coldly. "I don't know who your sources are, but I can assure you the Company has no dealings with anyone beyond the Wall, other than the other Sister Cities."

"How do you know that?" asked Zsuzsi.

Marci hesitated. "I just do."

"That's not an answer, it's just your opinion—unless you work high up in the Company. And if you do, why are you here?"

Marci felt his face flush. "I—I'm a guest, that's all."

Zsuzsi addressed Erin: "Who is he?"

Petros spoke: "Marci, Erin, you needn't answer. Zsuzsi, you know the rules. Our identities are private. Such questions are off limits."

"I don't see why," Zsuzsi objected. "If he has inside information, I'd like to hear it. And if he's a Company mole, I think we should all know. I don't want to put SIN at risk for expressing my beliefs."

"Ha!" barked Attila. "Now who's the hypocrite? You hate the Company but you want to keep your slope."

"I don't want to be liquidated," Zsuzsi snapped. "It's not a crime."

Petros removed his glasses and cleaned them on his shirttail. "I think at this point it's probably best to move onto tonight's topic. Last week we began the first in a series on the value of SIN-enrichment programs. Some of you argued that they serve little purpose, and that the investment they require would be better spent working overtime. Zoli, I believe you've prepared a presentation for us?"

Zoli took the floor and addressed the group in a didactic style devoid of all intonation. Marci slid down in his seat, silently berating himself for his outspokenness. He'd come here to please Erin but had ended up letting his pride and temper to get the better of him. Had the group guessed? Even now, Zsuzsi might be putting two and two together. So strict was their Code of Conduct that merely the act of arousing suspicion regarding an Adjudicant's vocation was a crime. An embittered Employee could, at risk to their SIN, report an Adjudicant to the Executive Team for doing so. But if Petros's preamble about security screening was true, Marci had little to worry about. The word of an Adjudicant was unimpeachable and could trump a thousand assertions to the contrary. If necessary, he'd deny everything. The knotty issue was second skin. Marci closed his eyes and let out a deep sigh at his stupidity. What was he doing at a political debate in the first place?

Zoli's monologue reached its tepid conclusion. Petros, springing to his feet, thanked him with a cheerfulness incongruent with the evening's events and brought the meeting to a close.

Marci made his way toward the exit, wanting nothing more than a coffee and a cigarette somewhere far away from Club Bohém. At the door he turned to see that Erin was behind him. Erin, however, had gone to talk to Zoli and the bitch with the green hair.

Marci stared at them in dismay. Was this some kind of snub for his spat with Zsuzsi? Out of earshot he watched as Erin raised her hands in what might be a gesture of conciliation. Was she apologizing? To hell with that! He'd done nothing wrong; in any case, he didn't need a delegate to convey his remorse.

Bristling, Marci strode toward them, but was intercepted by Petros who, grasping his hand, performed the Hungarian cheek-to-cheek kiss; something that always made Marci uncomfortable, but especially now, given his mood. "Marci, dear chap, I'm so glad you could join us. Erin's spoken about little else since you agreed to attend."

Marci drew back and reclaimed his hand; Petros's breath was rank from coffee and his palm moist with sweat. "I'm glad to hear it," he said, looking past him to where Erin consorted with the enemy.

"You certainly put the cat among the pigeons this evening," Petros chuckled. "I don't think we've had a run-in like that in quite a while."

"At least I've added something to the proceedings," Marci said, side-stepping him. "Excuse me, Erin and I are leaving."

Petros's face fell. "So soon? I'd hoped you'd stay for coffee. We usually spend an hour or so networking. It's good for the soul, you know."

"There's no one here I want to network with, although I'm sure the Justice Board wouldn't mind a word with some of your members."

Petros winced. "Ah, here I presume you refer to Zsuzsa? She means well but can be a little brisk at times."

"That would be a generous appraisal."

"Don't let her concern you. She's young and headstrong, but quite innocent."

Marci spoke primly: "Innocence is established by MARTHA, who rarely makes mistakes." He checked himself. *Rarely.* Had he just admitted her errancy? Moreover, who would say such a thing except someone who worked with her?

Petros seemed not to notice. "True, true, or so we're told. Who are we to argue with her?"

Marci, still preoccupied with the *ménage à trois*, caught Zsuzsa's eye. She scowled back at him and resumed her conversation. "Zsuzsi, apparently."

Petros suppressed a smile. "As the coordinator of Club Bohém I am, by necessity, impartial. However, you fought your corner with vigor and impeccable rhetoric." Less certainly he added, "I hope we haven't deterred you from another visit? We could do with fresh blood, especially someone willing to stand by their principles."

Marci caught Erin's attention. He tilted his chin to show they were leaving. "I'm afraid my blood isn't all that fresh, and my vigor quickly runs out when dealing with dimwits."

"It's a shame," lamented Petros. "Apart from Attila, who's truculent for the fun of it, Zsuzsi has the run of the place. I'm afraid Club Bohém has become something of a soapbox for her unorthodoxy."

"Unorthodoxy? I've never heard such seditious nonsense. I take it your comment about security screening was true?"

Petros nodded in regret. "One can never to be too careful these days. Even the most innocuous remark can be twisted into something sinister, forever changing the course of one's SIN."

"Some remarks require no twisting."

Erin approached and, to Marci's bewilderment, slipped her arm through his.

Petros, with great politesse, bowed before her. "My dear lady, thank you for your input this evening. You were a pacifying force among us."

Erin spoke demurely. "I feel silly compared to everyone else here. I'm only an artist."

"'Only an artist?'" Petros said in dismay. "You spoke with the sweet voice of reason and a wisdom far beyond your years. Your insights are like fresh air to this moldy chamber—"

"Time to go," Marci said, donning his coat. "Excuse us, Petros. I have an early start tomorrow."

"Of course, how remiss of me." Petros kissed Erin on the cheek and would have done likewise to Marci had he not already left the room.

At Fővám Tér the tram was late. The hail had ceased. A bitter northerly wind now blew along the Danube.

Marci watched Erin sidelong. She seemed none the worse for his spat with Zsuzsa. Should he go through with his plan to reveal his occupation? Given the liberal slant of her comments tonight, she was hardly going to take the news well. He rummaged around in his pocket for some Kqalms, then decided against it. He'd take something more potent at home.

"I'm sorry you didn't enjoy the meeting," Erin said.

"I'm sorry if I embarrassed you. It wasn't my plan."

"You don't like Petros, do you?"

"I don't trust him. He has the silver tongue of a snake."

Erin giggled. "Did you make that up yourself?"

"It's true, isn't it?"

"He's rather charming."

"I can't read him," Marci admitted. "I'm not sure if he's a socialite or a fraud, or perhaps both."

"I think he's just a social climber, like the rest of us. He's witty and intelligent and probably wants to improve his SIN."

"By running a political dissenter's club?"

"Hardly that. In any case, since Club Bohém is secret, who will know? From his point of view, he's making contacts, and contacts can help boost slope."

Marci felt his mouth twist at the irony of that, but maintained wise silence.

At last the tram rumbled out of the gloom across Szabadság Bridge. They alighted at Astoria and tramped, shivering, back to Marci's apartment. The courtyard was quiet; Norbert Tóth's shed was dark and silent.

While Marci made them hot chocolate, Erin wandered the living room, pausing at an antique glass-fronted cabinet that housed some framed photographs. One in particular caught her attention: Marci in his late teens, with two adults and a young girl.

Marci returned with their drinks.

"A sweet boy," Erin said. "Perhaps a touch serious looking."

"Nothing's changed," he said, handing her a mug.

Erin swapped the picture for another: the same girl, now around twelve, dressed in a school uniform. Her long, auburn hair was brushed straight down, and the lighting, pose and mottled brown backdrop suggested a studio shoot. Her expression was severe, as if she found the photo shoot an unnecessary inconvenience.

"Another eidolon? Who is she?"

Marci glanced at it without interest. "It doesn't matter."

"She's very pretty."

"She's dead."

"Oh. I'm sorry. What happened?"

"It's a long story." Marci went to the bathroom and opened a packet of Candormax. He hesitated. Did he really want to do this? He was going to have to tell her sooner or later. Why not now? Perhaps she'd take the news better than he expected. He swallowed one of the pills and returned to the lounge.

Erin, warming herself before the Living Wall, smiled and patted the sofa beside her. Marci sat down, wondering how long it would take before the drug loosened his tongue.

"I'm so glad you came this evening," she said, leaning her head on his shoulder. "It means a lot to me. Was it really very awful?"

"Do you agree with what Zoli and Zsuzsi said?"

"Some of it. I don't believe the people on the Outside are barbarians. And I'm intrigued by the Underground, if they exist. Also..."

"Also what?"

Erin made an incomprehensible gesture: perhaps a combination of angst and frustration. "Are you happy in life?"

"Happy?" Marci blinked. "In what way?"

"In any way. The Company, the Hangman, the SIN system. We spend all our lives from the day we're born until the day we die striving for a goal someone else has chosen for us and which hardly anyone's achieved. Don't you think it would be better if we could just be left alone to live normal lives like the sub-SINners?"

"Don't forget the Outsiders."

"Sure, or the Outsiders. They don't have to fight or strive like us."

"They do little else, but not for SIN. Compared to them, we've got it easy. Human history is one long record of struggle."

"But it's all so unfair!"

"I disagree. Everyone has a chance to reach the top if they work hard enough."

"But what's at the top?"

It was a silly question, but he answered it calmly. "Empyrean, of course. The chance to live forever."

"And you really want to live forever?"

"It's better than being dead forever."

"That's not a very good answer. What if it's like it is now? Or what if it's not real at all?"

Marci shifted in his seat, his body flushing as the Candormax crossed the blood-brain barrier. The sofa suddenly felt softer, the heat from the Living Wall comforting rather than oppressive. Erin's head became a pillow as his neck went lax. Pleasant torpor overcame him. Within a few minutes, the drug would desensitize his brain's prefrontal cortex, releasing him from inhibitory control. He would, in common parlance, spill his guts. Again: was it wise? Maybe it would be better all round to walk her to the taxi rank and put an end to this irritating evening. He still hadn't forgiven her for persuading him to attend Club Bohém.

Sleep took him unnoticed, followed by a jerk of wakefulness. What had she asked him? Something about Empyrean being real or not. "Of course it's real," he slurred. "You must have seen the advertisements."

"Zoli said it's a lie. He said it's a carrot and donkey situation, trying to keep us too busy to see the big picture."

"And you believe everything Zoli says?"

"No," said Erin calmly, "I have my own opinions. Which is why I don't automatically trust everything I hear. It's not a crime."

"Insurgency is. If the old bat upstairs could hear you you'd already be on your way to Nyugati."

"Then it's good I'm talking to you, not her," Erin said. "Unless you want to inform on me?"

Marci sat up sharply, forcing her head off his. "What kind of question is that? I'm not a spy."

"Then what are you?" she snapped. "You never talk about your job. For all I know, you're a Hangman. At the meeting tonight you said you did clerical work. But what kind of office worker is SIN 29?"

Marci, taken aback by her temper, fell silent. The Candormax was loosening up his composure; nevertheless, he maintained restraint. "I'm a senior Employee in the Executive Team. Does that answer your question?"

Erin shook her head furiously. "No it doesn't, not at all! Are you a director? You must be. Or something even higher?"

Marci went to the kitchen and poured himself a whiskey. On his way back his legs lost their strength. He sat down heavily in the Chesterfield opposite her and drank half the glass.

"Well?" Erin said. "Are you going to tell me what you do?"

"I'm not a director," he said. "I outrank him by three points."

"Then who are you? You can't be a Hangman if you work for the Executive Team. In any case, Hangmen don't make high SIN."

Marci spoke languidly; speech was becoming an effort now. "If you love me, why does it matter? You know who I am and what I'm like."

"I know what you've chosen to tell me. Ever since we met it's been me doing all the talking. I feel like a fool, a silly, chatty girl, and I'm afraid you're going to tell me something horrible!"

Marci picked up his packet of Winterbournes from the table and lit one, pleasantly unconcerned what Erin might think. "I've told you plenty. Maybe you haven't been listening."

"Oh, what rubbish! Marci, I hardly know anything about you! You're like a puzzle. Maybe I'm a bit too talkative and maybe I ask too many questions, but it's because I want to know all about you. Isn't that what normal people do, tell each other the truth? Remember that we promised no more secrets?"

Marci watched her as if removed from himself. She suddenly seemed quite pathetic. Angry and frustrated and immature, but also tragic, because through no fault of her own she'd fallen for someone who could add nothing to her life. Soon she would know the truth, and he would lose her, and that was all right. Everything was all right, damn the pill. He felt a stab in his stomach, the pain of an ugly emotion: pity.

He didn't know why he asked the question. He already knew it. It was the one that had overshadowed their whole relationship.

"What do you want to know?"

Erin sighed, the sound of expired patience. "I want to know what you do for a living. It's not too much to ask, is it? Then we can spend a nice evening together, and I promise I'll never mention it again."

Marci finished off the whiskey. The Candormax had finally reached its full efficacy. When he spoke, it was in a brittle, spiteful voice, as if this was his moment of revenge against her and everyone else who'd ever tried to bully, nag or cajole him into revealing his occupation. "Fine," he said. "Just remember, you asked for this. I'm Márton Kovács, Adjudicant Level 3."

Erin sat back and raised her hand to her mouth. In the light of the Living Wall her eyes seemed to well immediately, as if she already knew the truth at some subconscious level and had been waiting for the word that confirmed it.

Adjudicant.

In that same light, Marci watched her tears spill onto cheeks from which all color had drained. She looked, he thought, as fragile and as beautiful as a china doll. In spite of the drug, he instantly regretted his decision.

"You're an Adjudicant," Erin whispered. "That explains your SIN."

"I'm sorry I couldn't tell you before. It's against protocol."

"Protocol," she repeated to herself.

"Please don't be angry with me," he said, touching her knee. I can't tell anyone. It's the rules."

She flinched as if shocked by static. "Get off me! I don't want your—your murderous hands on me!"

"Murder?" Marci's mouth sagged. "Is that what you think I do?"

"What else would you call it? You send people to their deaths. You're no better than a Hangman!"

"I'm not a Hangman. I've never killed anyone!"

Erin went to the window to stand with her back to him. "No, you're not a Hangman. You're worse. A Hangman follows orders. You give the orders."

He followed her across the room with difficulty. "That's not true. MARTHA gives the orders. I make sure her decisions are fair."

"You choose who lives and who dies. How is that fair?"

"I spare just as many as I—"

"Exterminate? You must be very proud of yourself."

"—as I refer to the Justice Board." It was a lie; Marci's kill-pardon ratio was slightly below the median.

"I suppose you like playing God with people's lives. Does it give you a sense of power?

"It's not like that, I swear." He tried to embrace her but she shrank back in loathing. "Get away from me! I don't want your filthy, murderous hands on me, you—you Monster!"

Marci flinched; it was a sobriquet children used when describing the Hangman. If anything, it carried more sting than the adult pejorative. "I'm not a Monster. You know me better than that."

She was crying in earnest now. "Why didn't you tell me this at the beginning?"

It was a stupid question, and it deserved a tart reply, which he avoided making. "I was afraid of how you'd react."

She removed a tissue from her sleeve and wiped her eyes, smearing mascara across her cheek. "Yes, and with good reason. You lied to me. You made me think you're a good man. I was falling in love with you. But how can I love an Adjudicant?"

Feebly he said, "I didn't lie; I just didn't tell you. It's not the same thing."

"You've played a horrid game on me ever since we met. You knew I'd never go out with you if I thought you were a Hangman."

"I'm not a Monster and I'm not a bloody Hangman!" he yelled. "Is that what you learned at your stupid club?"

Erin cowered. "Don't shout at me."

Marci went to embrace her, but she shrugged him off and strode across the room.

"Where are you going?"

"Home."

"Please don't go. Can't we even talk about this?"

Erin's voice took on a businesslike tone. "We've had our time for talking—months of it—but you never told me what you did. If you had, I'd never have fallen in love with you."

Marci staggered behind her to the hallway. "Please, try to understand. I'm not supposed to tell anyone. I told you because I love you."

"You love me? You tell me that now? Why, Marci? Why, now it's too late?"

"Don't say that! It's not too late!"

Erin opened the front door. She wore that cold, aloof expression he'd seen the first time they'd met at Objet d'Heart. "It's over, Marci."

He reached out to stop her. "It's not over. I tell you, it's not!"

Erin's words rang with finality. "For me it is."

Outside, rain that couldn't be bothered to snow fell as sleet. In his narcosis she was already halfway toward the stairwell before he realized it, marching with that peculiar, jaunty gait that had once appealed to him as sassy but which was now ruthlessly intent.

Heedless of his neighbors, Marci shouted after her, "I love you!"

It was her turn not to look back.

11

It is Christmas.

Candles burn around the living room. The scent of pine needles and spiced cake fills the house. A Christmas tree, festooned with tinsel and fairy lights, occupies a corner, guarding presents wrapped in red, silver, and gold paper and tied with ribbons and bows. A carol crackles on the gramophone: "The First Noel". Outside, snowflakes drift silently, incessantly, past orange streetlights. It is the eve of St Nicholas'' Day, when good Hungarian children wait for Szent Miklós to visit with gifts. Red socks hang in anticipation above the fireplace.

Two children sit beside the tree. The boy, in his late teens, plays with an old cube puzzle made of many-colored squares. Beside him, a girl of five with long, chestnut hair grooms a plastic doll with a miniature hairbrush. On a nearby sofa their father reads a newspaper and smokes his pipe.

The doorbell rings. The girl looks at her brother, then to her father, but neither hear the sound and neither stir. Doll in hand she walks to the hallway, passing the kitchen where her mother prepares dinner. She hums a tune that is not known, a sound of haunting beauty.

The door is locked. The girl turns the key and reaches for the handle. She hesitates, looking back toward the lounge. Something is not right. She ignores the feeling and tugs at the door, which swings open.

Standing on the walkway are three men. From their visored helmets to their jackboots, they are dressed in raven black. Each wears an insignia on their chests: weighing scales and the initials J.C.B.—the Justice and Cessation Board. Behind them, the sky is a pool of livid flames that swirl and distort as if encased in curved glass. They are not the flames of an earthly fire. This is the fire of hell.

The man in the middle raises his visor and looks down at the girl. It is Marci.

He came to, roused by his own hoarse yelp. He was lying on his side, and across his bedroom the wan light of dawn was picking shapes out of the darkness. In the dimness he fumbled in his bedside locker for a bottle of Kqalms. When he sat up, his damp bedsheet clung to his skin. He peeled it off, wrapped himself in a dry blanket and wandered into the lounge.

"Alice, make coffee."

The living room smelled of violets and jasmine. Marci sat on the sofa where, hours before, Erin had listened to him make his confession. It had, he thought, been a disaster beyond imagining. He had relied on two presumptions: Erin's feelings for him, and a modicum of charity on her part. He'd overestimated both.

She was wrong about one thing: he was no Hangman. Judge and jury, yes—and a good one at that. In seven years of adjudication, he'd never sent anyone to an unjust death. Unlike Erin, forty million Employees trusted him with their lives. His conscience was clear—so he told himself. But it meant nothing. The only person whose good opinion of him mattered thought him a Monster.

Erin, dear Erin! Was she also awake, thinking of him? More than likely she was fast asleep. It was how women were. She'd reached her decision based on emotion and had settled the matter once and for all. Would things be different if he'd made Club 30? No, but the logic was false. If he were a Patrician he wouldn't be an Adjudicant, and the matter would be moot. His past was less flexible.

Marci reached for his cigarettes. On the coffee table lay a metallic business card. It read:

Stella Kennedy, PhD, Psychocerebral Therapist

Sándor had been complimentary about the woman. He had also been insistent. If she could help him make Club 30, everything else would follow. His resignation as an Adjudicant would be seen as an act of repentance and might conceivably sway Erin's opinion of him. If she loved him, it might win her back. And if not? His ascension to The Society would be something to rub in her face.

Marci lit his cigarette. The Kqalms was taking effect. He had a plan. He would proceed as before.

Hope dies last.

*   *   *

Balázs and Edit Vamosi lived in a squalid, damp apartment that smelled of boiled cabbage and stole electricity from a tangled web of power lines that hung above their walkway.

Balázs was retired. For the last forty-four years he'd worked for the Water Board as an Engineer Level 1, scraping together a living for his wife, daughter and himself. Since his pension was all but token, Balázs peddled mobile phone accessories from a booth in Eden One.

Edit, an impractical woman lacking common sense and people skills, sold bread at the local *pékség*. Their marriage had weathered thirty-nine loveless years of poverty, but for Edit it was expedient. Since she earned even less than Balázs, the union ensured her basic needs were met. Balázs gained less, but was philosophical about the arrangement.

Alex had, by now, conducted several interviews in Eden, and was becoming more familiar with the complex's baffling layout, although he still relied on his HUD glasses. Arriving at the sixteenth floor of Eden Four that afternoon, he'd steeled himself for a frosty reception from the Vamosis, whose notes he'd read in advance. In this he was not disappointed. The couple were even less welcoming than sad Viktor Romanov, and Alex was forced to take a more officious tone to gain access to their flat. At last he was led through a malodorous kitchen to the living room and instructed to sit in an armchair that smelled of wet dog.

Balázs and Edit, neglecting the courtesy of refreshments, sat on the sofa opposite him. This suited Alex; the kitchen suggested hygienic carelessness.

"Thank you again for your time," Alex began. "As I mentioned, this is an informal inquiry regarding an interview you took part in fifteen years ago at the Justice Board. Our discussion will hopefully clear up some inconsistencies in the Executive Team database. Rest assured that everything you tell me will be treated with the strictest confidence, and your SIN will not be affected."

Alex waited for a response. Edit stared blankly at him. Balázs adjusted his trousers at the crotch. Alex realized he'd not put a question to them. "Please, in your own words, tell me what transpired at Nyugati."

Balázs shrugged. "They asked many things. We were there for eight hours. I lost a day's wages because of it. Why are you here?"

"I'm trying to establish why they called you in," Alex explained. "We have no record of the event because the files were lost."

"That's very careless," Balázs said. "Very careless indeed."

"I agree. Fortunately, the mistake was not mine, and my SIN is safe."

"I imagine you feel very relieved," Balázs said without sympathy. "If only everyone's was so resilient, eh Edit?"

Edit watched Alex as she might a fly trapped in a spider's web.

"Edit agrees with me," Balázs said. "Her SIN is borderline. She stays alive only because she's an Informant."

Alex felt his stomach twitch; somehow he'd overlooked this in her file. "Informants are a vital part of the Company," he said with forced nonchalance. "We couldn't function without them. But back to my question: what was the purpose of the interview?"

Balázs shrugged. "They wanted to know about our daughter. They asked a lot of stupid questions. I told them that if I knew where she was, I'd have given her a damn good hiding. Edit's been driven spare with worry, and I've not done much better."

"Your daughter is Judit, yes? What happened to her?"

"She disappeared."

Alex waited. "And?"

"There's not much to say. Judit lived with us. She was twenty-three when she disappeared. She didn't earn much, but the money helped us pay the bills. One evening she didn't come home. I called the club where she worked. They said she hadn't shown up. I called her mobile. I suppose it was switched off. That's all we know."

"And you haven't heard from her since?"

"No. I called the police. I even went to the police station in Eden One. They said it was too early to file a missing person report, and that I should come back in a week. When we tried calling her again, her phone had been disconnected. I went to the club one night and got the numbers of her friends. Two were disconnected. The others worked, but nobody knew where Judit had gone."

"It must have been very distressing for you," Alex said. "Were there any clues where she might have gone?"

"Edit's not as daft as she looks. She played detective and found some of Judit's clothes were missing, along with make-up and some photos from her mirror."

"Perhaps Judit had planned to leave?"

"It would appear so."

"And you have no idea where she went?"

"Like I said, if I knew, she wouldn't be missing."

Edit rose and shuffled into the kitchen.

Alex stood up. "Thank you for your time. You've been very helpful."

Balázs remained seated. "Will we get any SIN points for this?"

"I'm afraid not. My visit is off-the-record. In any case, I don't have jurisdiction to recommend them."

"Too bad," Balázs grunted. "I haven't checked my slope in months. I imagine it's not good."

"There are many ways to boost SIN," Alex advised. "Your local booth can provide advice on how to do this."

"My days of chasing slope are over," Balázs said. "Soon the black van will arrive, and Edit will become a widow. Or maybe she'll go first. Either way, it doesn't matter." He inclined his head to the hallway. "Please see yourself out."

Alex hesitated. "One last matter: since this is an unofficial investigation, the Executive Team would appreciate it if your wife refrained from reporting my visit to the Justice Board."

Balázs's brow furrowed. "And why would that be?"

Alex licked his lips. "The case concerns Executive Team data management errors which would cause us considerable embarrassment if leaked to another agency. I'm sure you understand."

"Still," Balázs said, "it's a shame we can't sweeten the arrangement with some SIN. It would make Edit a happy woman."

Alex doubted that. "Very well. I'll have words with the relevant people."

Balázs appeared satisfied. "Is that all?"

Alex filed his paperwork, got up and bade him goodbye; the offer of a handshake would probably be declined. Holding his breath against the smell, he hurried through the kitchen and made his way back to the metro at Eden One.

*   *   *

An Adjudicant's suite, or cubicle, as it was more aptly described, was a darkened, soundproof cube ten feet deep, ten high and ten across. Six recessed ceiling fixtures provided token lighting, since most of the room's illumination came from a battery of monitors which curved around the Adjudicant's chair like spectators staring into a Roman *odeon*.

If the layout placed the Adjudicant in the limelight, the effect was misleading. At the swipe of a virtual slider he could access any one of the million surveillance cameras that watched the comings and goings of Budapest's beleaguered Employees. Cell phone transmissions, credit card transaction data and second skin tracked those who strayed beyond the range of all-seeing video eye. These, rather, were the stars of the show. It was a resource terrifying in its scope and power, and yet it remained for the Adjudicant largely unused. Data was his lifeblood and history his *modus operandi*. For these he turned not to live feeds but to MARTHA, whose subterranean memory banks stored the minutiae of forty million lives. Here, at the speed of light, the present added to the past to form the Employee's lifeline. A separate algorithm prognosticated life choices days, months and even years ahead.

Although Adjudicants were forbidden to base their decisions on an Employee's latent behavior, they were, inevitably, influenced by MARTHA's probability models. At the core of these was the predictive interval, a measure of an Employee's behavioral deviation from her projection. A narrow interval was good; said Employee was acting out his life as expected. Fluctuations within reasonable limits were acceptable; MARTHA had already factored these into her computations on a case-by-case basis.

A larger deviation from the norm would broaden the interval. Theoretically, this should exert no influence on an Employee's SIN. In reality, it did. MARTHA, who didn't like surprises, regarded anomalous behavior as a threat to the stable functioning of society, and revised SIN forecasts accordingly. Thus, the predictive interval served as the proverbial canary in a coal mine for anyone who cared to look.

One such person was Marci Kovács, who continued to build the sham case he hoped would persuade Data Analytics to release Alex's predictive interval. After three weeks of fabricating the inquiry, he submitted the request.

The reply came within the hour. Marci apprehensively clicked on the email's attachment, which opened to reveal the profiles of fourteen Employees: four money launderers; three embezzlers; two suspected Undergrounders; an Informant turned blackmailer; a SIN tout; and a couple of arsonists for good measure. All blue-collar stuff, apart from the pyromaniacs. Alex Pimenov, Adjudicant Level 2 and alleged political dissenter, completed the file. It was a motley and degenerate bunch who undoubtedly deserved a visit from some black-clad, visored gentlemen—all except Alex, Marci hoped. He printed out the documents and placed Alex's profile in his briefcase. The other records he shredded; they had served their purpose.

Marci resumed his casework. In the weeks following Erin's departure he'd adopted a new approach to work. She'd described him as a Monster. It was a childish insult, probably the harshest word she'd ever used—why did she never swear?—and one that, out of sheer perversity, Marci decided to embrace. His judgments remained fair, but where once he might have exercised leniency or compassion, now there was none. The soft-hearted Marci was gone. He was cruel, heartless Márton Kovács, the vicious taker of life! Yes, let him be everything she thought he was. Worse than a Hangman: an Adjudicant!

At 17:00 he logged off and emerged from the Executive Team building into a bitter wind laced with rain. For once he'd timed his departure perfectly. 20E, engulfed in its own diesel cloud, pulled up in front of him as he reached the curb. Inside it was warm and half empty, and his favorite seat was free. Marci made a window in the condensation with his coat sleeve and stared sadly out.

This was, by his reckoning, the nadir of his life. Erin had gone, and her leaving had broken him more thoroughly than he could have imagined. His outlook on life, which might at best be described as optimistically misanthropic, was now so bleak that the only thing keeping him from a Rapture pill was the note he kept in his wallet. On it were three bullet points: join The Society, quit job, get Erin back. The same, writ large, occupied the front of his fridge.

The plan did nothing to appease his OCD, which had returned with full force. Incessant handwashing left his fingers so dry that he could barely flex them. Ordering obsessions devoured his time. He slept poorly, barely ate, and was hitting the bottle more often. With no friends beyond the circle of *We Happy Few*, Marci buried himself in his work and in rewriting his speech, but neither helped fill the void. In dismay he saw his future for what it was. He would live and end his days lonely, afraid and unwanted. No amount of money, SIN, antiques, or even a life in Empyrean, would compensate him for his unhappy solitude.

Marci alighted at Keleti and was heading for the underpass when his phone rang. He snatched it from his coat, hoping the image on the screen might belong to a certain brunette with a mouth that wilted at the corners. But the face was Alex's, and so was the voice.

"It's me. Are you doing anything?"

"No. Any news?"

"Lots, and none of it good. I'm leaving Eden now. Can we talk in person? I think I'm getting a little paranoid."

"Sure. By the way, I've got news for you too."

"Go on."

"Not over the phone."

"Can you come to mine?" Alex asked.

"I'll be there in twenty minutes."

Marci took a cab to District IX and was buzzed into the building.

"Lei and the kids are out," Alex explained. "It's my mother-in-law's birthday."

"You're not going?"

"Are you crazy? I'm married now; I don't need to earn her blessing anymore. Drink?"

"Bourbon?"

Alex checked the cupboard. "Half a bottle."

Marci went into the lounge. "I'll have a double."

Alex followed with tumblers. "No ice?"

Marci downed the liquor in one go. He held out his glass. "It's a distraction."

Alex poured another shot. "Don't let her drive you to drink."

"I don't need driving. Besides, it helps me to liquidate people without compunction."

"If only I lacked your indifference. This morning I had a welfare case. An eight-year-old girl lost both her parents in a car crash. No siblings, no grandparents. The district care home is full, and the kid had an IQ of 76. Obviously, her SIN forecast was dire. MARTHA recommended liquidation. I tried overruling her on compassionate grounds, but she vetoed me."

"Tragic," Marci. swirled the whiskey around his glass. "Speaking of liquidations, what's your news from Eden?"

Alex disappeared into the bathroom and returned with a folder.

Marci raised an eyebrow. "Spy games?"

"Lei's been on at me to fix the tiling for ages. Good job I put it off. Take a look."

"I'd prefer a summary."

"Fine. The good news is that a trend's emerging. The bad news is it points to more mysteries. I've quizzed eighteen relatives of the eighty-three who croaked and it's the same story: they all had sons, daughters, brothers or sisters, or significant others who vanished into thin air. No calls. No postcards. Radio silence. All the families reported them missing. The cops replied with two letters, one to confirm the cases had been opened and another six months later saying they'd closed them for lack of evidence."

"Odd, but not surprising for Budapest police," Marci reflected. "Go on."

"It gets odder. I checked their lifelines, all six hundred and twelve of them. When I say they disappeared, that's literally what happened. They vanished just from MARTHA's tracking system. Second skin, CCTV, biometrics, the lot."

Marci frowned. "That's impossible. Second skin's programmed to send MARTHA our coordinates at the moment of death. There's no circumventing it."

"Agreed. But she never got them."

"How many were Edenites?"

"Fifty-four percent. And despite what the mafia claims, MARTHA still maintains some functionality there, including CCTV feeds. Mainly because the cameras are welded into the walls."

"Informants?"

"Proportionally more than in Budapest. I hear their life expectancy in Eden isn't sensational."

"There is a God."

"Quite. In summary then, we'd know if they died there."

"That leaves 281 Employees whose second skin was working well and who still pulled a magic trick." Marci's eyes narrowed. "Wait a minute, how can you know about their lifelines without access to MARTHA? You're not hacking her from home, are you?"

Alex grunted. "I'm not that stupid. Remember my backup? I downloaded their records from Data Analytics before IT. blocked me. The rest I got from the Eden Police Department's mainframe."

"Don't tell me: protection racket spreadsheets and donut tabs?"

"That comes next week. What I did learn was that the Exec Team took on all the missing person cases, not just those from Eden. Given the fact that E.T. and the Justice Board are more concerned about reducing the population, it's strange they should launch an investigation in the first place."

"Agreed. Why open a can of worms when it's doing your job for you?"

"Get this: Eden P.D. then asks both departments to send everything they have on the Edenite vanishings. E.T. agrees, and transfers the complete, unredacted profiles of all the missing persons."

Marci sat up. "They can't do that. It's a breach of data privacy."

"They can and they did. So I checked the second skin broadcasts. The transmissions ended throughout the capital, but the majority in eastern Budapest."

"I don't get it. What's so important to E.T. about six hundred missing people?"

"You're asking the wrong question. The million-credit question is: where did they go?"

"It's kind of the same." said Marci.

"Kind of, but not quite. I have a theory, if you're interested."

"Are you asking permission?"

"It's a little crazy," Alex said. "I'm embarrassed to say it out loud."

"Don't let that stop you. You can't lower my opinion of you any further."

"They could leave Budapest."

"That's crazy."

"I warned you," said Alex.

"Even for you."

"I kept drawing a blank until I reread my notes. Some of the left-behinders told me their loved ones mentioned the Outside before they vanished." Alex unfolded a spreadsheet and slid it over the table. "I made a chart." It sounded like an apology.

Marci gave it cursory attention. "It's just as hard for us to reach the Outside as it is for them to get in. They must still be in Budapest."

"Okay, but where?"

"Some kind of seclusion, below MARTHA's radar."

"The Underground?"

Marci lit a cigarette. "I thought you didn't believe in them?"

"I thought you didn't."

"So where does this lead us?"

"Nowhere new. Six hundred Employees fall off the face of the earth and the Company hasn't a clue where they went. Then they liquidate anyone who might have the answer."

"Thirteen percent," Marci reminded him.

"Which brings us here." Alex tossed the folder on the table. "I wish I'd never known."

"I wish you'd never told me."

"It's not enough to prove murder, and I doubt it counts as genocide. But Kruger's and Morrison's emails make them complicit in whatever happened."

"I need another drink." Marci refilled his glass. "What will you do?"

"More of the same. If I interview sixty relatives, that's 10% of the original interviewees. That's if they're all still alive; fifteen years is a long time. Now let's talk about something else."

"Your predictive interval."

"I was thinking more of you. I'm worried about you, Marci. You've been hitting the bottle pretty hard the last few weeks. Is this about Erin?"

Marci raised his tumbler in an alcoholic's salute. "Whoozh Erin?"

Alex tutted. "The first sign is denial."

"Give me a break. Erin's left me, the OCD's crippling and none of my meds are working. I'm having a few drinks. What's wrong with that?"

Alex held up his hands in appeasement. "I'm not judging you. I'm just worried, as a friend."

"I'm fine. Really." He took Alex's profile from his briefcase. "Anyway, while you've been mooching around Budapest drinking lattes, I've been risking my life getting you your predictive interval."

"At long last."

"All bad things come to those who wait." Marci winced at the witticism; given his findings, it wasn't the wisest quip. "The good news is your SIN hasn't changed: you're still a respectable 24."

"I know. I checked it this morning."

Marci shifted uncomfortably. "I'm not sure how to tell you this. Your predictive interval's changed. It's increased to 16%."

"Sixteen?" Alex snatched the file and began turning pages. On the last but one his predictive interval, represented as a graph, flared like the muzzle of a blunderbuss.

"I cross-checked the dates," Marci said. "It was 2% the day before you went to carrot-top with your anomalies. It jumped a couple of percent when you handed over your MARTHA model. From there it's steadily widened."

Alex stared at the page, dumbfounded. "It has to be an error. I'd just been promoted. How can I gain SIN and have my interval widen at the same time?"

"Then there's this." Marci reached over and showed Alex the penultimate page, the page he wished his friend had discovered for himself. "It seems there's a flag on your profile."

"A flag? What type of flag?"

Marci hesitated. "Alex, it's from the Justice Board. They put a risk marker on you. It's been active for the last few weeks."

Alex read the summary in silence, the blood draining from his face. "This can't be real."

"That's what I thought, so I called Justice and Cessation. In their words, they don't make mistakes."

Alex checked the graph's x-axis again and looked like he was going to be sick. "The flag was added the day I accessed Morrison and Kruger's emails. My God, Marci, they knew! They've been watching me all the time!"

"Relax. There's nothing to suggest it's active surveillance. They probably put it there to scare you off your crusade."

Why would they put a marker in a document they know I can't access?"

"I guess they knew someone else would get your profile for you."

"So they know about you."

"Of course. I requested it."

"May I have one?"

Marci tossed him his cigarettes.

Alex paced the lounge. "Six months it took me to create that model of MARTHA, six months and almost five hundred of my own credits. And for what? A P.I. of sixteen and a security marker? My

MARTHA model was meant to benefit the Company, not harm it. Lei and I, we've brought the kids up to love the Company. Lucinda and Huang are at the top of their citizenship classes. Why put a marker on me? It's not fair!"

"I know. No one loves the Company more than you guys." It was a lie; Réka and Takumi next door were Company zealots.

Alex waved his cigarette wildly. "A marker, like I'm some kind of criminal. What am I going to tell Lei?" He turned to Marci in horror. "My slope! Oh my God, think about how it's going to affect my SIN. I'll never make Club 30 now!"

"Calm down. We both know how predictive intervals work. Sometimes they widen, sometimes they contract. Give it a couple of months and it'll be back to normal. The same goes for the flag."

"That's rot, Marci, and you know it! Whatever good I do in the future this will always be on my lifeline, and you know it."

"Alex, it's temporary. Once it's erased you'll begin to make slope again. Alex, listen to me: I broke every rule in the book to get you this paperwork, and I'm still going to be elected to The Society."

"Yeah, unless they've flagged you too, in which case you can kiss Club 30 goodbye." Alex cringed at the gaffe. "Sorry, I didn't mean that. I'm sure you'll still make it." Then: "They wouldn't dare, would they?"

Marci shrugged as if to say, "I hope not." It hadn't occurred to him until now. "Alex, sit down. You're giving me neck ache."

Alex sat on the sofa and ran one hand across his five o'clock shadow. "What do I do now?"

Marci topped up their tumblers. "Think about it from the Company's perspective. You're a SIN 24 Adjudicant, a good one at that, who did a bit of hacking on the side and dug up something the corporation's been keeping under wraps. You've widened your interval and earned yourself a security flag. Neither are permanent; your future's just as open to you as it was before you found the anomalies. But this is where you need to draw a line. No more hacking, and no more investigations."

"So, you're saying I'm not at risk?"

"Yes," Marci said. "That's what I'm saying."

"And my career's still open?"

"You've as good a chance at SIN 33 as me. Talent excepted." He held out his glass. "A toast: to a quiet life."

"There's one last thing I need to do."

Marci looked heavenwards. "Oh, please."

"It's only an errand. Something I want to put right."

"Whatever it is, be done with it, and soon. And no more detective work. Agreed?"

Alex raised his glass. "Agreed. To a quiet life and high SIN."

Marci rose, draining his glass. "Speaking of which, I need to go. My nomination speech won't write itself. Every time I read it I want to rip it to pieces."

"If it's half as good as your pep talk," Alex said, "you'll wing it." At the door he said: "You never told me exactly what happened with Erin."

Marci shrugged. "There's not much to say. I went with her to her political club. It was a bloody circus show, scandalmongers and conspiracy theorists the lot of them. The worst part was that she actually defended them. Afterwards we went home. I took a Candormax and told her I'm an Adjudicant. She burst into tears, called me a Monster and walked out."

"I'm sorry. I know how much she meant to you."

"She wasn't exactly a model of discretion. That's a dangerous person for an Adjudicant to fall in love with."

"It's an occupational hazard," Alex said. "I was lucky with Lei."

"Luckier than you deserve."

"Women are funny creatures," Alex reflected. "Sometimes they just need to process things. Give Erin some space. Let her think the relationship over. She might change her mind."

Marci slipped on his jacket and felt the weight of his wallet in the breast pocket. Inside was his bullet-pointed master plan. It suddenly struck him as a pipe dream and a hypocrisy at the same time. "I doubt it. I stand for everything she hates. I'm conservative and predictable, a Company man. She's an artist, a free spirit, maybe a dissenter. No, she won't be back. And I won't chase her." He managed a smile for Alex's sake. "Don't look so worried. I'm doing ok."

"You're a terrible liar."

"That's what she said. If I really cared for her I'd be happy she's gone. She deserves better. A lot better."

The kitchen light dimmed, then failed.

Alex checked his mobile. "AirNet's at one bar. Must have been a lightning strike somewhere."

"My cue to leave."

In the courtyard, the wind had picked out trash from the communal bins and was busy sending it scurrying back and forth in a futile game of shuttle run. Thunder rumbled in the far distance, perhaps over Budaörs.

"Perfect weather for Undergrounders," Marci joked.

"I'll believe in pretty much anything now." Alex extended his hand. "Thank you, Marci. I owe you everything."

"I agree. Now give up your hunt for justice. We have to think of ourselves. And our families."

"Message received. And Marci—don't let her change you. You're worth more than that."

"Easier said than done."

12

Marci ordered an air cab and in due course disembarked outside his apartment on Gyulai Pál utca.

The elevator was busy. Taking the stairs, he arrived at the third floor sweating and out of breath to find the walkway blocked. Between him and his apartment a mob had gathered, intent on a commotion unfolding at the end of the passage. The group, he noticed, comprised neighbors not only from his floor but every other, who with loud cries were remonstrating whatever was occurring ahead.

Marci sidled through the crowd to his apartment and had almost reached the door when a single, shrill scream pierced the clamor. The voice was familiar: Satomi Nagy.

He pushed his way to the front and was confronted with his own reflection framed within the clam-shaped visor of a cessation officer. Body armor that accentuated natural human musculature lent the man an appearance of superhuman brawn. Beside him stood a colleague. Both barred Marci's way.

Marci peered between them to a scene of horror. Takumi Nagy, bent double, stood in his pajamas, dressing gown and slippers. His hands were cuffed behind his back and his spectacles lay at his feet, broken.

Pinned against a wall by two more officers and dressed only in her nightgown was Réka. One of the Hangmen pressed a truncheon against her throat; the other held a medi-pen ready. Desperate to reach her children, she railed violently against the men with inarticulate, choking sobs.

In their apartment doorway, Satomi and Noémi Nagy clung to one another, wailing inconsolably. They were kept from their parents by a female officer, who restrained both children in headlocks. Cuffed to the walkway railing, Akira looked on, helpless and pathetic.

Marci called out: "Takumi! What's happening?"

Takumi tried to look sideways. "Marci? Is that you? Help us, please! There's been a terrible mistake. We've done nothing wrong!"

Marci considered the Hangman in front of him. Apart from the Nagy family, none of his neighbors knew he was an Adjudicant. To disclose his position publicly would not only breach protocol—a small consideration at this point—but would endanger himself. Instead, he felt inside his jacket pocket, hoping to discreetly show his Adjudicant badge.

With savage speed the officer grabbed his wrist, at the same time reaching for his gun. A voice disguised by filters issued from his suit: "Keep your hands where I can see them, Employee."

"I'm getting my ID," Marci stammered.

The officer twisted Marci's hand to one side. "I said, take your hand out of your jacket."

Marci cried in pain. "Let me go, damn you! Do you know who I am? These people are innocent!"

"I don't care who you are, sir. If you reach for anything again, you'll be sorry."

Marci wrenched himself free. From the direction of Rákoczi Út came the sound of sirens: backup was arriving. Satomi, Akira and Noémi Nagy were herded inside the apartment and the door shut. Réka, now cuffed, was frog-marched down the corridor, shrieking for her children at the top of her lungs, with Takumi following quietly behind her.

A minute elapsed. The crowd milled uncertainly.

The front door opened. Noémi, Akira and Satomi, drugged and bound, were carried out. Outraged by the sight, the mob surged forward, pushing Marci into the officer, who in turn shoved him to the ground. Marci picked himself up, turned and fought his way back to the stairs, speed dialing a number on his phone.

"Justice and Cessation Board."

"Kovács Márton, Adjudicant Level 3. Put me through to Mike Blacklock."

"Please hold."

Marci reached the ground floor and burst onto Gyulai Pál utca. A single air cab, its lights turned off, sat on a landing pad. "Executive Team building, Dózsa György út," he said, climbing inside.

"I'm off duty," the driver said, turning a page in his e-paper. "Air Traffic Control's grounded everything."

Marci placed his badge in front of the man. "State emergency. Let's go. Now!"

"I'm sorry, Adjudicant, but rules are rules. I could lose my license."

Marci noted the driver's registration document on the dashboard. He pressed twenty credits into his hand. "You'll lose more than your license if we don't get going, Zoltán. Now move it."

Zoltán stared at the money, which was easily a day's wages. "I should really radio my controller," he mumbled.

Marci handed him another ten.

Zoltán muttered something, pocketed the money and engaged the craft's engines.

A voice through the phone: "Blacklock here."

"Mike, it's Marci Kovács… Yes, yes, just listen. A cessation squad just picked up my neighbors and their kids. The parents are Takumi and Réka Nagy. I don't know their Employee IDs. I need you to cancel the order."

A pause. Then: "Márton, it's MARTHA who decides liquidations, not us. I can't overturn a cessation order."

"Mike, I know them personally. Their SIN is above threshold. The cessation order's wrong."

"Are you saying MARTHA's at fault or that your department's screwed up? Because either way, I can't help you. You need to speak to—"

Marci hung up and dialed Fraser Morrison's office number, which diverted to voicemail, then his cell phone, which after several rings was rejected by the user.

Marci noticed City Park pass beneath them a second time. "Why are we circling?" he asked the driver.

"ATC. We're in a holding pattern."

Marci grabbed a handrail as the craft hit turbulence. What now? The Nagy family would already be in transit to Nyugati. It was ten minutes away by van, faster if the transport was using its sirens. Marci thought of diverting the taxi there, but to call in person would be just as gainless as his conversation with Blacklock. His only chance of saving the Nagy family lay with MARTHA herself.

For three awful minutes the taxi circled the high-rise towers of downtown, buffeted by storm winds and pelted with rain, until finally ATC approved their descent. The craft swooped low, skimmed one last time over City Park and touched down before the Executive Team building.

The duty guard stopped him. "Good evening, Mr. Kovács."

"Evening, Hans. I need to get through quickly."

"Sorry, Mr. Kovács. If you'll just hop into the chamber. It's the rules."

Cursing with frustration, Marci entered the security vault, held his breath and waited for the door to seal him in. From the ceiling came the sound of gagged suction, like an obstructed vacuum cleaner hose. Marci's ear popped. Seconds later, the air pressure returned and the far door opened.

At the lift, a matrix display showed the location of the car as floor 10: Records. Who the hell was in Records at 21:00? He pressed the call button, but the car remained stationary.

Cursing, Marci turned to the stairs—a daunting prospect. In his condition, it would take at least six minutes of non-stop climbing to reach the Adjudication floor.

There was no help for it. Skipping steps, he was halfway up the first flight when he heard the lift chime. The numbers on the screen had started to fall.

Marci returned to the lobby and began to pace. By now, the Nagys would have reached Justice Board HQ. Liquidation processing times varied. On a good night, Cessation could dispatch an Employee within fifteen minutes. Since workplace removals were bad for morale, Justice favored residential visits. Weekends were busiest. Weeknights were quieter, which meant that Takumi, Réka and the kids might already be in a medical wing.

Finally, the car arrived. Marci stepped inside, and to the sound of nondescript jazz rode to floor eighteen.

The admin office lay silent. He ran to the Adjudication Suite, placed himself inside the floor's annular bioreader, waited for it to turn green, and finally entered his cubicle.

MARTHA brought her monitors to life. "Good evening, Adjudicant Kovács."

Marci said: "Employee profile of Takumi Nagy, Rákóczi út 29."

Takumi's profile appeared, complete with his SIN: a safe 21. Marci swiped to the following page, which displayed his neighbor's predictive interval. He leaned close. In the last month, it had expanded from a healthy 2% to a staggering forty-eight. A code accompanied the increase: PATR.

He dialed Alex, who from the background noise was bathing his kids. "Alex, I don't have much time. The Justice Board's picked up Takumi and Réka Nagy for liquidation. I'm looking at Takumi's profile. Does the code PATR mean anything to you?"

Alex spoke to Lei, then left the bathroom. "They took Takumi? I thought he was a copywriter with a big agency?"

"Yes, and SIN 21. I think the code's significant, but I've never seen it before."

"PATR? I've never heard of it. Should I come in?"

"There's no time. I'll call you later."

Marci opened Takumi's second skin data, which placed him alive and inside the Justice and Cessation headquarters at Nyugati.

"MARTHA, open CORE. Override cessation of Takumi Nagy and authorize release by executive order."

"Cessation procedure overridden."

"Profile request: Nagy, Réka, spouse, same address."

Réka's details now occupied the screen. Marci scanned the summary page. At the bottom was her SIN: 16.

"Override cessation for Réka Nagy by executive order."

MARTHA spoke without emotion. "Unable to comply. Employee is deceased."

The words hung in the air. Marci brought up her lifeline. A thirty-six year-long waveform represented Réka's existence. Running through the middle, rising and falling, was a threadlike red line, which represented those events in her life deemed significant to the Company. At 21:23:09, the waveform ceased. The lifeline fell to intersect the abscissa, and Réka Nagy was dead. Her second skin transmissions—three vital signs oscillations—had stopped ten seconds earlier. Both indices—lifeline and second skin—bore the hallmarks of death by intravenous Rapture shot. *Quick. Painless. Peaceful.* For Réka Nagy, however, there would have been no peace. Strapped to a gurney and fighting for the sake of her children, her life would have been taken from her by force.

The kids! Were they with Takumi, or had Justice handed them over to welfare? As preteens, their profiles were nascent and only accessible from their parent's profiles. Marci switched back to Takumi's file, and was about to open Satomi's subfolder when he suddenly ceased typing. A new entry had appeared below his neighbor's name:

EMPLOYEE DECEASED

For a single, sickening moment Marci stared at the words. A shiver, gathering in the center of his spine, spread down his back and along his arms, setting the hairs on end. In the command log, below his instruction to cancel Takumi's cessation, MARTHA had issued five fateful directives of her own:

21:22:56 Adjudicant cessation override command revoked
21:22:57 execute original cessation order for Nagy, Takumi 961DT127R558
21:23:16: cessation executed
21:23:17 execute cessation order for Nagy, Akira; Nagy, Satomi; Nagy, Noémi.
21:24:05 cessation executed

"No, God, no!" Marci leaped up and struck the console, sending his chair tumbling backward, then sank to his knees. It was over. In less than two minutes, the Nagy family was no more.

As if in a dream he returned to the lobby, walked out onto Dózsa György út and took the SpeedWalk to Palotanegyed, whose narrow streets thronged with evening revelers. Too numb to notice, Marci would remember nothing of his journey.

At home, he forgot his OCD and went straight for the Yamazaki. He filled a dirty tumbler from the sink to the brim, set the gramophone to play a Chopin nocturne and sat at one of the bay windows.

Marci raised his glass, staring at the amber liquid. Alex was right: he was becoming something of a drunk.

"Alice, lights out."

On Gyulai Pál utca a breeze had picked up, twisting the rain sidewards in the light of the streetlights. Marci sipped his whiskey, then swallowed the rest of it. He considered a Seromax, but felt rooted to the spot by grief. Tonight, there would be no drugs to ease his pain. Tonight he would cry for them, for Takumi and Réka, for Akira, Satomi and Noémi. It was the least they deserved.

Friday came, cold and overcast. Marci overslept and fought through a hangover to arrive at work late. In the office pool, Tony Jackson, back on form, greeted him with exaggerated cordiality. Marci walked straight past him to his cubicle without noticing. Tony, nettled, raised a hand in cheery farewell before slinking back to his desk.

Marci logged in and began to address his casework, aware of a strange and unwelcome emotion towards the computer: disgust. Her voice, so professional and impartial, now sounded indifferent, even callous, and the data she presented him with now lacked the unquestionable veracity it once had.

In a spirit of spiteful revenge, Marci decided to adopt a different approach to his work. Today, no one would die. Remedial programs, self-improvement classes, official warnings—these were the tools he used to thwart the system.

Late in the afternoon a message appeared in Marci's inbox. It was from Morrison, who with extreme brevity requested Marci's presence in his office as soon as convenient, if not sooner than convenient, on a matter of urgency.

Marci logged off, left the building and strolled toward the SpeedWalk, smiling to himself. Carrot-top must be having a duck egg over his casework rulings. Let the miserable git spend all evening trying to undo a Level 3 Adjudicant's work. There might be hell to pay tomorrow morning, but Morrison deserved to stew awhile.

Back at home, Norbert Tóth's shed emitted a warm glow and the jarring stutter of an impact wrench. Marci rode the lift to his floor, and with sadness noticed the dark windows of the Nagy residence. A sticker affixed to the door provided official notification of yesterday's events, as if it was needed. Aside from Tóth, no one else was abroad. The building was desolate, with every curtain drawn.

As he entered his flat the landline rang: Morrison. Marci let it go to voicemail, then played a queue of missed calls from him which differed only in their tone of urgency. With a choice vulgarity, Marci removed the phone cord from the wall, switched off his cell phone, undressed and took a shower.

A microwave dinner joined him in front of the Living Wall, which showed a tropical sandbar bathed in the dying light of day. A wooden rowing boat nuzzled the beach, nodding with the swell of the tide.

Marci ate without appetite. Takumi, SIN 21. Réka, SIN 16. Why would two model citizens be liquidated above threshold? Takumi's predictive interval had exploded but his SIN hadn't changed. The same was true of Réka's. It made no sense, but the answer might lie in the acronym. PATR. What did it mean? Marci knew MARTHA's shorthand by heart. This one wasn't even in the handbook.

Alex was right: the system was sham. In overturning Takumi's repeal, MARTHA had denied her own protocols and proved herself as culpable as Kruger, Morrison and anyone else massaging the numbers. Together with the anomalies and the elimination of the surviving relatives, it all pointed to the proverbial tip of an iceberg. How deep it went he didn't want to know.

Marci pushed his plate away and opened the file he'd brought home from work. The cover read:

PETROS GARAI
EMPLOYEE ID 712AV445T598

For the next twenty minutes, Marci flicked through fourteen pages of clean, tedious living made remarkable only by its vapidity. True to his word, Petros worked for architectural firm DeLane Westland. His SIN was 20. Good, but no big deal. He had no dependents, drew an average salary and evinced no political leanings—on paper, at least. His notes made no mention of Club Bohém, nor even regular visits to Café Primo. If he was a dissident, he'd done a fine job keeping it a secret.

At a little before seven, Marci caught the tram to Fővám tér. It was snowing, big, goose down flakes that see-sawed groundward in the still of the evening. At Sóház utca he stopped to light a cigarette, and in a mood of abject wretchedness watched the smoke convect away like a wraith in the frigid air. It wasn't too late to turn back. In fifteen minutes he could be soaking in a hot bath with a Seromax coursing through his veins.

Another force, more insistent, pulled him in a different direction. Images formed unwanted: Takumi bent double and imploring him for help; Réka frog-marched away, wailing for her children; Akira, Noémi and Satomi, their small, drugged bodies carried to a waiting van. Yes, he could turn back to lose himself in booze and medication, and perhaps for tonight these would suffice. But tomorrow would be no different, and what then? He needed answers. Petros Garai might not have them, but at least Marci could spend an hour or two among those who despised the Company as he now did. The thought gave him a surge of hope, and would have hastened his steps to Café Primo were it not for a single catch.

Oh God, please don't let her be there.

He turned the corner at Csarnok Tér. Approaching from the opposite direction was the very person whose presence he coveted and dreaded in equal measure: a slight figure in a red beret, red scarf and a dark overcoat. A cell phone, held in both hands, lit her face, which was pinched in concentration.

Marci froze. A pang of longing, so compelling it was visceral, overcame him. Had she seen him? Could he slip into the shadows unnoticed? After all, what right had he to impinge himself on her presence?

Erin, perhaps sensing him, looked up and faltered for the briefest of moments. She stopped a safe ten feet away: too far to signal intimacy, far enough away to flee from a Monster. She was, Marci thought, even more beautiful than he remembered. He felt suddenly old.

"I... I was going to Club Bohém," he explained.

Erin nodded and looked away. "How have you been?"

"Not the best. They took Takumi and Réka," he blurted. "They even took the kids. I checked their SIN. They were way above cut-off. I—I tried to save them, but it was too late." His voice became ragged. "You were right all along."

"Right about what?"

Marci fumbled in his pocket for the handkerchief he never carried. Why did only women and old men carry tissues? "About the Company," he said. "I…I was too close. I couldn't see it. And you were right about me. I'm a Monster."

"Oh, Marci"—she reached out, then checked herself—"you're not a Monster. I should never have said those awful things."

"Can you… can you forgive me?"

"Forgive you for what?"

"For who I am. For what I do."

She took his hands. "You're freezing. Will you come inside?"

Marci lowered his head and wept.

"Come inside," Erin soothed. "We can sit in a corner of the café. You don't have to go into Club Bohém if you don't want to."

"Please," he insisted, "will you forgive me?"

Erin took a tissue from her sleeve and wiped both their eyes. "It's not me who needs to do the forgiving. You're not a Monster. You're a good man." She stepped close and hugged him. "And yes, I forgive you. I love you."

I love you. Three words. Enough to change a man. Enough to save him.

His breath came in ragged gasps. "No one's… ever told me… that before."

He held her close, his face nuzzled in her hair, until his vision became bright behind his closed eyes and he wondered if he was dying from joy or whether this was what falling in love was like and why no one had ever told him it was like this.

A noise from above: the flutter of angelic wings.

Erin, her face as bright as the sun, was looking into the sky. Two hundred feet above them, suspended in the snowstorm like a flashing glittering Christmas ornament, was a security drone. From its belly shone a cone of celestial light which raked their shadow across the cobbles of Csarnok Tér.

Marci, wincing at the brightness, held aloft his ID. "Kovács Márton, 311AV761H442."

A voice issued from the machine: "Identity confirmed. My apologies, Adjudicant. Pleasant evening."

The light ceased. With a soft purr, the machine ascended into the clouds, leaving behind it even deeper darkness than before.

"Bloody Justice Board," Marci muttered, blowing his nose.

Erin put her arm through his. "At least being an Adjudicant has some perks. Do you mind if we walk?"

They headed south, a block parallel to the river, along back streets silent and empty and glistening with the sheen of melted snow.

"Do you remember," Erin said, "when I asked us not to keep any more secrets?"

"How could I forget? It's been hanging over me like the sword of Damocles."

"Yes. Well, I didn't really apply that to myself. For months I've been nagging you about your job, but I haven't told you much in return. There are things about me, things you ought to know, so that you can make a decision."

"About what?"

"About us."

Marci felt a twinge of dread. "That sounds ominous."

"I hope it won't be," Erin said. "But at least this way we won't have any more…"

Marci grimaced. "Nasty surprises."

"Exactly. And maybe it will help you understand why I've treated you so horribly. Did I ever mention my sister to you?"

"Once, at your apartment. Sophia?"

Erin patted his arm in commendation. "Trust an Adjudicant to remember. Well, Sophia isn't my only sibling. I used to have a brother."

"Used to? Was he…"

"Not as far as we know. At least, we never received a letter from the Justice Board. His name was Tomi. He was three years older than me. He was clever, like you. My parents hoped he'd study medicine, but he took after Grandpa. Between the two of them they could repair anything. Tomi wanted to study Engineering, but my parents couldn't afford the fees. Grandpa said if he got a job and started saving up he'd give him five hundred credits towards his course. Tomi found work in a warehouse near Tatabánya and commuted on an old motorbike Dad bought him."

One evening he didn't come home. My parents called him, but his phone was dead. Then they called the factory, but they'd closed for the day. At midnight Daddy rang the police. They said it was too early to register Tomi as missing and that we should wait. That night there was a curfew, so we couldn't go looking for him. I remember lying in bed and listening to the storm, wondering where my brother was.

The next day, Daddy went to the warehouse and spoke to the manager. He said Tomi had come to work the previous morning but never returned from his lunch break. Daddy found his motorbike in the parking lot. We called Tomi's friends, but no one knew where he was."

Marci's attention, still caught up in the ecstasy of their reunion, snapped into focus. "Wait. Are you saying he disappeared?"

"Please, Marci, let me finish; I need to get this off my chest. Days passed, then weeks. Mummy made posters with Tomi's photo on them. Daddy took a sabbatical. He bought an old car and spent all summer driving the route Tomi took, putting up the posters and looking for clues the police might have missed. He even went to Nyugati to speak to the Justice Board."

Flatly Marci said, "Don't tell me. He asked for Tomi's biodata. They didn't have it because his second skin never transmitted the end-of-life signal."

Erin stopped walking. "How do you know?"

"It doesn't matter." The streets had become anonymous. Erin's story had robbed him of his sense of place. "Let's turn here. What were you saying?"

Somewhat diffidently, Erin continued. "Three months later we received a letter from the police. They were closing the investigation. Tomi was missing, presumed dead. Daddy hid the letter in a drawer. Mummy found it a week later and went to pieces. Sophia couldn't cope. She dropped out of college and became as hopeless as Mummy. Daddy managed to keep his job, don't ask me how. We sold the car. We didn't need it anymore.

"The following year, we received another letter, this time from the Justice Board, calling us to an interview at Nyugati. Mummy tried to make light of it, saying we could go shopping afterwards and that Daddy would have to tag along, whether he enjoyed it or not. I'd never been to Nyugati before. When we arrived they split us up. They took me to a room and asked me lots of questions about Tomi and our family. There was a machine there. I can't remember the name: MIP?"

"NIPS," Marci corrected. "Non-invasive polygraph scan. It's a lie detector."

"They said I'd better tell the truth, because the machine would know if I wasn't. It made me feel dizzy and a little bit sick."

"They should never have used it on you," Marci grumbled. "NIPS require permission from Health Budapest. Not to mention probable cause, which they didn't have."

"Anyway, eventually they brought me back to reception. It was dark outside. Mummy, Daddy and Sophia were already waiting for me. They made us sign a document promising not to tell anyone what had happened, then let us go. We'd been there all day. Nobody wanted to go shopping after that."

They had reached Nehru Part, that narrow strip of parkland that hugged the Danube. Along the waterfront, old sodium vapor streetlights stretched north-south, contending with the night. Marci tried to ignore the unpleasant sensation that had gathered in the pit of his stomach. Against his better judgment, he'd asked Alex for a copy of the folder he kept hidden in his bathroom and had read it all. Erin's story was sounding much like Viktor Romanov's and a good many others.

"The next year, on the anniversary of Tomi's disappearance, my parents had a huge fight. Daddy said that Mummy had made a shrine of Tomi's bedroom and that we should get rid of everything. Mummy said how could we, and if Daddy hadn't bought Tomi his motorbike, he'd still be with us. Besides, what if he came home one day? Daddy got mad. I remember him shouting, "He's dead, and he's never coming back!" Mummy ran out of the house and didn't return until dark. We did a lot of crying that night, but after that we gave most of Tomi's things away. Daddy went back to work, Sophia resumed college and Mummy learned to get through each day with her new friend, Seromax. Everything seemed like it was back to normal, except it wasn't. Tomi was gone, no one knew why and we were too busy coping to ask the question."

Marci asked: "How does this affect you? I mean, now?"

"That's what I wanted to talk to you about. I suffer from depression. Most of the time I'm fine, but then it hits me out of the blue. Tomi was marvelous. He couldn't make it go away, of course, but he always knew the right things to say." She hesitated. "I wish I had him now."

Marci said politely: "He sounds like the perfect brother. I'm not good at finding the right words to say."

She patted his arm. "You have other talents."

"Yes. Killing people. What happened next?"

"After Tomi disappeared, my mood swings got worse. Sometimes I'd spend whole days in my room curled up and wanting to die. Once, I took some of Mummy's pills. Daddy found me collapsed on the bathroom floor and called an ambulance. After that, Mummy kept the Seromax locked up."

Marci lifted their hands, kissing hers. "I'm sorry."

"Thank you. It's funny; people say time heals, but it doesn't; it just pushes the pain deeper inside where you can't see it. A few years later I got into art college. Life took off again. But I never stopped thinking that something strange had happened to my brother and that someone knew about it."

"Is that why you started going to Club Bohém?"

"Yes. Petros invited me but the seed was already sown. And the more I learned at the meetings, the more questions I had. Then I met you. I remember in the park when you defended the Company. It made me a bit angry, but afterwards I started thinking that perhaps you were right, and that I'd been silly all along." She looked up at him. "Marci, are you okay? You look a little peaky."

He wasn't. Fragments of information from across the years were coalescing into something far less abstract than Alex's research. "Let's go to the river."

At the towpath, a fence twenty feet high and topped with razor wire hindered those seeking life's final resolution from polluting the city water supply.

"I'm telling you this so you understand why I've been so horrid towards you," Erin explained. "After Tomi went missing, I became so afraid of losing someone else I love that whenever I meet someone nice I either act too clingy or run away in a fright, as if the same thing's going to happen to them. Then the depression hits. Sometimes I can't even get out of bed. I've missed so much work it's a wonder I haven't been liquidated. That's why I run my wretched self-development class. Nobody wants to be there; we're all just trying to avoid the Hangman. So you see, Marci, I'm quite messed up. I don't know what to think except that I don't trust the Company and I don't want to be alone anymore and in the last few weeks I've really missed you." She waited, then laughed: a nervous sound. "You're very quiet. Please tell me I haven't scared you off."

"June, 2117."

"I'm sorry?"

"Fifteen years ago last summer," Marci said. "That's when you were called to Nyugati. Tomi would have disappeared sometime in the previous two years."

Erin disengaged her arm from his. "Eighteen months. How did you know that?"

"Did he ever express any interest in the Outside?"

She frowned. "We used to talk about it, but only in passing. Doesn't everyone?"

"And no one else in the family was interviewed?"

"Someone from the Justice Board visited Grandpa. He was too old to travel to the city center."

"Were he and Tomi close?"

"They were best friends. Why?"

"What happened to him after the interview?"

Erin watched him a whole five seconds. "Grandpa was liquidated a week later."

Marci turned away and sucked in a lungful of cold air. He felt inside his pockets for a Nauselief but had forgotten to bring them.

"What is this about, Marci? Ever since I mentioned Tomi you've been acting strangely."

Marci closed his eyes. The pieces, the memories, had fused. Kristoph Romanov. Judit Vamosi. Tomi Macsy. They were all the same. Strings to be parsed, numbers to be crunched, grist for the digital mill. The format didn't matter. To the likes of Erin and anyone else left behind they meant the world. To the Company they, like forty million others, were anomalies to resolve or human commodities to be traded—a life spared here, another taken there—and he was part of it, a cog that turned a larger cog, and precisely what the machine achieved few on this side of the river would ever understand.

Erin was speaking. Absorbed by his thoughts, Marci failed to hear her words. He didn't need to. Her intonation carried questions, questions he'd asked himself long ago, before time and ambition and denial had pushed the pain deeper inside where he couldn't see it anymore. To the list of victims, another was added. Two, if he counted himself.

"Marci, are you listening to me?"

"Sorry. I—I was distracted."

"I've bared my soul to you. Aren't you going to say anything?"

Still distracted, he said, "What do you want me to say?"

Erin straightened. "This isn't about Tomi, is it? It's about that little girl in the photograph, the one with the red hair."

Marci pulled away from her and reached for his cigarettes. "I don't want to talk about it."

She caught his hand and spoke slowly, articulating each word. "I need you to be honest with me. No more secrets."

Marci pressed his face against the latticework of the river fence. Below, the Danube rolled past like liquid slate on an endless conveyor belt. It would flow the same tomorrow as a thousand years from now, and it would remember neither of them.

At last he spoke. "Her name was Carla. She disappeared fifteen years ago. She was my sister."

13

The metro train hurtled through the darkness.

At the far end of the last carriage sat a lone figure. His head was bowed; his hands, clasped together in his lap, suggested prayerful supplication. A tracksuit hood concealed his features, adding to his mien a sense of the monastic. To the casual observer, his bearing marked him as a man of faith. This was not so. But Alex Pimenov was afraid, and he was taking no chances.

Since leaving work for Eden he'd changed direction twice: once at Népliget and again at Mátyásföld. The route was deliberate and his logic simple: no one else taking such an oblique excursion would do so without intent. Alex had, in effect, eliminated the navigationally inept from the equation. Whoever still accompanied him was, to all intents, a Company spy.

He studied his fellow passengers. Common sense suggested a Justice Board agent would want to appear as inconspicuous as possible. But wasn't that too obvious? Should his criteria include the flamboyant, or even the roguish? On a train bound for New Babylon there were few candidates. Most of his travel companions were low-level clerical workers or city center retail staff unable to afford downtown rent. A double bluff could of course be feasible, in which case everyone was a suspect. Alex reached inside his breast pocket and felt the heft of the envelope he was carrying. He'd be glad when this last mission was over and he could resume his old routine.

At Eden One he disembarked, donned his HUD glasses and set his destination. Two SpeedWalks later he arrived at Eden Nine, with its gravity-defying housing units, frosted glass stairwells and window boxes that spilled dry tendrils into space.

At the familiar graffiti-covered staircase he looked back the way he'd come. A concrete passageway, arrow straight and dimly lit by strip lights, stretched with reassuring emptiness as far as he could see. Satisfied, Alex ascended to Viktor Romanov's floor.

He stopped short of the front door. The placeholder, which had previously designated Romanov's apartment, was empty. Odd. He pressed the doorbell and prepared for a long wait. Hopefully, the foreman wasn't sleeping ahead of a night shift.

Alex moved to the kitchen window and peered between the security bars. The glass, hitherto opaque, was now transparent, and gave onto a room bare except for a stepladder whose toe cap supported a tin of paint. The walls, he noted, were white. Had Romanov experienced some kind of domiciliary enlightenment?

Alex returned to the front door and was about to knock a second time when, from the stairwell, came the sound of labored breathing and the regular *thunk, thunk* of something heavy dragged over steps.

Into view huffed a dumpy woman in her eighties. A woolen Lenin cap, pulled low, forced her blue rinse into a frame around a moony, embittered face. The gilet she wore against the cold added girth to a large bosom which heaved with exertion, and she moved with the exaggerated swinging of the hip typical of the arthritic. Behind her trundled a tartan granny trolley. The woman was out of breath, but not enough to prevent her cursing the stairs, or her health, or both.

Alex watched her covertly. Informants tended to be a cadre comprised exclusively of old women, and he didn't want to take any chances with this one. Feigning preoccupation, he held his phone to his ear and strolled towards the other end of the passage, realizing as he neared it that it was a dead end.

"Mit akarsz?" the woman said.

Alex ignored her.

"What do you want?" she repeated. She'd stopped in front of Romanov's door.

"Kit? Engem?" Alex asked.

The woman nodded in disgust. "Who else was I speaking to? If you want Viktor, you're too late. They came a week ago for him."

"They? Who are they?"

"Those bastards in black, that's who. I'm surprised they dare show their faces around here. I hope someone lynched them on the way out."

Alex felt the skin on his neck prickle. "A cessation squad?"

"Who else?" Her face puckered in concentration. "Haven't I seen you before?"

"I don't think so," Alex stammered. "In fact, I'm lost. I was looking for a Mr. György Sepa."

The woman's eyes slid from Alex's shoes to his face as if assessing a joint of meat. "I remember now. You passed me on the stairs a week ago, like you'd seen a ghost. There are three apartments on this floor. One is mine. This is Viktor's. The last one's empty. What do you want with him?"

Alex laughed nervously. "You're mistaken; I've never been here before. You must be Veronika Takács?"

"How do you know?"

"It's on your front door."

Takacs's face puckered some more. To Alex's surprise she pulled a bundle of keys from her pocket. "We were good neighbors," she said, unlocking Romanov's door. "He told me he'd had a visit from an Adjudicant. You might as well see what your little visit did to him."

Alex tried to sidle past her. "That won't be necessary. I must have the wrong address."

Takács propelled him over the threshold. "Go on in," she sneered. "Take a good look around."

Alex reluctantly stepped into Romanovs kitchen, which had been refurbished beyond recognition. The fridge and shabby countertop, with its miscellany of cheap utensils, were gone. High up in a freshly plastered wall the old extractor fan had been swapped out for something modern, which was busy sucking the smell of paint from the room. The strip light was missing; bare wires protruded through a ceiling rose. The garden chairs and dining table where Romanov had spent dismal nights in vigil for his missing son were no more. Romanov and everything about him had been expunged, save the lingering odor of stale cigarettes. Not even the new Xpelair could purge the place of his fatal pastime.

Takács inclined her head toward the living room. "It's the same in the rest of the flat. When the plumbing around here breaks, nothing gets done for weeks. When the Justice Board shows up, the place is fixed up in days."

Alex, realizing his part in Romanov's liquidation, held his hand to his mouth.

"If you're going to be sick," Takács said, "do it outside. You brought him enough harm when he was alive without puking in his apartment now he's dead."

Alex rushed onto the walkway, leaned over the railing and emptied his stomach.

Takács locked the door behind her. She handed him a tissue. *"Jol van?"*

"No." He removed the envelope from his breast pocket. "You'd better take this. It was for Mr. Romanov, for his treatment. He won't need it anymore."

Takács inspected the contents. If she was shocked by his generosity she hid it well. "I'll buy some flowers for his grave. The rest I'll keep for Kristoph, if he ever comes home."

They shared a moment of uncomfortable silence at the unlikelihood of it.

"I'd better be going," said Alex.

Takács seemed in no hurry. "It wasn't the cancer that killed him. He should've given up on the boy years ago."

Alex wiped his mouth. "Would you?"

She shrugged. ""'The heart knoweth its own bitterness.' Only Viktor could tell us what it was like."

Viktor and several hundred others, Alex thought.

Takács put the envelope in her coat. "You should leave. Eden's no place for an Adjudicant, especially not at night. And forget your fancy glasses. Turn left at the bottom of the stairs. There's a SpeedWalk a block away. It'll take you to Eden 10. You can walk to One from there."

Alex nodded in thanks and hurried toward the stairs. He had seen all of Eden he ever wanted to.

"He was dying anyway," Takács called after him. "You did him a favor."

Some favor, Alex thought.

*   *   *

On Saturday morning Marci strolled to Deak Ferenc Square, and with Erin boarded the driverless limousine Sándor had arranged for them. They were conveyed to Széchenyi Bridge, where their day passes, also organized by Sándor, were scrutinized, scanned, cross-checked and stamped. With security formalities taken care of, the car carried them over the Danube and up Istenhegy, with villas on one side and expansive views over Pest on the other.

The sun had warmed and, hanging low in the sky, cast deep shadows in the folds of the hills. Protected by its Weathershield, fall had come late to Buda. Its wooded slopes now showed off a glorious palette of russet oaks, golden aspens, and the brilliant scarlet of rare red maples growing here and there on private grounds. Beyond, evergreens lent verdancy. Erin, who had never stepped foot on this side of the river, viewed the panorama in rapt wonder. Marci had only seen it from the air, and was equally taken by the vistas. Their presence here was no small matter; sub-30s were forbidden from treading on Society lands. Sándor had pulled some very long strings.

Near the top of Svábhegy the limousine stopped. The two stepped out into quiet made more profound by birdsong—a sound foreign to Pest, which few would ever hear. Neither of them moved; both were awed to silence.

"Are they real birds?" Erin whispered.

Marci shielded his eyes from the sun. "They must be in the trees or the bushes. That's where they're supposed to live."

"Are the trees real, too? I'd love to see them."

"We will. But first—" he drew her into his arms, closed his eyes and let his other senses inform him.

Erin spoke at last. "I wish this could last forever."

Marci spoke with sudden enthusiasm. "Maybe it can. I'll make it to Club 30. We'll leave Pest and move here—nothing showy, perhaps a little cottage in the woods with a studio for your art. We'll buy some land and grow our own food, real food. We'll never have to worry about anything again."

Erin laughed. "Marci Kovács, you have the soul of a poet. You've figured it all out."

"Are you mocking me?"

"Of course not! I think the fresh air has got to you and it's only ten o'clock. But I don't want to think about the Company or the future or anything else. I just want to enjoy this moment."

Marci cradled her face in his hands and kissed her again.

Finally, she pulled away. "My, my, it seems the mountain air has a magical effect on us. Whatever will the locals think?"

Marci glanced around. "I think they're too busy looking for worms."

"It's just as well. This is my first visit to Buda, and I don't want people to think me a hoyden. Come, Mr. Kovács, before your amour leads us into more trouble."

"That's what I was hoping for," Marci mumbled.

"Tra la! As for that, we'll see."

A footpath led in twists and turns up through a forest of birch, beech and oak, traversing the side of János-hegy until it brought them out on an open hilltop with views across Buda's sylvan landscape. To their right, crouching under a pall of rust-colored smog, lay Pest, with the Danube glinting silver-blue in the morning sunshine.

At the edge of the clearing lay a patch of scorched earth encircled by stones. Here Erin shook a picnic blanket out to settle on the ground and watched Marci return from the tree line with armfuls of wood. This he sorted into two piles: kindling and branches; the latter he cut into fire sticks. From a tin box he took a hunting knife, a magnesium block and a strip of old sock. He shaved filings onto the sock, added birch bark peelings, then struck the flint edge: once, twice, a third time. Sparks, alighting on the metal flecks, ignited them, creating bright-burning flames that consumed tinder, then kindling, then branches, until a small fire burned. What it lacked in heat, it made up for with good cheer.

Erin poured them coffee from a flask. "You're not so useless after all. I wonder what other secrets you have?"

"Many," Marci said, lighting a cigarette. "But I'd have to kill you if I told you."

"A man of mystery. I like it, but not too much. It sounds scary."

"Tell me how much mystery you want and I'll try to oblige."

"For now, none." She patted a space beside her. "Come and keep me company."

For a time, the two listened to the hiss and crackle of the fire and the colloquy of robins in the woods behind them.

"Isn't it strange?" Erin said. "All my life and I've never heard birds singing."

"They say during the First World War there was a battle in a forest where many men died. For years afterwards, no birds sang there. So the story goes."

"That's a bit creepy. Maybe they stopped because all the trees were gone?"

"It's certainly possible," Marci said, "and more logical than any other theory."

"I don't like thoughts like this," Erin decided. "They're gloomy. I like the sunshine on my face and the smell of the leaves. I quite like the smoke, except when it blows in my face. You're not too bad, either."

"Thanks. I nearly forgot: something Dad and I used to do when we went camping. These are marshmallows. Use the fork and toast one over the fire for a few seconds, like this. Dad called it a "pick me up." He also carried a flask of pálinka, which he referred to the same way."

"Tell me more about your family. You've never really spoken about them. To be honest, I'm a little jealous of that counselor woman, Roma."

"Stella," Marci corrected. "And you needn't be." He'd had his first appointment with her a couple of days ago in a fancy mansion on Honved utca. The practice, sterile white and devoid of aesthetic stimuli, reeked of vanilla and profit. Kennedy seemed proficient enough, but refused to provide Marci with the quick fix he desired.

"There are no shortcuts to wholeness," she told him, which worked well in her favor but not in his. In the end he'd left with a new prescription, a large hole in his wallet and enough homework for a school semester. They would meet three times a week, which was three times more often than suited Marci. At least he was keeping Sándor happy. "Psychologists and I don't gel," he added, "although she did manage to pry my life story out of me."

Erin nudged him in the ribs. "That's not fair! I'm more important than Stella. At least, I think I am."

"That depends on whether she gets me into Club 30."

Erin took Marci's marshmallow from him. "In which case, let's hope you don't make it after all. Now tell me all about yourself. No secrets."

Marci chuckled. "No more secrets doesn't mean unrestricted access. What do you want to know?"

Erin pulled a menacing face. "Everything!"

"Fine. But I reserve the right to embellish certain events."

She considered. "Poetic embellishment is permitted."

"Fine. I was born in Budapest in April 2093. My mother was Marya and my father, Péter. Mum was a radiologist, Dad a civil engineer. They met at a Christian summer camp when the Company still permitted religious freedom. A year later they married and moved to the city. I came along the year after."

"They're not alive?" Erin asked.

"Dad was liquidated in 2116. Mum died of hepatitis the following year."

"Oh Marci, I'm sorry."

"Mum's death wasn't a shock; the surprise was that lived so long. She contracted anemia in her childhood and had to receive blood transfusions. One of them hadn't been screened properly and contained hepatitis B. It didn't show up until she was in her thirties. By then it was too late to treat. Dad's death is still a mystery. He was SIN 28."

"Twenty-eight? That's nearly as high as you."

"If he'd built Eden nowadays they'd have made him a Patrician."

"Your father built Eden?"

"I know it's not much to brag about, but back then Eden was something special. The Company touted it as the eighth wonder of the world. We'd just come through the worst century in history, so I guess a little pretentiousness can be forgiven." Marci chuckled. "Dad became a minor celebrity overnight. He hated it."

"Hmm, your parents were clever! Tell me what it was like growing up."

Marci impaled a marshmallow and held it over the flames. "I was an only child until I was twelve; that's when Carla was born. I was good at school but a bit of a loner. Apart from some bullying, life was good. Mum made such a lovely home for us all that even my worst days were tolerable. Dad had a good income. We lived in a large apartment in District VIII. I spent a lot of my holidays with him at the river, or in the woods near Gyöngyös. We used to camp there every summer, when there was still some forest left. I believe it's all been built on now."

"Is that where you learned to make a fire?"

Marci laughed. "We did more than that. Dad taught me how to hunt. There were rabbits and even a few deer back then. I don't know how they'd got past the Wall; maybe they'd been inside the city all along. Most were irradiated or deformed, but sometimes we caught healthy-looking coneys and cooked them over the fire. At night, Dad would teach me the constellations. Once upon a time I knew them all by heart."

Erin lay her head on his shoulder. "He sounds like great fun."

"He was," Marci reflected. "Between us, I'm not sure who was the biggest kid. Mum despaired of him."

"Tell me about her."

"She was beautiful and smart with it. I remember she told me once, 'There aren't enough books in the world.' Dad said, 'Yes there are, and they're all in my bloody lounge!' He doted on her. I'm glad he didn't get to see her at the end." Marci tossed his cigarette into the fire. "Your turn."

"My life is awfully dull by comparison," Erin said. "I was born in Györ. Daddy's a draftsman. He does technical drawings for the medical industry. Mummy is a sort of part-time artist, which means she's unemployed but thinks she actually has a job. Sophia I already told you about. We're best friends, and I can't imagine life without her. None of us care about our SIN so long as it's above 5. Apart from what happened to Tomi, our lives are unremarkable, which suits me well. I guess we're just your average family. For artists I suppose we're fairly sane."

"You sound a pretty together lot."

She hesitated. "Marci, did you read my profile?"

"What profile?"

"My profile, silly. The one in MARTHA. If it were me, I'd have read yours. "

Marci picked up one of the firesticks and plucked off one of the feather-like edges. "I printed it out," he confessed, "but I didn't read it. It seemed wrong."

She kissed him.

"What was that for?"

"For being a gentleman. You could have found out all about me but you decided not to. It's one of the reasons why I love you."

"If I were a gentleman, I wouldn't have printed it out."

Erin patted his hand. "It's good enough for me. There's something else I wanted to ask you. The other night, when we met near Café Primo, you said I'd been right about the Company all along. What did you mean?"

"Does this fall under the 'no more secrets' policy?"

"Only if you want it to. I don't want you to get into any trouble."

"Thanks to Alex and his anomalies, I think we're past that stage."

"Anomalies?"

"Didn't you want to enjoy Buda and its bucolic idylls?"

Erin pursed her lips. "I changed my mind."

Marci gazed out across hills which, many years prior, he and his father had stared at longingly from the Pest shoreline. "Somehow it feels safe to talk about it here. But you have to promise not to tell anyone—not Petros, not your friends at Club Bohém, not even your family."

"I promise," Erin said, "but I don't like the sound of it."

"You won't." As concisely as possible, Marci related Alex's findings; his initial discovery of MARTHA's missing persons; his sudden promotion; Rieks' and Morrison's incriminating correspondence; and the evidence his friend's own investigations had brought to light. "When you told me about your brother, it opened up a narrative I thought I'd dealt with long ago. It's like an old, unfinished jigsaw puzzle that's coming together, but with a big hole in the middle."

Erin gazed broodily into the fire and said nothing.

Marci popped a marshmallow in his mouth. "I said you wouldn't like it."

"So Petros was right," she said. "There is a big conspiracy, after all."

"It would seem so. Minus Lydia's marauding cannibals."

"Do you think the Company took my brother?"

"It's unlikely. Why would they interrogate your family if they knew where he was?"

"Maybe it was a bluff."

"I don't think so. They gave Eden P.D. free access to over 600 Employee records. That's a big deal, and it reeks of desperation. The question is, why are they desperate? What's so important about 83 missing persons?"

Erin asked, "Marci, would you mind telling me what happened to your sister?"

He did mind. Wasn't it enough that he'd mentioned her disappearance? "I think I've covered the basics already."

"You told me she went missing, but not how. Maybe there's a pattern that explains why Tomi disappeared."

"Of course there's a pattern. That's what we've been talking about."

"There's no need to be rude."

"Sorry, it came out wrong. Look, if you really want to know, Carla and I weren't on speaking terms at the end."

"Why not?"

Marci saw that further evasion was pointless. "Fine. Two years before she died, Mum went on sick leave. She told us she'd picked up a virus and wasn't allowed back until she was better. For a while we believed her, until the jaundice appeared. Carla was thirteen. She'd always been an inquisitive kid, and blunt with it. I remember her asking Mum, "Anya, why is your skin yellow?" and "Anya, why are you always sick? Sometimes I hear you and it scares me." Mum told her it was the side effects of the medicine, but when the pills didn't work, even Carla started doubting.

"Mum got worse and quit her job. Dad was working overtime to pay the medical bills, and I'd just started my third year in the Executive Team. One evening, Dad called Carla and me into the living room. I'll never forget the smell. The linden trees were in bloom, and the house reeked of musk and honey; to this day the scent makes me ill. Mum had Carla sit on her lap. Dad sat crumpled in the corner, like someone who'd fought too long and given up. It turned out the hepatitis had done its work: Mum had cirrhosis of the liver and was dying.

"When Mum became bedridden, Carla dropped out of school to care for her. We thought things couldn't get much worse. The next summer a cessation squad took Dad. Mum lasted another year. We buried both of them in Szeged, in the graveyard of their childhood church. That's when Carla and I stopped talking."

"Why?"

"Carla blamed me for Dad's death. She said that if I'd cared I would have quit my job at the Exec Team. Never mind the fact I was an office clerk and had no contact with MARTHA, nor that I was now the family breadwinner."

"That seems very unfair," Erin said. "You were doing everything you could to support both of them."

"Carla didn't see it that way. She resented the fact that she'd given up her studies while I pursued my career. Maybe she had a point. Anyway, two months after Mum died I was walking home from work. It was March, the first nice day of the year, and for some reason I was feeling good about life—I don't know why. I remember passing a florist's and I decided to buy Carla some freesias. When I got home the house was empty. There was a letter on the kitchen table. I can still quote it verbatim: 'Dear Marci, don't ask where I've gone. I love you, but I can't stand the ghosts here anymore. We used to laugh and have such happy times, didn't we? All I can think of now is Dad not playing his records and mother slowly dying in the kitchen. Please forgive me. And forgive yourself. Love always, Carla.' She'd taken her clothes, make-up and a suitcase from the attic. That was the last I heard of her. The next year, I sold the family home and bought my place. She was right: there were too many ghosts."

Erin hugged his arm. "I'm so sorry, Marcim. It must have been awful, losing all your family. Weren't you tempted to ask MARTHA what happened to Carla?"

"Tempted, yes. But I didn't make Adjudicant for another decade. When I did, I swore to uphold the Adjudicant Code of Conduct, which precludes me from using MARTHA for personal reasons."

"Except for me," Erin smiled.

Sheepishly Marci said: "Except for you and a few others."

"If you haven't read her profile," Erin said, "how do you know Carla disappeared? Maybe she's still alive."

"Two years after she left I went looking for her. I still had her share of the house money, and I'd hoped by then she might have forgiven me. She'd had a boyfriend in Eden, so that's where I headed. But by then it was too late. No one had seen her in months."

"That doesn't mean she went missing like Tomi."

"True. And until a few days ago it never occurred to me that Carla might have vanished like the others. Then you told me about Tomi, and it occurred to me that Alex's research might include her disappearance."

"Does it?"

"In a manner of speaking, yes."

Erin spoke excitedly: "Then she's alive?"

"That depends on whose conspiracy theory you prefer. According to MARTHA, Carla Kovács's second skin ceased transmitting data in District XVII on February 21st, 2120. Technically, she expired. But since MARTHA can't reconcile a missing person with a dead one, that means everyone, the Company included, is left with the same knotty paradox."

"So we're no closer to finding out what happened than we were before," Erin said, "even with Alex's report?"

"I'm afraid not. The worst part is that reading Carla's profile opened up an emotional Pandora's box, not just about her but about Dad's death and the Company's part in it. I want to believe that Alex is wrong, but I know he isn't. That puts me in a difficult position."

"Why?"

"Because if I make waves, not only will I risk admission to The Society, but I might well end up dead."

Erin's mouth fell at the corners. "Surely they wouldn't kill you! You're an Adjudicant!"

"Adjudicant or not, if I'm seen as a liability then I'm as expendable as all the others. Once I'm inducted into Club 30, the Justice Board can't touch me. Patricians are immune to liquidation."

"Then you should wait," Erin said. "Sándor sounds like a nice man, and powerful. Once you're in Buda you can ask him to help you expose the Company."

"'We,'" Marci corrected. "If you think I'm leaving you behind you're very much mistaken."

"In which case," Erin said, "I'd better learn some airs and graces. Otherwise, your Society friends will think me a shameless hussy."

"Fat chance. They'll be smitten by you at first sight."

"Thank you. Marci, can I ask you something else?"

"Anything."

"If something happened to you, I mean something bad...would you inform on me?"

Marci looked at her in dismay. "Inform? How can you even think that?"

She laughed, nervously. "I'm sorry, it was silly of me. It's just that—well, you know the rumors about Nyugati. I was talking to Zsuzsi from Club Bohém about how mean they'd been to me back when Tomi vanished."

Marci grimaced. He hadn't forgiven the green-haired trollop from his first encounter with her. "Don't tell me: she said they have a special wing devoted to torturing Employees."

"Something like that. That's what lots of people say. Or at least wonder."

"It's a myth. Although having read Alex's dossier I wouldn't put it past them."

Erin pulled away. Her expression had undergone a transformation. She looked, Marci thought, suddenly fragile and vulnerable and very frightened, and when she spoke, it was with an earnestness that stung him deeply, for he knew it was because of him and every Adjudicant in whose steps he'd followed that she asked the question, and because, despite knowing him, she felt the need to ask it. "Then promise me," she said, "promise me you'll never betray me. I know that you won't and that I'm being silly about this, but I need to hear you say it. And please, Marci, for once don't think. Just say it. For me."

"I promise," he said, embracing her. "Whatever happens to us, I promise I won't betray you."

"Nor me you." The mask slipped back in place. Brightly she said, "And now let's not talk about it anymore. We've got the whole day here, and the only things I want to think about are the hills and the birds and these delicious marshmallows, which I see you've polished off. "

"Me? I've barely had any. And now—"

His phone chimed.

"Marci, it's Alex. Are you busy?"

"Yes, sort of. What's up?"

"Fraser's on the warpath. So's Rieks. Something big. Are you at work?"

"No, it's Saturday. I'm in Buda with Erin. Can it wait?"

"Man, I'm sorry to bother you. All hell's breaking loose. Fraser said to get you here ASAP. I told him you're ill. He wants to see you tomorrow, 08:00 sharp."

Marci's voice sounded half an octave higher than intended. "Did he say why?"

"No, but I've never seen him so frantic. Let's hope it's one of his moods. Gotta go. Say hi to Erin."

Marci hung up and stared at his phone.

"Is everything ok?" Erin asked.

"Not really. I think Alex and I have been found out. SIN 30 might not be on the cards after all."

14

Marci sat in silence, listening to the rain beat a steady tattoo on the window.

Fraser Morrison, his tie loosened and top button undone, reclined in his office chair staring at his monitor. Since he always wore an expression of irritated disdain, it was hard to gauge his state of mind, and Marci had long given up trying.

The interaction had begun before they'd even met. Morrison had kept Marci waiting forty minutes before summoning him to the shark tank—a gesture Marci correctly inferred as a power play between the Head of Department and his least favorite Adjudicant. Marci had borne the insult well, mainly because getting angry with Morrison was counterproductive and would provide his boss with the entertainment he craved.

Morrison finally dragged his eyes from his screen. "Well?"

"Well what?"

"Well, what the bloody hell do you think you're doing?"

Marci replied with innocence. "I don't follow."

"You realize interfering with a cessation is a capital offense?"

"I'm an Adjudicant. I interfere with cessations every day."

Morrison made a dismissive nasal sound. "I'm talking about the debacle at your apartment complex."

"I'm more inclined to call it a crime."

"In your case, yes. You're lucky Justice isn't pressing charges. This from the report they sent me. I quote: 'Subject'—that's you—'Subject forced his way to the front of the mob that had gathered to protest extraction. Subject used proximity to attempt physical intimidation. Subject attempted to draw concealed weapon.

Concerned he was armed, I restrained him and gave verbal warning. Subject intimated violence against me and made threatening remarks about his social status. Subject tried breaching barrier to interfere with said extraction, requiring use of non-lethal force.'"

"Threatened an officer?" Marci laughed in derision. "Who the hell wrote that?"

"Someone else in life you managed to piss off," Morrison said, "this time a Hangman. It seems to be a habit of yours."

Marci stifled a snort of laughter at the hypocrisy of the remark.

"Problem?"

"Catarrh."

Morrison resumed reading. "'Call received at 21:18 by Justice and Cessation Liaison officer Aaron Temple. Subject attempted to thwart a cessation, implying intimate knowledge of targets' SIN ratings and disputing validity of MARTHA's decision processes. Subject made patronizing and intimidating remarks to said officer.'"

"I did nothing of the kind! Aaron's a friend of mine. An acquaintance, at least."

"You then headed to the Adjudication suite and attempted to overturn the liquidation yourself."

"Of course I did!" Marci snapped. "Takumi and Réka were well above cut-off. MARTHA confirmed their SIN when I ran the kill-desist. Check it yourself if you don't believe me."

Morrison turned his computer monitor around. "I already did."

Marci stared at the numbers.

"It's the tip of the iceberg," Morrison continued. "November 3rd, 13:43. You submitted a request to Data Analytics for the profiles of fourteen Employees including Alex Pimenov, breaching Adjudicant protocol section c, 1.3: 'An Adjudicant may not, under any circumstances, request or access the profile, lifeline or SIN data of any other Adjudicant unless expressly authorized by an Executive Team Head of Department.'"

"You changed their SIN score," Marci mumbled. "You can't do that."

Morrison picked up his Biro, which at some point he'd bitten down on hard enough to fracture it along its length. Holding it with fingertips at both ends, he rotated the barrel to inspect the writing on it as a jeweler might assay gold. Nonchalantly he asked: "Are you accusing me of doctoring Employee data?"

Marci spoke in a slow dull monotone of disbelief. "Takumi was SIN 21. Réka was SIN 16. I saw the numbers myself."

"MARTHA doesn't liquidate Employees below SIN 5."

The statement, Marci thought, was redundantly obvious, as if Morrison were making a point. "But I saw them."

Morrison enunciated each word, as if expressing an irrefutable truth: "You saw wrong."

Marci slumped back in his chair. The sound of the office outside had become suddenly loud.

"So again," Morrison asked, "what the hell were you doing requesting Pimenov's profile?"

Marci wiped his palms on his trousers and tried to recover his composure. The story he'd concocted for the meeting wouldn't fool anyone—not least the savvy Scot—but he had nothing else. "Two months ago, I began an investigation into thirteen Employees who showed seditious tendencies. At the time, Alex Pimenov mentioned that he'd created a replica of MARTHA, which, of course, is illegal. I included Alex in the caseload for convenience. As part of my inquiry, I requested his profile from Data Analytics. When I determined Alex had, in fact, created the simulation to test her predictive interval routines I closed the case. None of it constitutes any kind of irregularity."

Morrison barked in laughter. "D'you think I was born yesterday? He's your friend. You made the whole case up to get his predictive interval. I'm not bloody stupid."

"That's your opinion," Marci muttered.

"Your timing's all wrong, Kovács. Pimenov created the replica in September. You created your case three weeks ago. If you're going to break the law, at least cover your tracks better."

"Like you did?" Marci retorted, instantly regretting it.

Morrison placed his pen on his desk and, without removing his gaze from Marci, lifted the handset from its cradle and speed-dialed someone. After a dozen unsuccessful rings he hung up. Marci watched him work the computer keyboard, wondering who he might be messaging, and was almost relieved when a hologram of his employment work record appeared in the air between them.

"Márton bloody Kovács," Morrison said, "aren't you a paragon of virtue? 2112: graduates from the Weber Institute, Applied Judicial Administration, summa cum laude; joins Executive Team. 2119: promoted to Assistant Adjudicant, the youngest in Company history. 2125: promoted to Adjudicant and makes SIN 27. Again, a record. You're thirty-nine years old and SIN 29. I know men twice your age who've been stuck at SIN 26 for the last two decades."

Marci decided silence was his safest response.

"I don't give a toss what the Justice Board wrote," Morrison said. "They're so stuck up their own arses I'm surprised they can see daylight. But I do care when my top Adjudicant goes wonky on me. Your case is obviously a sham, so let's have the truth."

"I already told you. When Alex first mentioned his model, I took him at his word. That's why I didn't submit the request immediately. Then I started having doubts."

"Why?"

Marci hesitated; he hadn't planned for such a question and didn't want to risk inculpating his friend any further. "No particular reason."

"Bullshit."

"Replicating MARTHA's algorithms was reason enough."

"And what about the other thirteen?"

Marci decided a leavening of honesty was his best option. "They're innocent. I was only interested in Alex's profile. I included them so that he wouldn't think I'd singled him out if he ever got wind of it. As you say, he's a friend."

"Again, bullshit. The only way he'd find out is if you told him. You didn't bulk up the case to protect his feelings, you did it to cover your tracks."

"Fraser, you read my employment record. It speaks for itself. I'm on the verge of Club 30. Why would I jeopardize my nomination by breaking the law?"

"You've already broken the law. By your own admission, you solicited a friend's profile from D.A. That's a breach of Adjudicant protocol and a capital offense."

"It's not like I altered anything," Marci stammered. "I only—"

"If I thought you were fudging data," Morrison said, "you'd be talking to Taggart, not me. And to be frank, if you weren't invaluable I'd have had Justice run a NIPS test on you long ago. You're the best Adjudicant I've got, Kovács, but you're becoming a liability. If you want to make Club 30 you'd better keep your nose clean; that's coming from Rieks. As far as I'm concerned, this is the end of the matter. But no more poking around in the state computer. Got it?"

Marci stood, and in a mood of relief mixed with disgust, stalked off to the quadrangle to smoke.

Morrison waited two minutes, then tapped his keyboard. The computer spoke: "Sub-NIPS[19] analysis complete. Subject's delta brainwave function shows strong empathy for colleague. Theta waves indicate acute anxiety when questioned about workplace practices. Alpha waves suggest fear. Lo-beta shows intense activity, suggesting duplicity regarding expressed motives. Skin moisture, heart rate, blood pressure and neurological activity all suggest anxiety. Skin secretions contain traces of Motiv and Cortiquell. Verdict: inconclusive. Subject's medicated condition has hindered a conclusive NIPS result. Recommend full NIPS test."

Morrison opened up a dialogue box and typed:

Rieks, I ran a basic NIPS on Kovács as requested (see attached results). Not sure why Intelligence wants this, but I've done my job here. I don't like this cloak and dagger stuff—not what I signed up for. I hope the powers that be know what they're doing. He's our best man and I don't want to lose him.

Morrison, chewing the end of his pen, sat for a time staring into space, then sent the message and resumed his work.

---

[19] NIPS: non-invasive brainwave and physiology scan. A lie detection tool which records changes in brain wave activity and other physiological responses to external stimuli. Highly controversial, it is widely feared by many Employees.

*　　*　　*

Marci spent the rest of Sunday at home trying to ignore the incessant noise that now issued not from Norbert Tóth's shed, but his apartment, three doors away. The reason for the change in location was unclear, but Marci decided that speaking to the old bugger would be an exercise in futility. At best, Tóth would ignore the doorbell. At worst, Marci would be instructed in no uncertain terms to leave. Either way, his neighbor would keep up the racket.

At lunchtime Marci's phone chimed. A text from Erin appeared:

Szia! What happened at the meeting? xx

Marci replied:

Got off lightly. Time to keep my head down. xx

Unable to work any further on his speech, Marci put on his coat and was about to leave the flat when the doorbell rang. Outside stood Alex, his wet raincoat flapping about him in the wind.

"Were you going out?" Alex asked. "The weather's rotten."

"So it seems," Marci said. "I was about to throw myself off the balcony, but you saved me."

"What are friends for? I might have joined you. May I come in, or shall I set up camp here?"

Marci swung the door wide and walked into the kitchen. "Drink?"

"Anything strong."

Marci fixed Alex a whiskey and himself a coffee.

"I thought you'd resigned yourself to a life of booze?" Alex asked.

"I had second thoughts. But there's always tomorrow."

"True enough. What happened this morning?"

Marci sank into the Chesterfield. "Apparently, my little ploy about a caseload of deviants didn't fool anyone. Morrison even mentioned a NIPS test."

"The bastard! He wouldn't dare. You're a Level 3 Adjudicant; he's just some squirming SIN 24 pen pusher."

"Twenty-five, but who's counting? He also showed me Takumi and Réka's SIN. According to MARTHA, Takumi died at SIN 5 and Réka SIN 4."

"I thought Takumi was SIN 21?"

"He was. Someone changed it."

"And carrot-top showed you it?"

Marci lit a cigarette. "He'd have known I'd seen their real scores for myself. It was as if he wanted me to see through it."

"Then my theory has a hole."

"How so?"

"Takumi and Réka had their SIN downgraded to make the kill orders look valid. The anomaly victims still show SIN above cutoff. That means MARTHA's being selective about whose SIN she plays with."

"Or someone behind her is." Marci noticed Alex's hands were trembling. "Are you okay? You look like you've seen a ghost."

"In a way I have. Remember how Romanov was liquidated a week after I interviewed him? I started wondering if the same thing had happened to the other 'left-behinders.'"

"Bloody hell," Marci groaned, "don't tell me you went back to check on them?"

"Just hear me out. I picked three groups: a middle-aged couple, a family of four, and a widow. The couple and the widow didn't answer, but the doors were new and their nameplates were empty. At the family's place I was received by some guy in overalls. He said he'd moved in two days ago and knew nothing about them. And I could smell fresh paint, like at Romanov's. So I checked with the housing manager. Apparently, a cessation squad came on Monday night and took all of them away." Alex gulped down his whiskey. "If I hadn't gone asking questions, they'd still be alive."

Marci spoke without conviction. "You don't know that. It might be a coincidence."

Alex refilled his glass. "There's something else. I'm pretty sure I'm being followed."

"What did you expect? You've got a security marker on you. Who else knows about your social calls?"

"Apart from you? No one. I haven't told Lei, at least not the details. She must wonder if I've got a mistress."

"In your case, that's unlikely. Anyway, the Justice Board hardly ever runs feet-on-the-ground surveillance details. There's no need."

"That's true outside Eden," Alex said. "Inside, it's a different story. The Eden mafia, I've learned, has found a way to prevent the Company from operating any kind of electronic surveillance system there. That means Justice has to send in flesh and blood operatives. Last year they caught a Company spook nosing around Plaza One and lynched him from the ceiling. Now Justice gives the place a wide berth except for liquidations, when they go in packs."

"So you're being tracked by the mafia and the Justice and Cessation Board?" Marci asked.

"Definitely by the latter and probably by the former." Alex accepted a cigarette. "What have I got myself into, Marci? A couple of months ago my life was simple. I thought my MARTHA replica was a golden ticket to Club 30. Now I'm checking everyone's feet for black jackboots."

Marci spoke quietly: "I don't know why you haven't dropped it."

"Don't you? Innocent people—whole families—wiped out just because they had relatives go missing. Doesn't it at least make you angry? Or at least curious?"

Marci remained silent; Alex knew nothing about his sister. He watched Alex walk across the lounge trailing a thread of silver smoke from his Winterbourne, only to turn back into it again.

"Oh," Alex said, "and what about your meeting with carrot-top? Did Morrison mention me?"

"No. I told him the story we agreed on, which he didn't believe for one minute."

"Good, good. But he didn't say anything about me?"

Marci sighed in irritation. "Alex, you're becoming a nervous wreck. For your own sake, please drop this. Let's suppose there is a conspiracy—"

"Suppose?"

"—and that you're getting close to the truth. Who are you going to take this to? Morrison? Rieks? They're already implicated. Ron

Taggart? If the Exec Team's manipulating MARTHA's data, he's hardly going to welcome you with open arms."

"There must be someone who'll listen." Alex's expression brightened. "The Society! You could give my findings to Sándor. They're virtually above the law."

"Don't even think about it. I'm not taking this to the Patricians."

"Why not? We have to do something!"

"No," Marci said, "we haven't. You've got a wife and kids and another on the way. I've got Erin and my Club 30 nomination. I'm not jeopardizing them for this."

Alex regarded him with disgust. "I think you're afraid."

Marci took Alex's whiskey from him. "And I think you've had too much to drink. Go home, Alex. Burn the paperwork. Report to Morrison. Tell him you lost your way but that you're back with the program. Then live out your days with Lei in peace."

Alex brushed past him and stalked to the hall.

Marci trailed behind him. "Alex, you're my best friend. Please, just drop this. One day all of this will come to light. Even if we hate the system, we still have a duty to the people of Budapest."

Alex swung the front door open, and with a final withering glance of reproach strode away.

Marci locked up and went for the whiskey.

15

Marci had long ago decided he was a misanthrope, and twenty years of Employee profiling had done little to change his opinion of either himself or humanity. To the contrary, he disliked people all the more for knowing what it was that made it so obnoxious. Yet he possessed a remarkable aptitude: he could, with considerable accuracy, determine the SIN score of any citizen based on their appearance and mannerisms.

Spotting a Company mole was a different matter. Fifteen years ago, the Exec Team had sent him on a Justice and Cessation Board training course. Having spent the afternoon feigning wakefulness, Marci was roused and, along with the other delegates, tasked with picking out two spies from a thirty-strong lineup. A wild guess proved wrong. The real operatives stepped forward: one resembled Trotsky, complete with tea shade spectacles and a pointed beard; the other was an adolescent girl in whose mouth butter wouldn't only have melted, it would have curdled. The former was too Machiavellian and the latter too comely to be secret agents. In the end, Marci decided the event was a complete waste of time and dismissed the recondite art of spy catching from his thoughts. It was a topic that had no bearing on either his professional or private life, and never would.

Until three nights ago.

Alex had many strengths, but imagination was not among them. If he reckoned he was being followed, chances were he was. And if Alex, why not Marci? Morrison had already expressed doubts about his top Adjudicant. Having Taggart put a tail on him was no more inconvenient than organizing a NIPS test.

Marci chided himself; Alex's paranoia was getting to him. How he wished he'd never heard about the whole damnable affair.

He checked his watch. As usual, Erin was late. Marci carried his coffee through Café Primo into the meeting room and grabbed two empty seats near the exit. Across the aisle, a bobbing dome of pus-green hair marked the presence of Zsuzsa, no doubt ready to put the world to rights tonight in her own, special way. Marci laid his jacket on Erin's seat and checked his watch again. It was her idea to come to Café Primo. Tonight's meeting, she'd told him, would be an event of such rarity that they simply had to attend. He'd refused, of course. But Erin had a way of making his most resolute decisions infinitely elastic, and in the end he'd buckled to her will. He scolded himself anew. So much for flying under the radar. This would definitely be his last visit to Club Bohém until after his election.

He glanced over to where Zsuzsa was making an embarrassment of herself. An image came to mind, and he chuckled at the absurdity of it.

Beside him, a presence. Erin leaned down and kissed him. "I'm sorry I'm late," she said, a little out of breath. "A cessation squad took the mother of one of my SIN enrichment class students last night. We must have got through a whole box of tissues between us. What's funny?"

"I was imagining myself sitting here dressed in a toga and sandals, discussing the finer points of meritocracy with the green-haired bitch. Do you think Petros would allow a Patrician into a meeting?"

Erin shrugged her eyebrows. "You never know. Petros enjoys living on the edge, in a dandy kind of way."

"He's on the edge all right," said Marci. "The greatest danger Petros will ever face is when his crème brûlée's caramelized at his table."

"After tonight you might change your mind about him."

"I doubt it." Marci thought about the two spies, but could see neither an aging Marxist nor a grown-up *femme fatale* among the crowd. The regulars, however, were here. Attila sat in the second row, his arms folded and a sneer already on his face, no doubt in anticipation of hearing something disagreeable; near the front,

Marysia chattered nervously with a distracted Petros; to right, talking loudly, were the liberal art students Zsuzsi and Zoli. Both held thermos mugs adorned with the logo of the latest, most fashionable cause. Marci watched them with a condescending sneer. Credit where it was due: the halfwits could maintain a conversation and sip their coffees almost at the same time. Soy lattes, probably.

In the center of the room were two chairs, one empty, the other taken by an unassuming figure of small stature and stocky physique sporting a crew cut. He wore tan slacks and a heavy navy pullover, military in style, complete with elbow patches. A striped beige tie added a modicum of awkward formality. His appearance conveyed neither elegance nor bohemian panache. A bus driver, perhaps? Whatever his trade, Marci thought he resembled a working-class man out of his depth.

Petros disengaged himself from Marysia and brought the meeting to order. "Good evening, everyone. Tonight is a special occasion, and you'll no doubt be pleased to learn I plan to speak as little as possible. Instead, someone far more qualified than I will chair our meeting. Without further ado, I shall step aside and ask you to welcome Peti."

The man with the crew cut rose. "Thank you, Petros. My name, for our purposes, is Peti. I won't mention my job, SIN or anything relating to my personal life, for reasons which will soon become obvious. Petros has assured me this is a closed-door event, and that appropriate security measures are in place. I'm here to speak on a topic I'm told has been the focus of this group in recent weeks: the Underground. Many of you may wonder if it exists, what it does and whether it's responsible for the bombings and riots that plague Budapest. Tonight I hope to shed some light on its activities, because I'm a spokesman for the organization."

Marci's stomach knotted: a rush of adrenaline, followed by a shiver of dread across his skin at the thought of being discovered here. Once again, he ran his eyes across the faces in the room.

"We begin with a history lesson," Peti said. "Thirty years ago, Grisha Ossian, the last of the Patricians, was alleged to have died. Ossian, like his contemporaries, was regarded as a genius, and for good reason. Vladimir Kolchenko's DOME spared Budapest the atom bomb, but Ossian developed the Red Plague vaccine and the cure for radiation sickness. The original Wall, which was also their doing, protected us from the anarchy of the Outside. The Patriarchs were heroes, and who could replace them? Finding a substitute would be like supplanting one's own doting parents.

"In 2096, Grisha was a frail eighty-nine-year-old. With his human cloning research still incomplete, people began asking questions about his future. Who would fill his shoes when he died? Budapest needed strong leadership; without him, the city would become a rudderless ship. From the ranks emerged an ambitious young administrator called Jean-Pierre Trauffaut.

"Trauffaut was an able bureaucrat with powerful connections in both government and the business world. In 2097 he ran for office with a radical agenda: replace the existing political structure with a form of meritocratic corporatocracy which would reward the successful and execute the weak or inefficient. The parliamentary model was scrapped in favor of a new form of government called the Company, with The Society of Patricians acting as a kind of Roman Senate. At the top of the pile was Trauffaut, the Prefect of Budapest.

"Trauffaut somehow sold his vision to the public. Overnight, the political landscape changed. Ossian stepped down from office and was replaced by Trauffaut, who now presided over a secretive council which would benefit from his decrees and approve his edicts without exception. Trauffaut would enjoy re-election in perpetuity, not by the will of the people but by his paid-off Club 30 cronies. And we, the ordinary citizens of Budapest, were now "Employees" in this new corporate world."

Marci, offended by the slur on the Prefect and The Society, folded his arms and decided he didn't like this Peti character.

"Budapest now faced an existential threat even greater than the Fuel War," Peti continued. "The fences, watchtowers and gun emplacements that kept the world at bay were preventing the city from expanding. At the same time, raiders from the Outside were attacking our plantations, killing our agricultural workers and stealing produce. Trauffaut, not one for half measures, had The Society rubber-stamp a directive that would address both problems at once.

First, the Company would extend the city limits fifty miles in every direction. For two weeks, heavy artillery pounded an area around Budapest the size of former Slovenia. What the shelling didn't destroy, incendiary bombs finished off. In a fortnight, the Prefect had purged the city's hinterlands of all life. While the ash was still settling, the Company laid the minefield we call the Field of Blood and began erecting the new Wall.

"The second prong was the SIN system. Despite its expansion, Budapest still needed to control its population. Trauffaut's brainchild was at once just and merciless: work hard and live or meet the Hangman. The Company sold it as a necessary evil, and work began on building MARTHA. All seemed well until the first cessations began."

Marci's focus drifted from Peti to the audience, which to a person sat in rapt attention. Even Attila had lost his characteristic smirk of disdain.

"In 2105, MARTHA went online and immediately began liquidating Employees. There was public outcry. Crowds, taking to the streets, tried to storm the newly formed Justice and Cessation Board at Nyugati. The Company responded quickly. The ringleaders were identified, taken inside and never again seen. Enforcement drones issued warnings, then gunned down those who refused to leave the area. Trauffaut appeared on News24 and pleaded for order. The Company would award every man, woman and child 10 SIN points, to use or squander as they wished. A six-month grace period would allow Employees to accumulate further SIN without fear of liquidation. MARTHA's cessation program was temporarily shelved."

Peti turned to Petros. "Forgive the preface, but it's necessary to understand how we got where we are today."

Petros waved away the apology. "Please, this is indispensable. Do continue."

"This brings us to the Underground. In 2107, a handful of students at the Weber Institute formed a secret society to discuss alternatives to the New Way. News of the group soon spread to other universities, attracting undergraduates and academics alike. When the Company got wind of it, the meetings shut down—or so it seemed.

In fact, the movement had gone dark, becoming a collective of city-wide home groups whose members included manual workers, lawyers, housewives and even politicians. Thus, the Underground was born.

"As it grew, it began attracting other, less wholesome elements. Our vetting process is stringent, but it isn't perfect. In 2122, local anarchists infiltrated a cell group in Debrecen. Before we could identify them they'd hijacked several demonstrations, turning what should have been peaceful protests into looting sprees. The Company seized on this and has portrayed us as insurrectionists ever since. However, I can assure you that the Underground has no part in any of the city's riots."

Marci made a sardonic sound, which Erin ignored. She seemed to be soaking it up like a sponge.

Petros asked: "Some have described the Underground as a political faction. Do you agree with the label?"

"The clue's in the name," Peti replied. "A faction implies membership of a ruling body. The Underground exists outside the political framework and has no interest in supporting the status quo. We're ordinary folk, united by our disgust for the system."

"You mentioned cell groups. How large is your membership?"

"It's in the low millions, not including staff. Each of the 47 districts has a Divisional Director. They report to Regional Directors, who answer to City Commanders. Despite Company propaganda to the contrary, we believe many more citizens are sympathetic to the cause but are afraid to join us."

Petros arched his fingers into a wigwam. "And what would you say are the Underground's ultimate goals?"

Without hesitation, Petros answered: "To remove the Company from power, abolish the SIN system and restore Budapest to a constitutional democracy."

Marci leaned over to Erin and whispered: "I knew that was coming."

Peti checked his watch. "My time here is short. I hope this potted history has provided an insight into the birth of the organization. I'm happy to take questions."

Petros rose and paused an unnecessarily dramatic moment. "Thank you, Peti. I, for one, am speechless. I open the floor for discussion."

"You mentioned Grisha Ossian's death," came a voice from the back of the room. "It sounds like you don't believe he died."

"Correct," Peti said. "The Company maintains that Ossian died in 2100. As is our tradition, all the other Patriarchs—Pétersson, Weber, Kolchenko, Geerts and Garcia—had open-casket parades. Ossian was more revered than any of them, yet he received no state funeral, only a private ceremony."

"So you're saying they didn't have the body?" asked Attila.

Peti gave a hard smile. "Exactly."

Zoli said: "Then where is it?"

Peti's expression didn't flicker. "We believe Grisha Ossian is still alive and living in the Outside."

Marci, who'd been sulking at Peti's slight, sat up.

"How is that possible?" someone said. "Wasn't he ninety when he died?"

"Ossian cloned himself when he was ninety-three," Peti replied. "He re-emerged as a twenty-year-old before fleeing the city. That would make him fifty-two now."

"Hogwash," Attila sneered, looking around for agreement. "Everyone knows he kicked the bucket years ago."

Erin raised her hand. "Why did he leave Budapest in the first place?"

"For two reasons," Peti said. "To evade a second Company assassination attempt, and to deny it access to his human cloning program."

Zoli spoke uncertainly. "Then Health Budapest's cloning program doesn't exist?"

Peti, saying nothing, shook his head.

"This is an outrage!" a woman in the center row protested. "What about my DNA samples? What's the Repository been doing with them?

Others joined her. "My slope! Does it mean nothing?" and "All these years of toil, wasted!"

Peti raised his hands for silence. "Ossian's whole-person cloning process involved two phases. The first copied the physical body. The second sought to duplicate the 'soul': the mind, will and emotions. Each involved a different apparatus. The Crucible duplicated the body, while Solace captured and implanted the subject's memories, relational connections and emotional make-up. Grisha was the guinea pig. As soon as the Company realized the system worked, they took it for themselves. Grisha knew what they planned to do with the technology and had already prepared his own disappearance. When he left, he took Solace with him."

"Why didn't he take the Crucible?" Erin asked.

"He was in a hurry," Attila scoffed.

Zsuzsi asked: "Does that mean we can clone the human body but not personalities?"

"Not even that," Peti answered. "The Company has the Crucible but no instructions on its use; Ossian was careful to take them with him. And without them, it's impossible to operate the device."

Petros sat forward. "But they might be trying?"

"They lack all scruples," Peti replied. "Anything is possible."

"They're making zombies right on our doorstep!" Marysia blurted.

Marci, who'd been listening in incredulous silence, found his voice. "What you're saying is preposterous. If human cloning is impossible, then the entire SIN system's a lie."

Peti nodded somberly. "That's exactly what it means."

"What about those who've reached SIN 33? And what about Empyrean?"

"How many are we talking about?"

Marci hesitated. There was only one man, and he'd waived his right to paradise for the greater good of the city.

"Trauffaut is sick," Peti said. "Empyrean aside, if the technology exists, why hasn't he cloned himself into a younger, healthier version of himself?"

"What about the bombings?" someone asked. "Is the Underground behind them?"

"I've covered that. Besides, why would we bomb our own city? It's hardly good PR."

"So the Company's blowing up its own citizens?" Attila jeered.

"Every society needs a public enemy," Peti replied. "We have two. Both are fictitious."

"Just how do you know all of this?" Marci said. "You've offered no proof whatsoever. Why should we believe any of your claims?"

"I'm not here to convince you," Peti replied. "There's proof, if you know where to look, both here in Budapest and the Outside."

Attila asked: "So you're in league with Outsiders?"

Peti gave an easy laugh. "'In league with' isn't a phrase I'd use. We have little contact with them and even less in common, save a loathing for the Company."

Erin asked, "What did you mean when you said the Underground is waiting for an opportune time?"

"I'm not going to jeopardize the organization's safety by providing operational details. But I will say this: a time is coming when the people of Budapest will have their eyes opened to the truth and will take matters into their own hands. The Underground will help facilitate this."

The door to Café Primo opened. Three heavyset men entered. Peti muttered to Petros, who sprang to his feet. "On that note, Peti must take his leave. I'm sure you'll agree this has been a fascinating discussion. I kindly ask you not to bring any further questions, as he has pressing business elsewhere."

There was a patter of shell-shocked applause. Without further word, Peti and his minders left. After a moment of dazed silence, the room broke into excited chatter.

Erin turned to Marci. "Wasn't it amazing? Can you believe it? Maybe you can't. How are you?"

Before he could reply, Petros approached. "Erin, my darling"—he took her hand and kissed it—"*csókolom*. And Marci, dear fellow"—he bowed. "Tell me: what did you make of Peti's presentation?"

"Oh, it was astonishing," Erin gushed. "Is it really true? About the Underground and the Outside and Grisha Ossian?"

"Peti is a good man, and his sources are impeccable. I happen to believe him."

"But what about Empyrean? Do you think it's all make-believe?"

"The evidence would seem to point in that direction. As Marci observed, only Prefect Trauffaut has sufficient SIN to retire there. Why, then, hasn't he? No, I fear Empyrean is a pipe dream."

"What evidence?" Marci growled. "All we've heard is unsubstantiated hearsay. If Ossian is alive, why hasn't the Company found him? They've had thirty years to do so."

"I'm not the man to ask," Petros said. "But from what I understand, our aircraft have limited range, and our transport ships don't monitor ground activity. I suppose the Company could fit them with cameras, but why bother? It would be like finding the proverbial needle in a haystack."

Marci grabbed his coat. "It's all too much. I don't believe the Company's bombing its own people. And I can't believe Empyrean's a lie. Petros, it's been entertaining, but I won't be coming to Club Bohém anymore."

Erin stood on tiptoes and kissed Petros on the cheek. "Thank you," she whispered.

Marci and Erin stepped into the strangely normal world of Café Primo. Outside, the wind was blowing rain in sheets down Sóház utca.

"I need a drink," Marci said. "Shall we find somewhere?"

"I think I'd like to go home," Erin said. "Peti's talk was a lot to take in, and I'm not sure a bar would suit me right now." She kissed him. "Don't stay out too late. Remember, you're trying to make a good impression at work."

"If only they could see me now."

Marci watched her make her way back to Fővám Tér, then lit a cigarette. For an instant the overcast above him broke to reveal a cold half moon and what he thought were the blinking red and green lights of a Company drone. Seconds later he saw only clouds. Troubled, he hurried home.

16

Twenty-six adjudication cases later found Marci on a bus full of Friday people headed home. The day had been long, tedious and routine—everything he'd hoped for. Tony Jackson had greeted him with chummy impudence, Morrison was grouchy and overworked, and Alex had ignored him. He'd skipped lunch, taken fewer smoke breaks and, importantly, committed no crimes. In short, he was above reproach. If carrot-top was snitching for Kruger, his outbox was empty.

All of this left only two commutes and a microwave dinner before he could put the day to bed. It was a victory of sorts. He'd managed to not think about last night for almost twenty-four hours.

At home, Marci poured himself a glass of pinot noir and settled into the Chesterfield. The main thing he felt was anger. "No more secrets." Those were Erin's words. Why, then, had she invited—no, insisted—that he attend a Club Bohém meeting whose guest was a fully-fledged member of the Underground? Peti was clearly deranged, yet he spoke with such conviction. But what of it? Even lunatics believe their own delusions. Marci chuckled at the thought of Hangmen in civvies armed with petrol bombs. If the Company was setting fire to its own city, he might as well take a Rapture pill.

The second feeling was fear. Being placed anywhere on Café Primo's premises concurrent with Peti's visit would affect his predictive interval. Marci's only comfort was that if there had been spies present, he'd openly refuted Peti's warped version of reality. It didn't excuse his presence, but it might count for something.

He spun the wine around the inside of his glass. Erin had failed to reply to any of his messages today. He decided not to jump to conclusions. Catastrophizing, Stella Kennedy had called it. Perhaps Erin, too, was trying to process Peti's ridiculous speech. Or maybe András was keeping her busy at Objet d'Heart.

At 23:30 Marci checked his phone before turning in for the night. His sent messages had all been read but he'd received no reply. At the very least it was rude, but she was a woman, and caprice was her prerogative.

Rising early, he spent the following morning working on his nomination speech, now due less than a month away. By lunchtime he'd made little headway and turned instead to the homework Stella had set him. This comprised two parts. The first was a multiple-choice survey twenty pages long covering various periods of his life. After several minutes, Marci realized that each question was rephrased in such a way as to subtly repeat its antecedents, as if the author's intent was to bamboozle him into an error of contradiction. With casual insouciance, Marci flitted through the document, completing it before his coffee had gone cold.

The second assignment was even more onerous than the first. Stella had insisted he keep a daily anxiety journal. Dates, triggers and emotional responses each had their own columns, and neither brevity nor blank spaces were permitted. Since Marci lacked both the time and inclination to keep the record up to date, he resorted to mendacity. By early afternoon he'd cobbled together enough anecdotes to appease her.

Marci sat back in his chair and stared outside. Low December sunlight slanted between the stark frames of Gyulai Pal's naked, artificial elm trees. The day was unseasonably warm; the perfect opportunity to spend time with someone special.

On a whim, he picked up his phone and dialed a number. After five rings it went to voicemail. Odd. Erin's phone always diverted on the eighth. Had she turned down his call? Irked, Marci resumed work on his nomination speech.

Sunday came, as irritatingly as warm as Saturday. Marci worked on his speech into the afternoon. At 14:00 he threw down his pencil in disgust and considered taking the FATS to Kecskemét. He decided against it. To turn up unannounced would at best appear desperate and at worst sinister.

A final bedtime call to Erin's number went straight to voicemail.

Monday turned up unwanted, followed by an equally unwelcome Tuesday. Marci arrived early and left late, dispatching his casework with consummate professionalism, all the while trying not to dwell on Peti's speech. *Under the radar*, he told himself. The truth, whatever the hell it was, could wait until he was safely in Buda.

On Wednesday evening, Marci visited Stella for another counseling session, having completed his weekly anxiety diary on the tram. Despite her obvious proficiency, Marci had little confidence in the regimen she'd devised, hoping rather that a panacea of a pharmaceutical nature might be on the table.

Stella was less enthusiastic. "Medication is only an adjunct to psychotherapy," she told him. "You've lived with anxiety for many years. Now we must begin the process of retraining your brain's response to stressful stimuli." Nevertheless, Marci left with a prescription for something he couldn't pronounce and a list of side effects that would terrify a stoic. At least, he thought, it was progress.

On Thursday, having heard nothing from Erin all week, Marci swallowed his pride and risked a visit to Club Bohém in the hope of finding her there. Tonight the mood was different. Peti's presentation had stirred up a hornet's nest of debate. Petros, too busy separating combatants, failed to notice Marci at the door, and since Erin was absent, Marci left without word.

Late on Friday morning his routine was interrupted by a knock on his cubicle door.

"Are you busy?"

Marci swung around in his chair. "For you, never."

Alex, wan and unkempt, closed the door behind him. "I owe you an apology. I should—"

Marci raised a finger to his lips. "Not here," he mouthed.

"It's nothing hush-hush. I came to say sorry for the other night. You were right. And I was out of order."

"Apology accepted. And please accept mine. I can be brisk at times."

"The guys are meeting up for a few drinks tonight. You free?"

Marci made a sound of frustration. "I've got a counseling appointment." He tapped his fingers on his armrest. "To hell with it. One missed session's not going to make a difference."

"Great. Seven-thirty at my place."

"I'll bring whiskey. The good stuff, not your gut rot."

At 18:44 Marci stepped off the SpeedWalk at Népliget and made his way through heavy rain to the Pimenov residence. He was received by Lei, who was busy preparing Lucinda and Huang to go out. Lei, a plump but comely lady of early middle years and Oriental descent, greeted him with a traditional kiss.

Feeling guilty, Marci said: "You're not staying?"

"And intrude on We Happy Few? Perish the thought! We're late for their pre-SIN prep class. Then it's off to mother's for the night."

"Can I help?"

"You can help Huang with his laces, if you don't mind. He's getting the hang of them, but he's still a bit slow. There's *kakaós csiga* in the oven. Don't let Alex burn them. He's like King Alfred when it comes to food."

"When it's black, it's done."

"So long as they're eaten, I don't mind. Huang, Lucinda, put on your rucksacks, please."

"How's work?" asked Marci. "I don't know how you juggle the law firm and looking after two kids."

"Three," Lei corrected. "Two of them are under ten and cause me less trouble than the third."

"And we're kicking you out again."

Lei shrugged. "It's a welcome break, although sometimes I'd like to visit mother on my own; at least we could get drunk together. Alex tells me we'll have to start bowing and scraping before you before too long."

"Perish the thought," Marci said. "In any case, first I need to get elected. Every time I think of Prefect Trauffaut and the Synod I break into a cold sweat."

"I remember feeling the same way when I joined the firm. A colleague told me to imagine my boss sitting on the toilet."

"Did it work?"

Lei smiled mischievously. "Too well. Whenever he called me into his office I had to fight the giggles. Children, are you ready? Yes? Then let's be off." To Marci she said, "Enjoy yourselves."

"You too."

Marci rescued the pastries from the oven and took them to the lounge. Seated on the sofa, Alex and Csaba were busy making a dent in the evening's beer supply. They rose to greet him.

"You look bloody awful," Marci told Alex. "Have you slept this week?"

"Not much. What's your news?"

"Not much either. Where's Akito?"

"In the doghouse," Csaba said. "Turns out he spent half his salary at a bookie's in Little Tokyo. The missus threw a fit. No more going out for a month."

"Silly bugger. Still, at least it gives Csaba a fighting chance. Not that it'll be much of a game with the three of us."

"Four," Alex said. "Anton's coming."

"Anton? I haven't seen him for months."

"Don't ask me what he's been up to," said Alex. "In fact, don't ask Anton what he's been up to."

Csaba put on a sinister voice. "He's a Hangman!"

Alex slapped Csaba's hand away from the pastries. "Csaba, I swear you're obsessed by Justice and Cessation. Have you ever sought professional help?"

"Who isn't? I still remember the kindergarten nursery rhymes. But I'm safe! My SIN's 18."

Alex took a shoebox from under the coffee table. Inside were several packs of playing cards and a dealer's chip. "Your SIN's safe but your pocket money isn't. Time to kiss it goodbye."

Csaba wiped his hands on his trousers. "We'll see about that. Tonight, things will be different."

Alex looked at Marci. "Isn't that the mantra of all addicts?"

They were interrupted first by a pizza delivery, then by Akito, who had been granted parole on condition that he didn't gamble anymore. The game broke off for dinner.

At 20:00 the doorbell rang. Standing on the walkway was a man tall and spare. Blonde stubble covered his chin and jawline; eyes of delft blue shone with clever intelligence. His raincoat, which was sodden from the rain and thirty years out of fashion, clung to his wiry frame. The knapsack and wide-brimmed bush hat he wore were equally outmoded. He stood with a stoop, as if his height were an embarrassment to him. As he entered the kitchen, the fellows of We Happy Few gave up a cheer of welcome.

"Anton!" Csaba cried, "we thought you'd been liquidated!"

Anton smiled. "I'm working on it."

Akito embraced him. "Good to see you, brother. It's been too long."

"Good to be here." Anton extended his hand to Marci, who somewhat stiffly shook it.

"Pálinka?" asked Alex. "The good stuff."

Anton removed his coat and took a seat. "We're celebrating?"

"Alex is one step further from the grave," Csaba said.

Anton regarded Alex with mild surprise. "You made SIN 33?"

"Not quite," Alex said. "SIN 24, a couple of months ago. Marci's the hero: he's a whisker away from Club 30."

Akito slapped the table. "We Happy Few are on the up! Soon we'll all be sipping tequilas in Empyrean!"

"SIN 24's a big deal," Anton remarked. "What did you do?"

Alex carried the shot glasses to the table, one on each finger like thimbles, and set the bottle down with a thump. "Oh, just a little tinkering with the Exec Team database."

"It must have been some tinkering," Anton said.

"Did you tell Morrison about your MARTHA model?" Akito asked. To Anton he said, "You won't believe this. Alex only recreated MARTHA's entire database on his home computer."

Alex spoke over him. "Marci, will you be having pálinka tonight?"

"If the alternative's your whiskey, yes."

"Weren't you bringing a bottle of your own?"

"I forgot it," Marci lied; there was no way he was sharing the Yamazaki with five of them. "Anton, you look like you chewed a bee."

"It's nothing."

"Spit it out, man!" urged Akito. "We haven't seen you in months. We want to hear your views on life, the universe and how to gain more slope!"

Anton frowned. "I admit to some confusion. Alex, don't you and Marci work for Data Analytics? Then why would you need to show your model of MARTHA to Fraser Morrison?"

Alex pulled the cork free from the pálinka bottle, spilling some of the spirit on the table.

"Because Morrison's our boss," Marci replied.

"Really? I thought Marcus Behrman ran D.A. Doesn't Morrison head up Adjudication?"

Marci flushed. "That's Rieks Kruger. Morrison is Head of Data Analytics."

Anton nodded slowly. "My mistake. The mystery is solved, except for one last matter: if Alex works for Data Analysis, why would he need to create a model of MARTHA at home? Surely he'd have access to her files at work?"

Marci watched the neck of the bottle tremble as Alex tried to pour a shot. He took the flask from him and dispensed each of them a measure. "Alex was looking for anomalies. I assume he lacked the time at work. It isn't part of our job remit. Is it, Alex?"

"Absolutely not."

"You assume?" Anton asked. "Don't you guys work together?"

"What is this, the bloody Spanish Inquisition?" Marci growled.

"Guys!" Akito cried, "lighten up! Alex made 24 and Marci's about to join the high life. I'd say that's cause for celebration."

"Hear! hear!" Csaba said, raising his glass. "We're proud of both of you."

"Me included," said Anton. "A toast, then: to our friends Alex and Marci. May their SIN grow ever higher."

They saluted, drank.

"Bloody hell," Marci gasped, "what is this stuff? I've smelled paint stripper that's kinder on the palate."

Csaba, still savoring the fruit spirit, began to chortle and accidentally inhaled most of it, sputtering the rest into his lap.

"Csaba likes to enjoy his pálinka to the fullest," observed Alex. "Swallowing it isn't enough."

"You ok, man?" asked Akito. "You want a slap on the back?"

Csaba's face was scarlet. Too inconvenienced by coughing to speak, he shook his head.

"Another toast," said Alex. "To We Happy Few. An odd bunch, but decent fellows except for Csaba, who ate all the *kakaós csiga* before Anton got here."

The group, except for Csaba who was still busy choking, raised their glasses and toasted.

From his backpack Anton removed a rectangular slab of something wrapped in black and gold, and a blue-and-silver striped tin canister, placing both on the table.

Csaba recognized the first before the others did. "Chocolate!"

"And coffee," Alex said, inspecting the label. He looked up in something like awe. "It's real."

Marci, trying to sound casual, asked: "How did you find these?"

Anton tapped his nose. "Ask me no questions."

"The chocolate's Australian," Csaba said, sniffing the paper. "It's real too."

Akito snatched it from him. "What are you, a drug dealer? Of course, it's Australian. Where else does cocoa grow?"

"Coffee and chocolate," Marci mused. "You're full of surprises."

Anton smiled. "I have friends in low places."

"I don't doubt that," muttered Marci, pouring himself another drink.

"Anton's the black sheep of our happy flock," Csaba said. "I reckon he's a Hangman with good connections."

Akito buried his face in his hands. "Not this again."

"Or maybe an Undergrounder?" Marci speculated.

Anton fixed Marci with a hooded gaze. "Anything's possible. We all have our secrets, don't we?"

"Enough banter," said Alex, placing the chocolate out of Csaba's reach. "Akito, you're banker. Marci, you're small blind. Gentlemen, please have your credits to hand. Is everyone ready? Then let's begin."

The game resumed. Alex, Anton and Marci played with caution. Unusually, Csaba forsook his usual scare tactic of betting high on the flop, perhaps because of Anton's reputation as a card shark. Akito, who was lucky by nature, won a spate of rounds with good hands and sensibly adventurous wagers.

After an interlude of coffee and chocolate Marci began to win, on one occasion placing his cards face-up on the table. Anton, noticing their low value, commended him on his bluff.

Marci ignored him and changed tactics. The community cards were promising: a nine of spades and a pair of jacks. Pleasant silence settled over the table as each man weighed his options and devised his strategy. Csaba sat hunched over his cards, sweating; Akito lounged, lazy and unperturbed, with one arm slung across the back of his chair; Anton was inscrutable; and Alex sat enjoying his share of the chocolate.

Marci studied his hand, which included the nine of diamonds and the nine of hearts. His opponents would only need a jack to beat him; the chances of anything more sensational were very low. A straight, Marci calculated, ran a cumulative probability of 1%. In spite of the jack, he decided to bet high.

Csaba, who had not laid off the pálinka, matched Marci's three-credit gambit. On second thoughts, he slid his remaining eight to the center of the table. "All in."

Anton regarded his hand, then Marci, whose expression was inscrutable as his own, then Csaba's contribution to the pot, which amounted to twenty-four credits—a considerable sum of money. He counted out, stacked and moved a column of coins to the middle, watching Csaba's poker face disintegrate. "Call."

Alex leaned back in his seat. "Too rich for my blood. I'm out."

Akito stared at the pile of credits. "I've put most of my money in this game, but my missus will kill me if I lose. I'm out, too."

Alex looked from Anton to Marci to Csaba. "It's just the three of you reckless fools. Let's see who's going to be working overtime for a month. Marci, show your hand."

Marci turned over his cards.

"Csaba?"

Csaba twisted his cards over: a nine and a three of hearts.

Anton, without expression, tossed his hole cards on the table face-up.

Akito slapped the table. "Damn it, Anton, I swear you could bluff your way into Empyrean itself!"

"A full house," said Alex. "Marci, it seems you were bettered this time."

Anton scooped up his winnings. "Don't take it badly. If you hadn't shown us your lousy winning hand earlier, I'd never have met Csaba's raise."

Marci put his coat on and went outside. Night rain, red and blue in the lights of an overhead Zeppelin, fell with narcotic incessancy into the courtyard. He leaned over the railing and lit a cigarette, furious with himself for losing so much money. He was angrier with Anton. Who the hell was he to question his and Alex's line of work? And how had he known Morrison worked for the Executive Team? Unlike Data Analytics staff, Exec Team employment records were classified. A simple search on AirNet would have shown that Marcus Behrman ran D.A., but Morrison's role was off-the-record.

Then there was the obvious question, one that Akito and Csaba—well, Akito at least—had always been too polite to ask: why indeed recreate MARTHA at home if Alex worked for Data? Marci's was a sloppy answer based on a sloppier oversight. They should have created a more credible excuse months ago.

The front door opened and closed. Anton leaned on the railing beside him, a Sobranie hanging from his lips. "Do you have a match?"

"Yes. My arse and your face."

"That's an old one. Have a real cigarette."

They were Russian. Too good to pass up. Marci flicked his Winterbourne into space and acquiesced.

"Sorry about that," Anton said, accepting a light. "I didn't mean to take you to the cleaners."

"It's just chump change."

"If you say so."

"Csaba had it worse."

"Csaba's a mug. You're nobody's fool." Anton studied Marci. "Nice bluff, earlier. The poker one, that is. You had me fooled."

Marci resisted asking what the other one was. "Is that an accolade?"

"Maybe. You're good at reading people."

"Evidently not well enough."

"Well enough. It must come in handy in your profession."

"In Data? Not really."

"Data, still? I thought that one had died a death."

Marci turned to leave.

Anton motioned him to stay. "You're an interesting guy, Marci. SIN 30 at what? Thirty-nine? Only a handful of jobs offer slope like that, and Data Analytics isn't one of them. You'll be the first Adjudicant to make it into The Society. That's quite an achievement."

Marci spoke carefully: "I don't know where this is going, but if you're goading me for some kind of confession, you're wasting your time. I work for Data Analytics. So does Alex. So does Fraser Morrison. Now please excuse me: my palinka's getting cold."

"No confession needed. Your career's the worst kept secret this side of the Wall."

Marci let his Sobraine sizzle out on the wet railing and turned to leave. "Piss off, Anton."

"At least you've done a better job hiding your Club Bohém antics."

Marci stopped. A chill, forming at the nape of his neck, spread across his shoulder blades and down both arms. "Club Bohém?" he asked. "What do you know about Club Bohém?"

"Enough to realize you're no dyed in the wool Company man." Anton strolled over to the front door and opened it a crack—wide enough to let out a draft of rowdy bonhomie, too narrow to allow

Marci inside. "You're playing a dangerous game, especially for an Adjudicant."

Marci tried to push the door open. Anton held it closed.

"I don't know what you're talking about," Marci said brusquely.

"You realize," Anton said, "that Morrison ran a micro-NIPS on you for accessing Alex's profile?"

Marci stepped back to take Anton in whole. "How do you know all this?" he stammered.

"That doesn't matter."

"Then what do you want? Money?" Marci fumbled for his wallet and pulled out a sheaf of banknotes. "Here, take it. I have more, much more."

Anton said almost with pity: "Put it away. I came to bring you a message. The Company isn't the only one watching you. When the time comes, we'll be there for you."

"What time?" Marci asked, "and who is 'we'? I don't know what you're talking about."

Anton let himself into the kitchen. As he closed the door behind him, he spoke two words: "You will."

Marci stepped back from the threshold. His legs gave way. Stumbling, he grabbed the walkway railing and turned to overlook the quadrangle below. The Zeppelin, floating closer, cast an infernal shade of crimson from its billboard which smothered the building, courtyard and the rain around it.

He squeezed his eyes shut as a rush of vertigo engulfed him. His pills! Where were they? Everything was in his backpack in the lounge. More than his medication, even more than fleeing home, he needed alcohol.

His blood pulsing an allegretto in both temples, Marci entered the kitchen, grabbed the whiskey from the table and took it to the lounge. Lacking a glass, he downed a Cortiquell from the bottle in two unpleasant gulps.

The effect was immediate. Heavy with sudden fatigue, he sank to the sofa and drifted off to the sound of banter, which had resumed in the other room.

When he came to, Alex was saying his name. "You're awake, thank God."

Marci wiped his face with the heel of his hand. "What time is it?"

"Midnight. Shall I call a cab or do you want to crash here?"

"Where's Anton?"

"He left soon after you stole all the booze. How much have you drunk?"

"I don't remember."

"I thought you didn't like it."

"I don't."

Alex sat down opposite. "Did you two have words or something? You looked pretty shaken up when you came in."

"Something like that." Marci shielded his eyes from the ceiling light; his head was killing him.

"It couldn't have come to much," Alex said. "He left you a whole pile of credits. You don't like him, do you?"

"Are the others here?"

"Only Csaba. Akito lost all his money and went home. He'll be eating gruel for a month of Sundays."

Marci pulled himself upright with the coffee table's help. In the kitchen, a very drunk Csaba crooned the Hungarian national anthem with the help of half-remembered chords from Alex's guitar.

Outside, the rain had stopped; the night dripped silently with runoff below a sky full of stars.

"Don't forget your cash," Alex said.

Marci glanced at the table. Anton had left him more coins than he'd come with. "You keep them," he said. "Buy us some decent whiskey for next time."

"I will, but I'm worried. Do you want to tell me what happened earlier?"

He didn't. He didn't want to think about anything. The Cortiquell was working, and he was loath to break its spell. He checked his watch: 23:47. Cinderella still had a little time to get home.

He bade Alex farewell, hailed an air cab and was asleep in bed before he could remember anything Anton had said. Reality would come in its own bad time.

17

Arriving groggy and late to work the following morning, Marci went directly to his suite, locked the door and slumped in his chair to stare at the ceiling. The Cortiquell had worn off, but not the booze, and he nursed a headache Trotsky would have been proud of.

Marci let out a slow, sighing curse. Anton had cast the die; circumstance now forced Marci's hand. The question was how to play it with the least damage. Morrison hadn't minced his words. If suspected of misconduct, Marci would be hauled before Intelligence Director Ron Taggart to explain himself. They'd met once, which was once too often. Taggart disliked Adjudicants and would gladly send him to Nyugati a full NIPS test, a painful and invasive procedure requiring Marci to fast his medication 48 hours prior. Yet, if handled correctly, the risks should be minimal.

Marci wheeled his chair over to the console. MARTHA slept. Ranged above him, eight black monitors stared blankly down at Márton Kovács, an insect trapped inside a spider's web. He tapped a button and looked into a camera set in her fascia. Eight eyes came alive.

"Biometric scan complete. Good morning, Adjudicant Kovács."

Marci's fingers hovered over the keyboard long enough to have second thoughts. The Company was watching him? Let them. Morrison and Taggart could run all the NIPS they wanted; the truth would exonerate him.

He tapped a succession of keys and hit return. For good measure, he dictated a command: "Hide last request from public records. Recipient access only." The last thing he wanted was Alex finding out.

It was done. Marci leaned back in his seat. All he had to do now was wait.

At noon a message appeared. Marci downloaded the attachment, hid it in his backpack and, skipping lunch, applied himself to his caseload.

At 18:00 he logged off and walked to the E.T. office. The shark tank was dark.

"He went home early," Moira said, her eyes on her monitor. "Can I take a message?"

"It can wait."

Back at home, Marci ordered pizza from the one restaurant his fear of poisoning allowed and spread Anton's profile on his desk.

Anton Aslanov's life was remarkable only in its mediocrity. The single event of note was the liquidation of his parents, who were discovered attending a church house group during a wave of religious persecution. Along with a handful of other believers, they were sent to Nyugati for interrogation but refused to deny their Christian faith or swear fealty to the Company. Both were charged with treason and liquidated the same day.

Overnight, Anton and his sister Saskia were orphaned. Saskia had gone to pieces. After a period of disbelief, then rage, Anton dropped out of university and found menial work to pay the mortgage on the family home. It wasn't enough. Three months later they moved to a bedsit in the Eden complex. Saskia found lucrative work in Nursery Three, a soy processing plant. Her earnings enabled Anton to resume his university studies in Heavy Air Mainframe Support. On graduating, he landed a job working for Atlas Heavy Air, Inc. Their days of poverty were over.

Marci poured through the rest of the document, although there was little else of interest. Anton had vacated Eden as soon as possible, married, raised two children, divorced, and been promoted three times. He taught "success visualization" at a community center two evenings a week, played competition chess and lacked both a social presence and cell phone number. His SIN was 20, his predictive interval 9%. No flags, no red lights, no klaxons. On paper, he was as inculpable as a librarian who moonlighted for the Sally Army.

Marci dropped the file into the bin. Had he really risked Morrison's wrath for this? Anton's biography failed to address the very reason he'd requested it. But what had he expected? If the Company believed Anton an Undergrounder he'd already be dead.

One other question remained. How did Anton know about Club Bohém?

The answer came, quick and painful: Alex. The pair of them were friends. All it would have taken was a lapse in discretion—something he was prone to— for Alex to mention it. The NIPS remark was a throwaway line from a man who bluffed for a second income. Anton had simply put two and two together and scared the hell out of him. Cursing his folly, Marci picked Anton's file out of the bin and flung it across the room, followed by his whiskey glass.

Now what? Damage limitation was key. He'd have to intercept Morrison early tomorrow and explain the whole matter. All except Club Bohém, of course.

For most of Friday morning Marci wore a groove in the floor between his suite and Fraser Morrison's office. Morrison was busy—so a notice on his door attested in unmistakable terms. Moira, with customary focus on her monitor, would shed no light on when he'd next be free.

Late in the afternoon, Marci rode the elevator to the rooftop, a terrace of potted palms and cigarette butts which afforded views of Hősök tere and Városliget. A dust storm had blown in from the Adriatic. The sediment, mingling with rain, streaked the sky with glowing shafts of gold. It was a glorious sight, although a little too ostentatious for his liking, as if God was gilding the lily.

Marci walked to the guard rail and sagged against it, overcome by a feeling of such sudden, desolate loneliness that he wondered if he was finally losing his mind. An image of Erin seated on the ground with her knees clutched to her chest and her head bowed in sorrow entered his mind, as distinct and palpable as the cityscape before him. A moment later, the vision and mood lifted, leaving him a deep sense of unease. Was he sharing in some kind of telepathic misery of hers? He checked his phone: she was offline. His messages, all six of them sent today, were unread.

He leaned over the guardrail. Far below, Friday afternoon traffic crawled along György Dózsa út. A thought occurred. Not quite ideation, more a fleeting fancy. It would be a spectacular end to a meaningless existence. Perhaps, if he timed it well, Morrison would emerge from the building to break his fall: a final act of kindness to the world.

Marci returned to the Adjudication office, where the lights in the shark tank were out. Moira caught sight of him and shook her head by way of apology; apparently, carrot-top had left for the day. Perhaps, Marci thought, he should have jumped after all.

Loath to head home, Marci went to his suite, locked himself inside and sat staring at MARTHA's screens, holo-projectors and console buttons. Across the deep, kidney-shaped desk, MARTHA watched him. Almost sentient. Almost human. Here was his true north. No matter what the warp and weft of life yielded, she would never leave him.

MARTHA, OH MARTHA! If only you were flesh and blood. But in the end, you're just as faithless as the rest of them.

He returned to the roof garden. Dusk had settled on the city. Along Andrássy út, the well-heeled enjoyed their reflections in shop windows while shawled gypsy women lay prostrate begging for change. A waning moon, low in the east, fought to pierce the aura-glow of sand and streetlight.

Erin! Again she came to him, but now as an intense, visceral longing. Marci stepped up to the parapet and peered the edge. Three hundred feet of gloom eventually collided with Dózsa György út. At his weight, around 4.3 seconds. Long enough to have second thoughts several times over.

In a mood as bleak as he could remember, Marci went back to his cubicle. On this occasion, he didn't hesitate.

Ten minutes later he was riding the SpeedWalk with the nervous anticipation of a schoolboy carrying his first pornographic periodical. Inside his briefcase was his own forbidden fruit: Erin's profile, her whole life in impartial, explicit detail. Disembarking at Rákóczi tér, the attaché felt heavy with significance, and Marci wondered if those around him could somehow sense the dirty secret it contained.

In his apartment hallway, Mária Földi was peering inside someone else's mailbox. Seeing Marci, she straightened and showed a remorseless, gappy smile. *"Jó estét,* Marci! *Hogy vagy?"*

Marci ignored her and trudged upstairs. On the third floor, Norbert Tóth was busy in his kitchen with a new toy: a bench grinder. Marci considered yelling an expletive, but it would have been swallowed up in the noise. Besides, he was in no mood for a confrontation.

He retreated inside his flat and washed his hands until his fingers bled. Despite his appointments with Stella Kennedy, his OCD had relapsed, the skin on his hands now a latticework of paper cut lesions that no amount of ointment could relieve.

Marci took a tumbler full of whiskey to the lounge and spread Erin's profile across the coffee table to create a chronological centerfold of her life. School reports, social media activity, medical and employment records, spending data, friendships and romantic attachments—together these painted a portrait of the person that was Erin Macsy.

Toward the end of the document, MARTHA had taken the minutiae of Erin's twenty-nine years and applied to them her predictive algorithms to produce behavioral projections of such detail as would shame the most gifted seer. The remainder of her days were already mapped out.

Impelled by loneliness and rejection, Marci gathered up the pages and began to feed on the details of her life, at once greedy with an insatiable hunger for the most intimate details of her life, and also wholeheartedly disgusted with himself for his secret violation of her privacy. With each page he felt more and more pained: pained because she had trusted him not to do this, and pained because she would probably forgive him. Damn her forgiveness! He hoped she wouldn't. Offering him grace would only debase her even further. Her words, spoken at Normafa, came alive. He was a gentleman! He was a man of honor! It's why she loved him.

After eight pages he could stand it no more. He tossed the document onto the tabletop. The pages spread out like a dove's tail across the surface, with one falling to the floor. Marci picked it up and was about to put it with the others when his eyes fell on the final page.

SUMMARY:
ERIN REBECCA MACSY
EMPLOYEE ID 492FR973A688
SIN 5
PATR

Subject recommended for expedited cessation on grounds of political deviancy.

Marci stared at the words. A knot the size of a fist formed in his solar plexus.

Five. The number every Employee dreaded. The number he'd scrawled in the writing pad in his dream.

His father's number.

He scooped up Erin's paperwork and began rummaging through it. There—her SIN development sessions. Over the last two years, they'd boosted her slope by a meager quarter point. Her employment records were equally mediocre. A series of low-paid, short-lived jobs had done little to improve her prospects.

Marci turned to her lifeline, which showed a slow but positive four-year trajectory from SIN 13 to SIN 14. In June 2131, the bullish trend ended. Her line plateaued, then began to fall. For the next eleven months, Erin's SIN had tumbled 28% to SIN 10. Her predictive interval was just as shocking; a rise from 3% to 21%. To Marci the connection was clear. A year last June she'd started attending Club Bohém.

What didn't make sense was what followed. Since the time of their first date in September her SIN had entered free fall, losing over half its value. Fifty-one percent in 91 days. It was an unprecedented decline. Why? And why hadn't she checked it? Erin's words, spoken on their trip to Buda, returned to him: "None of us care about our SIN so long as it's above 5."

Marci hurried to the hall, then returned to the lounge to dither a moment. Time was of the essence. MARTHA had issued the kill order this morning, but Justice and Cessation would wait for her to get home from work. That could be any time now. He dialed her number. A chirpy voicemail greeting wasted ten seconds.

"Erin, it's me," he said. "I need you to get out of the house. Go somewhere public—a café or the library or somewhere. Don't ask me why. I'll call you back."

Marci put her profile in his briefcase and ran down to the street, where an air cab was discharging its passengers. "Executive Team building, Hősök tere," he said, climbing in. "As fast as you can."

Three minutes later, the taxi discharged him on Dózsa György út. Marci cleared security and stepped from the elevator on the eighteenth floor. The administrative office was quiet; a few late workers toiled in pools of isolated screen light.

Marci ran to the Adjudication suite and entered his cubicle.

MARTHA's screens flickered into life. "Biometric scan complete. Good evening, Adjudicant."

"Request profile of Erin Macsy, Employee ID"—he read off the printout—"492FR973A688."

There was a pause.

"Unable to comply."

Marci frowned. "Open Employee file: Erin Rebecca Macsy."

MARTHA spoke in a stoic monotone. "Unable to comply. Access to this file has been restricted based on your personal connection with the Employee. Your request to access this file has been flagged."

Marci struck the keyboard. "Damn you!"

"Warning," MARTHA said, "violation of Company equipment is a criminal offense. This incident has been logged."

Marci ran back to the elevator. He dialed Alex and spoke in a tumble. "I checked Erin's profile. She's SIN 5. There's an expedited cessation order and the same PATR code Takumi had. I tried canceling it, but MARTHA's blocked access to her file."

Alex spoke a muffled aside to someone, then asked, "Are you at work?"

"Yes, but I'm leaving for Kecskémet. Maybe I can beat the Hangman there."

"I'll try to hack my way in from here. If that doesn't work, I'll rescind it from the office."

"I can't ask you to do that," Marci said. "They'd figure out the connection in an instant."

"Don't worry. If they ask, tell them we haven't discussed it. We can work out the consequences later."

"They'll come down on you like a ton of bricks."

Alex laughed: a bitter sound. "I'm already a marked man. Besides, I owe you for checking my predictive interval."

"Checking your interval isn't the same as changing someone's SIN."

"Let's just call it even."

"I don't know what to say."

"Nincs mit."

On Dózsa György út Marci waved down a taxi. On second thoughts, it would be better for them to meet halfway. He tried Erin's number again. This time he got through. "Erin, it's me. Did you pick up my message?"

She sounded half asleep. "What message?"

It doesn't matter. I need you to meet me. Can you get to the playground under Margit Bridge?"

There was a pause. "Yes, I suppose I can, but—"

"Please," Marci urged, "get out of the house. I'll explain everything there."

"Is everything all right? You sound scared."

No, it's not all right. Take the SlideWay or an air cab. I'll pay the fare. Okay?"

"Okay. I'll leave now."

Marci hung up and boarded the cab, which rose swiftly to merge with an air corridor. Above Nyugati it banked hard over the Justice and Cessation Headquarters and its smoking incinerator towers, then descended to one of Margit Island's landing pads.

A rubber jogging track encircled the island. Marci followed it south to where it ran a semi-circle beneath the abutment of the bridge's southern embranchment. A children's play area and calisthenics station occupied a space near the bank of the Danube and harkened to simpler years. Both of them he'd played on as a kid; both now lay corroded and broken.

Marci found a bench. Feeling sick with dread, he patted himself down but found only the apple peel-like twist of a Kqalms wrapper. In lieu, he lit a cigarette and listened to the sound of cars crossing the viaduct. They were Buda-bound, of course, the luxury sedans and exotica of the smart set. At night, the rich flew in; these were day-trippers headed home with their District VI spoils. He recalled that, in his childhood, he'd sat here with his father playing a guessing game: "whose car is this?" With great gusto he would portray the personage of each occupant as he imagined them—kings, queens, perhaps even Prefect Trauffaut himself—with dramatic, often operatic enactments of their lives and deeds, to his father's amusement. Marci had always assumed his *apa* knew everyone in Buda because he knew a lot about pretty much everything. Looking back, neither of them had a clue what went on over there. Thirty-two years later, Marci still didn't.

Five minutes passed. How would he break it to her? He'd sit her down. Better still, they could go for a walk. That way he wouldn't have to look her in the face when he confessed to reading her profile. He wasn't sure which she'd take harder, that or her SIN. If Alex called with good news it would make telling her easier. But even if he managed to change Erin's SIN, they were only buying time. Within a day or two, MARTHA reset it. The Hangman would come, and he would find her no matter where she hid.

Marci closed his eyes. Sounds and images came unwanted. Pillangó utca, lit with the pulsing strobes of a Justice Board van. Heavy footsteps pound along her walkway. How will she receive them? He sees her now, curled up fetus-like beneath her bed, trying not to cry at the sight of jackboots moving through her room. The boots stop. A knee appears, then a visored face, then a gloved hand reaching for her hair. Trussed like an animal, she is frog marched past gawping neighbors to the waiting transport.

At Nyugati they process her. Nyugati: spartan, sterile, warm and over bright; ripe with the tang of disinfectant and the stench of bodily emissions. The interview is cursory. Her crimes are certain, the penalty death. There is no appeal.

In an anteroom she is stripped and led along a passage bright as day to a chamber where Vivaldi plays from the ceiling and where Rapture does not come in white-and-cyan packets. A nurse waits, syringe ready. Two male orderlies loll in a corner, eyeing Erin with undue interest. The cessation officer stands aside as the judicial yields to the medical.

A plastic gurney is her deathbed. The orderlies strap her down, a band across her chest, another above her knees. One grabs her arm and bends it straight. No alcohol swab is offered; there is no need. As the needle punctures her skin, Erin cries out. The fluid enters her like a violation.

The nurse and orderlies retreat and wait. Thirty seconds to narcosis, death around one-twenty. The drug, reaching her brain and spinal cord, takes immediate effect. As life slips from her body, Erin's face softens. Even Nyugati cannot deny its victims the joy of Rapture.

A minute passes. The nurse inspects the body. She nods to the cessation officer, who turns and leaves the room.

The restraints are removed. An orderly operates a lever. A hatch in the wall opens to reveal a steel chute. He pulls another lever. The pallet rises, tipping the corpse through the hatch into darkness.

Four storeys below, her descent is broken by a trough of bodies. In the flicker of firelight, men, women and children, piled high in undignified nakedness, move along a conveyor belt that encircles a ring of outward-facing furnaces. At each, silhouettes of men like flickering demons toss the corpses onto belt feeders, which stoke the flames day and night with human fuel.

Closer now he watches her. As she draws near he sees her move: a twitch of her hand, a jerk of her leg. Her chest rises with sudden force. She moans and turns her head to face him. Reptilian pupils, narrow and vertical, glare at Marci. From her dead lips issue forth a diabolical baritone: "You killed me! You killed me!"

You've killed her. You're an Adjudicant. You know the rules. Never get close to anyone. You've destroyed her, just like you've destroyed everything.

Marci roused himself. He got up and began striking his ears to quell the inner voice. "No I haven't!" he shouted. "Shut up, shut up!"

From somewhere close came hurried footsteps. Erin rounded the corner of the embankment out of breath. "I got here as soon as I could," she said. "Is everything all right? Who were you talking to?"

Marci collected himself. Taking her hand, he led her to the bench. "You're SIN 5," he said. "MARTHA's flagged you for liquidation."

"Liquidated?" Erin stared at him. "Marci, if this is some kind of joke it's not funny at all."

"I wish it was. I checked your profile. I know I shouldn't have, but I did. Last summer you were SIN 14. Then it began falling. Since we first met it's dropped to 5. I tried canceling the order, but MARTHA's locked me out. I—"

"Really, Marci! I don't know what's got into you. Did you really drag me all the way here for some cruel joke?"

Marci looked at her, slack-jawed. "A joke?"

"I know what this is about. You're cross because I didn't reply to your messages. This is your revenge, isn't it? I was busy when you called. In fact, I've been busy all week. Just because—are you listening to me?"

Marci had opened his briefcase and was sorting through the pages of her profile. He handed her the summary. "It's at the bottom," he said. "In bold."

Erin reluctantly took it to the light of a nearby streetlight, and holding the page with both hands as if it were the hymn sheet to her own dirge, read it.

Marci tried to watch her eyes move across the paper, but her face was in shadow. Two tears rolled from her nose and landed on the foolscap, loud enough for him to hear.

When she fell, he caught her. He took her back to the bench and she placed her head against him and sobbed until he thought she'd make herself sick, and her perfume, that sweet, familiar redolence of jasmine and violets, rose from her skin to engulf them both. He wondered if he'd ever smell it again.

She pulled away and wiped her eyes. She had, Marci observed, undergone that baffling metamorphosis of hers, apparently at will, to bring her emotions in check.

"When will they come?" she asked, quite calmly.

"I don't know. Today or tomorrow."

She began to cry again. "My family! Oh Marci, I'll never see them again!"

Hating his cowardice—didn't she deserve the truth?—he said: "Yes, you will. Alex is restoring your SIN. If he can't breach MARTHA's firewall, he'll reinstate it at the office." An idea occurred to him, something desperate, probably futile, and certainly something he would have thought crazy a week ago. But it was a straw, and right now he'd draw any. "Look," he said, "we'll speak to Petros. Maybe he can talk to Peti. The Underground will help. Didn't he mention cell groups? They must have places where people can stay."

"And then what, Marci? I live in hiding for the rest of my life?" Erin reached in her sleeve for a tissue but found none.

"Sándor!" Marci said, suddenly encouraged. "I'll call Sándor. If anyone can help, it's him."

Erin took a vanity mirror from her handbag and inspected her face. The mask had fallen into place again. "That's kind of you." She rose. "I should be going. I need to phone Mummy and Daddy and Sophia."

"Do you want to stay at my place tonight?"

"I think I'll go home to Győr. But I don't want the Hangman visiting me at my parent's. Do you think I'll be safe?"

"That depends on Alex."

"I suppose I should thank you for checking my profile."

"Please don't."

Erin embraced him fiercely. "I'm very afraid," she whispered, but her voice carried no emotion. "And I'm sorry for worrying you. The last Club Bohém meeting put me in a bit of a tailspin. But you mustn't go worrying every time I need some space."

Every time. She spoke it like they still had some left.

His phone rang. "It's done," Alex said, "but there are complications."

"What complications?"

"I'll tell you in person. Can you meet me at The Celtic Cross?"

"Give me ten minutes."

To Erin's unspoken question, Marci said, "He restored your SIN. How long it will last I don't know."

She hugged him again. "Thank you. For everything."

"Don't. I should never have read your profile."

Erin gave a bittersweet laugh. "At least now we can skip the 'getting to know each other' phase of our relationship."

"I should print you a copy of mine," he said, "If MARTHA will let me. At least then we'd be on an even footing."

"I'd enjoy reading that, I think. When you're a Patrician, you can do anything you like."

On the bridge Marci hailed a ground cab to Rottenbiller utca and hurried inside The Celtic, a lively Irish pub inhabited by career drunks and a perpetual pall of cigarette smoke, which hung like a magic trick twenty feet in the air. He made his way across the room, wincing as his shoes stuck and unstuck on a floor tacky from cheap beer and a sloppy cleaning rota.

Alex sat hunched over a half-finished pint, with another to keep it company. He was a sorry sight. His face, unshaven, was drawn and pallid. Dark semi-circles hung below bloodshot eyes like bruises from a fistfight.

Marci drew up a vacant barstool. He was about to offer Alex a Winterbourne when he saw there was no need; Alex had smoked his way through a pack of his own and was lighting one off the tip of another.

"It's done," he said through a cloud of smoke. "I had to go into the office after all; MARTHA's firewall is impenetrable these days. Like I said on the phone, she's back to SIN 14."

Marci clasped Alex's hand. "Thank you so much."

"Not that it'll do much good. MARTHA already knows that something doesn't compute. She'll have to figure out how to reconcile a kill order from on high with an Adjudicative repeal. We both know which one will win."

"Complications?"

"The PATR code isn't the only thing in her notes. You didn't tell me she's under Special Directive 18."

Marci frowned. "She's not. I printed out her summary this afternoon. There's no mention of it."

Alex slid his copy across the table. "I printed it out twenty minutes ago."

Marci stared at the page. Below her PATR code was another acronym: SD18.

"Seeing as I'm certain for the chop," Alex continued, "I pulled up your file, too."

Something in his Alex's tone suggested reticence. Marci took the file from him slowly and opened to the summary.

MÁRTON KOVÁCS

EMPLOYEE ID 311AV761H442

SIN 29

PATR

SD18

He turned back a page. His predictive interval, hitherto a narrow line running left to right, now resembled a door wedge. In three months it had grown from 2% to 22%.

Marci's world contracted. The Celtic and its noise felt suddenly small and quiet and distant, as if their corner of the room had been plucked and separated from the continuum of time.

Special Directive 18. As an Adjudicant he'd seen it often enough. There was no higher level of state surveillance.

"... not customary for an SD18 flag to have any explanation," Alex was saying. "The security service doesn't like to show its cards. Do you know why they might be watching you?"

"Oh dear God," Marci said, rubbing his face. "This can't be happening."

Alex offered him a Winterbourne, the antidote to all problems. "What will you do?"

Marci lit up and drew on the cigarette like a drowning man sucking air through a snorkel. “I don't know. I thought I was saving Erin, not both of us.”

“At least your SIN's still intact.”

“With my predictive interval? Not for long.”

“The sooner you quit whatever you're up to, the sooner your P.I. will revert.”

“Where have I heard that before?”

“I should have listened to you in the first place,” Alex said. “Anyway, it's too late for me, maybe also for Erin. But not you. You've everything to live for.”

“Really?” Marci said. “What, exactly? A Roman toga and a house in the country?”

“Come on, Marci. It's what we've spent our whole lives working for.”

“And look where it's got us. We're like mice inside a wheel. I'm not sure what's crazier, killing ourselves for slope or believing in Empyrean.”

“You think it's real?” Alex asked.

“We're statisticians, Alex. Zero in forty million isn't the best of odds. Besides, I won't stand by and let them take Erin.”

“Then we need a plan.”

“I already have one. Two, in fact; and if Petros can't help Erin, maybe Sándor can.”

“Talk about chewing the carrot from both ends.”

“I'm not exactly big on options, am I?”

“Not exactly.”

“What about you?” Marci asked. “You've risked everything for us.”

“I'm not sure.” Attempting levity, Alex added: “There's always a Rapture pill.”

“Don't even joke about it.”

“There are worse ways to die.” Alex stubbed out his cigarette and got up. “I'd best get home to Lei and the kids. I've a lot of explaining to do and not much time.”

"Let me speak to Petros," said Marci. "Maybe the Underground can house you guys, too."

"A family of four? It would be a prison sentence, especially for the kids. No, I'll visit Rieks in the morning and sweet-talk my way out of it." He grinned. "You know me–the gift of the gab."

Marci rose, offering his hand, but Alex embraced him.

"You're a good friend, Marci. The best."

Marci's voice broke. "Please don't say goodbye."

"No chance; I don't believe in them. But if there is a hereafter—and I don't mean Empyrean—let's have a beer together and reminisce about the bad old days."

"You can count on it."

They stood there a moment, awkwardly, neither wanting this to be the last time they'd see each other.

Finally, Alex turned away. Marci watched him weave his way through the crowded pub until he was lost to sight. A minute later, Marci also made his way out into the night.

At home, his first call was to Sándor. The phone rang three times and went to voicemail.

He phoned Erin. "You're SIN 14 again. MARTHA will revert you to SIN 5, probably in the morning. But unless Justice is subcontracting weekend liquidations to Vulcan, you're probably safe for a few days."

"Probably," Erin said bitterly.

"I dread to think what will happen to Alex."

"Will he get into a lot of trouble?"

"Apart from exposing mass murder, he's broken every rule in the book to save you."

"Oh my God, this is so terrible. And what about you, my love?"

"Fine," he lied. "Just trying to think at a hundred miles an hour."

"I called Petros and told him everything. He—"

"Not over the phone," Marci interrupted.

"If anyone's listening in, they already know about the plan."

"There's a plan?"

"Well, an idea, at least. "Did you speak to Sándor?"

"He didn't pick up. I left a message."

"I see. I doubt he'd want to save a silly girl like me." She started to cry. "Oh Marci, what have I done? I've brought all of this on you, not to mention poor Alex and his family. I wonder if Petros is in danger too?"

"It wouldn't surprise me. Will you go to Győr?" He hoped she'd say no, then silently reprimanded himself for his selfishness. Didn't she have the right to spend her last hours with her family?

"I'd like to, but I don't want the Hangman coming to my parents' house."

"They don't know?" Marci asked.

"I'd like to tell them in person. In fact, I think I'll go in the morning."

"It's almost morning now."

"So it is. Good night, Marci."

"Good night."

Marci poured himself a nightcap and returned to the lounge, where the Birch and Gaydon was playing its Westminster Quarters. Suddenly bone-tired, he fell into the Chesterfield and listened as the clock struck midnight.

He didn't hear the twelfth chime. He dreamed he'd made Patrician and that Stella Kennedy presided over the ceremony. Petros handed him his Club 30 card, written in crayon on a piece of tatty cardboard. When Erin took him to their new home, it was the rusting exercise station below Margit Bridge. She wore a Roman toga. He walked naked beside a Hangman.

18

When he rose at dawn there were no messages and no missed calls. Erin's number was busy, Sándor's phone rang to voicemail and Alex didn't pick up.

Marci showered, dressed and took coffee to his study, where his nomination speech glared at him from his computer monitor. Ten weeks in the writing, it now stood at a modest two hundred words. He ran the timer on his watch and read it aloud. It took a minute to recite. A panic attack, should one occur, would add further brevity.

By lunchtime, neither Sándor, Erin nor Alex had returned his calls. Gritting his teeth, Marci resumed his work, and in the fading light of midafternoon printed the final draft. As he narrated it to himself the phone rang.

"Thank God," he said. "I've been worried sick. How are you?"

"I'm at my parents," Erin said. "We had a long walk and I told them."

The question made him feel foolish, but he asked: "How did it go?"

"Not very well. Mummy cried a lot and Daddy was silent. I was scared because Daddy always knows what to say and do."

"I wish I knew what to do, too. When will you be back in town?"

"I don't know. I'm… exploring options about the future."

"That sounds profound."

"I suppose it does, but everything's profound right now. How are you?"

Marci wandered into the kitchen looking for whiskey. He found the empty bottle in the trash. "I finished the speech, for what it's worth."

"It might be worth a lot, especially if it gets you into The Society."

"If that happens, I'll take you with me to Buda."

"Thank you, Marci. Did you hear from Sándor?"

"Not yet. Will I see you this weekend?"

"I think, no. I need some time with my family. I hope you don't mind?"

"No. I'm glad you're with them."

"Szeretlek."

"I love you too."

On Sunday afternoon, Marci called Csaba and Akito, but neither could shed any light on Alex's whereabouts. Feeling restless, Marci took an air cab to Margit Island and returned to the bench by the broken playground. A northerly squall was shunting tattered clouds across the sky like dirty rags. At sunset they died in a bed of carmine and marigold. He lingered for the afterglow, which hung like an aura over Buda.

Imminence hung in the air. Marci hugged himself, but not for lack of warmth. Events beyond his control were unfolding, with no means to arrest their development.

The following morning he reached the office at sunrise and went directly to Fraser Morrison's office, hoping to catch him before duty or temperament indisposed his Head of Department to conversation. Since admitting the truth would mean instant dismissal, lying was both expedient and unavoidable. Preoccupied with his failing romance, Marci had inadvertently called up Erin's profile by mistake. It was laughably, patently bogus, but he couldn't think of anything better. As for his bungled effort to cancel her cessation, he had no defense. He would have to rely on his supervisor's latent sense of compassion and human decency.

His duplicity was wasted. Morrison was already busy when he arrived and would remain so for the rest of the day.

Marci trudged to the Adjudication suites and knocked at Alex's door was locked, and knocking elicited no response. The time, he noted, was 07:09, which was far too early for Pimenov to show up, anyway.

After a protracted cigarette break, Marci logged into MARTHA and immediately checked his emails, half-expecting a summons from Ron Taggart's secretary. But his inbox was empty—unusually so—and after sending Morrison yet another meeting request, Marci began tackling the casework that had accumulated over the weekend.

At noon he broke for lunch. Alex's cubicle door remained locked. A call to Sándor went unanswered.

Tuesday and Wednesday were notable only for Alex's absence from the office and Morrison's continued preoccupation. Erin, who had remained in Győr with her parents and sister, was faring as well as might be expected. "I miss you very much," she told Marci on Wednesday night. "I also miss my family, even though I'm here with them. It's like I'm grieving for them ahead of time." Marci tried to console her but had little positive to offer. Of the two individuals who could save her, one was unreachable and the other one of questionable sanity. The matter of Petros's rescue plan was still left unspoken; they would discuss this when next they met.

Early on Thursday afternoon, Marci sought out Alex's PA, Emese, who told him what he already knew. "He hasn't been in this week," she said. "He usually sends me a message if he's sick, but I've heard nothing."

Marci collected his coat and briefcase and logged off. Instead of heading home he took the Metro to Népliget. A short stroll brought him to Elnök utca, where he gained access to the Pimenov building and rode the elevator to the third floor. In the stairwell he passed a stack of heavy floor tiles; evidently one of the apartments was being renovated.

At the Pimenov's apartment there was no answer. Marci waited a respectful ten seconds and tried the door, which was locked. *Odd*, he thought. By now, Huang and Lucinda should be back from school. That meant Lei, too. The kids usually played on the walkway in their school clothes, which meant he should have encountered them as he left the lift.

He cupped his hands and pressed them to the kitchen window. A vague outline of disorder presented itself. He let his eyes adjust to the gloom. The room took on detail. Lei was houseproud, but not excessively so. Doubting his own vision, Marci wiped away the fog his breath had left and cowled his face against the glass again. His breath came sharply. His eyes had not lied to him.

Marci ran to the stairwell, picked up one of the paving tiles and carried it back. With his hand wrapped in his coat he swung the tile at the pane, breaking it, then tapped the shards from the frame. He checked the walkway: no one had stirred. Before the neighbors noticed him he climbed inside.

His shoes met with liquid. Water, something milky, other fluids. The fridge freezer was on its side, its doors wide open and its contents a heap of thawing sludge that had spread across the floor to produce a sticky, squelching sound when he raised his foot. Cabinets, ripped from the walls, lay smashed atop the broken crockery they once contained. The table where We Happy Few played poker, lacking two legs, had submitted to gravity in a posture of obeisance. The air was thick with the stench of rancid meat and spoiled dairy. Everything, from food cartons to cleaning products, was either ripped apart or emptied out and gone through.

In the hallway, five coats still hung on their pegs but the shoe rack was empty. Lying faceup on the parquet was the family portrait Lei was so fond of. A starburst of cracked glass radiated from the center where someone had trodden on it.

The lounge fared no better. The sofa Marci had fallen asleep on a week ago was in tatters, the work of a box cutter. Dolls, jigsaw pieces and other toys, emptied out of their tubs, littered the carpet. Alex's computer was gone, along with his AirNet tracker. The television, however, remained intact on the wall.

Unsure if he was alone or not, Marci tiptoed into the children's room, which equaled the lounge in destruction. Both the kids' bunks were bare; their mattresses, sliced lengthways, rested on the floor. The wardrobe stood empty. Clothes still on hangers felt soft underfoot.

The master bedroom was equally disarranged, but with a chilling new detail. Large sections of plasterboard, presumably broken by the same sledgehammer that had pockmarked other parts of the wall, were torn away to reveal the brickwork behind it. Dust like coarse talc coated Alex's and Lei's possessions which, like the children's, were scattered across the room.

Marci followed the sound of running water to the bathroom. The light switch didn't work. His Zippo did. The linoleum floor was wet.; the culprit was the toilet, whose tank and bowl were rubble. The washbasin had fared better: only half of it remained. Rising out of the pedestal, the faucet drooped like a heavy flower on a wilting stem. A sliver of vanity mirror in the basin caught the light from Marci's Zippo and dazzled it back at him. The walls were stripped to brickwork or plaster. Pieces of drywall and a broken medicine cabinet filled the bathtub.

Marci crouched before the stopcock and shut off the water. His eyes fell on the bathtub enclosure, which was intact but for a single missing tile on the side. In its stead was a carefully chiseled away square of plaster carcass.

Something tugged at Marci's memory, something Alex had said about getting the bathroom fixed up. The hole was there for a reason. Marci extended his Zippo into the cavity but found only empty space and the side of the tub itself. Whoever had sacked the place had found what they were after. Alex's research was gone. More pressing, so were Alex, Lei and the children.

Marci sat back on his heels, steadying himself against a flush of vertigo. The destruction was wanton, excessive even. Could it be a warning? But from whom? Certainly not Justice and Cessation; home invasion wasn't their remit. Nor, for that matter, the *rendőrség.*[20] Half the police force was on the bottle and the other half on the hustle. In any case, why? Alex's wake-up call had already been delivered as a four-letter word spelled PATR. Even that, Marci reflected, wasn't really for his friend's eyes. Darker thoughts began to gather, but were interrupted.

The voices, both male, had come from the walkway. The words were lost but the pitch suggested caution, possibly alarm. Marci snapped shut his Zippo shut and froze. He'd recognize Alex's in an instant, and the timbre precluded Huang. If it was the neighbors, it

---

[20] Budapest police force.

spelled only bad news. Residents to housing manager to the Justice Board—this was the chain of events. The forensics would quickly prove Marci's innocence, but mobs cared little for such niceties. If it wasn't the neighbors, it was worse.

Marci grabbed a chunk of the broken porcelain and went to the hallway, where he waited. The voices had ceased. As he entered the kitchen, his feet made contact with something sticky. Grimacing in disgust, he traded the masonry for the chef's knife and went to stand parallel to the window. The walkway was empty. In a rush of adrenaline, Marci clambered through the frame and dashed for the stairs.

He reached the street unhindered. Heedless of the direction, he ran through the dusk and soon became lost. On a corner he stopped to catch his breath.

An elderly man attached to a small, trembling dog approached.

"How do I reach Népliget?" Marci asked him.

The man's eyes fell on Marci's right hand. In his haste, he'd forgotten to relinquish the chef's knife.

Marci tossed it into a nearby bush. "Sorry."

The man extended a bony finger. *"Menjen egyenesen a Könyves Kálmán körútra, majd forduljon jobbra—"*

Before he'd finished speaking, Marci was halfway up the street. A blur of avenues brought him to Népliget, where he rode the escalator down to Metro Five, where a train was waiting to depart. Marci squeezed through its closing doors and collapsed on a bench. A call to Alex's cell phone yielded a long, unbroken tone. Lei's number was the same. He started to feel queasy.

At Keleti he alighted and caught the SpeedWalk home. The building was quiet; Norbert Tóth had ceased his ruckus days ago. Marci locked himself in his apartment and washed down a Seromax with some flat lager. He tried Alex, then Lei, again, but got the same dead exchange tone. It was probably a line fault, maybe storm damage somewhere far from downtown.

Marci went to stand by the window. On Gyulai Pál, a few mothers with strollers chatted in lamplight. A jogger in fluorescents huffed his way past the dog park. Two tramps bickered over loose change.

Nobody suspicious, and certainly no Company spooks. Just to be sure, he closed the window shutters.

There was no logical explanation for the state of the Pimenovs' apartment. An act of revenge was out of the question. Nobody hated the Pimenovs. Burglary? What self-respecting thief would leave behind a big screen TV? And why were the family coats and shoes still in the hall? If there was a sensible explanation, it was eluding him.

His phone rang. He rushed to the kitchen where he'd left it. When he answered, he was almost disappointed to hear Erin's voice.

"*Szia.* I'm back in the city," she said. "How are you?"

Marci thought better of mentioning the break-in. "I'm surviving. Do you want to come over? I'll order food."

"That sounds nice, but I'm quite tired. Telling Mummy about my liquidation was very draining. Did Sándor phone?"

"No. I'll keep trying."

"At least I have some breathing room, thanks to you and Alex."

"A little." Something told him Erin thought she had more. "We need to meet. Are you free tomorrow?"

"I think so. Or Saturday for certain."

"The sooner the better."

Friday brought drizzle. Arriving early at work, Marci went to his cubicle, hung up his damp coat and waited for MARTHA to grant him security access. On this occasion, however, her screens remained blank.

With ill grace Marci waited. The delay was almost certainly due to System Services running one of their ill-timed housecleaning routines. Why the hell couldn't they do it at night? He still hadn't caught up with last weekend's casework. The last thing he wanted was to spend the coming one fretting over an ever-growing pile of jobs.

Unwilling to indulge any further delay, he spoke into the microphone. "MARTHA, log me in."

There was a pause. Then: "Unable to comply. Please consult your line manager."

Tutting in irritation, Marci leaned over his keyboard and entered his twelve-digit login code. For good measure, he placed his right hand on the desk's bioreader panel. But the panel remained dark, and the code elicited nothing in response.

Marci spoke slowly, articulating his words as he might to a wayward child. "MARTHA, run security bioscan."

MARTHA spoke without emotion. "Unable to comply. Access to Adjudication system is denied. Please consult your line manager."

Marci felt his stomach turn. "MARTHA, log in Kovács Márton, Employee ID 311AV761H442."

"Unable to comply. Access denied. Your Adjudication privileges have been withdrawn."

Marci stormed from his suite into the office, where Moira had just arrived for the day and was settling herself at her desk. Beyond her, the shark tank's privacy glass had been set to an opaque crimson. It meant one thing: Morrison was in residence, but was already unavailable.

Taking pity on Moira, Marci descended to the quadrangle to cool his heels, which happened quicker than he imagined. Outrage became reason. Given his activities the last few days, it was no wonder MARTHA had locked him out. Why, then, hadn't Morrison called a meeting?

Reason became fear. Marci began to feel clammy. He loosened his tie. He told himself: *if they wanted me dead, I'd be dead already. Maybe it's just a warning.*

Back in the office Moira stopped him. "He's gone out," she said, "most likely for the day."

Marci cursed something vile. "Do you know anything about Alex?"

Moira locked eyes with her computer monitor again. "Not really."

Something in her voice suggested duplicity. "Moira?" he said.

Moira glanced across the room at Emese, who was busy pretending not to listen. "I really don't know for sure."

Marci looked from one to the other. "Fine. If Morrison asks, I've gone home. He can call me back any time."

He didn't go home. In City Park he bought *kifli* from a kiosk and sat at the bench where he and Erin had watched the boy play with his sailing boat two months ago. It seemed a lifetime ago. How had they got here? He'd been a rising star in the Exec Team. Now he had the security service listening every time he broke wind and a predictive interval that resembled a door wedge. For Erin it was worse, Alex too. Their days were certainly numbered. All because neither would take no for an answer, she with her bloody Club Bohém meetings and he with his anomalies.

No, Marci reflected, that wasn't fair. If he hadn't screwed up his Society speech, he'd be safe in Buda and Erin with him, and none of this wretched business would have happened, except for Alex's investigation, which Marci might have stopped had he tried harder. But damn, hadn't he tried?

He tried some of the *kifli*. It was dry and impossible to swallow—drier than usual—and he wondered why he'd bought it and why he hadn't bought a coffee as well.

He took out his phone and scrolled through the address book to P. When he called, a recorded Petros invited him to leave a message using twice as many words than necessary. He hung up. If the Company was monitoring his cell phone, he wasn't going to give his firing squad any more ammunition.

Marci tossed the bread to the ducks and returned to Heroes' Square. As he approached the SpeedWalk, he was overcome by a sensation of such intense calamity that the hairs on his arms prickled. The premonition, if such it was, again related to Erin.

On Dózsa György út he spotted an air taxi parked outside a pizza kiosk with its duty light was off. He climbed inside.

The cabbie scowled into his mirror. "Can't you see the light? I'm on lunch."

Marci held out thirty credits. "Pillangó utca, Kecskemét. It's an emergency."

The driver put his meal aside. "Where's the fire?"

"Just get me there."

With uncommon alacrity the taxi rose through the clouds to emerge in hazy sunshine at odds with Marci's mood. He leaned forward and checked the airspeed indicator.

"I'm doing three hundred," the cabbie said. "I can't get any more from her."

Marci sat back and opened the air vent. The reek of pepperoni filled his nostrils. He closed it again and dialed Erin's number. It rang to voicemail.

Ten minutes brought them to the Great Plain. The taxi circled Kecskemét and landed on Pillangó utca.

Marci ran through hail to Erin's apartment building, which lay in eerie silence aside from the patter of hailstones. At her front door the bioreader ran his DNA. The door chimed three tones and opened.

The smell of linseed oil and turpentine welcomed him. He considered announcing himself. If he surprised an interloper, at least the exit was near. If the place was vacant it would make no difference. Given Erin's predicament, his impromptu presence might scare the hell out of her. In a voice lacking vigor he called, "It's me, Marci."

Silence.

Mindful of the Pimenov's apartment, Marci pulled an umbrella from its stand, and holding it high he crept from room to room. But the flat was reassuringly tidy—Erin's kind of tidy—and empty. So much for his presage of doom.

In the kitchen he brewed chamomile tea and sat at the table where, months ago, Erin had hosted her dinner party. Marci wondered how Lydia was faring. Not well, hopefully. One day he should check her profile if MARTHA ever granted him again.

Fixed on the fridge door by Kalocsa flower magnets were various pieces of memorabilia he'd failed to notice before: a family portrait from many Christmases ago; a poem penned by Sophia; the exhibition flier featuring Erin's art. Marci removed a Polaroid she'd taken of them on their trip to Buda, embellished around the edges with a chain of interlocking flowers and hearts around the edge. In the thick white border at the bottom was a single word: "Szeretlek!"

Overwhelmed with sadness, Marci replaced the picture and with slow deliberation moved from room to room. Each one seemed to release memories imbued within it as sounds that, by some vicarious means, he recalled as his own: the chirp of crickets in the drowsy heat of summer; the rise and fall of dinner party chatter; rain like silver dragées chattering against the shutters of her bedroom window. The house was dormant but alive; timeless, yet pervaded by a sense of quiet, tragic finality.

The alarm clock in her bedroom corroded time in sixteenth notes. Marci sat on the mattress, closed his eyes and listened to its remorseless, hateful countdown. He must face facts. There would be no rescue. Petros had the will to help and Sándor the means, but neither possessed both. Even if he could, would the President of The Society repeal a cessation order? Marci knew the answer. Prefect Trauffaut? Asking either of them would make a mockery of the system he'd sworn to uphold.

Erin, dear Erin! Why hadn't they met years ago when life was simpler? Yet perhaps he wouldn't have been ready for her, or her him. No, fate had conspired to merge their paths when it did.

Marci thought of her reading her profile summary in the lamplight under Margaret bridge, and realized that for the first in his life he cherished someone else's existence above his own. Now it was too late. He might still make it to Buda, but he'd do so alone.

On the bedside table lay a book. The cover was handmade from wallpaper: an embossed, floral William Morris affair. Resting on it was a silver picture locket. Marci held it up. Cheap and mass-produced, it was the kind of junk András might fob off as Victorian. Erin wouldn't know the difference and wouldn't care. Inside was a miniature version of the photograph taken at János-hegy.

Marci turned to the book. Across its center, a strip had been torn away to reveal a white underbelly. In this space Erin had inscribed:

My Journal, 2132

Marci became aware of a sudden quickening of his pulse. At the same time, he felt the same wayward thrill that had accompanied him home with Erin's profile. He touched the fore edge of the book, lifting the cover a fraction, his finger charged with sensual tactility at what the pages might reveal.

In a sudden impulse of self-restraint he returned it to the nightstand. Wasn't it enough he'd read her lifeline? To trespass on her diary would be beyond contemptible.

Seeking distraction, he went to the window, which overlooked a park of poplars, maples and large-leaves limes, framed within a quadrangle of tenement buildings. In the center, a Socialist-era playground added a dash of drab nostalgia.

Marci turned away. The bedroom seemed suddenly also very bland, except for Erin's journal. A frayed pink ribbon hung like a snake's tongue from between the pages.

The temptation was too great. He crossed the room and opened it at random, trying not to land his vision on anything in particular. The format was simple: a series of entries in chronological order, completed in Erin's delicate, childlike handwriting.

In an outburst of rage against himself he slammed it shut, with such force that the diary slipped from his hands and landed with its pages splayed and its spine upmost. Marci sat on the floor beside it, hooked his finger between the parted pages and opened to an entry made three days earlier.

Tuesday 9th December

I'm writing this a few days late because I couldn't think straight last weekend. Daddy picked me up from the station on Saturday night. I wanted to tell everyone the bad news as soon as possible, if "wanted" is the right word. But when we got home, Mummy had dinner ready and Sophia was so excited to see me she was like a little puppy, and I couldn't bear to tell them.

After the meal we went for a walk. Bad news is always easier to tell someone when you're walking. It took half an hour before I could speak, listening to their news, their ordinary, everyday stories, wondering how they'd react to mine. Mummy cried a lot. Sophia wouldn't believe me and begged me to say it wasn't true. Daddy didn't say anything, which scared me most of all.

When we got home we talked until morning. I don't know if it was because we had a lot to say, or whether we were making the most of what time I have left, or maybe because nobody wanted to be woken up by a Hangman. It seems that unless Petros or Marci's friend can help me I'll soon be dead. Poor Marci. How I wish I'd never brought him to Club Bohém. I don't think he'll ever make it into The Society now. I've probably ruined his life. He deserves so much better than me. I hope one day he'll meet someone who loves him as much as I do. Maybe they'll bring him good instead of harm.

His throat tight with emotion, Marci turned the page.

Thursday 11th December

I feel like I'm living through a horrible nightmare I can't wake up from. The blackness wants to return, but I'm fighting it. Mummy's worried I'll do something silly again, but I'm not depressed, only frightened. I've never seen Daddy like this. I'd hoped we'd talk and that he'd make everything all right, like he always does. But he can't make it all right.

Everyone wants to spend every minute with me, like it's the last time they'll see me. I suppose it is. Much as I appreciate them, it's a bit suffocating, as if I'm taking part in my own funeral.

This evening I came back to Budapest. I'm sure I'm becoming a little paranoid. The only place I feel safe to express myself is in this book. At least the Company can't read it.

I miss Marci very much.

From the hallway came three high-pitched beeps and a click: the sound of the front door. Marci froze. Erin was at work; of this he was certain. Who else had an access key? The Justice and Cessation Board, for sure. They carried DNA samples of every Employee. They posed him no risk, unless... No, he'd checked his SIN that morning. Besides, Hangmen always knocked before letting themselves in. That left her Sophia and her parents. But they were in Győr. It also left whoever had wrecked the Pimenovs' apartment.

Marci scanned the room. Dignity prohibited him from hiding under the bed. He tiptoed to the door, then remembered Erin's journal, which still lay on the floor.

From the hall came the unmistakable sound of jackboots. Cursing under his breath, he returned diary and locket to the table, ran to her studio and closed the door behind him.

The room was an obstacle course of canvases, easels and work benches. Marci tiptoed his way through the mess to the window. From here on the third floor it was a thirty-foot drop to the footpath—a bone-breaker, for sure. Shimmying along the ledge to a neighbor's balcony was another option. He tried the window latch. It was locked.

The footsteps had stopped in the kitchen. Marci remembered his tea on the dining table and winced; the cup would still be warm. He might as well have assembled a marching band to announce his presence. He looked around for a weapon but could find nothing more intimidating than a palette knife.

Marci returned to the door and took up position behind it, from where he could strike or run or both. He clenched his fists with his fingers wrapped over his thumbs and wondered how to punch someone. Perhaps, he thought, he should have practiced. Several candidates came to mind.

The clunk of boots grew louder and stopped outside.

The door flew open. Marci pushed back, slamming the intruder against the wall and knocking something from their grasp, which struck the floor with a metallic clang. Without thinking, he bore them to the ground and raised his fist as a waft of jasmine and violets enveloped him.

Cowering beneath him was Erin. Her eyes were squeezed shut and her face tilted her away from him in anticipation of the blow. When it didn't land she opened her eyes a slit. "Marci?"

Marci, primed with adrenaline, stared down at her with his fists still raised. "Erin?"

"Are you crazy? You almost killed me!"

"Bloody hell, Erin! I thought you were a Hangman."

"Do I look like a Hangman to you? What are you even doing here?"

Marci felt himself go limp. He unballed his fists and dropped them to his side. "I—I had a premonition. I thought you were in danger."

"You weren't wrong." She hit him on the chest. "Get off me, you oaf."

He was straddling her. He rolled off and lay at her side. "Did I hurt you? I'm sorry, I didn't mean to hurt you." She was wearing, he noticed, a pair of lace-up, knee-length military boots. Lamely, he said: "You're wearing boots."

Erin gave him a look of irritated bemusement. "Aren't I allowed to wear boots?" She felt the back of her head.

Marci gently rubbed her arm, as if the gesture might both remove the pain and make amends. "Are you all right?"

"Yes. And no thanks to you." She started giggling.

"What are you laughing about?"

"You," she said. "It's bad enough having the Hangman to worry about without you trying to kill me."

Whatever Erin had dropped when he attacked her lay uncomfortably beneath his back. Marci propped himself up on his elbows and pulled out a length of lead pipe two feet long and an inch across. "Bloody hell, were you going to use this on me?" he said.

"Of course. I thought you were a burglar. Better that than be to murdered by you in my own home."

Marci chuckled. "Don't worry, I only kill people at threshold." He cringed. "I'm sorry. It came out—"

His phone interrupted him and he answered it gladly. "It might be Sándor," he told Erin. "Maybe he's got good news. Hello?"

"Kovács? It's Rieks Kruger. Moira told me you've gone home for the day. We'll need to see you on Monday morning in H.R. It will be a formal hearing, so please dress appropriately for once."

"H.R.?" Marci repeated dumbly.

"08:30 prompt, if you please." Kruger hung up.

Marci stared at the phone.

"What is it?" Erin asked.

"It's work. I think it's the end."

19

"You can come in now, Márton."

Marci roused from his slumber. It was 08:40. He'd been dozing in the HR suite for forty minutes. Before him stood a short, dumpy woman of early middle years. Her hair, brunette, was cut into a bob, which made her moony face seem rounder.

Marci spoke with the candor of the freshly woken. "You're new."

She smiled—something strained, and with a trace of offense. "Maddy Clarke," she said, extending a hand, "acting Director of HR. I'm sorry we've kept you waiting."

Marci immediately perceived the purpose of her appointment: she was here to oversee dismissals. HR always brought in temps to fire staff. It dented staff morale less when a stranger did it.

Clarke, whose handshake had gone unrequited, gestured to a boardroom. "This way, if you please."

Marci followed her into a room square, lacking windows and ventilated from the ceiling by a noisy air conditioning unit. Four people sat around a crescent-shaped table. A single chair inhabited the concavity, which Marci was instructed to occupy.

Clarke took her place with the others, and with a surfeit of warmth unbecoming the circumstances welcomed him. "Thank you for coming in this morning, Márton. I'm sure you're already familiar with everyone, but for the sake of the recording, those present are Ron Taggart, Head of Executive Team Security and Intelligence; your line manager, Fraser Morrison; me, Madeline Clarke; to my left, Rieks Kruger, Executive Team Director; and László Szűcs, Company psychologist."

Marci regarded the five with cool detachment. The combination of pills he'd taken earlier, including Ketamax, Nrjize, Kqalms and Cortiquell, was working with uncommon vigor; given the apparent gravity of the meeting, he felt unfazed by the lineup. Morrison, Kruger and Taggart he knew. Taggart, a little man with cropped graying hair, had a face scarred by congenital smallpox which rarely betrayed emotion. Morrison was fiddling with his pen and already looking bored. Kruger wore the pinched expression suggestive of one suffering from hemorrhoids. At the cusp of the table, a thin, bespectacled man with black beads for eyes and a neatly trimmed beard observed Marci with scientific curiosity. Marci nodded a greeting in return, which was ignored.

Maddy continued less buoyantly. "For the record, this morning's proceedings are being taped. At this point I'd like to hand over to Rieks Kruger, who will act as Chair."

Kruger, tall and heavy-set with equine features and a tedious, nasal voice, dragged his eyes up and down Marci in distaste. "What Maddy hasn't told you is that this is an official tribunal regarding breaches of professional conduct carried out by you over the last several months." He pressed a button set into the tabletop. A particle camera projected a green, three-dimensional image in the air. "The following is a list of incidents taken from MARTHA's activity log. Since the case is clear-cut, I see no reason for preamble.

"We start in September. On the 16th you entertained one Erin Rebecca Macsy, a known dissident and member of a subversive political organization called 'Club Bohém' at your home, contravening Adjudicant Code of Conduct section C and placing you in collusion with said person. On the 19th your colleague Alex Pimenov, deceased, discussed with you the MARTHA replica he'd created—"

Marci jerked out of his torpor.

"—in order to access confidential data. Pimenov confided in you that he'd discovered alleged errors relating to adjudication decisions within MARTHA. You failed to report his activities to Fraser, making yourself complicit in your colleague's crimes.

"On 24th September you again fraternized with Erin Macsy, with whom you were now relationally involved, at the Museum of Fine Arts, afterwards engaging in seditious dialogue about the Company at Városliget. October 4th: requested file of said Erin Macsy in violation of Company policy, section E, item two, forbidding access to the profiles of personal acquaintances. October 7th: you consorted with one Petros Garai, political activist and leader of Club Bohém, at Macy's residence in Kecskemét."

Marci started to speak but was cut short.

"October 12th," Kruger continued. "Pimenov visits you carrying email correspondence allegedly written by Fraser Morrison and myself. The emails concern a morally repugnant conspiracy within the Executive Team. Said content was derogatory and slanderous. Pimenov shared these with you, but your failure to inform either Fraser or myself makes you party to the offense."

Marci stared unfocused at the list of allegations that hung in front of him. Kruger's litany had become just noise.

Alex was dead.

Kruger flicked his fingers over a control surface. "For the sake of our longevity, I'll abbreviate the list. October 22nd: you met with Garai at an art exhibition at the Weber Center. The following Thursday, you and Macsy attended a Club Bohém meeting, the first of eight such visits. The group is known for "espousing anarchic philosophies detrimental to the security of the Company," according to the Intelligence Service.

"In November, Pimenov began an unauthorized investigation into what he believes to be illegal cessation orders. These so-called deaths were, in reality, clerical errors, a fact confirmed by Marcus Behrman, head of Data Analytics. Despite being fully aware of Pimenov's activities, you refused to disclose them to your superiors.

"Throughout November, you continued visiting Club Bohém with and without Erin Macsy. On 13th, you interfered in cessation proceedings at 29 Rákóczi út." Kruger swiped his touch pad; a document from the Justice Board appeared. "I quote the cessation officer concerned: "Subject approached me as I was holding back mob. Subject made intimidating remarks about his authority and reached into his coat, possibly for a weapon, whereupon I restrained him. Subject cursed me, spat in my face and attempted to reach for my gun. Subject then tried to force his way past me. I responded with non-lethal force. Subject retreated, making threats against my person. Cessation targets were removed and crowd dispersed with gas." Following this, you proceeded to the Executive Team building and attempted to annul the kill order."

The drugs were wearing off. Marci blinked as sentience returned. The Hangman's account of events was far from accurate. Come to think of it, it seemed to have been embellished since Morrison cited it.

Kruger's voice became a monotonous drone. "On 14th November, after requesting the file of Petros Garai, you attended a meeting at Club Bohém, where the guest speaker was one 'Peti,' an Underground spokesman, where you not only entertained his propaganda but actively engaged in subversive dialogue with him. Further, you refused to report his presence to the Justice Board, either during the meeting or subsequent to it.

"Throughout November, you built a sham case to cover your request for Pimenov's predictive interval and lifeline. This is in direct violation of the Adjudicant code, section B, item seven. On 26th November, you requested the file of one Anton Aslanov, another political subversive and a friend of yours." Kruger looked through the hologram and fixed Marci with a derisory smile. "A member of your little gang, 'We Happy Few.' Two days later, you printed out Macy's profile. With Pimenov's help, you illegally manipulated her SIN and revoked her cessation order, despite an expedited liquidation advisory."

Kruger, apparently finished, sat back in his chair and studied Marci with contempt. Taggart, Morrison and Szűcs watched him like predators eyeing up quarry.

Maddy Clarke spoke soberly: "Márton, these offenses are a matter of record and constitute serious breaches of Executive Team protocol, the Adjudicant Code of Conduct and the law. Do you wish to say anything in your defense?"

Marci tried to speak, but his mouth had dried up. Unlike the panel, he'd been neglected the courtesy of water.

"I take it your silence is an admission of guilt?" Kruger said.

"The charges are wrong," Marci said.

"All of them?" asked Clarke.

"Takumi and Réka Nagy were well above cut-off," Marci said. "I revoked the kill order because it should never have been issued. You can check MARTHA's record if you don't believe me."

"We don't need to," said Kruger. "Both of them were barely scraping SIN 6 for the last two years."

"That's not true," Marci protested. "I saw the numbers myself."

"Are you saying," Kruger asked, "that MARTHA made a mistake?"

Marci considered the question. Conviction prevailed over tact. "Yes."

Crisply, as if making a point, Kruger said: "MARTHA doesn't make mistakes."

Marci's words. The ones he'd used in the canteen to describe Alex's ridiculous anomalies theory. It had turned out to be neither ridiculous nor theoretical, but had killed him nonetheless. MARTHA doesn't make mistakes. They'd been listening in even back then. It was that or uncomfortable coincidence. Either way, Kruger had uttered the perfect confession. Piqued by his hypocrisy, Marci asked, "Then why exactly were they liquidated?"

Kruger, unaccustomed to giving an account of himself, spoke haughtily: "I see no reason to field questions from you, especially in light of your libelous slur on my character."

Taggart answered. "Your access to official records is revoked, but since it's germane to this hearing, the Nagy family was engaged in extracurricular activities deemed a threat to the Company."

Despite himself, Marci sneered at the absurdity of the statement. "That's absurd! They were the most ardent Employees I've ever met!"

"Unlike you and your friend Pimenov," said Kruger. "Both of you abused your public office to further private agendas. That's a capital offense."

"That's not how it was!" Marci protested. "The anomalies have nothing to do with me!"

"And the profiles?" Taggart asked. "Pimenov, Macsy, the others? You don't deny accessing their records. What was your motive?"

Marci licked his lips. "Suspicion. I—I had reason to believe they posed a security risk."

"Including your girlfriend?" asked Taggart.

"She's not my girlfriend," Marci blurted.

"Don't lie to us," Kruger snapped. "We know you're involved with this woman."

"Besides," said Taggart, "You printed out her profile twice. The first time was before you'd attended any Club Bohém meetings."

"She'd mentioned it in conversation." Marci ran his finger under his collar and glanced at the air conditioner. He was burning up. He went to wipe his brow but found his hand was even moister.

Kruger leaned over and muttered something to Taggart, who moved his fingers in the air, swiping and scrolling the hologram's control surface like a mage working an incantation. Marci watched, hypnotized, as the space between them became a giant video image through which he could vaguely see if he tried. He wasn't trying. He was watching Erin's apartment from across her courtyard. A patch of blue-black sky at the edge of the frame indicated early morning, as did the dressing gown she wore as she waited for him in the doorway. Into shot trudged Marci. Erin, standing on tiptoes, kissed him and led him inside.

Taggart tapped his keypad and the scene changed. Warm with the glow candles, the Weber Center's Grand Hall appeared. Beneath its chandeliers, three hundred guests milled around works of art as diverse and cosmopolitan as themselves. Near the middle of the room, dwarfed by a Moorish man in a silk kaftan, stood Erin.

The camera panned across the crowd to a latecomer standing in a corner and wearing a navy suit: Marci. Erin, spotting him, excused herself and hurried over to embrace him.

Next, CCTV tape captured under Café Primo's archway showed the two of them sheltering from a storm. In this case, audio accompanied the footage.

"Not bad," Erin said, brushing hailstones from Marci's jacket. "You're quite a catch. A little grumpy, but still a nice prize for me to show off."

"I hope I stack up well against tonight's political heavyweights," Marci complained.

"You'll do. I know you don't want to be here, but thank you for coming."

"Don't expect me to say anything. And please don't tell anyone else I'm SIN 29."

"I promise." Erin kissed him. "Are you ready?"

Taggart pressed the button again. A swirl of flecks like white noise occupied the screen. The pixels changed direction and came into focus: snow. At two hundred feet, the drone broke through the cloud cover to reveal a cobbled street: Csarnok Tér. Two figures, their forms indistinct in the evening darkness, stood locked in a clinch.

The drone descended further and activated its beam projector; the street became bright with the power of ten thousand lumens, arousing the couple from their ardor. One of them, the man, raised his ID card. The camera zoomed in on the badge. It read: Kovács Márton, 311AV761H442.

The image froze. Silence hung in the air like a question.

"It's not what it looks like," Marci mumbled. "I was running an investigation."

Taggart leaned his thick forearms on the table. "Go on."

"When we visited City Park she told me she thought the New Way was unfair. She said she was interested in different views, whether they were popular or not."

"So you suspected her of treason?"

"Yes, but I needed proof. The only way I was going to get it was if I could earn her trust."

"Then your relationship with her was a cover?"

Marci nodded vigorously. "Yes. A cover."

"And your involvement with Club Bohém was part of the ruse?"

Believing he was starting to sway Taggart, Marci spoke on with a little more enthusiasm. "Exactly. I realized that if they accepted me into the group I could expose not just her but the entire membership."

Taggart looked down the table. "Doctor Szűcs?"

Szűcs worked his keyboard. A cross-sectional image appeared. "This is a scan of the frontal lobe of Mr. Kovács' brain," Szűcs explained. "Note, if you will, the anteriormost portion. The colorization indicates neural activity. As you can see, when asked about his relationship status, the prefrontal cortex evidenced a substantial increase in function. Compare it with his brain activity at the beginning of the meeting." Szűcs added a second image, side-by-side. "Bearing in mind changes in his skin conductance, pupil dilation and my professional observations, it's my belief Mr. Kovács has been frugal with the truth."

"NIPS result?" asked Kruger.

"Inconclusive. He's highly medicated."

"That in itself suggests premeditation," Kruger muttered. "Ron?"

"NIPS result or not, the evidence is overwhelming. Sedition, treason, criminal facilitation, falsifying official records, defamation, assault on a cessation officer—"

"Any one of them will suffice." Kruger regarded Marci as he might a noxious insect. "Well?"

He was shaking now, trembling with such force that his teeth chattered when he spoke. "Please," he urged, "you've got this all wrong! I've dedicated my life to the Company. Whatever I did, I did it for the city. My record is exemplary!"

"Your recent actions prove otherwise," said Kruger. "Any comments from the panel? Fraser?"

Morrison, who was playing with his pen and who'd barely made eye contact with Marci, shook his head.

"Ron?"

"Nothing further to add."

"In which case—"

"Wait!" Marci cried. "What about the Nagys? You said they were SIN 6. How could MARTHA issue their kill order?"

"That's none of your affair," said Kruger.

Taggart indulged him. "PATR," he said. "Political Activity Tendency Risk. MARTHA added it to their profiles the day before their cessation."

Kruger tapped his keyboard. The hologram disappeared. "The panel has determined your actions in recent months do not befit those of an Adjudicant. Furthermore, several of the indictments are capital charges. Maddy?"

Clarke folded her hands on the table and affected an expression of austerity. "Márton, the crimes you've committed are serious, and under normal circumstances would warrant cessation. Nevertheless, taking into account your years of service, the panel has agreed on a remedial program. You are hereby removed from the office of Adjudicant. A penalty of nineteen points has been applied to your Social Index Number. With immediate effect you are now SIN 10. On successful completion of a psychiatric rehabilitation program, you will be assigned a junior clerical grade in the Executive Team's Records department. However, due to the nature of your actions, you will never again hold the office of Adjudicant."

"Nor any other office," Kruger added.

"You may, of course, choose to leave the Executive Team altogether and pursue a new vocation elsewhere," Clark added, "but it will prove impossible for you to recoup your current Social Index Number. Your SIN 29 perquisites are now revoked, and you are relieved of all duties. Please relinquish your ID."

Taggart beckoned. "Your warrant."

Wordlessly, Marci removed his badge and placed it on the table.

"Doctor Szűcs will be in touch with you to set up your first session." Clarke paused. "Márton, I hope you appreciate the gravity of your conduct and the leniency we're showing you."

Marci stared back at her but could find nothing to say.

"Kovács, you're free to go," said Kruger.

Marci nodded vaguely. Dazed, he shuffled from the room.

Taggart spoke: "Everyone except Rieks, please also leave."

Clarke, Szűcs and Morrison got to their feet and departed.

"Well?" asked Kruger. "What now?"

Taggart brought up Marci's profile. "He's in shock. MARTHA predicts he'll go to Városliget and place calls to various friends." He took out his phone and dialed a number. "Petros, it's Taggart. Find Kovács and proceed with the plan."

20

Marci trudged across Hősök Tere, passing Gabriel and the seven Magyars chieftains towering unseen above him in his single-minded desolation. In City Park he found his usual bench and stared into the leaden waters of the lake.

It was over. In fifteen minutes his career had been destroyed. There had been charges. Some of these were blatantly false; elsewhere, the truth had been skewed to portray him in the worst possible way.

He'd been told he'd got off lightly. A trip to Nyugati would have been kinder. Already MARTHA would have processed his demotion and adjusted his predictive interval. His crimes were now a matter of public record and would be stored for the rest of his life, frustrating every attempt he made to regain slope.

The implications of his punishment began to crystallize. His stratospheric rise to SIN 29 was more than equaled by his fall from grace. His new grade placed him one rung above an intern. He would outstrip his peers and managers in years of service and accumulated SIN but would play second fiddle to them all, a laughingstock even Tony Jackson would eclipse in rank. The demotion was an act of such obvious spitefulness that it was as if the panel wanted him to see through the sham of it.

The facts grew worse. Joining The Society was now out of the question. Admittance rules were stringent, and no amount of maneuvering on Sándor's part would sway the Synod. Even if Marci started over in another field, Maddy Clarke had made it clear he'd never recover his SIN. And without Patrician immunity, he had no means to shield Erin from the Hangman. What his botched Society speech had failed to accomplish, Kruger's kangaroo court had. Empyrean, and with it eternal life, was forever out of reach.

A sense of uneasy shame, vague and indefinable, tugged at his conscience. Taggart had asked questions about his relationship with Erin. What were they, and how had he responded? Shock, combined with the secondary effects of his medication, were having an amnesic influence on him. All he could recall was a montage of surveillance footage, months in the making, to which he had no defense. Except he'd tried.

I was running an investigation.

An investigation. How quickly he'd folded under pressure! Taggart had pressed him further, and like a fool he'd elaborated. Her crime was treason. In the eyes of the Company there was no greater trespass. Murder, rape and molestation were merely crimes against the person. He who sinned against the Company sinned against Budapest itself. All it had taken were three suits, a girl Friday and a quack to make him denounce the woman he loved.

Treason. It carried the death sentence. For the sake of his own neck, he'd inculpated the woman he loved. Her life for his.

You vile, craven bastard.

Too woebegone even to cry, Marci lifted his eyes to the huddle of skyscrapers rising above the tree line. The sun had broken through the overcast, sending long, low shafts of light to rake across the structures. In the glare, the Executive Team's facade of blackened mirrors glinted dully. For years the structure had instilled in Marci a sense of unshakable self-importance. Now he saw it through the eyes every other ordinary Employee: esoteric, inscrutable, ominous, a distended obelisk annexing earth and heaven.

Without thinking, Marci took out his phone and scrolled to Alex's number before realizing there was no point. Poor Alex! Had they stopped him on his way home from The Celtic or taken the whole family at once? The latter would explain the home invasion, even though it wasn't the Justice Board's *modus operandi*. Marci didn't know enough about Intelligence to decide if Taggart's goons had a hand in it. And what of Lei, her unborn child and the kids? Were they dead, too? Lucinda and Huang's school grades were good. Maybe Welfare had them now. He'd never find out.

A breeze picked up, blowing through the bare branches above him and hustling park trash nowhere in particular. Distantly, on the path circumventing the lake, a stranger approached.

Marci lit a cigarette and watched as ripples formed and fluttered on the surface of the water. Had he the chance to reverse time would he do things differently? The question was moot. He could certainly have visited Stella Kennedy sooner, and might even have refused Erin's invitation to join Club Bohém. But Alex would still be dead, and Erin's fate, written by her own hand, would have led to the same futile conclusion with or without him.

The figure on the footpath drew near. To Marci's surprise and intense relief he saw it was Petros Garai.

Petros stopped and peered the final fifty yards. "Marci?"

"Thank God," Marci said, hurrying over to clasp Petros's hand. "You couldn't have timed things better."

Petros appeared equally astonished. "My dear fellow, what a remarkable coincidence! I was just coming back from a client meeting."

"Have you seen Erin?"

"Today?" Petros frowned. "We spoke last night on the phone. I've been working on a solution to her problem. I assume you're privy to it?"

"Not yet. We haven't met since she got back from Győr."

"I see. Excuse my asking, but is anything the matter? You appear a trifle peaked."

"Do you mind if we sit?" Marci asked. His limbs had lost their strength and he felt suddenly very tired. At the same time, his skin tingled as if bubbles coursed through his blood. It was a typical Cortiquell comedown. In the vernacular, *Corti-crash.*

Petros helped him back to the bench, where in detail Marci described the events of the tribunal, including the demise of the Pimenovs and the trumped-up charges he'd faced, careful to omit references to Club Bohém. "I'd hoped that I could take Erin to Buda with me," he lamented. "Now Alex is dead and there's nothing I can do to stop them from taking Erin."

Petros looked to the east, where the sun had cleared the park's distant woodland boundary in smoldering overcast. For a while he chose not to speak, appearing to weigh something of import. "As a matter of fact, there is."

"What is it?" Marci asked. "I'll do anything to help her."

"It won't be easy. In fact, it will cost you much more than you can imagine."

"I've nothing to lose."

"To the contrary, you will lose everything except Erin."

Marci watched him closely. "Tell me."

Half an hour later, as he was crossing Hősök tere, Marci's phone rang. Erin said, "how was your meeting?"

"Not the best. Can we meet?"

"Of course. The same place as before?"

"It'll do."

Marci took a cab to Margit Island. The wind had picked up. Rain resembling soot trailed over the hills of Buda. He followed the path around the bottom of the island and arrived at the old playground. Erin was already there, leaning back and pulling herself upright against one of the calisthenic beams, as a child might. Marci fought back an unpleasant, choking sensation of grief mingled with guilt.

She ran over and embraced him. "How are you?" she asked. "Tell me what happened."

"Where do I begin?" he said. "For one, you're not looking at Márton Kovács, Adjudicant Level 3. Behold the new Marci: a SIN 10 junior records clerk. Apparently, I'm lucky to be alive."

"But that's preposterous! You're on the verge of joining The Society!"

"Not anymore." He took her hands. "I'm sorry. I wanted to help you. I wanted to take you with me to Buda."

"Then it's over? Our dream of a life there?" Erin let go of him and walked over to the riverbank fence. "So, the Hangman will come for me and we'll never be together. That's our fate."

"No!" Marci cried. "You'll live, and I'll live with you. They won't separate us. I won't let them!"

"And where will we go, Marci? The Underground doesn't hide people."

"Petros said he had a plan. He said we should be ready to travel light."

"Travel where, Marci? There's nowhere we can go. It's hopeless."

"Of course it's bloody hopeless!" He began to pace, a step forward, a step backward. "Damn this OCD!" he cried. "Damn the Company. And damn you!"

Erin flinched. "What did you say?"

"You!" he yelled, pointing his finger. "It's because of you all this has happened! You and your damned Club Bohém! You and your idiotic friend Petros! I should have called it quits after our first date in City Park."

Her eyes looked stung with the pathetic injury of a rebuked child. "Why are you saying these horrid things?"

"Because it's all your fault! If I hadn't met you, none of this would have happened. I'd be in Club 30 by now. I'd be safe, away from my job and away from Morrison and Kruger and bloody Tony Jackson!"

"No you wouldn't," Erin said coldly. "You can't get into Club 30 because of your mental health problems. Do you think you're the only one who suffers? Yes, you suffer. But you also live like a king. When was the last time you wanted something you couldn't afford, or had to choose between buying food and paying the rent? Do you know what it's like to work in a dingy little junk shop with a boss who's a bit of a pervert? To wake up every morning already hating the day and wishing you were dead, or cry yourself to sleep so hard it makes you sick to your stomach? Of course you don't! You're too busy wondering when your next bottle of whiskey from Japan is coming. You're going to get a nice desk job for a few years. Even if you work in Records the rest of your life, you'll make more than enough to survive. I'm 29 and I'm about to be liquidated! They could come for me now, tomorrow or in a few days—it doesn't matter. Soon I won't exist, and my parents won't have a daughter. And why? Because of the Company you serve!"

Marci started to stutter something in reply, but Erin cut him off.

"You're as bad as they are," she continued. "I bet the only reason the Hangman's coming for me is thanks to you. Because nobody would care about some stupid, depressed shop girl if she didn't know someone important. So tell me, Marci, who has it worse? Yes, you've lost your job, but I'm going to lose my life."

"Erin, I—"

"Don't touch me! I don't want your murderous, bloody hands on me. I should have known you were trouble when you told me you were SIN 29. People like you don't care who you step on to get to the top. I bet you'll go back into the office tomorrow with your tail between your legs like nothing ever happened. Won't you? Well, what about Alex? What about your neighbors?" She stepped close and shoved him in the chest. "You know what, Marci? I wish I'd never met you!"

"I'm sorry," he stuttered. "I didn't mean those things, really. Let me speak to Sándor. He'll be able to help us."

Erin turned to leave. "There's no 'us' anymore."

He grabbed her arm. "Don't go. Please!"

Erin pulled herself free and stumbled backwards, falling to the ground.

Marci rushed to help her. "Are you hurt? Why did you cower from me?"

But she'd scrambled to her feet and was striding away and dusting herself off, back towards the bridge ramp. Marci ran after her, but she only walked faster.

"Don't follow me, Marci," she said. "And don't call me. Let me die without your tears and your self-pity."

He thought to do just that, to follow her, to let her know again he'd find a way to make everything okay. But something told him what she'd said was right, that there really was no longer any them. She was leaving, and nothing he could do would change that. As she walked away, he was consumed by a choking, heartbreaking sense of grief that it had all been for naught and that he never see her again.

21

Marci, gaining access to 29 Rákóczi út, climbed to the third floor. As he neared his apartment Norbert Tóth emerged from his own and approached. Marci hurried under the bioreader and willed Alice to let him inside; he was in no mood to speak to anyone, especially not Tóth.

Tóth, a little self-conscious and preceded by a fanfare of body odor, forewent the courtesy of a greeting. "You stay inside tonight. Igen?"

Marci looked at him in irritation. "What are you talking about?"

"Inside," Tóth repeated slowly. "You stay inside tonight. Important!"

Sometimes, Marci thought, it was just better to humor the old fool. "Okay, Norbert. I'll stay inside." Marci closed and locked the door on him. He kicked off his shoes, lined them up with the others and ran his hands under the bathroom tap, wincing with pain; they were raw and bloody from too much washing.

His reflection looked back at him in pity.

Take the pill. You might as well.

At the back of the medicine cabinet, behind expired cough syrup bottles and some fancy razor blades he never used, was a small, white-and-turquoise carton embossed in flowing script: Rapture. Marci tore away the wrapper to reveal something like a jewelry box. A silk ribbon protruding from the front opened a velvet-lined tray. Couched on a pillow was a small, oval pill. An inch-thick booklet, hidden beneath the tray, denied responsibility for every eventuality.

He checked the expiry date: December 2140. As if a suicide pill needed one.

Marci took the box to the lounge. Beside the Chesterfield was a luxury he could no longer afford but which he poured into his tumbler with a generous hand: Yamazaki 18-year-old single malt. Tobacco, alcohol and potassium fentylcyanide. All a downwardly mobile man could want.

He removed the pill from its tray. Striped white for purity and cyan for peace, it was as harmless looking as a jelly bean but more costly than all the gold in Christendom, for its value was exactly equal to the life of its user.

Take it. You've lost everything. Why suffer any more?

He reached for the tumbler. Beside it lay his phone. For no particular reason he dialed Sándor's number.

"Hello?"

Marci jumped to his feet. "Sándor!"

A slight pause, then a guarded greeting. "Hello, Marci."

"Thank God you called. Did you pick up my messages?"

"Yes. My apologies for not replying; I was away on business. What can I do for you?"

What can I do for you. A bizarre response.

As succinctly as possible, Marci relayed the events of the last week, including his demotion and Erin's plight. "We canceled the kill order, but it's just a matter of time before MARTHA reissues it."

"I heard something of your predicament through the grapevine," Sándor replied. "To be honest, it's put me in rather a delicate situation, as I'm sure you'll understand."

"What situation?"

"This is very difficult for me, Marci. You're like a son to me, but this goes above my head."

Marci felt his stomach twist. "I don't understand."

"I'm sorry, Marci. I can't help you with The Society anymore. As you know, we only accept nominations from SIN 29ers. You're an intelligent young man. I'm sure you'll carve out a niche for yourself when this storm's blown over."

"But what about Erin?" Marci cried. "Can't you at least help her?"

"I'm sorry, but my hands are tied. Now please excuse me: I'm a little late for a dinner engagement."

"But Sándor, we—"

"I really must go now. Good night, and good luck."

The line went dead. Marci lowered the phone, then let it fall to the floor. Slowly, he walked to the window and sat beside the gramophone.

Time passed. Marci stirred. From the bookcase he took a heavy Bakelite pressed two centuries ago, the 78 record Alex had picked out but never got to hear. The label read *His Master's Voice* but the track details had worn away. He removed the sleeve, placed the disc on the turntable, cranked the handle and lowered the tone arm.

The needle rode the lead-in groove. From the flared horn came the hiss of static. Rising from silence, strings: violins, violas and cellos, pianissimo, non-tremolo. A harp joined them: three notes, descending: C, A, C. Slowly, longingly, the Adagietto built.

"Lights out."

Marci's breath came quickly. He filled his whiskey glass to the brim and rushed it to his mouth. Liquor ran over his fingers; the glass slipped from his hand and broke. Falling to his knees, he released a wail of grief that broke into shuddering sobs. He cried for Alex and Lei and the children. He cried for his mother and father. He cried for his dreams, stolen from him and forever out of reach. But most of all, he cried for Erin.

He was already half-awake, nauseous and shivering, when the explosion sounded, and when he reached for his bedside clock it was gone. Marci fumbled for his watch and lit up the display: 01:38. He'd been out for three, maybe four hours. He waited for Alice to raise the house lights. When she didn't, he sat up quickly and regretted it.

"Lights on."

There was no response.

"Alice, lights on."

For once in seven years, Alice was silent.

Cursing, Marci swung his legs over the bed and stood up. The floor struck his shoulder. He found the bed frame with his hands. A point of reference. Then the bedside table. In the top drawer was a flashlight he never used but which still had enough power to show him his own nakedness. Somehow, he'd undressed himself—no mean feat in his inebriated condition. An empty tumbler and a half-drained bottle of Yamakazi on the floor confirmed his suspicion.

He swung the beam of light across the room. Glass shards like many rodent eyes glinted back at him all the way to the shattered bay windows. The curtains were shreds; they danced like pennants over Gyulai Pál utca, stirred by a musty, sulfurous draft which was blowing from the lounge. The odor was familiar, but in his drunken stupor Marci couldn't place it.

On the street, a brass section of car horns was waking up the neighborhood. Marci used the bed as a prop and gained his feet. He dressed, wriggled his feet into some slippers and staggered to the window. A hundred yards down Stahly utca a line of parked cars blinked their hazards like so many highway roadwork lamps. The streetlights on Gyulai Pál, he noticed, were out.

The flashlight dimmed, then died. Marci shook it back into life, losing his balance and landing on all fours. He yelped in pain as something sharp punctured the heel of his left hand. He tried to pluck it out but only embedded it further. A second reason to visit the bathroom. The first took precedence: he was about to vomit.

He stumbled into the *en suite* and when Alice failed to switch the mood lights on he felt along the wall for a switch that wasn't there because of the concierge. What he wanted more than a pair of tweezers was a Nauselief.

A second explosion, something like a Chinese firecracker lit at arm's length, was quickly followed by a third. Marci dropped to the floor as a rush of hot air filled the room with the same acrid stench as before. This time he placed it: Thököly út and the blown-up trolleybus.

In the lounge, the air was a pall of choking black dust. Marci groped his way to the hall, and here the source of the draft became clear. His front door stood ruptured and sagging on one hinge. The central windowpane and transom above it were missing; broken glass sparkled on the parquet. From outside, the chemical odor blew stronger now, and the breeze carried something else: the bloodcurdling, high-pitched screaming of men. Marci found his running shoes halfway down the hall and swapped his slippers for them. He forced the front door aside, stepped onto the walkway and immediately shielded his eyes.

A dozen yards to Marci's right the walkway branched left and led to Norbert Tóth's apartment. Suspended from a hanging basket bracket near his neighbor's door, a work lamp illuminated a scene of horror. Between the two flats the iron guard rail was missing or bent as if made of licorice. Half of Tóth's apartment wall was gone. The other half was black with soot and spattered with something crimson. In the lamplight it resembled a fresco fashioned by a maniac.

Marci, still unbalanced from booze, took a corrective step into something wet. A spreading puddle of blood, almost fluorescent in its luminosity, followed the grooves in the old tiled floor beneath his feet to where the railing used to be, before dribbling into the courtyard.

The source became clear. Six black-clad bodies littered the landing, their contorted forms resembling the playthings of a petulant child. All wore the jackboots and insignia of cessation officers; all varied in stages of sentience. One was clearly dead, blown apart at the waist. His torso remained; the rest of him lay in the courtyard. Another was decapitated but otherwise intact. A third lacked human form altogether.

The others were alive, barely. One man, lacking legs, tried to claw himself upright using a section of guardrail. Another hung half-in, half-out of the Nagy family's kitchen window, an apron of blood fanning out on the wall below. Closest to Marci, a cessation officer naked to the waist was making shrill, inarticulate sounds. The flesh on his back was missing; his spine shone white in the glow of Norbert Tóth's work lamp.

Marci stepped back in revulsion. The scene was too much; he bent over and vomited.

From across the walkway came yelling. Framed in his doorway, robed in a dressing gown and brandishing a shotgun stood Norbert Tóth. His voice was hoarse, perhaps from the dust, or maybe it was how he sounded when he shouted. "Bastards!" he cried, "I got you, you filthy bastards! How do you like your own medicine?" Catching sight of Marci, he leveled the gun and picked his way through the human debris. As he passed the work lamp his shadow fell over the carnage like a ghoul looting a battlefield. "You!" he shouted. "They were here for you!"

Marci spat bile from his mouth. "Me?"

Tóth surveyed his handiwork. "I thought my time was up," he murmured. "It is now."

Marci, transfixed by the weapon, backed into the wall. "You did this?"

Tóth nodded proudly, but his voice was soft. "I've been waiting many years for this night."

"How do you know I was the target?" Marci stammered.

Tóth gave him an incredulous look. "Are you thick? That bitch Mária let slip you're for the chop."

"Mária? How could she know?"

"She's an Informant, remember? Probably let them into the building herself. But don't you worry, I've got something special lined up for her."

"So that's what you were doing in the shed."

"Well, I wasn't making a bloody spaceship, was I?"

From the distance came the wail of sirens.

"They'll be here for me soon," Tóth muttered, heading back to his flat. At the door he turned, fixing Marci with a look neither boorish nor truculent, but almost affectionate. An unspoken understanding pass between them. "You'd better get going, son. I'll slow them down."

Marci nodded and stumbled back inside his apartment. In the hall, the backpack Petros had advised him to prepare was waiting. There was still a little room at the top. What had he forgotten to pack?

Marci ran to the display cabinet in the living room and took a family portrait from its frame. Under his bed he found the biscuit tin András had given him. On the coffee table lay his cell phone and the Rapture carton. These and the other items he stuffed into the pack and returned to the hall.

The sirens were growing louder. At the front door he looked back. His home, his dear home! Never would he see it again. A terrible melancholy rose in him. With great effort he turned away.

Outside, Tóth stood with his shotgun, looking up into the clear night sky. "Emese!" he called. "Did you see what I did? After all these years, my darling, I got them back! And now I'll join you." His eyes fell on Marci. He smiled. *"Isten veled*[21]*."*

Marci ran to the stairs, leaving a trail of bloody footprints and the sound of Tóth's rich, gentle crooning in his wake. As quickly as his hangover allowed, he descended to the side entrance and burst onto Gyulai Pál utca. Which way? To the left, Rákóczi út was ablaze with red and blue strobe light. The sirens had ceased; presumably a cessation squad had entered through the front of the building.

Marci turned right, and with a loping stagger reached the intersection with Stahly utca. Here, the remnants of a cessation squad van belched black smoke from its mangled interior. The tires had popped; the vehicle's rims rested in pools of smoking rubber. Tóth must have known exactly where they'd pull up. The man had thought of everything.

Out of breath, Marci reached Kőfaragó utca, pressed himself into the shadow of a shop porch and placed a call. "Petros, it's Marci. A cessation squad came for me. My neighbor killed them. I'm in the Palace District and I don't have anywhere to go."

"Head towards Rákóczi Tér metro," Petros instructed. "I'm sending you a waypoint on the other side of the city."

"What about Erin?" Marci asked. "Is she safe?"

"She's with me and she's fine. Just get to the marker. And watch out for drones."

Marci stepped back into the street. The night was clear; a handful of stars contended with Pest's light pollution. More significantly, there were no drones visible.

He looked back down Gyulai Pál utca one last time. A flash of light, supernaturally brilliant, illuminated the far end of the street, turning the artificial elms outside his apartment as white as dead salt

---

[21] "God be with you."

pan trees. Channeled by the narrow street, a wall of energy resembling kettle steam raced toward him. Marci jumped back into the shop porch as the heated wind carried debris and the reek of ammonia past him. A crack like a bull whip but as loud as close thunder followed. When he peered around the corner, the top floor of 29 Rákóczi Út was a rising ball of fire. Norbert Tóth's revenge was complete. Mária Földi was no more.

Through the dark backstreets of Palotanegyed he fled, his footsteps loud and resonant in the predawn torpor. In spite of his drunken state, something shrewd occurred to him. Thank God for the whiskey! If he'd gone to bed sober, he'd be running through the city in his underwear. A bleaker thought occurred. He'd left most of his medication in his bathroom.

As he reached József Körút his phone chimed and a map of the city appeared. A blue dot showed his current location. Far to the east, a glowing green circle indicated his destination.

Marci crossed the boulevard and rode two escalators down to the station. The platform was empty. He moved to the end and sat on a plastic bench to inspect his wounded hand. A quarter-inch shard of glass lay flush beneath the skin in the fleshy area above his wrist. It hurt worse than it looked.

A rush of warm wind heralded an approaching train. Marci stepped up to the marker on the platform's edge where the carriage doors would open. The train slowed, stopped. A handful of late-night revelers disembarked further down.

Marci stepped into an empty compartment and took a seat near the driver's cab and waited. A minute passed. What was the holdup? His second skin transmissions would already have pinpointed him here. If he really was the target of the kill order, Justice could have ordered Transport Budapest to hold the train for them. What if, at this moment, a cessation squad was descending the escalator?

He went to the doors and peered along the empty platform. An air cab would have been a more sensible option. Was it too late to return to Rákóczi Tér and catch one?

The light strip in the threshold began flashing amber. Before he could change his mind, the doors closed and the train eased away into the tunnel.

Suddenly tired, Marci returned to his seat. When he closed his eyes, an afterimage of Norbert Tóth's explosive finale bleached his vision. Norbert Tóth the bomb maker! Small wonder he'd been so furtive about his workshop activities. How had he done it? Marci recalled that Tóth worked at the ammonia plant at Veszprém. It would explain the odor carried by the final bomb's shock wave, but not the walkway booby traps. Presumably, the old man had access to other materials.

There was a larger question. Why tonight? Marci was under no illusion that Tóth had intended the bombs for his own extraction. Why, then, had he wasted them on a neighbor he despised? Perhaps Marci had misjudged him. Or maybe one cessation squad was as good as another. Regardless, Tóth had finally avenged his wife's killers and would already be with her in death. Either that or in pieces.

A ride of twenty minutes brought him to Miskolc. The journey had been uneventful—remarkably so. If Justice wanted to apprehend him, they'd had thirteen metro stops to do it. Had he underestimated their ineptitude? A welcoming party at the top of the stairs would exonerate them.

Marci checked his phone. The blue dot representing his location had shifted 12 miles east. His destination, pulsing green, lay close at hand. In trepidation he rode the escalator to Kandó Kálmán Tér but emerged to neither a Justice Board committee nor anyone else.

The square lay dark and vacant under a full moon and a sky free of drones. The green dot was 150 feet away. Marci strode through a small park past a statue of Kandó Kálmán and into a deserted bus terminal. Here the dots rested, green obscuring blue. He had reached his destination. Neither Petros nor Erin were anywhere to be seen.

He lit a cigarette and took in his surroundings. Sixty feet away, water flowed along some kind of man-made conduit, too dark to see but perhaps a flood relief channel. It cut through a landscape of single-story housing, with a warehouse or two to spoil the neighborhood, then disappeared under a road bridge.

The beginnings of two people crested the brow of the riverbank, one lanky, the other short, female and a few steps behind. At the sight of Erin, Marci felt a pang of bittersweet emotion: longing, with a twist of intimidation.

Petros forewent his usual superficial affability and handed Marci a small, yellow pill. "Take this. It won't remove your second skin, but it will interfere with the signal. Erin's already taken hers."

Marci glanced at Erin, who paid him no heed.

"Very good," Petros said. "Let's start moving. And please, remain silent."

At Kandó Kálmán Tér they rode the escalator down to the metro platform and boarded a train about to depart. Petros, stood by the doors, watched the platform disappear behind them before taking a seat next to Erin. Marci sat opposite and stared at his feet, unwilling to meet her eyes.

Petros, perhaps sensing the tension, leaned forward and spoke over the noise. "Listen carefully. Both your lives are in grave danger. You must put aside your differences here and now. You will soon be traveling in less amenable conditions."

Marci risked a glance at Erin, who was staring disconsolately nowhere. "Where are you taking us?" he asked.

"A safe house. You will remain there until the next phase of the plan can be executed."

"What plan? All you told me was that we're being sent away somewhere."

Petros indicated the carriage's video camera, recessed in the ceiling. "She can't hear us above the noise," he said, "but MARTHA can read our lips. I'll tell you what you need to know later."

Marci stared at the floor, trying to block out memories of the gruesome destruction wrought by Norbert Tóth's IEDs. He lifted one of his shoes. The toe cap and outsole were stained crimson. The tread was a deeper shade of red.

The train slowed and pulled into a station.

"We're here," Petros said. "Let's be off."

They emerged from the subway into an industrial suburb of single-story buildings lining a long, vacant road. Sodium vapor streetlights stretched away into the blackness. Far away, a dog was barking.

"Follow me," Petros whispered. "Stay silent and keep close."

For an age, it seemed, they crept along side streets, through alleyways and past endless rows of dismal terraced houses bordering a set of fenced-in railway tracks. Finally, Petros stopped outside one of them and knocked twice, then three times.

The door opened immediately to a wisp of her woman in her late twenties, who ushered the three into a narrow hallway and bolted the door behind them.

Petros made introductions. "This is Bogi. She'll be looking after you for a day or two. Bogi: Marci and Erin."

Bogi smiled. "Nice to meet you."

Petros motioned down the hall. "Shall we?"

Bogi led them to the rear of the property, where walls painted tangerine orange enclosed a space sixteen feet by ten. Two gray sofas faced each; between them was just enough room to approach a bricked-up hearth and a plastic wall clock marking the passing seconds of the night. The carpet, stained in places, was black, as were a pair of curtains hiding most of a patio door. A single bare bulb hung from the ceiling and cast filament shadow over everything. Marci surveyed the room in disgust. If rooms could talk, this one was apologizing.

Bogi brought tea and pogácsa. Marci and Erin, divested of their coats and rucksacks, sat on opposite couches ignoring one another for different reasons. Bogi lit a cigarette, something menthol, and looked uncomfortable.

Petros sipped from his mug and placed it on the carpet. "Now we can talk. To anticipate your question, you're in Nyíregyháza. You're in a safe house run by the Underground."

Marci tapped a Winterbourne free of its carton. "So, what now? Do we stay here?"

Petros glanced at Bogi. "No. You're going to be transported to the Outside."

Marci's mouth gaped. "The Outside?"

Petros made a placating gesture. "You're not the first and you won't be the last. We've helped many to escape before now. You'll be quite safe."

"Safe?" Marci cried. "What are you thinking? We won't last a day out there!"

"You can and will. We have people there who will look after you."

Erin said, "Why can't the Underground hide us here in Budapest?"

"Live?" Petros smiled sadly. "My dear Erin, what kind of life would that be? Moving from house to house, hunted down like a fugitive, watching the world from the sideline but never able to be part of it again?"

"But isn't it worth trying? I mean, there must be a way somehow." It was a plea more than a question.

"And how long could you stay in hiding? Every day would be a day closer to discovery, not just yours but the entire organization. I'm afraid the Underground can't take that chance."

"We stand no bloody chance if we're sent Outside," Marci growled.

"I beg to differ. There are communities, towns and cities, even, where ordinary folk live and work and enjoy productive lives."

"And how do you propose we reach this rural utopia? In case you haven't noticed, there's a 150-foot-high wall separating us from them, not to mention the Field of Blood. Or are they make-believe, like the Company's human cloning program?"

"No, they're very real. We won't be able to skirt them."

"Then how will we get past them?" Erin asked.

Petros showed a faint smile. "You'll go under them."

Marci laughed flatly. "Now I know you're crazy."

Petros took a pogácsa from the plate and nibbled on it.

Erin shot Marci a dark look. "Please, Petros, tell us your idea."

"It's quite simple. You'll travel on the freight train to Plantation One. Once there, the Underground will transport you to the Wall. A tunnel runs beneath the Field of Blood. Our contacts on the other side will rendezvous with you and take you to safety."

Marci lit his cigarette. "It won't work. We'll never reach the Green Zone. The terminal's a fortress and all outgoing cargo's scanned for life signs."

"We have a contact at the depot. He'll administer something to put you to sleep. We call it a pulse blocker. You'll travel in a shipping crate and pass by the scanners undetected."

"A pulse blocker?" Erin asked.

"Yes. It's a drug formed of two parts. The first stops your heart. The second oxygenates your blood and keeps it circulating at the same rate it would naturally. The scanners are essentially heartbeat monitors. Since your hearts won't be beating, your presence won't be detected."

Silence hung in the air.

"Would you care for a pogácsa?" Bogi asked.

Erin said: "What happens next?"

"The drugs last less than forty minutes," Petros continued. "When you reach the terminus at Plantation One you'll be given the reversal agent and revived."

"Let me get this straight," Marci said. "Your plan is to kill us, ship us out dead and bring us back to life at the other end?"

Petros looked earnestly between Marci and Erin. "In a nutshell, yes."

Marci got up and went to the door. "You're crazy."

"Don't be so rude, Marci," said Erin. "He's trying to help us."

"To what end? To be eaten alive by cannibals or wild dogs? At least the Hangman would've finished us off quickly. This nut job wants to put us in a coffin and ship us to the back of beyond."

"It's easy for you to criticize," Erin scolded. "You're not the one with SIN 5. You've still got your cushy desk job in the Executive Team."

You're a little behind the times," Marci replied. "The Justice Board came for me tonight. I'm as dead as you are."

"All the more reason to take Petros seriously."

"Are you in on this?" Marci asked. "I mean, there has to be a reason why you wouldn't tell me over the phone."

Petros answered for her. "Erin knew no more than you, and for good reason. Our calls are being monitored, and I didn't want to risk jeopardizing the mission."

Marci sucked a lungful of smoke and blew it across the room. "No. No, I don't buy it. There's more to this than meets the eye."

Petros opened his hands wide as if to say, "Such as?"

"What's in this for you?" Marci said. "Why are you so keen to send us Outside?"

"Why must you think badly of everyone you meet?" Erin snapped. "If it weren't for him—"

"If it weren't for him, we'd never have gone to Club Bohém and we wouldn't be running for our bloody lives."

Erin spoke coldly. "You chose to go."

Petros removed his spectacles. "You ask me why I do this, why I risk my own life to save yours, as if I'm somehow in your debt. I am not. My life is comfortable and my income is sufficient. My SIN, while not stellar, is respectable. In short, I have all I need except eternal life, for which I care nothing. Club Bohém was not your downfall; it was your enlightenment, had you only eyes to see it and ears to hear. You ask me why. I'll indulge you with a question. Did you ever wonder why you never met my wife?"

Marci, abashed by Petros's censure, said nothing.

Petros turned to Erin. "Her name was Elena. She was tall, like many Hungarians, and beautiful, like our women. Six years ago, a cessation squad came to our apartment in the middle of the night. I was in Sopron that weekend when I received the text message—yes, a text—telling me my wife had been liquidated in my absence.

"I immediately flew to Nyugati in the hope of seeing her one last time. It was too late. I was told her body had already been 'disposed of'. They gave me no reason given for her murder. Her SIN was high and she had no political ax to grind. We were normal people living ordinary lives until they stole her from me. So to answer your question, the truth is that each person I smuggle out of Budapest is a victory against the Company I couldn't win for her."

Erin squeezed Petros's hand. "I'm so sorry. I can't imagine how awful it was for you."

"It was her death that led me into dissident politics. I joined the Underground soon after. And now you know."

"You were a member all along?" Marci asked.

"I'm afraid so. I'm sorry for my duplicity."

"You don't need to apologize," Erin said. "You've done so much to help us already."

"The drugs you mentioned," Marci said. "How safe are they?"

"Very. We've used them for several years without incident. You'll feel a little strange when you're revived, but this is quite normal and should only last a few minutes."

"And afterwards?"

"Once you reach the Outside, you'll be taken to a medical center to have your second skin removed. Even though it doesn't work beyond the Wall, we like to do it anyway. Belts and braces, and all that. There'll be work for you both, real food and a life without surveillance. To tell you the truth, I almost envy you."

Marci said: "So when does this happen?"

"Tomorrow. The second skin disruptor I gave you isn't 100% effective and won't last long." Petros rose. "Now I must finalize the arrangements. Bogi will take care of you until my return."

"One last thing," Marci said, handing Petros a list he'd penned on the train to Miskolc. "When I left home, I left behind most of my medication. Can you get these for me?"

Petros read it and gave it to Bogi. "She'll get them for you."

"Once we're in the Outside, how will I find more?" Marci asked.

"Most things are available," Petros assured him, "including medication. I'll make sure your hosts know about them. Until tomorrow."

Bogi led them to the front door, unlocked it and looked outside. "It's clear."

Petros was about to leave when Marci stopped him. "I owe you an apology. You've put your neck on the line for us. Thank you."

Petros patted his arm. "Don't thank me. Thank Elena."

"I must go too," Bogi said, putting on her coat. "There's food in the kitchen and beds upstairs. Lock up after me. Don't go out and don't answer to anyone except Petros or me. The code is two knocks, then three. If a squad comes, use the bedroom window. Climb out, turn left and walk along the ledge to the roof. There's a gap between the houses; the next has a flat roof you can jump onto, then to the ground. I'll be back tonight. *Sziastok*."

Marci locked the door after her. In the lounge Erin sat drinking tea. She was, he noticed, wearing her locket. He slumped opposite her and tried to keep his eyes open.

"You should sleep," she said, watching him. "What happened to you?"

"A squad came. My neighbor blew them up. The apartment's gone, along with half the building."

"I'm sorry. I know how much you loved your home."

"Not to worry. According to Petros, a bright future awaits us in the great outdoors." He lit a cigarette, as much to stay awake as anything. "You do realize Petros's plan is insane."

"I'm sure he knows what he's doing. He said we're not the first."

"Let's pray we're not the last."

They fell silent.

"I can't believe it's come to this," Erin said.

Marci went to the window and parted the curtains. The moon, now low in the west, illuminated a long, unkempt garden; beyond it, rows of terraced houses, black against an ink-blue sky, obstructed further view. Marci felt as though he were in a dream from which he would at any moment wake. He wanted to say something, anything to fill the gap, no matter how trite. All that came to mind was the tribunal and his betrayal of her to Ron Taggart. He hadn't told her, of course; events had moved so fast he'd barely had time to dwell on it. Now, in the brooding silence of theirs, the guilt was gnawing at him. He had to tell her. How could he make things right between them unless he told her?

"It looks like the end of the world outside," he said feebly. "I never knew such a place existed."

Tell her. Tell her, you coward.

"Erin, I need to say something" he began. "It's about the tribunal. You see, they asked about you, about us. They wanted to know why I printed out your profile and why I went to Club Bohém. There were other questions, so many I've forgotten half of them. Anyway, they asked about us and why I'd gone to Club Bohém with you. I told them... I told them that the only reason we'd been together was because I was running an investigation on you and Petros because I suspected you of treason. I know it was despicable, but they were trying to set me up, and I thought that if I could keep my job and my SIN I could take you to Buda with me. So I lied."

He paused, waiting for her response, hoping she'd understand. He pictured her staring at him in dismay but couldn't bear to turn around and face her. "That day we spent in Buda you asked me if I'd ever betray you. That's exactly what I've done. I wish it hadn't happened. I wish none of it had ever happened except meeting you. You're the only good thing I have in my life. My SIN, my place in The Society, even eternity in Empyrean—I'd give up all of them for you. Instead, I betrayed you." He turned from the window. Erin, her chin on her neck, sat on the sofa, fast asleep. She'd dropped her drinking mug, and her tea lay in a pool, soaking into the dismal black carpet. Marci stared at her in dismay. He'd made his confession to himself.

He fetched comforters from the bedroom and draped one over her, wrapping the other around himself before taking to the spare settee.

He woke in a narrow oblong of dull daylight which spilled through the crack in the patio curtains, over the other empty couch and up the wall. His watch read 11:08. Somnolence gave way to reality. His sleep had been for naught. To the contrary, he felt wrecked.

Outside, daylight hadn't improved the view of the garden. Three brick walls boxed in a strip of weed-choked backyard beneath a sky of steel-blue overcast.

From somewhere close, a rumbling sound grew, then receded; presumably a cargo train like the one that would soon carry them, dead, to the Outside.

Marci found Erin upstairs, rolled up in a duvet and fast asleep. In the dimness of the bedroom, her face was soft, angelic. One day he would have to repeat his confession to her, but not now and not until they'd reached safety.

In the kitchen he brewed chicory coffee and heated porridge, which he ate without appetite.

From the front door came the sound of two knocks, then three more: the code. Marci left his food, unbolted the door and allowed Petros in.

"I was followed," Petros said, walking to the lounge, "but I managed to lose them. Where is Erin?"

"Asleep upstairs."

Petros removed his rucksack and handed Marci a ziplock bag. "Your medicine and other supplies, courtesy of the Underground."

Marci counted two boxes each of Kqalms, Seromax, Cortiquell and Nauselief, plus four packs of Winterbournes. Everything he'd asked for.

"There's enough medication for a few weeks," Petros said, "depending on your needs. I'm only sorry I couldn't get more."

"How easy is it to find this stuff in the Outside?"

"That depends on circumstances I'd like to discuss with you both. I think you should fetch Erin now."

Marci went upstairs and reappeared with Erin to a room resembling a Doomsday cult yard sale.

Petros greeted Erin and surveyed the miscellany before them. "First, your escape. Bogi will take you to the transit depot at 21:00 tonight. The janitor is Franz. He's one of us. He'll administer the drugs, put you in a container and send it to the train. Once you arrive at Plantation One, our people will dispense the reversal agent and drive you to the Wall. You'll rendezvous with a military escort on the other side of the tunnel sometime around midnight and be escorted to safety. From there you'll need to travel, and this is the part I want to discuss."

"Wait a minute," said Marci, "I thought you said we were being taken to some kind of settlement?"

"All in good time. For now, we need to address more immediate concerns. What you see before you is a survival kit assembled by our Employee migration team. There are two sleeping bags and a tent, a four-season type, which means it's rather heavy. You'll sleep in your clothes, inside the bags. Next, two magnesium fire starters. Then we have water purifiers and a test kit. Use the analyzer on the side to test water quality. Green means it's safe, red means contaminated. Use one tablet per liter of water. There are better systems, but they're heavy, and I don't want to weigh you down any further. The silver pouches are MREs: meals ready to eat. Some you need to boil, others you add hot water to. I'm told they're edible, but I've never been brave enough to verify this."

"What's that?" Erin pointed to something that looked like a chainsaw.

"It's a magma saw. It can cut through anything, including hands, so take care. Something else you might want to treat with respect is this." Petros picked up a leather holster. Inside was a handgun. "Have you ever used one?"

Both shook their heads.

"It's quite simple, I'm told. Point and shoot. It fires pellets of some self-regenerating substance with the same force as a traditional bullet but will never run out. There's a safety catch, here. There's one for each of you." Petros put it down with a shudder. "I hate even touching the thing. The rest of the kit comprises clothing, footwear, a compass and a map of the region. Do either of you have any questions?"

"It's absurd," Marci said.

"What is?"

"The whole situation! Look at us, Petros! We don't know the first thing about living in the wilderness!"

Erin said: "I thought you and your father used to go hunting together?"

"I was nine, and it was hardly hunting. And it wasn't in the Outside."

"You need to face facts," Petros said. "Neither of you can remain in Budapest. Soon the Company will discover your whereabouts. The Underground can't move you from house to house indefinitely, for reasons I've explained. I'm sorry, but this is the way of things. It's this or Nyugati."

"Or a Rapture pill."

"Don't say that," Erin scolded. "We can't give up so easily."

"Can't we?" Marci cried. "How long do you think we'll last? A week? A month? Have you ever killed for food? Have you killed a man? We've no skills, no training and not enough supplies to last beyond Christmas. We might as well take the pill and be done with it."

"That attitude," Petros said, "will not help you. There are many who have made the transition and now live beyond the Border."

"Scraping grubs from dead bark?"

"Do you have a better idea?" Erin said.

"No," Marci snapped, "and that's the problem. But I won't give them the bloody satisfaction of topping myself. Not yet, anyway."

Erin asked: "Petros, yesterday you told us we'll be taken somewhere safe. Why do we need these camping things if we have an escort?"

"An excellent question, and one I was getting to." Petros made space on the sofas and invited them to sit. "The infrastructure in the Outside is, shall we say, substandard. Simply put, your escort vehicle can only take you so far. The remainder of the journey you must make alone."

"How far away is it?" Erin asked.

Petros made an airy gesture. "A day or two."

Marci and Erin studied the equipment with new interest.

"That's a lot of gear for a two-day walk," Marci said.

"It is," Petros said, "and I'd be lying if I let you believe otherwise. The truth is, the Underground's role in your bid for freedom isn't quite as altruistic as it might seem."

"Here's the kicker," Marci snorted.

"You will recall Peti's visit to Club Bohém. As you know, Peti—and I, for that matter—believes that Grisha Ossian might still be alive somewhere beyond the Border. If it's true, the Underground wants to locate, make contact with and somehow return him to Budapest. Since Grisha cloned himself in 2100, he'd be fifty-two now."

"Why would you want to bring him back to Budapest?" Erin asked.

Petros chose his words with care. "To facilitate a realignment of the city's leadership structure."

"By 'realignment' you mean a revolution?" asked Marci.

"Yes, if you will. Although we prefer to describe it as a 'non-violent people's movement'."

"And we're the gophers."

Petros leaned forward in excitement. "My dear boy, you are far more than gophers! Think of yourselves as our Joshua and Caleb, scouring Canaan and reporting back on the Promised Land. With Ossian at the helm, we will retake Budapest and bring an end to the Company and all it stands for."

Marci nodded to himself. "At last I understand you, Petros. The art exhibition, Club Bohém, the soiree at Erin's place—you had this whole thing planned from the beginning. I thought you were just another dilettante, but you're actually pretty slick."

"Marci!" Erin protested, "Petros is my friend, long before I met you."

"Then why don't the two of you team up? I'd like to see him mincing around the Outside."

"At least he's offering us hope, which is more than you're doing."

"What hope?" Marci cried. "That somewhere in half a million square miles of Ukraine we'll stumble across an octogenarian holed up with a cloning machine?"

"It's a little more—" Petros began.

"And then what? We drag him back to Budapest and live happily ever after? Damn it, Petros, I always thought you were a bit loopy, but now—"

"Please," said Petros, "let's not cover old ground. If we can effect your safe evacuation from Budapest and locate Ossian by the same means then where is the harm? If you stay here, you die. If you commit to the plan you'll live, and in so doing may well find the answer to all our problems."

"I agree with Petros," Erin said. "We've nothing to lose. Marci?"

Marci lit a cigarette. "It's the plan of a madman."

"It's the only one we've got. Petros, what should we do?"

"Split the equipment into two parts but share essentials—water, rations, bedding, the fire kits and the guns—just in case you become separated. When you reach the Outside you'll be given further instructions." Petros rose. "I'm late for work; I can't afford to blow my cover. Bogi will return soon. As for us, unless you find Grisha Ossian, we will never meet again."

Erin hugged him. "I don't know how to thank you."

"My dear Erin, it is I who thanks you. You've brought great joy to my life and I'll miss you terribly."

Marci and Erin followed Petros to the front door.

"I almost forgot." Petros reached into his coat, took out a brass petrol lighter much like Marci's and removed the metal sleeve. Flush against the body of the Zippo was a minute red button. "If you find Grisha, he may lack the means to contact us. This activates a homing beacon and will provide the Underground with your location. Please use it only when you've made contact."

Marci eyed it warily and put it in his pocket.

Petros opened the front door and let himself out. "One last point, and an important one," he whispered. "If you reach Ossian and his organization, under no circumstances mention me. We don't know how far the Company has penetrated the Outside, and it might blow my cover here." He extended his hand. "*Viszontlátásra*, Marci."

"Goodbye, Petros."

"*Viszontlátásra*, Petros," Erin said, hugging him again.

"Remember," Petros added, "let no one in except Bogi. Goodbye, and good luck."

Marci closed the door and locked it. He turned to face Erin, who looked as scared as he felt. Wordlessly they embraced.

22

The rest of the day dragged interminably. Marci spent the early afternoon checking the equipment and dividing it based on weight and content. Erin was able to carry more than he'd supposed, which came as a relief; his own pack, fully laden, was almost too heavy to lift. When she offered to take more of the equipment he ruled against it, on the basis that what seemed comfortable now would be burdensome in the field.

Their clothing, which consisted of thick thermals, high pile fleece layers and breathable waterproofs, proved stiflingly indoors: a good sign. Stout walking shoes completed the ensemble, which the two wore around the house to break in.

The gun was a trickier issue. "I hate it and won't be able to use it," Erin protested, and none of Marci's efforts could persuade her otherwise.

In the lounge, time ate away at the afternoon. Erin slept until, overwhelmed with grief, she returned to bed. Marci spent the rest of the day alone, trying to figure out an alternative to Petros's plan that didn't exist. If there was anything to thank the man for it was the medication he and Bogi had acquired. Already Marci had made a dent in the Cortiquell.

A little before 16:00 he went outside to stand in the yard beneath a mackerel sky. The sun, dying somewhere out of sight, had painted the clouds a shade of macaroon pink, so that they resembled myriad pieces of shredded cotton daubed in rouge. Heedless of Bogi's warning to stay indoors, Marci watched his last sunset in Budapest until he could bear it no more.

At 20:00 Bogi arrived bearing fresh bread, butter, kolbász sausage and pickled gherkins. The three ate a simple dinner in silence.

Marci, whose anxiety had been growing worse all day, was about to take another Cortiquell when Bogi warned him off. "The pulse blocker is strong. You should avoid sedatives until it's worn off." In the end, he settled for a Kqalms and sat by the patio door, smoking and listening to Bogi washing up, and to the wall clock's angry chattering. This, along with the sunset, he was already missing, as if living ahead of a moment whose passing he already mourned.

Bogi entered the lounge. She had changed clothes, and now wore military boots and night fatigues which looked odd on her slim frame as if she were the last hope of the conscripted. The smile she gave them might have been pretty were it not for what it denoted.

Marci and Erin donned their backpacks and followed her to the front door.

"No talking from now on," she said, stepping into the street. She looked to the left, then right, then up, then whispered, "Follow me."

Beneath a moonless sky they crept, along end-of-terrace alleys, under brick railway arches and along the empty cobbled streets that lined the gray hulk of the Nyíregzháya Transit Depot. Several times Bogi had them stop as video cameras, mounted high above razor wire fences, swept the perimeter.

At a gully choked with pyracantha bushes Bogi took a flashlight and pair of gloves from her pack and pulled at the prickly shrub. It was loose, and came away easily. Behind it lay a dry ditch deep and wide to conceal them all. "Get in," she whispered, "and stay low."

With the three of them on the other side of the firethorn, Bogi pulled the vegetation back into place and began digging away loose earth at the base of the fence with a trowel until there was a gap sufficient to pass underneath it. "There's sixty-three amps of electricity running through this fence," she whispered, wiggling under the bottom rail. "It's designed to kill you, and it will if you touch it." On the other side she beckoned. "Slide your coats and packs under. Carefully."

Marci and Erin did as instructed.

"Now, you first, Erin."

Erin wriggled under the fence with ease.

"Marci, your turn."

Marci regarded the opening with suspicion.

"Bigger men than you have made it."

Marci lay on his stomach and inched his way through the gap. "Out of three deaths," he muttered, "Hangman, Outside or electrocution, this one seems the most merciful."

"No talking," Bogi hissed.

Covered in soil, Marci emerged on the other side in a stand of hawthorn bushes. Three hundred feet away, beyond a floodlit expanse of lawn, stood the Depot.

Bogi scoped it with night vision glasses. "Cameras are clear. Put on your packs and follow me."

The three, crouched low, followed the ditch several hundred feet to a culvert hidden from view. A storm drain grate barred entry to a two-meter-wide pipe, bored horizontally into the earth. Bogi took a gully key from her pack. "The way in," she explained. "The smell is bad, but it's not a sewer. Marci, please help me catch the grate." She turned the key and the grill fell forward. Marci caught it and lowered it to the ground.

"Listen carefully," Bogi whispered. "The tunnel is long, and there are sentry guns inside. Franz has switched off those that guard our route, but the rest are active. Stay close and do not stray! The guns will kill you, and I will be caught. Do not speak; the sound will echo." With that, she climbed inside.

Marci and Erin exchanged glances, then followed.

The tunnel, like its entrance, was two meters across and formed of smooth concrete that carried just enough foul-smelling water to slosh loudly over their boots. Silhouetted by the torchlight bouncing off the tunnel walls ahead of her, Bogi's slight form led them forward at a pace Marci and Erin struggled to keep up with. Since their packs rubbed against the ceiling, both were forced to move at a bent-kneed shuffle that made speed impossible.

Here and there, tunnels of equal or smaller diameter adjoined theirs. At these intersections, automated sentry guns nested in the walls stood inactive. Marci eyed them with apprehension; were they active, all three of them would have cut them to ribbons.

At a larger intersection Bogi turned left. The tunnel sloped up, and after several minutes led them to a chamber with enough headroom to allow them to stand upright. The air smelled of stale water and bleach. From somewhere unseen came the low rumble of machinery. Above them, a grill identical to the one at the drain's egress let in enough murky light to prove the interlopers that they'd reached a dead end.

Marci stood on tiptoes and pushed up against the grate. It was locked.

Erin said: "Should we use the key?"

"It doesn't open from this side." Bogi tapped her flashlight against the lattice twice, then three times. They waited.

"He's a little deaf," Bogi explained, with a hint of nerves. She tried again, louder.

Somewhere above them a door opened. Footsteps, then the dazzle of a flashlight.

Bogi shielded her eyes. "Franz, it's us."

The torchbearer turned the light on himself. "It is me, Franz."

"Let us out, please."

Franz duly released the three of them from the sluice into a cramped janitor's closet. He greeted Bogi with a traditional kiss, then looked Marci and Erin up and down as an undertaker might. Marci returned the favor. A portly, silver-haired gentleman sporting dungarees and a walrus mustache, Franz's countenance suggested the roguish affability of a disgraced grandfather whose name was taboo at family gatherings. This was the man on whom their lives would soon depend.

"Franz will look after you from now on," Bogi explained. "He can't speak much English, but he's done this many times before, so follow his instructions." She embraced Erin, then Marci, then lowered herself into the chamber. "I wish you all the luck in the world."

Franz dropped the grating back in place and locked it. "So," he said, climbing to his feet and smiling kindly, "you go Outside like others? Franz look after you. Everything will be nice."

Marci glanced at Erin, who stood staring down at the sluice grate with a face bled of color. He asked Franz: "How long will we be asleep?"

"I load you last. Train take seven minutes. Others unload you first. Twenty minutes?" He went to the door and looked out. "Everything is nice. You follow Franz now. Okay?"

They emerged from the storeroom into a space so vast that at first it defied comprehension. In every direction, chutes, ramps, flumes, conveyor belts and escalators carried steel shipping containers at breakneck speed, seemingly at random here and there. At junctures, turntables received, scanned and discharged the crates in new directions, down live rollers or to vertical carousels for further sorting. Automated forklifts attended shelving towers 100 feet tall, moving consignments to and from the sorting network, or stood idle, awaiting orders. Far away, perhaps five football pitches distant, waited a cargo train. Here, robots formed, stacked and loaded pallets into open-sided rolling stock. The effect was of an enormous spider's web overrun by innumerable scuttling silver bugs. Marci now realized why Franz was hard of hearing.

Franz led them under one of the storage towers and into an aisle where a steel container lay on its side. The top was hinged and hung open. "We are here," he yelled above the noise. "You go in now."

Marci and Erin studied the crate with skepticism. Eight feet long and six feet across, it was little larger than two coffins placed side by side.

Franz read their expressions. "Strong box. Safe box. Now, please—" he gestured.

Erin held back. "I'm not going."

"What do you mean, you're not going?" Marci said.

"I can't do this. I can't leave my family."

Marci spoke as gently as the noise would allow. "We don't have a choice. If we go back, we die."

Franz patted the crate. "*Nincs probléma.* You go in, you sleep like baby. Many have."

Erin looked longingly back the way they'd come. "Please let's go home."

"Erin," Marci said, "there is no home anymore."

"I can't," she cried, "I can't do it!"

Marci unwrapped and pressed a Kqalms lozenge into her hand. "Take this," he said. "It will make it easier." On second thoughts, he took one too. Whatever was in the pulse blocker would knock him out, but it couldn't come too soon; if she didn't bolt for the cleaning closet, he soon would.

Franz glanced nervously along the aisle. "Please, you go in crate now."

Once again, she looked back.

Firmly Marci said: "It's over, Erin. There's nothing left for us here. One day we'll return."

"Promise me! Promise me we'll come back!"

"I promise," he said. "I promise we'll come home again one day. Now please, take the pill."

Erin took the pastille and bit down on it. "Hug me," she said, gripping him tightly.

Franz manipulated a control box on one of the storage tower posts. A pair of robotic forks descended the column to stop four feet off the ground.

With terrible reluctance Marci loaded their backpacks into the crate and helped Erin inside before joining her.

Franz knelt beside them. From a plastic tub he took four miniature hypodermics and pointed to his forearm. "Now, please, here."

Marci and Erin rolled up their sleeves.

"One," Franz said, injecting Marci. "Two"—he did the same for Erin, then dispensed the contents of the other syringes. "Very nice. Now you sleep."

"Marci," Erin said, "I don't feel very well."

"It's fear," Marci said. "The Kqalms will work soon."

"No, it's something else. I think something very bad is going to happen."

Franz motioned for them both to move deeper into the crate, then aligned the cover and crossed himself. *"Isten áldjon,"* he said, sealing them in.

Blackness engulfed them. Marci tried to reach for his Zippo, but his arm was constrained at his side. He found her hand. Softly, he sang:

Búza, búza, búza,
De szép tábla búza!
Annak közepébe
Kinyílott a rózsa.[22]

"Marci?" Erin asked, "do you think we'll wake up?"

From somewhere nearby came a whining sound, followed by a jarring motion as the robotic forks lifted the crate. There was movement, the rattle of live rollers. The hum of the warehouse grew louder. Another jarring motion and they were pitched headlong as the container began climbing a slope.

Nausea washed over Marci like a wave. He gripped Erin's hand ever more firmly. "It must be the conveyors," he said, trying to visualize the beach scene he knew so well. "How are you feeling?"

"Very sleepy," Erin said. "In a strange way."

"I guess the drug is working."

Moments later they were dead.

---

[22] "Wheat, wheat, wheat, what a pretty wheat field! In the very middle of it a rose has blossomed."

23

"—responding well."

"And the girl?"

"No vitals."

"Get me an I/V with 0.5 of epinephrine and a BVM."

He was cold, colder than he'd ever remembered. The three blurred faces that hovered somewhere before his expanding consciousness might have been real or the stuff of dreams. For a time he wondered if he might be dead. Did the dead see visions, or shiver like their bones might break? To consider the question implied sentience. He must be alive.

Pain confirmed his suspicion. It came suddenly, an intense pulsing in the brain that kept time with his pulse, so forceful he could hear it, like the muted sound of water drawn from a hand pump. He breathed deeply and uncomfortably and sat up. His vision swam; the three faces became one. Someone pressed a mask to his face, and he sucked chilled air into his lungs until his head cleared and he could take stock of his surroundings.

The loading dock was a hundred feet of gray concrete attached to a warehouse, a yard and a railway siding, with space for a dozen vehicles. Only two were present: an old sedan and a 6×6 army truck with a canvas roof and a tailgate backed up against the bay. A wire fence, lit by the glow of the truck's lights, ringed an abandoned compound. Beyond were fields. Resting open on the dock was the crate that had carried them here. Beside it lay Erin.

She was dead. They'd taken off her winter clothing and cut away her blouse. Now, twelve wires attached her to a vital signs monitor that had flatlined. Kneeling at her side, a paramedic and a doctor were trying to revive her while the corpsman prepped a hypodermic. One performed chest compressions. The other waited with a bag mask.

The doctor, winded, paused; the medic placed the mask over Erin's mouth and squeezed. Her chest rose, but not of her doing.

The doctor resumed compressions. "I need that adrenaline."

"I'm setting up the cannula."

"Forget it. Go for intramuscular."

The corpsman handed over the syringe.

"Fetch the AED."

The medic gave the shot and checked the screen. "She's not responding."

"Damn it," the doctor muttered. "We can't lose them. How's the male?"

"Conscious and mobile. Should we give her more reversal agent?"

"It won't help." The doctor yelled to the soldier: "Where's that defibrillator?"

The corpsman returned at a run. "It's charged."

"Stand clear."

Erin's body rocked with the counter-shock.

All three turned to the monitor, whose wave forms had sprung to life.

"The paramedic placed his ear to Erin's mouth. "She's breathing."

"O^2 level's climbing. So is blood pressure."

"Heart rhythm's stable."

"Good job. Clean her up." The doctor noticed Marci. "She made it."

Still woozy, Marci started crawling toward Erin, but the corpsman stopped him. "We'll take care of her," he said, helping Marci to his feet.

Marci flinched; his left shoulder twinged with pain. "I'm not leaving her."

"I said we'll take care of her. Get in the truck. We need to leave."

Marci shrugged him off and staggered to where Erin lay, conscious but trembling even more violently than he was. "She can't travel like this."

"She'll be monitored in transit."

Marci shuffled over to the lorry and watched as the corpsman and medic carried Erin inside. A row of opposing benches ran the length of the interior. A pallet occupied the space between them, near the tailgate. As they laid Erin down, a soldier with a face like old leather brought blankets.

The corpsman departed. Marci watched him leave. "Where's the doctor?"

"Not coming," the soldier said. He attached a pulse oximeter to Erin's index finger. "They only come for the resus."

Marci took a blanket for himself and covered Erin with the rest. "She needs a doctor."

The soldier, whose name patch read "Varga," whistled. Six other men, all armed, climbed aboard and lifted the tailgate. "The doc signed her off as fit to travel," Varga said, walking over to the cab wall and kicking it. "That's good enough for me."

The truck's engine fired into life. With a blast of black exhaust smoke it rolled out of the compound and down a dirt track.

Marci knelt beside Erin and cradled her head. "Can you hear me, darling?"

Erin might have been nodding but he couldn't tell. "Why… am… I… sh-shaking?"

Marci asked Varga: "Why is she shaking?"

"It's the pulse blocker. Like coming round from anesthesia. You're just cold, that's all." Varga checked the monitor's screen. "Her heart rate is irregular."

"What does that mean?"

Varga shrugged. "Maybe something, maybe nothing. Too early to say."

"Where… are we?" Erin asked.

"Plantation One," Varga said, lighting a cigarette.

"Then… we… made it?"

Marci smiled. "We made it."

Erin closed her eyes and appeared to sleep.

Marci ran his hands across his face. His head was still pounding from the pulse blocker. He asked Varga, "How long were we out for?"

"No idea. Depends when they gave you the shots. From the time we pulled you from the crate, five minutes, give or take. The girl took longer. It's not unusual."

"You've done this before?"

"Not for a while. A few years back we were shipping 'em out like there was no tomorrow. You must be special. You don't look like an anarchist, and I've met a few. What did you do?"

Marci realized anonymity no longer served any purpose. "I was an Adjudicant. My colleague and I discovered the Company was falsifying MARTHA's records. He was killed. I'm alive."

Varga spat over the tailgate. "Sounds about right. I've smuggled all sorts over the years. You're the first Adjudicant."

Marci, suddenly tired, lay down beside Erin and was soon asleep.

"Get up."

Varga's less than gentle kick to his side roused him. Erin was gone. Marci threw off his blanket and turned to see her sitting close to the cab, drinking hot chicory from a thermos mug. She looked pale and haggard but wasn't shivering anymore.

He joined her. "How are you feeling now?"

"Very tired. Are we near the Border?"

"We can't be far."

"Did you ever wonder," Erin asked, "why Petros didn't just get us uniforms and passes for the Green Zone?"

"There's a lot of things I wonder about Petros," Marci said. "Maybe there wasn't enough time. Then again, he seemed to have everything planned out. When I see him next I'll be sure to ask him, just before I punch his face."

"I'm glad to see you're back to your normal self," Erin said. "Just think: soon we'll have the whole world as our backyard."

"I'm trying not to. If you had your paints you could make a fortune selling authentic artwork from the frontier."

"It would certainly raise my SIN," Erin said. "Maybe they'd even make me a Patrician."

"That's impossible. Only men can be Patricians."

"Surely they'd bend the rules a little bit for me?"

"If I were the Prefect, you'd be in like a shot."

Someone in the driver's cab tapped the wall twice. The truck stopped.

Varga slung his rifle on. "Gear up, we're here. Did they tell you about the tunnel?"

"Not much," Marci said.

"God knows how the Company hasn't found it. We built it a couple of decades ago. Couldn't risk setting off the mines with boring equipment so we dug it by hand."

Marci wasn't interested. "What are our chances out there?"

"About slim to none, unless you find Grisha Ossian and a big pile of weapons. You have military training?"

"No."

Varga lowered the tailgate and jumped out. "Then you're screwed."

Marci bowed his head, eyes closed and wondered how much worse things could get. He thought of Petros, by now probably fast asleep. One of Norbert Tóth's bombs, strategically placed beneath his bed, would prove a fitting wake-up call for the Club Bohém anarchist.

Varga clicked his tongue impatiently, as if urging on a horse. "Sleep time over. Let's go."

"Can you walk?" Marci asked Erin.

She rose, gingerly. "My legs feel weak."

Marci helped her to the ground. They'd stopped in a small clearing of Douglas firs silhouetted against the night sky. The truck's lights were out; flashlights stayed low across a track littered with pine needles. He inhaled deeply.

"First time?" Varga noticed. "Nothing like the smell of pine forest. Contaminated as hell, but better than city smog. Follow me."

Marci and Erin fell in. Two hundred feet ahead, an aura of light rose above the tree line, blotting out the stars. Varga sensed the unspoken question. "No-man's-land," he whispered. "They run the lamps all night long. Makes Little Tokyo look like a Chinese lantern. We're near the substation. You'll hear it soon. Stay close."

The track ended at a gully. Beyond, through thinning trees, a wall of sheer concrete rose 150 feet. From somewhere unseen, the buzz of high voltage electricity carried menace. The group turned left, following the ditch with the Wall parallel. After a hundred yards they stopped. Recessed into an earth bank was an iron grate similar to those Marci and Erin had seen outside the Depot.

Two soldiers worked it free. Varga shone his torch inside the tunnel and sniffed. "I smell something dead. Watch your step."

"You're not coming with us?" Erin asked.

"Why would I? I'm not your chaperone."

Marci asked: "How far is it to the other side?"

"Just over a mile. At the other end's another grate and someone else with the key. If not, you'll add to the smell in a few days."

Erin looked back the way they'd come. Far to the west and out of sight, Budapest's skyline would be glowing with radiance more familiar to her. "I suppose it's the last time I'll ever see Budapest," she said.

"It's done us no favors," Marci said, inspecting the tunnel with his own flashlight. "Take off your pack; this rat hole's too narrow to wear it in."

Erin, glancing back one last time, followed him inside.

24

Varga had been right on two counts. The tunnel was narrow, less than the span of Marci's outstretched arms, and reeked of something long-deceased. Underfoot was dry clay, hewn away to form a shallow trench. The walls and ceiling had been covered up with sheets of corrugated metal. Marci hoped there was something more substantial behind them girding the duct. No doubt the Underground, chary of making noise or setting off the minefield, had simply relied on the diameter of the bore and the density of the soil.

From behind them came a metallic clang as the grate was put back in place. Marci didn't stop. He wondered if Erin had, but didn't check to see. To look back now would be more than he could bear. Whatever fate awaited them at the other end of the tunnel, he knew they would never again see their beloved Budapest. For all his bravado moments earlier, the thought began to choke him. He forced his attention on the trembling torch light a few feet ahead of him.

Bent double, their packs dragging like deadweight behind them, the two fugitives moved at a stooping shuffle, their progress impeded by Erin's frequent need to rest. She looked, Marci thought, as deathly as anyone he'd ever seen, and were it not for the diameter of the tunnel propping her up she'd have probably fallen over by now. But she refused him to take her rucksack, which more than anything irritated him; there was no guarantee that whoever might be at the other end would wait.

He switched off his flashlight. The way ahead showed only blackness. If there was anyone at the other end it was impossible to tell.

After twenty-five excruciating minutes, a pinprick of light appeared in the distance. The source grew: ten minutes later, the size of a golf ball; another five, the size of Marci's fist held before him. Finally, the exit grew large enough for them to see the grill was missing. Shielding their eyes and overwhelmed with thankfulness, Marci and Erin stumbled out of the conduit and collapsed in the headlight of a military truck. They would not end their days entombed below the Field of Blood, after all.

Marci caught his breath and took in his first view of the Outside. Four military vehicles lit up a waste ground of broken asphalt, burned-out cars, and tall weeds. Concrete pillars, emblazoned with graffiti, supported a decaying six-lane viaduct high above, unused in more than a century. An off-ramp led somewhere, perhaps to the highway. A handful of soldiers milled around smoking cigarettes and eyed the newcomers warily.

Marci's exultation was short-lived. Striding toward them was a lean-faced young woman dressed in fatigues and carrying a Kalashnikov. Her hair, scraped back into a bun, accentuated features narrow and snub. A mouth like a thin scar was already pursed in disapproval. She greeted them without warmth. "My name is Zita. Welcome to the Outside. Get in the truck. We're late."

Two soldiers replaced the tunnel grill and helped Marci and Erin into the back of a personnel carrier. Zita climbed aboard and yelled a command. The remaining troops boarded the convoy, which trundled up the ramp onto an arrow-straight road cut through dense conifer forest. Behind them the night was an incandescent glow.

Marci watched his homeland recede into the night. When he glanced at Erin he was relieved to find her asleep. This was a view he didn't want her to remember.

Time passed. The road rolled under the truck's dim red taillights through a landscape so unchanging it might have been glued to the inside of a hamster wheel. There was no traffic; no one approached from behind and no one passed from ahead. The glare of the Border receded to a faint glow on the horizon, then faded from sight.

Zita had so far resisted conversation and seemed bored by the evening's proceedings, instead preferring to exchange coarse anecdotes with her platoon until the stories ran out.

Marci addressed her: "Where exactly are you taking us?"

"One hundred and twenty miles east. Another team will take you further."

"Is there a destination in mind?"

Zita gave no response. Clearly, she had her orders and would not offer anything more.

Marci leaned back against the canvas wall and dozed, waking up cold and hungry. The truck had stopped, lights out, at the side of the road, and from outside came small talk and the sound of emptying bladders. Sore and shivering, he jumped down and marched around, flapping his arms under a sky as dark as ink but as bright as he could remember with the burning a thousand distant suns.

Erin was still asleep when they set off again. Soothed by the rocking of the truck, Marci soon fell asleep.

He came to under a dome of indigo blue. Someone had lit an oil lamp fixed to the ceiling with coat hangers and the men were checking their weapons and looking like they had purpose. A minute later, all four vehicles made a U-turn and came to a halt. The tailgate was lowered; the troops disembarked.

Zita appeared. "Time to go."

Erin woke with a gasp of breath. "Where are we?"

"God knows," Marci said. "How do you feel?"

"A little dizzy and very tired. And a bit strange."

Marci left her brush with death go unspoken. "Maybe it's the pulse blocker."

"That was hours ago," she pointed out.

Two soldiers helped them down. Marci dragged their packs past the truck and into the high beams of an armored personnel carrier crowned with a .50 caliber gun turret.

Zita made a facetious flourish. "Your new ride."

Marci watched her return to her convoy, which promptly departed in a cloud of grit and diesel fumes.

A brawny man in his late forties approached. A golden oak leaf ensign sewn on his breast suggested officer rank. He spoke in Hungarian but his accent was foreign. "You are Márton and Erin?"

"Yes," said Marci. "Who are you, and where are we?"

"I'm Oleksander. You're in Ukraine—what's left of it. The girl looks like death. Is she ok?"

"No, she isn't," Erin replied. "I hope you're taking us somewhere that has a doctor?"

Oleksander chuckled. "In the Outside? Here you're your own doctor. Come, let's get moving. It's almost dawn. "

"I'll kill Petros," Marci muttered, climbing on board.

With a roar the APC set off. Marci and Erin sat beside the tailgate across from Oleksander and watched Zita's convoy disappear westward until distance consumed them.

Marci turned his attention to his fellow travelers, who unlike Zita's lot spoke quietly in a tongue akin to Russian. None slept; all held their guns at the ready.

Erin asked Oleksander: "How much further do we have to travel?"

"About two hours. What's the hurry? You're not in the big city anymore."

"There's no hurry," Erin said politely, "it's just nice to know. We've been traveling all night."

"You've a lot more ahead of you."

Marci decided to try his hand. "Do you live out here?"

Oleksander made no reply.

"Why the military escorts? It's not like we're VIPs."

"Someone important wants you alive."

"What's our destination?"

"We're to get you east. Those were the orders."

"Who gave you those orders?" Marci asked.

Oleksander showed a faint smile. "What does it matter? Whatever life you had before, it's over."

"We were told we'd be taken to some kind of town or city. Do you know anything about this?"

"Whoever told you that's a liar. We're dropping you at a waypoint. If you want my advice, head east. There's nothing between here and Budapest except hills and forests and bandits." Oleksander's gaze fell on Erin, who had fallen asleep again. "The girl is your weak link. She won't survive."

"You don't know that," Marci snapped.

Oleksander shrugged and looked away.

Outside, the sky had lightened to lapis lazuli. Still plumb line straight, the road resembled a dark gray scar that intersected the unceasing forest.

The sedative effect of the pulse blocker had worn off. Marci washed down a Cortiquell with some flask water.

Oleksander watched him. "You should hide those, unless you want your throat slit," he said. "Those things are worth more than gold."

"You mean no one makes them out here?" Marci asked.

Oleksander laughed. "Make? We make clothes from hide. We make pots and pans and knives from old tin cans at the smithy. We're three thousand years behind you." Seeing Marci's reaction, he added, "Sure, there's medicine to be found. The question is, can you afford it?"

There was a shout from the gun turret and the APC slid to a halt. Someone lowered the tailgate. The soldiers jumped out, taking up firing positions in a ditch.

Erin jerked awake. "What's happening?"

"Roadblock," Oleksander said, climbing out. "We'll finish them. Lie on the floor."

Marci pulled Erin down as the .50 caliber opened fire.

In ten seconds it was over. Oleksander reappeared. "You're safe. We're going to loot the bodies. Stay here."

The APC inched along the road, passing two sedans whose bodywork had failed to shield its occupants from the big gun. On the ground lay four more corpses.

The soldiers, laughing in triumph, returned to the carrier with their spoils. The words were foreign, but their tone carried a sense of the macabre.

Oleksander barked something gruff and the men fell silent.

"Who were those people?" Erin asked.

"Local bandits," Oleksander said. "They hadn't reckoned on meeting us." He tossed Marci something. "A gift."

Marci inspected the cigarettes. The paper was almost as thick as the cardboard they came wrapped in.

"Bogdan found a bottle of samohon," Oleksander said. "We'll have some when we drop you off."

The first rays of sunlight raked along the highway and cast a single shadow twice their length behind the truck. The road now began to rise and fall to undulating hills. Marci watched the forest transform from a place of menace into crumpled folds of shadow and light in a receding strata of greens. It was, he thought, the loveliest landscape he'd ever seen, raw and brutal and enchanting at the same time. Buda's manicured hills were tinsel and fakery by comparison.

And with this, to his great surprise, his spirits rose. If the night represented the death of their old selves, this dawn—crisp and bright and chaste as the first morning—was their resurrection. Yes, they would die here, and probably soon. But they'd do so not as numbers spewed from a SIN booth but as authors of their own fate. It brought Marci a joyful, ridiculous anticipation at what lay ahead.

Without warning, the APC stopped, released a wheeze of air from its brakes and cut out.

Oleksander jumped to the ground. "This is as far as we go."

Marci sat Erin on the tailgate, climbed down and lowered her into his arms. When he let her go of her, she lost her balance and fell against him. He glanced at Oleksander, who turned away and yelled, "Samohon!"

The troops let up a cheer. One of them who was busy urinating said, "Let's hope it doesn't taste like this."

Oleksander took the moonshine off Bogdan and offered it to Marci and Erin, who shook their heads. He shrugged, drank, and handed it on. "Now we leave you," he said. "It's not safe to stay still. In the Outside you keep moving."

"Where should we go?" Erin asked.

Oleksander pointed east. "That way. Or another way. It's all the same. Just stay off the road. No good comes from the road. You have weapons?"

Marci nodded.

Oleksander turned to his men and barked an order. With poor grace they trudged back to the truck.

"Is that it?" asked Erin. "You're just going to leave us here?"

Oleksander made a conciliatory gesture. "Orders. This is where we always drop them. I wish you success."

"Do you think Grisha Ossian's base is near here?"

Oleksander climbed aboard. "If I knew that, I'd have joined him years ago."

The APC fired up, swung around and departed. Oleksander, sitting at the back, raised a hand in farewell. Marci and Erin watched the lorry until it became lost to the horizon.

"So much for Petros's further instructions," said Marci.

"So much for the medical center," Erin said.

"I wonder how it is to the nearest settlement."

"Petros said a day or two."

"Petros said many things." Marci sat down in the middle of the road and removed his pack. He handed Erin one of the handguns, then put it on the ground beside her when she refused it.

The sun felt warm against his skin. He closed his eyes and began to laugh.

Erin gave him a peculiar look. "What's funny?"

"If only Tony Jackson could see me now."

Erin sat down beside him. "If only András could see me now."

"At least the air is clean," Marci said. "If Mária were here, she'd report us for enjoying it."

"So what do we do? We've got food for a few weeks and water for a few days. Without the water we can't eat the food."

"Damn Petros," Marci said. "There probably isn't a town within five hundred miles of us."

"I'm quite disappointed with his behavior," Erin said.

Marci began to chuckle again.

You've lost your mind.

He didn't care. The voice had lost its power over him. He could have stopped himself. Instead, he laughed until his ribs hurt. Maybe the voice was right after all.

"What's got into you?" Erin asked.

"I finally got what I wanted," Marci said. "I'm free! Free of the rat race, free of SIN and free from the Hangman."

Erin shook her head in bemusement. "You're a strange one, Marci Kovács. We're stuck in the wilderness and you're laughing like a madman."

"Look around," Marci said in elation. "The world lies before us! We might only last a week, but at least we'll die the way we were meant to."

Erin came over and joined him. Together, they listened to the sound of birds welcoming the new day.

Appendix

An excerpt from "A Short History of the World"
by Miklos Nagamuri

In the infancy of the 21st century, Europe was in chaos. Inefficient, bureaucratic and divided, a series of acrimonious secessions had rendered the EU politically impotent. The mid-2030s brought a new threat; under President Mednikov, Russia revived its expansionist policy, first with a successful reinvasion of Ukraine, then the subsumption of Belarus. When Bulgaria and Romania ceded to their mighty neighbor, it became clear the continent faced the biggest challenge to its sovereignty since World War II.

Meanwhile, turmoil in the Middle East escalated. Desperate for oil, America redeployed troops to Iran, Afghanistan and Iraq, a move matched by the Russian Federation. Assailed on two fronts, Iran's blusterous Ayatollah Mousavi threatened the invaders with nuclear retaliation, but was removed overnight by an ingenious Russian *coup d'état.*

With Iran subdued, Russia and the US turned their attention to Afghanistan, striking it from the south and west. The Afghans fought bravely but in vain. The Taliban was routed and the country carved up. An uneasy tension between the two superpowers settled into amicable equanimity. Each had a finger in the pie, and there was plenty to go around.

In other spheres, things were less congenial. The Kyoto Protocol and Paris Agreement had been abandoned years ago. By 2050, new data revealed that previous climate change predictions had been conservative, to say the least. Despite this, mankind continued to drill for black gold, further contaminating the atmosphere until even the most optimistic ecologists despaired of finding a solution.

The answer came from an unexpected quarter. In 2078, Russia announced to the world a radical discovery: Heavy Air. Expanding on the laws of gravity, electromagnetics, and acoustic and molecular physics, engineers were able to manipulate the density of air and create "virtual ground." In effect, Heavy Air created a resistance platform against which normal propulsion systems could fire with minimal energy expenditure to create lift. Its applications were endless, from agriculture to medicine to transportation. Heavy Air was the new electricity. The Age of Oil was dead.

Russia, ever expedient, offered its Schengen neighbors Heavy Air charters and blueprints in return for their vassalage. Like iron to a magnet, European politics immediately gravitated into the sphere of Muscovite influence. The remaining patents were auctioned to the highest bidders, all except America.

Within six months, Russia's national net wealth exceeded the aggregate income of all the G7 since its inception. It next struck a deal with OPEC: Heavy Air technology in return for worldwide oil extraction rights in perpetuity. The response was unanimous. With the flourish of a pen, the United States was denied access to petroleum beyond its own borders. Pumping the ground dry, Russia shipped, cracked and stockpiled crude in its own vast underground reservoirs.

By April 2085, the U.S. had exhausted its own reserves. At the World Fuel Summit, it issued an ultimatum of breathtaking brinkmanship: Heavy Air blueprints, or war. Russia's response was truculent. Its delegation walked out, and its armed forces were mobilized.

On May 7th, 2085, America launched a conventional ICBM from a silo near Büchel, Germany. The target was Ufa in Bashkortostan, a key Heavy Air tech manufacturing city. The attack achieved two outcomes: a temporary halting of production, and the commencement of the Fuel War. Within the hour, Russia retaliated with a single, low-yield nuclear missile, destroying the Pentagon and irradiating nearby Arlington.

An emergency UN summit convened but failed to halt the escalation, since representatives of neither the United States nor Russia were in attendance. Instead, America responded with a full-blown nuclear assault against Moscow, Saint Petersburg, Vladivostok, Yekaterinburg, Novosibirsk, Rostov-na-Donu, Nizhny Novgorod, Samara, Omsk, and Kazan, as well as several Central and former Eastern European capitals. Many of these cities produced Heavy Air or ancillary systems; all of them had large populations.

Russia counter-attacked with its own atomic weapons, hitting Washington DC, the significant East Coast cities, Chicago, Los Angeles, the Gulf of Mexico's offshore oil platforms, and key military establishments in New Mexico and the Appalachians. US bases in the UK and Germany, from which some American missiles had originated, were also destroyed[23].

In January 2086, the bombs stopped falling. Russia and Europe had lost many tens of millions of people; the United States had suffered even greater casualties, while availing itself of no Heavy Air technology. Spent, fuel-less and irradiated, lacking even the time to lick its own wounds, the U.S. now turned on itself, descending into anarchy as a second civil war ensued.

On June 3rd, 2086, the bombs stopped falling. Spent, fuel-less and irradiated, the U.S. turned on itself, descending into anarchy as a second civil war ensued.

The earth was ravaged. Untamable nuclear pollution swirled through the atmosphere, killing millions and contaminating nations without regard for culpability. The planet's oceans swam with crude oil released from destroyed wells, nuclear fallout, and the dead. What the world needed was time to heal. What it got was the Red Plague.

Nobody knew its origin. When the entire staff at a Marseilles hospital fell ill, tests were run. The findings were conclusive and horrifying. Mankind's ancient adversary, smallpox, had re-emerged in the nuclear winter as a super variola. Resistant to treatment and more

---

[23] Russian targets included Pine Bluff Arsenal in Arkansas; Rock Island Arsenal, Illinois; Redstone Arsenal, Alabama; Fort Derrick, Maryland; and the Center for Disease Control's repository in Atlanta. Among notable U.S. targets were Biopreparat's facilities near Moscow and Koltsovo; Novosibirsk Oblast; the Ivanovsky Institute in Moscow; and Porton Down in England.

contagious than its progenitor, it infected refugee camps, field hospitals and anywhere else humanity had regrouped for its survival, killing millions.

There was a ray of hope in all of this. In 2087, a handful of corporations joined forces to find a cure. After eighteen months of trials at a research lab in Budapest, Hungary, Professor Grisha Ossian announced the discovery of a successful vaccine: Nulleukin.

International response was immediate. Desperate governments snapped up the drug, making the consortium the richest organization in history. With a public image of heroic proportions, the CEOs ran for office and were elected with a landslide majority.

Slowly, the Red Plague receded into painful memory. Humanity united into six Sister Cities, each one bulwarked from the barbarian wasteland by walls, minefields and a host of other defenses. Here they thrived. For those born to the Outside it was a different story. Irradiated, diseased and forgotten, they were left to fend for themselves.

One by one, the Patriarchs become memories, revered names and park statues. Budapest became a ship without a captain, a fortress with a population too large to contain. A new system and a new leader were needed. The system was the Company and its leader the Prefect. Together they would change the way people thought, lived and died.

From the embers of world conflict, the dream of a thousand sociologists at last came true: history's true meritocracy. It would prove to be anything but the utopia they had longed for.

Nagamuri, M., 2129 *A Short History of the World.* 3rd ed. Sydney: Ashton, Miller and Associates.

About the Author

Christopher Valkenburg lives in Eastern Europe. His interests include classical music, Art Deco and Soviet Brutalist architecture, and mountain biking.

To subscribe to his newsletter and receive updates on the Empyrean series and other novels, visit:

www.christophervalkenburg.com
Twitter: @Valkenburg_C
Facebook: www.facebook.com/groups/christophervalkenburg

Printed in Great Britain
by Amazon